BLIND SIDED

EMMANUELLE

USA TODAY BESTSELLING AUTHOR

SNOW

Smart Lily
Publishing

Emmanuelle Snow
www.emmanuellesnow.com

CARTER HILLS BAND UNIVERSE
(SUGGESTED READING ORDER)

Carter Hills Band series
False Promises

HEART SONG DUET
Blindsided
Forevermore

Whiskey Melody series
Sweet Agony

SECOND TEAR DUET
Cruel Destiny
Beautiful Salvation

BREATHLESS DUET
Wild Encounter
Brittle Scars

Upon A Star series
Last Hope

Midnight Sparks

Love Song For Two series
<u>Lonesome Heart Duet</u>
Fallen Legend
Rising Star

<u>Two of Us Duet</u>
Snowbound

Wicked Love

All titles available at
emmanuellesnow.com

For the best experience, read in the order as shown above

WHAT THE REVIEWS SAY

- "DAAAMN. This author can write! I mean, wow. It is not often I enjoy musician angsty romance books. But this blew me out of the park." **(Net Galley)**

- "What a rollercoaster ride! That had to be one of the most emotional and heartfelt books I've read in a long time because wow, that was both intense and sweet and just everything my romantic heart wants! " **(sara.reads.too.much)**

- "It was the sweet (and slightly steamy) little romance novel I didn't know I needed... I can see fans of Colleen Hoover enjoying this one." **(Net Galley)**

- "This romance novel had me entranced from the first chapter." **(Net Galley)**

- "Give me all the angst." **(Tanja - OMGReads blog)**

- "A little bit of Country and a whole lot of HOT. Angsty, fun, romance." **(Gina Rae Mitchell blog)**

- "It is absolutely brilliant. The emotions, the banter, the love, the chemistry - it all just works!!" **(Shalini's Books and Reviews)**

- "This book had so much heat and sizzle that I am surprised my kindle didn't melt." **(Carla Loves to Read blog)**

TRIGGER WARNINGS

Disclaimer

My books are realistic and emotional love stories.

I'm an advocate for mental health, and some topics could be sensitive for certain readers since they are portrayed as close to real life as possible.

I've listed the potential trigger warnings for each title on my website.

Be advised that those trigger warnings could potentially be spoiler alerts for the storylines.

Those sensitive topics have been written with the utmost care and respect. Please reach out if you have questions or comments.

All books contain sexuality, mature content, and language not intended for people under 18 years of age.
For other readers' sake, please avoid spoilers in your reviews.

Thank you and have a wonderful day!

Emmanuelle

emmanuellesnow.com

To my kids and husband.
This adventure wouldn't be as thrilling as it is if you weren't cheering
me on. I love you with all my heart.
Now and forever.

———

To all the artists in the world.
Follow your own rules.
Shine the way you were meant to shine,
not the way other people want you to shine.
It's your voice.
Never lose sight of who you really are.

Nobody else can tell your story the way you're telling it.
Embrace it.
Breathe it.
Live it.

BECOME A VIP

TO NEVER MISS A THING

Snow's VIP

Join **Emmanuelle Snow's VIP newsletter** for all the cool stuff, promos, new releases, giveaways, and gifts.

emmanuellesnow.com

Snow's Soulmates

Join Emmanuelle Snow's Facebook VIP group, **Snow's Soulmates**, to chat with her and other readers, get updates, and more bonus content.

facebook.com/groups/snowvip

PINK AND COUNTRY
THE SONG

I couldn't see the light
I thought I had it all figured out
But I didn't; I had no clue
And then you came my way
You disrupted everything I've always
    known
And there you were
That night on my front porch
I never planned to fall so hard so fast
I never thought it would last

[CHORUS]

Girl, I just want you to know
There's no one else like you
You are the sunshine in my storms
You color my night sky
You are the star I wish upon every
    night

You hold my heart; I'll never let
    you go
Babe, I'm blind without you.

I still feel your lips on mine
Even after all this time
Babe, you're special; you're the one
Now all I want is to make you mine
Watch you sleep every night
And breathe you in
And watch you smile
I want to live in your pink world
'Cause you're my favorite color

[CHORUS]
Girl, I'm mesmerized by you
You are the rainbow
I never knew I needed
You're my compass
My muse and my other half
Babe, I'll never let you go
This is my promise to you

[CHORUS]
Girl, I just want you to know
I want my life to be pink like yours
Babe, I'll never let you go
You're my absolute favorite color

Music and lyrics by Carter Hills

Chapter 1
April

My eyes flew open. I blinked a couple of times, letting my vision adjust to the darkness. Entangled in my bedsheets, I combed the web of knots my hair had turned into with my fingers. Great, my night had been another round of tossing and turning. I stared at the ceiling, the darkness swallowing me in, wondering what time it was. Through the small crack where my curtains didn't quite meet, the moon peeked at me, a thin crescent of silver in the night sky. I propped myself up on my elbows, angled my upper body toward the nightstand, and searched for my phone with a hand numb from sleeping in an awkward position. Once I unplugged the cord, I slumped back, my head hitting the fluffy pillows. Squinting at the phone screen, I held my breath.

Three forty-eight.

No. I cringed and dropped my device beside me, where

it landed on the mattress with a soft thud, praying I read the time wrong.

I needed the rest. More than ever. My novel wouldn't write itself. Right now, I had half a mind to look for a ghostwriter. But who was I kidding? I'd never go there. I sighed, dragging my hand over my face, still heavy with sleep. All I needed was to bring my brain on board.

A few years ago, I had my first meet-and-greet with insomnia, and it was a hard cycle to break. Believe me. We were in this long-lasting relationship. Sure, the sleeping pills I took for a while helped with the sleep part, but they also made me feel drowsy during the day. After I dropped them, I tried melatonin, magnesium, meditation, breathing exercises, and lavender essential oil. Anything to help me find sleep at night. The latter had even become Zen-April's drug of choice. So much so that I turned it into my personal fragrance. I sprayed it on my pillow, misted it in the kitchen using one of those little, ten-light-setting diffusers, and kept a roll-on in my purse.

Every night, my brain was stuck in the hamster wheel for hours, with thoughts of what could have been, but remained stalled and blank during the day. Forget being productive or at the top of my game. Not happening. My disturbed nights complicated my existence. In one word, they messed with my head. And my life.

Damn thing.

I pondered my options. Get up and get to work. Or force my eyes to stay closed and bury my head under a pile of pillows, hoping sleep knocked on my door and swept me away. Yeah, right. I snorted. Sleep never knocked twice on the same night. At least, not in my case. With a sigh, I tried the pillow thing anyway. Just in case. One could still be hopeful.

My brain would not win this round. No way. Not under my watch.

Four fifty-seven.

This was an impossible situation.

How early was too early to wake up and jumpstart your day?

If I had an athletic bone inside of me, I would be a runner. Or a high-performing triathlete. Those were the people who got up early with purpose—or I supposed they did. At this time of the day, I, April Simmons, had none. To focus on my writing now was asking too much from me.

Hours ticked by.

I flipped onto one side, then rolled on the other, doing a poor job of convincing myself I'd fall back to sleep.

My mind wandered to my third novel, which I hadn't even started writing yet. My agent Jill had given me a one-month deadline to submit the first draft…my fourth deadline extension. I'd been procrastinating for the last three months, unable to focus, my fingers too stiff to type, my brain blocking my creative flow. My head wasn't in the game. Nah, it was lost somewhere, far from the place it should be. And added to my sleepless nights, that was a deadly combination. Who would ever believe I was a twenty-four-year-old fantasy—enchanted kingdom, magic spells, elves, and all—author with two bestsellers? At this moment, I wasn't convinced myself.

Blame me for my lack of organizational skills. Every minute of every day, I managed to find more ways to be counterproductive than efficient. In the past few months, I'd shattered my previous low records and now should reward myself with a medal. "Procrastination Queen." My bubbly, spur-of-the-moment personality usually fueled my creative side and made up for my mental chaos: a cluster of grief, broken dreams, and lack of restful sleep.

It worked for my second book.

Not this time.

My brain turned into a blank canvas when it came to writing eighty-four days ago and counting. Every attempt to reboot it since then had failed. Baking chocolate chip cookies, going for walks around the block, singing my heart out. Once I even tried jogging. *Yeah. Crazy, right?* Anyway, the right side of my brain, the root of creativity, had gone on strike and refused to come back to work. Regardless of the reward at the end. Stupid gray matter. Or was it white matter? Who cared? Somewhere inside me, I had locked away every single disappointment and sorrow in my life. Losing Travis, having to reinvent myself, being on my own again. That was what fueled my insomnia. And now I was failing my agent with this book. Even when I tried to keep my pain out of reach, but it always resurfaced and toyed with my mind. I guess the lock wasn't sturdy enough, and my sleeplessness only amplified my sense of inadequacy, adding to the rambling inside my head.

How pathetic had I become? I was now talking to myself as if there were two of us.

Six eleven.

Sitting, my attention drifted to the dresser on the opposite wall. The paint was chipping on the side, and I made a mental note to repaint it. And change the knobs while I was at it. It was the only piece of furniture that had followed me around since college. It used to belong to my boyfriend when he was a kid, and for sentimental reasons, I had kept it when I moved here. It matched the teal bed frame and nightstands. My bedroom was big enough to host a queen-size mattress, flanked by dual nightstands and a large walk-in closet. A dozen black-and-white framed photographs of my friends and me over the years covered the wall above the dresser, and a freestanding mirror stood in one corner, next to a large potted plant. My eyes lingered on one of the happiest days of my life for a long moment. That perfect memory now had a sour aftertaste, so I blinked and looked away, not wanting a fresh surge of emotions to ruin my day. Insomnia had already taken its toll on me; I didn't need my sobs and broken heart to be added to the mix.

Deciding I had prolonged the inevitable long enough, I got up. I put on my favorite dark-purple sweatpants and slid my arms into a gray cardigan over the white T-shirt I'd slept in. With the elastic band I kept around my wrist, I tied my jaw-length baby-pink hair in a messy half-do on top of my head. I slid my feet into my sheepskin boots—the one expensive fashion piece I'd ever indulged in—and made myself a large mug of hot chocolate, with whipped cream. Not coffee, though. No matter how tired I was, I never yielded to caffeine. The smell alone was powerful enough to engage my gag reflex. Sure, I downed a cup or two—let's be honest—in college when I knew I'd be up all night studying for mid-terms or finals, but each attempt failed at keeping me awake and left a putrid taste on my tongue. Back when insomnia and I weren't acquaintances. I filed coffee under the *You'll have to kill me first* file in my head. Along with oysters, licorice, and kissing Stevie Broderick in high school. All things that made washing my mouth with bleach seem like a viable option.

In my own twisted way of thinking, I believed hot chocolate solved everything. Heartaches, headaches, menstrual cramps, writer's block. However, the latter hadn't turned out to be true. I remained hopeful it'd work its magic. One day. Eventually. The secret was in the whipped cream. A catalyst able to multiply the *hot chocolate cures everything* effect by ten. Or I wished it could.

With my head tipped back, I crossed my fingers and

mouthed a silent prayer to the God of creativity. Yeah, if he didn't exist, someone should invent him.

In the kitchen, I plopped down on a stool at the island and turned on my laptop, shutting my eyelids when the lit screen blinded me. *Ugh, too early for this.* I blinked to moisten my eyes, the back of them burning from the sudden assault of white light. Since when did I become a morning person? *April, get a grip on your life, move forward, and live a little.* How many times had I repeated the exact same words to myself in the early hours of the morning without success?

I sighed. I'd lost count.

I perused the space around me, anything to distract me and prevent me from staring at a blank page and the cursor blinking back at me. The room was small but inviting. Stainless steel appliances, chess-black-and-white tiled floor, mint-green cabinets. A wooden island topped with a concrete slab and two stools separated the kitchen from the dining room, which consisted of a square blonde wood table surrounded by four mismatched chairs in a spectrum of colors. A large window overlooked the neighbor's building and prevented natural light from getting in early in the morning. A steel-blue sofa, a square artisanal coffee table with a floor lamp, a small cactus in a pot, and a wall-to-wall bookshelf filled with my favorite titles made up the living room of the two-bedroom apartment. The whiff of lavender mixed with the sugary scent of the chocolate chip cookies I baked and left on the cooling rack last night filled the air, giving the place a homey feeling.

Bernice, my tabby cat, woke up from her slumber and jumped on the kitchen counter, her vibrant-blue eyes— almost the same shade as mine—staring at me, unblinking, as she padded on the keyboard. I pushed her to the side and caressed her head, her soft fur warming up my fingers.

"You hungry, sweet girl?"

She purred, and I rose to my feet to fill her golden bowl, set on the floor by the refrigerator. It was the one with a black fishbone etched on the side that I made in the ceramic class I took last year, when I tried to meet new people and start socializing again.

"You should grow fingers, you know. And learn how to type. Could be useful."

She arched her back and ignored me as she attacked her food.

"Keep ignoring me, Bern. Super useful." Why did I ever think getting a cat as a roommate would be entertaining?

Once back on my seat, I stared at the blank page on the screen and typed in big, bold black letters—

Amelia's Kingdom – Book 3
I can't even come up with a title
By April Simmons, lost but not found.

Before my brain could catch up, I opened a new browser tab. Procrastination much, right? I typed "Kitten pictures" and hit search. The image of a tiny black kitten yawning in the big palm of a firefighter, his gorgeous soot-covered face set in a determined expression, stole all my attention. The sight was just too damn hot. At least through the chaos my life had become, my hormones weren't dead. Good to know.

I rolled my shoulders forward, buried my face in the crook of my elbow, and let out a heavy sigh. Gone were the days when I impressed myself with my dedication. A series of yawns escaped my mouth, making my eyes water. I took a sip of my hot beverage, absent-mindedly watching Bernice groom herself.

"Hey girl, can you do that later? I need some encouragement here. Can't you see I'm struggling?" Our eyes met for half a second before she went back to licking her paws. "Never mind. I've seen beauty queens more enthusiastic than you. You won't be mentioned in my acknowledgments section this time. Shame on you." My words didn't rattle her. Not even a little.

My phone chimed, and the sound startled me. Perfect. As if I needed another distraction. I clicked open the text message my best friend Saunders just sent me as if she'd read my mind and knew I required some much-needed guidance. Or a kick in the butt. Such a seer. *Take this, Bernice.*

Wait. Why was she up at this early hour? Saunders should be all wrapped up in her boyfriend's arms at six in the morning. Not texting me. She wasn't even a morning person. Never had been.

SAUNDERS

> Hey, Bubble Head, call me when you get this. Love you xx

Bubble Head was the nickname Saunders gave me during our freshman year in college when I was in too many projects and committees during our first semester. Lacking time to hang out with my friends, I told her one night I pictured myself as a cartoon character with text bubbles popping up all around my head. The name stuck all these years later.

I read her text message for a second time, wondering what she wanted. My curiosity won, and my sleepiness vanished as I punched in my best friend's number.

She answered on the first ring. It seemed like I wasn't the only one feeling impatient this morning.

"Okay. I hope you're ready for this because I have great news for you. I've got your next adventure. Something to change your mind and give you that kick in the butt you desperately need."

Yeah, Saunders knew me too well.

My heart raced at the thought she'd send me bungee jumping or swimming with sharks. "Do I really wanna know?"

"Oh, April, just trust me. When did I ever fail you?"

I inhaled, bracing myself for whatever she was about to propose to me.

"One of my clients rented a two-bedroom luxury cabin in Green Mountain for the month. He can't go because his wife got sick, and she needs to stay in the city. Anyway, I thought you could use it. Fresh air. Great for inspiration. And, oh yes, it's rent-free. Since he canceled last minute, he couldn't get a refund. Anyway, what do you think?"

"You're serious? You want me to move to the country for an entire month? They probably don't even know what wi-fi is."

"Girl, you're being ridiculous. It's a five-star cabin, not a shack. Anyway, don't be a party-pooper. Imagine writing your new book without being distracted. You know I'm a genius in disguise, right?"

"Don't flatter yourself. Genius isn't your middle name, Saund. Your super ideas don't always turn out so great. At least not for me."

"Come on. It's not like we live in New York City. We're in Ginger Creek, Georgia, April. Most people would consider it a small town."

"Except here we have malls. We have more than just one main street, and there are no deer living in people's backyards. You know what I mean." I pinched the bridge of my nose, thinking. "What about Bernice? I know you won't watch her. You hate that litter box thing."

"I already checked with the renting company, and they

said you can take her along. So, you're going? You don't have any good excuses to avoid this opportunity. I'll give you one hour to think about it. If you leave tomorrow morning, you'll be there by sunset."

"Fine. Give me an hour." We hung up, and I dropped my forehead on the table. Did I just get set up? Saunders was right, though. I had no good excuses for refusing her offer. Damn it. I hated when she was right.

My phone pinged as a new text message came in. Two words.

SAUNDERS

Start packing.

I gritted my teeth. My best friend would never let it go. And telling her I feared bears wouldn't cut it. Saunders ran a vacation and retreat agency for rich folks. She booked vacation spots according to their needs in luxurious locations only they could afford, where they could unwind and have a good time without too many distractions. Over-organized—the opposite of me—she had vacation packages ready for all types of clients. Exotic destinations, mountain retreats, boathouse rentals, treehouses, or desert and jungle getaways.

Right now, she was offering me a cabin, for an entire month, all by myself. Why was I still trying to find reasons not to go?

I worked my jaw back and forth, making a pros-and-cons list in my head, weighing my options through the mental traffic jam that was my brain.

Could a change of air boost my creativity and engage my brain productively? *Yes. No. Probably.*

Plus side? No distraction. No noisy neighbors. *A definite pro.*

Would I feel lonely all by myself for an entire month? *Sure. Not so much. Maybe a little.*

No Saunders around. *A con.* No busy sidewalks. *Pro? Con? Tough call.*

Being on my own was my normal these days. Here or there wouldn't matter much. *Okay, a pro then.*

My mind raced through the possibilities. I rubbed my eyes with my closed fists. I hadn't taken a vacation in…huh… forever. When was the last time? I sighed. Too long ago. I massaged the nape of my neck with my fingertips, untying the knots in my upper back and shoulders. My pulse picked up as the idea of going on a mountain vacation took root.

I scanned my small apartment. With its ivory walls, dark ceilings, maple floors, and colorful accents, it wasn't much, but I liked it. It was home.

I'd moved here, an almost four-hour drive from Atlanta, three years ago, after graduating from college. After everything. When my life collapsed. This place was supposed to be my fresh start. The first step to moving forward. My apartment wasn't big by any means, but it suited me and it was all mine.

New me.

New life.

New career.

New home.

That was the plan back then. Did it work out? Honestly? *Not really. A bit…maybe.*

Bernice jumped on the counter and butted my cheek, purring into my ear. "You wanna go, girl?" She purred some more. "And *now* you have an opinion." Could a cat and my best friend know what I needed better than I did? With a huff, I shook my head. No, not going there. Even I had to admit it sounded silly. But maybe… *No, April. Stop.*

I dropped my shoulders and scraped my hand through my hair.

"Okay, girl, let's do this. Let's go on an adventure for a month." Bernice and I exchanged what could pass as smiles, at least in my mind.

In the last few years, I'd lost sight of who I was. It was time to get my power back. To redefine myself. To find where I belonged. To dream again. To do this whole new me, new life thing. And give it a real shot. I blew out a breath. The more I thought about it, the more enticing it sounded. I'd been waiting for a sign for so long. Could this be it?

Yeah. Time to get my groove back.

Straightening my spine with a new resolve, I typed a message to Saunders, letting her know I'd go to the cabin. I would do this. I would get out of my comfort zone. *About time*, the smart side of my brain screamed at me. For once, I agreed, and mentally gave myself a high-five.

The mountain air would clear my head. See? It was working already. Just thinking about it released years of pent-up tension from my back. I remembered reading somewhere, a while back, about how living in the mountains made you healthier and happier. Green therapy, they called it. I risked nothing by trying it out for a month.

The seclusion would help me focus. Yes, the idea grew on. A wide grin painted my face. "Time to pack," I said out loud, mostly to myself—or to Bernice, who had already retreated to the comfort of my bed.

I shut my laptop and sauntered to my bedroom with a pep in my step I hadn't experienced in a long time. Saunders's crazy last-minute idea didn't sound so crazy after all. On my tiptoes, perched on a plastic step stool, I grabbed my suitcase from the top shelf of the closet.

Yeah, I was doing this.

No more excuses.

No more procrastination.

The mountains were calling me, and I was answering.

Half-packed, I sat back in front of my laptop to find a dozen new messages from my best friend. I expected nothing less from her and imagined her doing a victory dance in her underwear when I agreed to her retreat idea. Saunders emailed me lists. Lists with an *S*. Itineraries, things to do in Green Mountain at this time of the year, the best places to eat on my way up there. She attached forms to sign, the cabin's rule book, and other documents I didn't dwell on, for now.

For an instant, I wondered if she sent these to all her wealthy clients or if she had compiled all this information for my sake only. Knowing my best friend, probably a mix of both. Part of her foolproof strategy to win me over.

I skimmed over the documents I printed and emailed back the signed forms. It looked official. It even included a non-disclosure agreement. I shrugged. Guess that made sense since Saunders only booked high-end, private destinations for her clients. Anyway, I trusted my friend. Back in my bedroom, I finished packing, adding more sweaters to my suitcase under Bernice's watchful eye, now curled up on my pillow.

Jitters filled my heart, knowing I'd enjoy one of Saunders's destinations for once. My best friend offered me a month-long vacation, and I intended to make the most of it.

Chapter 2
Carter

My smile was anchored to my face, and nothing seemed to chase it away. These days, running helped me put my thoughts in order. Not so long ago, it was a coping mechanism, to deal with stress. Not anymore. Lately, I started enjoying exercise for its health benefits. I nodded at the security guard holding the door of my building as I slipped through the opening. Instead of using the elevator, I climbed the staircase up to the top floor, adrenaline still coursing high in my bloodstream and needing to flush it out of my system.

My phone went off, and I reduced my pace, going from a light jog to a walk. My lips curled when I noticed the name flashing on the screen. "Hey, June. What's up?"

"Carter, can we talk?" Something was wrong. I could tell. Her voice was devoid of any hints of playfulness, which was unusual for our phone calls.

"Huh, sure. Gimme thirty minutes? I'll shower and eat something. I just came back from a run with Taylor."

"Listen, I just got off the phone with someone from your record label. They heard from Savannah Prince's people. Some things we need to discuss."

"The fuck."

"Call me when you have a minute. I'll see what I can do in the meantime, okay?"

I huffed my frustration. "Yeah, I'll do that."

With my fists clenched at my sides, I threw my head back and exhaled.

Once I reached my floor, I hurried inside my apartment.

My cheerful mood had vanished, replaced by an angst that sent chills down my back. The name of Savannah Prince never rhymed with good news, but rather with catastrophe.

Discarding my gym clothes on the bathroom floor, I positioned myself under the hot stream and let the water relax my body while the gears of my brain engaged. A dozen different scenarios played in my mind. Whatever Savannah wanted, I knew, for sure, it would piss me off.

Minutes later, dressed in a pair of faded denims and a simple white T-shirt, I downed a glass of icy water before returning June's call. Like a Band-Aid, I had to rip it off and fast, or else it would pollute my thought feed, and I'd become restless.

The moment she picked up and revealed the reason for her call, I regretted ever returning it. Now that I had the confirmation June wasn't delivering good news, I wondered how anyone with a sense of decency at my record label would ask me to partake in this circus.

"No, June, I won't do it. I'm done. D. O. N. E. Been there, done that. Bought the T-shirt. Burned it. From now on, they can talk to my lawyers." I scratched my forehead with the tip of my thumb. Anger simmered inside me. *Get a hold of yourself, Carter.* "It's a no. Everything has been explained already. If they wanna prove one of them is at fault, they don't need me. Isn't this why corporate lawyers exist?" Juniper, or June as I called her, my assistant manager slash personal assistant, was my go-to girl in my music career. Sometimes, I felt like her job description could be summed up as *Keeping Carter out of trouble.*

From her five-foot-four height, with three-inch heels on, Juniper Stewarts had a lot of attitude. She stood up for herself—and me—no matter what.

With long brown hair and exotic caramel eyes with dark-green rings around the pupils, she resembled a college student more than a twenty-eight-year-old assistant to Riley Burns, music mogul and manager of some of the biggest names in country music.

I trusted her with my career. Most times. Not today, though. Today, I didn't dig it. "We broke up officially weeks ago. I'm done with this episode of my life, and I don't owe her or anyone else anything. I thought I had been clear when we parted ways. She even signed the damn papers. What more do they want from me?" I balled my hands into fists as June delivered her spiel on the other end of the line.

"Listen, Carter. It's big. She claimed Carla paid her to gather as much intel on you as possible. Seems like Savannah wasn't the only one with paparazzi on speed dial. Carla was feeding them information too. About you."

"I told everyone from the start Carla was crazy. I never trusted her. Her irises were dollar signs. I never authorized her to publish that crap about me. Or to sell me to gossip rags without my consent."

"That's why the label requires your testimony. To settle

the case quickly. And to make sure it's not just another one of your devil ex's setups, but legit accusations. This is no joke. Only you can confirm the conversations that took place between you two in her office."

"Well, right now I don't care about Carla. And whatever Savannah says, it is usually a big lie. They make a great pair. Yep, two psychos I can live without." I paused to calm myself before I said things I would regret. "Without solid evidence and any other way to prove they teamed up against me, I'm not getting involved. I've turned the page. The label has enough means to deal with it on its own." A low grunt escaped my lips. I refused to be those manipulative witches' puppet any longer. "Whatever scheme they've come up with, I'm staying out of it. Both can rot in hell for all I care. And why is Carla still working if the label thinks she screwed me over? See? It's all a big joke."

June kept talking, but I turned a deaf ear, working extra hard to keep my calm.

"Tell the label's attorney I'm unavailable to meet with him or for video calls or whatever. I won't answer anyone's questions. They all know what I think of Carla. Riley does too. He can vouch for me. He was there and heard her nonsense. Where is he anyway? I would have thought he would get involved in this himself and put a stop to it before it even reached my ears."

Riley Burns was my manager. He had been by my side since before I made it big on the music scene. Over the years he had become a friend to me, a brother, someone I could always count on.

"He's been in and out of meetings all day. We're supposed to get together later, but he put me in charge in the meantime. It's over my pay grade, but for you, I'd run errands naked if it meant you wouldn't have to go through this on your own. Being the middleman is no fun, but I bark loud enough that the label is almost overnice each time they contact me."

"I get it. I swear. It's just… I thought we all had moved on and that I was free from their scheming. Word of advice. Tell everyone who wants a piece of me right now to keep me out of it. I really don't wanna have to come to the office and tell them what's on my mind. It wouldn't be good for anyone involved. Trust me."

"I'm sorry, Carter. I really thought we were done dealing with them too." June hesitated for a beat. "Let me see what I can do."

"You sure? I don't like the idea of your being stuck between all of us. It's not fair."

"I told Ry I would do it. And he knows he can count on me. I'm on your side. Always." She paused and seemed to hesitate for a moment. "And Carter, listen… I also wanted to inform you about something else." She lowered her tone. "So you're not taken by surprise when the news comes out. Huh…Savanna landed that lead role in Wesley's next movie. She'll be everywhere. Giving interviews. Rising to the top. I just wanna make sure you're ready for what it implies. Your relationship, or lack of it, will continue to feed the media. I would bet my next paycheck she'll surf on your fame for a little longer."

Evil manipulator. Torturous witch. Selfish huckster. I lacked adjectives to describe my ex-girlfriend nowadays.

"Seriously, can't I catch a break? I'm sure there are more exciting scandals out there than my personal life, which isn't interesting to anyone else right now. I'm almost a monk these days."

"Well, maybe. Some heiress will get divorced or some actor will be caught cheating soon enough, but for some reason, your love live is still the hot topic. You've always been so discreet about it in the past. It's like now the entire planet thinks they are entitled to every detail. I know it's not fair and you did nothing to deserve it, but that's the way things are. People live vicariously through you. The mysterious and brooding top-selling country artist who ended a relationship that fed the gossip trash for two years. You offered them a window to your personal life, and they jumped in with both feet. Wasn't it Savannah's plan all along? It's not like—"

"Just for the record, I don't care about her big, multi-million-dollar Hollywood contract. Or whose dick she sucked to get there. Or that she snitched to my publicist." As if my life hadn't been enough of a circus lately, now my label suspected my ex-girlfriend had been feeding info to my publicist and vice-versa. They both knew my position about fame, and they went behind my back to sell me to the press. Sharks with no respect for private lives whatsoever. "She got the part, good for her. And bad for everyone else involved. The truth is she probably did unthinkable things to win it." A chill crossed my entire self as I thought about how Savannah would do just about anything to get to her end. Yep, there were no lines she wouldn't cross for fame or money. "Whatever went down with any of them isn't my problem anymore. I'm over that bullshit, and I have no plan to revisit it anytime in the future. And, by the way, next time, tell whoever brings it up it wasn't a separation, it was a fucking breakup. I dumped her ass."

For the last fifteen minutes, I'd been pacing my penthouse back and forth from the kitchen to the living room in an attempt to calm the storm raging inside me. I stopped by the dining table and placed a hand over the backrest of one of the chairs, hanging my head low, wondering how my day had gone from amazing to this. With its high ceilings, straight lines, open floor plan, and honey-colored hardwood floors, I loved everything about my place, especially the panoramic windows overlooking the city of Nashville in every room. My own bachelor pad. My safe haven. One that suffocated me right now the more June kept talking about the devil and her crazy sidekick.

"Carter? Are you still there?"

Angst built inside me. Why had I endured that nightmare for so long?

My fist hit the table, and the vibration echoed through the room.

I wasn't the guy to lose his cool, not usually, but any mention of Savannah Prince took me back to a dark corner of my existence. A place I wished to never return.

Bile rose in my throat at the memory of the hell I had endured for those two years.

All this time, she wore the victim suit like a second skin.

I heaved at the reminder.

We were toxic together. Poison. Before her, I avoided all relationships, and she knew it. She took advantage. And I let her. I became the worst version of myself for the length of our relationship, pushing away all the people who genuinely cared about me. The ones who had my back.

Never again would I wish to revisit that part of my existence. The one where I became sexually frustrated. And castrated—in many ways.

It still angered me that I'd been blind for so long.

Being linked to her had been my first mistake.

Dating her had been the second.

And moving in with her had been the fatal one.

A prison that took me a long time to escape from.

"Talk to me." June sounded worried now. "Cart, don't give her power over you."

June was right. My grip loosened around my phone, and I unglued it from my ear. *Relax, man. Breathe in. Breathe out. Don't let Savannah Prince ruin another one of your days. Not after she wrecked the last two years of your life.*

"Carter, try to keep your emotions out of the equation. She's fishing for a reaction. Don't give her that satisfaction and let her antics affect you."

"Yeah, I hear you, and you're right." I pivoted on my heels, grabbed an apple from the fruit basket on the kitchen island, and juggled it with one hand until I missed, and it crashed on the floor at my feet.

"I will tell them you're unavailable. To be on the safe side, I'll run everything by Riley tonight to make sure we're all on the same page. By the way, I only found out about all this one hour ago."

A humorless laugh bubbled out of me. "Like she hadn't planned it ahead of time."

"I don't want you to suffer anymore because of her actions. She seems desperate to keep feeding off your fame and your name."

A new upsurge of anger simmered inside me, and holding back my anger, I forced my voice to remain steady as the next words left my mouth. "Miss Hollywood, like the narcissist bitch she is, can't stop painting me as the villain to gain all the sympathy and exposure she's always dreamed of by acting like a victim. Typical. Geez, why can't she set me free?" A guttural growl exited my mouth. "I'll die before I put my name next to hers of my own volition again."

"I know. Believe me, I do. It's like those two never grew a brain. Or a conscience. As long as I'm involved, they won't get away with it. I'll buy the shovel and bury them myself if I need to."

"That's why people in this industry fear you." Humor returned to my words.

"Yeah, well, I guess Savannah and Carla haven't gotten the memo they should stay away from your business."

"Well, their funerals." I breathed out, some of my left-over anger evaporating. "I'll stay put for a while and let the dust settle. When I come back, I'll be stronger than ever before."

"You promise you'll be fine?"

I swallowed. "Yeah. I'll be with my family. They always ground me. And the fresh air will do me good."

"Be safe, Carter. Just a sec, I'll be right back. Some unknown number keeps calling."

It still surprised me how I had played along with Savannah Prince all this time without questioning her motives. Either she was smarter and a better actress than anyone would give her credit for or I was so lost back then that I refused to see the warning signs.

A long sigh passed the rim of my lips.

What was done was done. I was self-aware now, and I wouldn't agree to any of her requests.

Our relationship had turned out to be the worst decision of my life. By far. Worse than the sophisticated snake tattoo I got on my upper back at sixteen.

The tattoo had been removed.

However, nobody could ever erase my relationship with the Evil Queen.

June's voice broke my train of thought. "She's relentless. I'm telling you, I bet she can feel the heat about to burn her ass."

"Who was it?"

"Carla. She just requested an emergency meeting. She just wants to save face."

My tone hardened. "I'm fucking over all of this. And I'm done with this conversation. We've already lost enough time today on a subject I have no interest in. Let's put an end to it. Get her on the phone." I barked the words at June and slapped myself mentally. *Come on, man, be nice. June is on your side.*

"Carter, forget it, you're not in the right state of mind to talk to her. She's not in her office at the moment. She said she'd be back this afternoon."

"I don't care where she is. Mars or in the middle of the fucking jungle. Get her on the phone. She has a cell phone. Call her." I paced the room, tugging at my hair. I exhaled through clenched teeth. "I'm sorry for yelling. You shouldn't have to deal with this shit. It's not your job. I'll fucking shut her up once and for all. She's done bossing all of us around like we're her puppets. But I appreciate your help, and I swear I won't punch anyone this time." Last year, I had punched a paparazzi who was following me in New York City for no apparent reason other than I had been dealing with one of Savannah's crazy episodes and he wouldn't let it go. Six months ago, I stormed out of an interview when the host didn't stop praising Savannah's talent and charitable endeavor. *Fucking idiot.* That was my fucking money she had pledged.

June sighed and kept her tone even. "Carter, listen to me. Calm the fuck down before you talk to anybody else. Nobody wants to deal with you when you're like this. Take that break, go to the countryside as you planned, spend time with your family, then we'll talk. Green Mountain usually helps you unwind. I'll clear your schedule, and we'll only keep the engagements you can't miss. Meditate, do yoga, or any other shit that'll help you relax. Stay away from the press, don't watch the news, and let the Savannah story wear out. I'll take care of it from my end. And please keep it in your pants. Don't fuck around. The last thing you need is another scandal."

"What about Ry?"

"I'll share the new developments with him later and keep you updated. We'll figure it out. All of us. Don't worry. I have your back. Always."

With both hands, I tousled my hair, my phone now on speaker.

"Fine. I trust you, June. You better be right about this. Never let Carla near me ever again. I can't promise I won't lose it next time. And if I wasn't clear enough before, she's fired. Tell the label whatever they wanna hear, but Carla isn't on my team anymore. Effective now." We agreed to talk later, the hair on my body standing on end, an unmistakable sign I needed to walk away before I had one of my episodes.

I strode back to the kitchen and kicked a chair off balance. Lava boiled inside my veins.

When did I become so restless? My emotions usually ran the game. Not my actions. But today, it all seemed too much to deal with.

I needed a release. Something. Anything to calm my nerves down.

My hand dragged along my jawline. My beard felt weird under the pads of my fingers. I'd never kept it this long, but now I used my scrubby face as a shield to hide from the rest of the world.

I changed back into my workout gear, and with red boxing gloves on, I pounded the punching bag hanging from the ceiling of the small gym. Along with a treadmill and a weight station, it was set in the corner of one of the guest bedrooms I had transformed into a man cave. It also hosted arcade games, a large screen mounted on the wall, and an oversized leather couch. Every time my friends came over, this was the room where we spent all our time.

The exertion burned my muscles, and sweat pearled on my forehead. With my shoulder, I pushed strands of hair falling over my eyes away. With both arms around the bag, I stopped its back-and-forth motion and leaned my forehead against the slick surface, catching my breath. Punching the sucker for one hour straight did nothing to ease my angst.

Riled and restless, I packed my guitar and a few things in the trunk, tossed a duffle bag filled with clothes on the backseat, and climbed into my SUV.

When I told Taylor, my bodyguard and chief of security, earlier that I was going to spend some time in Green Mountain, I didn't expect to leave today. But now that I thought about it, there was nowhere else I'd rather be.

The tires screeched as I exited the parking garage in a hurry.

As I replayed June's and my animated conversation in my head on a loop, I headed toward the mountains.

Once some of my wrath melted away, I gave myself a pep talk. *Get your shit together, Carter. Use this time to work on your next album and be with your family.* With the train wreck my life had become, it'd been too long since I released a new album. Yeah, the last one had been before Savannah. I had one scheduled last year but ended up pushing it back indefinitely as I worked on my dead-end relationship. The joke was on me now. It was long overdue to give in to my creative side. My fans were adamant about it. Time to go back on the road and bring the music back into my life. No more wasting my time in a relationship based on false promises and pretenses. Savannah had hardened my already icy heart and wrecked my mojo, and I was ready to leave my past behind and move forward with my life.

Jack and Dahlia were already there, waiting for me on the front porch, when I parked my black SUV in front of the three-story log cabin at the end of the road. Located atop the mountain, it offered the perfect view of the valleys and the sunsets. At night, the lack of city lights provided a glorious sight of the constellations sprinkling the black canvas. Back when Dahlia and I formed the Carter Hills Band together with our ex-bandmate, Stud Burgess, we used to play at Green Mountain Fest every fall. We started performing on the small stages when we were kids and ended up headlining the festivals only a few years later. After her life went through the wringer, Dahlia moved here full-time. Nestled in the Smoky Mountains, it possessed all the small-town charm one would expect while being just a few hours' drive from Nashville, Atlanta, and other big cities. Green scenery, fresh air, valleys, and a quaint Main Street, it was no wonder Dahlia chose to raise Jack here.

Over the years, I'd acquired half a dozen luxury log cabins all over town—most of them nestled in the mountains—and rented them to high-end businesses and wealthy folks craving some peace of mind. No other spots beat the mountains to evade your everyday life and forget about everything making you tick.

This one cabin where I had parked, I kept it as mine.

Nobody except close friends or family was welcome here.

Its location gave me some much-needed privacy, and no picture hunters could take snapshots of me when I relaxed on the deck over the steep mountainside.

Perfect spot.

When I bought the lot at the top of the mountain, I had a gate installed down the road and a fence put around the perimeter to keep bears and other animals out—and of course, stalkers. Let's be real. I'd had some following me around over the years. I had my mountain lodge, where the view was breathtaking, built first. The following year, I added two smaller cabins next to it, both of them sitting in the gated part of the property. I used them to lodge friends who stayed overnight, while the rest of the time they were rented through agencies that conducted thorough background checks on everyone, never compromising my security. They made sure everything was in working order and always left a handwritten note in the kitchen to welcome each new guest. I never revealed my identity, but I loved the idea of offering those who stayed in one of my cabins a personal welcome. It was one of the many little details that made up the experience I was providing within my rental business.

My other properties were spread all over Green Mountain. I bought them through the years and made minimal changes to them as they were already fully furnished and ready to be rented. They just diversified my real estate portfolio. Nonetheless, all guests staying at any of my cabins always received the same little attentions to make their stay unique and memorable.

"*Carrrter.*" Jack ran my way and jumped into my arms as soon as I climbed out of my truck.

I held on to him tight and twirled him around. The long drive had defused every remnant speck of my anger. Thanks to the wide-open countryside scenery, some old classic rock music, and peppermint tea.

"Hey, buddy. It's been too long, I've missed you." I ruffled his short dark hair and put him back on his feet. With my palm raised, I pretended to measure him to my body. "You're almost a man now. You've grown at least two inches since I last saw you." Jack, Dahlia, and I hadn't spent time together in months due to the fact that I was in a very dark place and was trying not to drown in the chaos of my love life and bring the ones I loved down the rabbit hole with me.

The boy giggled, and Dahlia mouthed *Thank you* from where she stood, her arms crossed over her chest, wearing ripped dark denims and a red flannel jacket.

"I could use some help. Show me those muscles of yours." Jack flexed his arms, and I handed him my guitar case with a grin. "Be careful. You're the only one I trust with it." I bent at the knees, leveling our faces, and whispered, "Don't tell your mama, or she'll be jealous." Jack snickered, and my voice rose as I added, "Put it in my studio."

The boy's eyes sparkled. He knew how much the guitar meant to me. I had gifted him a kid-sized replica last summer for his fifth birthday. He wouldn't treat diamonds any better. And the kid had natural talent. It flowed in his veins. He shared the same genuine passion for music that Dahlia and I did at his age.

His mama inched closer and rose to the tips of her toes to drop a kiss on my cheek. Our eyes met, and we exchanged more in our gazes than any words could ever do.

"I've missed you, Carter."

I wrapped my arms around her and pulled her closer. She felt skinnier than usual under my touch. I framed her face with both hands and leaned back to look at her. A lone tear rolled down her cheek, and I wiped it off with the pad of my thumb. "I've missed you too. So damn much. I'm sorry. I needed to heal and find my way. On my own."

Dahlia lowered her gaze, her hands stuffed in her pockets. "I know. Didn't mean I wasn't worried about you. It's okay, though."

"No, it's not, but I'll make up for it."

She squeezed my forearm, and her lips curled up.

Back when Dahlia, Stud, and I had a band together, Dahlia hated the fame, so after she found out she was pregnant with Jack, she walked away from it. Then everything went to shit, and she secluded herself here in Green Mountain and stayed out of the public eye. For good.

Lost in my toxic relationship with the devil herself, I let Dahlia and Jack down for a few months. I refused to involve them in the nasty turmoil my life had turned into. It was mine to fix. I promised myself it'd never happen again.

Was Dahlia's weight loss related to my messy existence? It wouldn't be the first time my antics affected her. I blew out a worried breath.

She stepped back, breaking our embrace, as Jack came trotting in our direction.

"Done. Your guitar is safe in your music room."

"Thanks, bud. I knew you were the man for the job." We fist-bumped, and I handed him another bag. "This is precious stuff too. Are you up for the challenge?"

"Yes, sir," he said, giving me a salute. A flicker of emotion tickled my spine. The small gesture reminded me so much of my big brother when we were younger. I chased the memory away.

"Hey, Dah. Where's your car?"

"At the mechanic's. Nick dropped us off an hour ago."

"I could've picked you two up. You know that, right?"

She flicked her hands as she added, "It's nothing. Nick had errands to run anyway. It's not like we live hours from here either." True. They lived a few miles from my cabin.

"When is he picking you up?"

"In two or three days. Haven't decided yet. Did I forget to tell you Jack and I are staying with you? Is that all right?"

The idea the three of us would spend a few days

together sent a soothing feeling through me. For a second, it felt like old times.

"Oh yes, it's perfect."

I opened the back door of the truck and swung the duffel bag over my shoulder, draped my arm around Dahlia, and we followed Jack into the house.

"Hope you're hungry. I've cooked dinner. We could eat early and get Jack to bed and spend some one-on-one time together. We're long overdue." She glanced at me, one brow arched, a small curve playing on her lips. My heart swelled as I took her in. *God, I've missed her.*

"I'm starving, and there's nothing I'd like more than spend some alone time with you, Dah." I winked and kissed her forehead before leading her inside and taking all my stuff to my room upstairs. The master bedroom occupied the entire third floor. It was decorated simply with a recycled barn-wood king-size bed with matching night-stands on either side, a dark charcoal bedspread, a walk-in closet, and an en-suite bathroom. A large black-and-white picture of my first solo show—the one Dahlia herself took and gifted to me—was hung above the bed. On the second floor, Jack had his own room with a guitar-shaped bed my ex-bandmate Stud Burgess handcrafted for him after he outgrew his crib. Next were a bathroom and three additional guest rooms—one Dahlia used every time she spent the night—down the hall. Toys and clothes filled Jack's closet because my home was his too. Even Dahlia had left some of her stuff in her bedroom, so whenever she decided to stay over, she was never caught off guard.

Stud and his wife now lived in Oregon with their children, and we barely saw each other, except for a couple of times a year. I missed my friend, but he was happy, and in the end, it was all that mattered.

When Stud quit the band, soon after Dahlia did, my

existence shattered. I had not seen it coming. The guy breathed music. Talented, he begged Dahlia and me to give him a chance to join our band back in the day. And he soon became family. Growing up in a fucked-up environment, I understood his need to build something else. A family. A stable future for him and his wife. Even if I wanted to, I could never blame him for offering his kids the chance he never got when he was a child himself.

While I showered, Dahlia and Jack busied themselves in the kitchen downstairs. Other than the den and my music studio, the kitchen had always been one of my favorite rooms in the cabin. It had state-of-the-art Sunset Bronze appliances, a large island with a walnut butcher-block top, and a panoramic window overlooking the valley. Like every other room here, it had hardwood floors, wooden walls, and twelve-foot-high wood plank ceilings. The cabinets were painted a soft shade of cream just like the L-shaped couch in the living room, the rug in the den, and the bricks dressing up the fireplace. A few teal accent items like pillows, vases, and paintings—the ones Dahlia insisted I needed—were scattered around. The cabin was a bigger replica of the two-story smaller ones down the road. It was a mix of rustic and farmhouse chic. Thanks to my best friend, it looked like a house and not just a bachelor pad with no personality.

On the walls were framed pictures of the happy memories of my life, and some of Jack's pieces of art through the years.

The smell of white wine sauce pasta with fresh herbs invaded my nostrils as I grabbed a clean towel from under the sink to dry myself off. Dressed in low-cut denims and a long-sleeved black shirt, I jogged downstairs. Not in the mood to tame the wild strands of my shaggy look, another side effect of my after-Savannah-Prince era, I raked a hand through my damp hair. It was freeing not to give a damn about trivial details of my appearance and just surf life for once.

"Ohmygod, Carter. Your hair," Dahlia teased with a tentative smile as I joined her by the stove. "It's so long and unruly. I wouldn't have been able to tell earlier." She studied me for an instant. "Never mind, I like it. It's a good look on you." For a second, I forgot I'd worn a beanie when I arrived.

I shrugged, half-smiling. "Let's just say grooming hasn't been a top priority lately. And it's easier to stay under the radar when I look like this." I shoved the carrot stick Dahlia offered me into my mouth.

Dahlia had always said I looked like a boy-man with my tousled hair. Like I knew she would, she ran her fingers through it, and loads of memories from our past resurfaced.

A shiver traversed me. Not sure if it was due to the mid-January crisp air or her familiar touch reminding me of my carefree days. When we used to be at the top of the world together. She and I living the dream we'd been cherishing since we were little kids. I loved my life now, but parts of me missed those early days. When everything Dahlia and I did felt like magic. Back when we still had that innocence about the rock star lifestyle and climbed the ladder to stardom one step at a time, having no clue what would happen when we reached the top. I understood the choices she had made in the last few years, but that didn't mean it sometimes still didn't sting to walk onstage on my own.

"I'm glad we're all here," Dahlia said.

"Me too. Gimme a few minutes, I'll light up the fireplace." I left the kitchen, crossed the living room and beelined toward the side door as a wave of nostalgia hit me. I wasn't in love with my best friend anymore, but sometimes, when we were alone, playing house,I got a picture of what life could have been if things between us had been different. Standing in the living room with my hand around the doorknob, I surveyed the space around me. On my right was a hallway leading to a home gym and my music studio, rooms no one visited except me, and the media room which consisted of a large screen and over-sized couch. The wooden staircase separated the living room from the rest of the main floor where the kitchen, dining room, and den were located. The latter had large windows that gave the impression we were standing outside and a second fireplace. I loved the room. It was one of my favorites, and every time it snowed, I sat there and looked outside for hours, playing music and losing myself in my creative side.

With a pile of wood in my arms, I shut the door with a kick. A shiver zipped through me. The winter this year was colder than usual.

The fire crackled as I contemplated the scenery from the bay windows in the den. A sense of calm washed over me. The sky, a pale shade of gray, threatened us with an imminent snowfall. A breeze lifted fallen leaves from the ground and twirled them around. From where I stood, I saw the silhouettes of the mountains in the distance, the peaks no doubt covered in snow. I rubbed my jaw. *Home.* Green Mountain was home. I blew out a shuddering breath. Maybe I should move here full-time. Sure, I'd miss Nashville, but here, I felt calmer. In control.

Happier.

Jack joined me and slid his tiny palm into mine. We stayed still for a fat minute, our gazes glued to the moun-tains afar. The tension in my back vanished. I closed my eyes, tingles of contentment rising inside me at the realization I had conquered my heartbreaks and was still standing strong. And tall. Just like those mountains that passed the test of time.

———

After I sang Jack one of my songs, at his request, Dahlia tucked him in bed while I attacked the dishes. A smile stretched my lips at the thought of being here with two of my most favorite people in the world. The ones who mattered.

No camera flashes.

No interviews.

No screaming fans.

No underdressed groupies or crazy stalkers after me.

No Savannah Prince or her toxic nonsense.

When Dahlia joined me, I handed her a glass of wine. Her floral fragrance, the same one she'd been wearing for the last ten years, reached my nostrils. The one reminding me I was home. "How are you doing? For real."

She offered me a hint of a smile. "I'm fine." Without taking a sip, she put the wineglass on the counter beside her, avoiding my gaze.

"Come on, it's me, Dah. You can tell me anything. No woman who says she's fine is ever fine."

She huffed a laugh.

"What is it?" I cocked my head to the side, meeting her watery eyes.

Her eyes brimmed with tears, and she fanned herself with a hand.

A weird sensation twisted my insides.

"I'm not sad. I swear."

I let go of the breath I was holding.

She swallowed a big gulp of air, met my eyes, and said,

"Carter, I'm pregnant." Cradling her face with my hands, I stared at her. I studied her moss-green eyes, the curve of her lips, the blush on her cheeks. My lips drew into a sad upturn when, for a second, I wished this could have been the news we could have shared together. The words felt like a *déjà vu*. Something we had uttered in the past.

I cleared my throat, my mouth as dry as California during a drought. "Are they happy or sad tears, Dah?" I usually had no trouble reading her expressions. Not this time. The flow down her cheeks confused me. A lot. Women's simplest emotions were always the hardest to figure out.

"Happy," Dahlia sniffled.

"Why the tears then?" I clamped her waist with my hands and dropped a soft kiss on her forehead.

"I was…I was scared to tell you. I didn't know how you'd react." She looped her arms around my midsection and buried her face into my chest. My hands traced circles on her back. "You and I, we went through this once. It makes me emotional thinking about the last time I told you I…I was pregnant…with Jack. And the aftermath of how it changed our relationship. You. Me. Jeff. It brings back so many memories. Good and bad. I swear I'm happy about it. Nick and I, we're ready for this."

My heart quivered in my chest, and a tightening sensation wrenched at my insides. I breathed slowly. The last time my best friend announced she was pregnant, it ended up being the beginning of a very traumatic episode in our lives. But she deserved her happily-ever-after. She'd been through too much not to come out stronger on the other side. And thriving.

"If you're happy, then I'm happy for you. It's all I've ever wanted." My pulse slowed down, and the knots in my chest slackened. Air flowed in and out of my lungs easier. I had faith that this time around, her pregnancy wouldn't be a bittersweet memory. With a finger, I tipped her chin up and looked into her eyes. "What about the weight loss? You don't seem so fine to me."

"Morning sickness. Remember how it was with Jack? I couldn't get out of the house for weeks."

A lopsided smile twitched my lips at the recollection. "How's Nick?"

"Ecstatic. He's a wonderful dad to Jack. I love him, and he's good to me." Dahlia and Nick had gotten married two years ago. The summer before I embarked on my ride to hell with the one I shouldn't mention.

They had an intimate ceremony here, in the mountains, with only a few people in attendance. I shed a tear or two that day. My heart had ached at the sight of my best friend in a white dress for the second time. However, it also allowed me to let go of the feelings I'd bottled up long ago. Dahlia, Nick, and Jack were a family of their own, and I trusted Nick to care of the two people I loved the most in this world.

I sighed. On their wedding day, I wished it could've been me up there at the altar. Today, this feeling re-emerged. I wished this baby were mine.

But the news also confirmed I had made my peace with this part of my past. As much as I still loved her, my feelings for Dahlia weren't the same that had clung to me for so long. We were best friends, and I was okay with the current status of our relationship.

Entangled in blankets, we sat on the loveseat before the fireplace, just like old times. Dahlia's head rested on my lap, and I smoothed her red hair, twisting strands around my fingers.

"I love you, Carter. That will never change. Time for

you to find your happiness too." She yawned, and I stayed silent. My pulse spiked at the thought.

Life would change for all of us. Things would never be the same again.

A baby.

Knots tied my stomach. Dahlia and Jack were no longer mine. Not like they used to be. Our family, as we'd known it, would be altered forever. Dahlia and Nick would have a baby. A child of their own. Even though I refused to panic at the idea, I wondered if I would still have a place in our unique family dynamics or if I would be on my own all over again. Unless… No. I refused to let myself think about the different scenarios tonight. I wasn't ready to deal with the consequences of my curiosity. Not before I was absolutely sure I could handle the outcome without the reality of it plunging me into another downward spiral. Perhaps someday I'd be ready to face the truth. Not today, though.

My throat closed, and I focused on my breathing to avoid getting unsettled by the emotions raging inside me. Now wasn't the time to have an episode.

Jack was sleeping upstairs in his bedroom, and Dahlia was here. With me.

Everything was fine. We were all fine. They would forever be my family. No matter what. That, I was sure of. Just in a different way. It was all good. The realization quieted the insecure part of my mind.

Pushing the thoughts of the unknown as far away as I could, I blinked fast to keep in the tears prickling the back of my eyes.

Tightness developed in my chest, and choosing to have faith in the unknown, I slumped back, my head sinking into the headrest, evading my flow of paralyzing thoughts, and fell asleep to the steady rhythm of Dahlia's breathing.

Chapter 3
April

"Girl, I'm in the middle of nowhere. The GPS is worthless," I said, hitting the steering wheel with the palm of my hand. "I'm driving around in circles. These roads lead nowhere. The navigation screen is a jumble of purple and white roads. My pantry is less messy, can you imagine? One moment I'm facing a cliff on a dead-end road and the next, I'm stuck in a labyrinth with no exit. Even the satellite is lost. Tell me again why I agreed to this."

"Relax, Bubble Head. Follow my directions, and you'll get there. It's trickier in the dark. I get it. But I'll assist you. You're lucky it hasn't snowed yet."

"Snow?" I repeated my friend's word. I sat up straight, forehead creased, scanning the pitch-black mountain road as if a bucketload of snowflakes would fall any second from the sky right on my path. "I've been on the road for eight hours. It's late, and I'm tired. Tell me you're joking."

"S-N-O-W, snow. You know, the fine white dust winter gods sprinkle on Earth during the cold months. I've heard it's quite common in the mountains at this time of the year."

I sighed through clenched teeth.

"Relax, April. You'll be fine. Don't panic over some sparkling white sprinkles."

I rolled my eyes. "I love snow. But it looks better on postcards, puzzles, or in Christmas movies."

My best friend chuckled, and I joined in.

Laughing relieved some of the tension in my back.

"Okay, I'm at the corner of Bear Crescent and Eagle Lane. Next thing I know I'll be on Weasel Boulevard. Who has given these streets their names?"

Saunders sighed on the other end of the line. "April, please focus. Stay on Eagle Lane up to Mountain Road. It should be about half a mile further on your right. Be careful, there's a sharp turn ahead."

"These roads are too narrow. Even for Miss Dolly. Tell me again why rich people vacation here. It's not safe. Don't be surprised if I drive off a cliff. Please choose a nice casket."

"Stop whining. Your car—Miss Dolly—is full of food, so you won't have to go out too much. I'm still confused you named your car. Each time you mention it, I believe, for a second, you have a passenger riding with you. Anyway, once you see the cabin, you'll never want to come back home."

"I doubt it. Remember you're lucky I still trust you, Saund." I carefully took the sharp bend along the mountainside and stopped breathing when all I could see for a second was the vertical drop of the cliff. "The last time I did, I ended up on a date with a podiatrist who had some foot fetish and asked me at least twenty times to show him my toes during dinner." I winced at the memory.

"There are no feet involved this time, and it's cold, so no one will beg you to take off your shoes. You're safe."

I uttered a bunch of curses. "You should've warned me before I came here that I needed to update my life insurance policy."

Saunders snickered but chose to ignore my quip. "Where are you now?"

I squinted and leaned forward to read the street sign on my left. "Huh, Mountain Road."

"Great, you're almost there. Make a right turn. Tell me when you see the gate."

"Gate? As in I'll be living in a gated community? In the middle of nowhere? Are you playing a prank on me?"

"Relax, girl. Blimey, I told you already. It's safe, and the view is to die for. You'll thank me later and dedicate your new book to your super-extraordinary best friend. Be real. You know I'm the most amazing girlfriend in the world." Saunders clapped her hands together on the other end of the line, sounding a lot more enthusiastic about the entire trip than I was at the moment.

What did I get myself into?

I steadied my breathing and reminded myself of the reasons I agreed to come here.

Mountain air.

Creative environment.

Free rent.

Hope for something new.

"What's the code?"

Saunders laughed, her attention not on me. She whispered something, and my cheeks flushed. Ohmygod, I had interrupted a fuck session when I called her in panic. If only I could lash myself. Not lash, ugh. Bad choice of words. No BDSM reference when my two best friends were fucking. Please… No… If only I could kick myself. There. Better.

"Saunders, I'll let you go back to your fuck marathon if you give me the code."

She giggled and brought her focus back to me. "Four-two-six-eight-five. Once you punch it in, it will be deactivated within five minutes and you won't be able to use it again. In the kitchen, you'll find an electronic key fob that will let you in and out of the gate for the length of your stay. Oh, and use your phone to unlock the cabin. I've already set up the digital key for you."

"Wait. What?"

"This morning, I added the digital key app to your device. You lock and unlock the front door with it. It's super easy, you'll see."

"*Thaannkks*," I said, stretching my word longer than I intended to.

"Call me in the morning or if you need anything before then. Love you, Bubble Head."

"Love you too, Saund. Tell Reed I'm sorry I interrupted whatever you guys were doing. I won't bother you anymore tonight." *Oh God, please don't let these images get etched into my brain.*

My friend moaned. Clearly, for my sake.

"Take care, April. Don't talk to strangers, and find yourself some testosterone-filled lumberjack to keep you warm at night," Reed said through the phone. I fought a smile. Saunders and Reed were family to me. The only ones I had left.

Once through the gate, three cabins appeared before my eyes. A three-story one so big it could be a mountain lodge, flanked by a smaller one on each side. Mine stood on the right side of the road, closer to the huge log castle.

Squeezing my steering wheel, I parked next to the front porch and killed the engine. Back steeled and chin up, I climbed out of my car and reached the steps. Even at this late hour, the lingering smell of barbecue wafted in the air. I congratulated myself for packing warm clothes. The chilly winter air sent shivers down to my toes. With my suitcase and Bernice's carrier beside me, I tried to unlock the door using my phone.

Nothing.

With fumbling fingers, I tried twice more.

Still nothing.

I rebooted my device.

Nope.

My nipples puckered and threatened to drill holes through the fabric of my light cotton shirt. My jacket was somewhere in my messy car, but I refused to empty the trunk to find it at this late hour. At my feet, Bernice meowed, no doubt also annoyed by the cold breeze.

"Sorry, girl. I'm trying here. Stupid technology."

After three more attempts, the green light of the door lock flashed in the dark.

Hallelujah.

I sucked in a quick breath and flicked the light switch on. A dim glow lit up the room.

A fervor spread through my body. I gaped. The interior of the cabin looked nothing like how I'd pictured it in my head. I freed my cat, who purred as she butted my legs. "Go explore, girl."

Hugging myself, still freezing, I scanned the room, taking everything in and blinking to make sure I wasn't dreaming. Hardwood floors, wooden walls, vaulted ceilings —wooden everything.

Anywhere else, it'd be too woodsy, but not here. Here, it worked.

The cream sofa, kitchen cabinets, and wool rug made it look classy. And inviting.

The soft aqua accessories gave the whole place a modern yet country charm vibe.

In the living room, there was a stone fireplace with a wooden mantel above. A black wrought-iron chandelier with a rustic charm hung above the farmhouse dining table, big enough to seat eight people.

With a straight back and a hand pressed to my heart, I emptied my lungs.

Love at first sight.

Saunders was right. One month here would never be enough. I felt at home and wanted to live in this cozy log cabin for the rest of my life. A hammock chair hung in a corner, facing the floor-to-ceiling window, giving the impression it floated in the air. Without a doubt, I knew this would be my writing spot.

Like a kid, I hurried around the cabin, opening the door to every room, wanting to uncover all the secrets this place hid between its walls.

The master bedroom occupied the second floor, a mezzanine overlooking the living room downstairs. The shower alone was bigger than the entire bathroom in my apartment. It had soft-gray tiles and a rain-style showerhead.

Flutters invaded my stomach. I jumped and landed on the mattress, on my front, arms spread, giggling. This was too good to be true.

The darkness outside engulfed me. Without any big city close by to light up the night sky, it was darker than anything I'd ever experienced before. I couldn't wait for the morning to come so I could admire the view. Saunders had promised it'd be spectacular, and I believed her. After all, she'd sent me to heaven.

Back in the kitchen, I added water to the kettle and turned the stove on, in need of some herbal tea to warm me up.

A handwritten note on powder-blue paper lay on the butcher-block topped island.

> Dear Ms. Simmons,
> Hope you have a marvelous stay.
> Enjoy the view and fresh air.
> Your host,
> C. H.

Whoever this C.H. was, he or she was kind enough to welcome me personally. Everything about this place drew me in. A lone tear streamed down my cheek. Somehow, I felt as if I belonged here.

Back in the living room, I added wood to the fireplace —someone had lit the fire prior to my arrival—to cozy up the cabin. Not quite warm enough yet, it served more as an element of decor than a source of heat. I cranked the thermostat up in the meantime and went to my room to empty my suitcase.

One cup of tea later, wrapped in the duvet on the bed, my eyelids heavy, I fell asleep on the soft mattress, dreaming I was lying on the fluffiest cloud.

———

The sound of a car engine outside woke me up the next morning. One quick look at the alarm clock on the night-stand told me it was thirteen past nine. Wait. No middle of the night *I can't sleep and the minutes are ticking by* episodes? No tossing and turning in bed for hours? I blinked twice to make sure I read the time right.

Curled on my side, my body buried under the white duvet, I failed to stop the grin growing on my face.

I'd been in Green Mountain for twelve hours, and already the mountain air was working wonders on my sleepless nights.

With lightness in my chest, I jumped in the shower. Singing at the top of my lungs, I enjoyed the hot water relaxing my knotted muscles. "Red dress, high heels, la la la." Dressed in faded blue jeans and a cropped fuzzy pink sweater, with a cup of hot chocolate in hand, I sat in the hammock chair, feeling as if I were at the top of the world. Without blinking, I took in the red and orange leaves covering the ground and the clear blue sky that let me see miles ahead. The view from here was breathtaking. I took a sip of my liquid cocoa indulgence, and heat traveled from my head to my toes.

Peace spread through me, and I felt calmer than I had in a long time. And happier too.

With my mug in hand, I ventured out onto the back deck. A hot tub occupied the right-hand corner, while two wooden Adirondack chairs and a small grill were positioned on the left. The mountain air woke up all my senses, and the cold breeze stung the tip of my nose.

Saunders truly had sent me to paradise.

I snapped a selfie and sent it to her with a heart emoji.

The reception wasn't that great up here, and it took a few minutes for the message to go through.

After devouring a light breakfast, I powered my brain, excited about where my creative mind would take me. Comfortably tucked in my now favorite chair, armed with a notebook and a pen, I scribbled notes for my new book. Before I knew it, it was four o'clock.

Buried in my work, I'd lost track of time.

For dinner, I fixed myself some chicken and noodle soup I'd brought from home and relaxed with a glass of white wine on the couch, my legs folded under a fluffy blanket.

The fireplace had warmed the air, and before I could make it to my room, my eyelids got heavy. And I dozed off.

———

The next morning, I woke up at eight, on the couch, entangled in the blanket, with Bernice curled up beside me. Butterflies danced in my stomach, and tingles of excitement spread through my chest. A faint aroma of pine lingered in the air. It tickled my nostrils in the most delicious way.

I stretched my arms over my head. "Good morning, Green Mountain."

I'd slept for over twelve hours. Whoa, I'd clearly misjudged how sleep-deprived I had been.

Could a change of air have been all I needed, all along?

I got up and reached the bathroom upstairs. My eyes widened when I glanced at my reflection in the mirror. *Oh my.* My hair was a tangled mess, and I had dried drool at the corner of my lips. Who cared, right? The smile on my face had turned into a permanent fixture I couldn't shake away.

I'd spent the last three years of my life in some kind of monotonous parallel universe. I lived through them, but instead of enjoying myself, I went through the motions. Days turned into months, and months bled into years. Except for my long-lasting friendship with Saunders, I lived a pretty lonely life. Now, for the first time since the day my world had been turned upside down, I felt free.

After Travis, the love of my life, passed away, I barely got out of bed for weeks. We'd moved in together during our junior year in college, living in his closet-sized apartment for ten months before making an offer on a house. A fixer-upper dream we had planned to renovate over the years until it fit our vision fully. A little house with banana-yellow wood siding and white shutters, a backyard, and a wrap-around porch. Nothing extravagant, but a place to call our own. It was like we both felt this urge to reach for our goals early on in life. Like we knew our story came with an expiration date. We shared so many dreams together. Backpacking a summer through Australia, adopting a dog from a shelter, going bungee jumping in Europe—Travis's dream, not mine. And raising a bunch of kids—somewhere down the line. But then Travis got sick. It shattered all our hopes and plans, every single one, until all that remained was dust.

His death threw me into a downward spiral.

A dark hole that sucked me in until I crashed and burned.

I lost a lot that year. Myself included.

Freshly showered, I draped a towel around my body, my hair piled on the top of my head in a messy knot. Something—or rather someone—caught my eye outside.

From the bedroom window, I noticed a tall dark silhouette of a man standing in front of the larger log cabin, the one I thought was a mountain lodge. The man was rummaging through the trunk of a massive black SUV. I took in the over-the-top log cabin behind him.

All of it screamed money.

Way out of my league.

I wondered if the man was a tenant like me or if he

owned the place. Not that it really mattered, as long as I could enjoy the sight of him.

His attention drifted to his left. He pushed back from the trunk and pivoted around. His plaid shirt clung to his ripped chest and defined biceps.

Even from a distance, I noticed how handsome he was.

Longish, disheveled dark hair, wild stubble, broad shoulders, and high cheekbones. And an ass worthy of a jeans ad.

All male and testosterone-y.

I would've paid good money to run my fingers over his couple-of-days-old scruffy jaw.

"Hello, gorgeous," I said to myself. The part of me I'd buried years ago awoke the moment I laid eyes on him. I grinned. Green Mountain was definitely everything I needed.

A beautiful red-haired woman and a little boy traipsed down the road, hand in hand, toward him. Handsome picked the boy up and twirled him around. They shared words and laughed hard. His arm curled around the woman's neck, and he pressed his lips to her temple.

"Aww," I exhaled with a huff. "Perfect family."

That's what Travis and I thought we'd have someday. Life decided it'd never happen for us. A strong pinch tightened my chest at the memory.

I'd made my peace about losing Travis, but somehow, seeing these people, all close and happy, played with the strings of my heart. My vision blurred for a second, and I blinked, chasing my emotions away.

Handsome turned his head as if he sensed my gaze on him, and his eyes found mine. He stared at me for a second too long, his gaze glued to my face. My mouth went dry. Feeling like a stalker, I moved to the side, away from the window, but the towel around my body caught on the window handle and puddled at my feet, exposing my bare chest for everyone outside to see.

"Fuck." I swore and folded my arms over me to hide my nakedness. Handsome's eyes flared, and the corner of his lips curled into a lazy smile. Exposed, I dropped to my knees on the floor, hoping he saw nothing from where he stood.

I snorted. Men had a sixth sense for naked chicks. No way had he missed my breasts.

When I raised my head a little to see if he still stood there after a long minute that dragged infinitely, Handsome and his perfect family had disappeared inside their cabin.

Heat flared in my cheeks. *I'd flashed a stranger.* Not just any stranger, but my neighbor. I crossed my fingers, hoping I wouldn't run into him or his family again in the next month, or I'd die of shame.

Me and my clumsy self.

Chapter 4
Carter

Filling my lungs with the distinctive and addictive mountain air, I was rummaging through the trunk of my SUV when I noticed Dahlia and Jack returning from a walk, sauntering my way. We exchanged grins before I turned to lift Jack into my arms, his laughter, as I spun him around, lighting me up inside.

With one arm, I pulled Dahlia closer and planted a kiss on her temple.

I could feel eyes on me. Jerking my head, I took a look around.

If paparazzi had found a way inside the gate, I would never feel at ease here ever again. Not as long as Dahlia and Jack were with me. When my best friend suggested I install a fence when I bought the lot, at first, I brushed it off as unimportant. With everything that had happened in the last two years and the woman I grew to hate probably perfecting a revenge plan, I had never been so relieved that I'd listened to Dahlia.

A group of businessmen occupied the cabin down the road, meeting once a year for a retreat. They'd been here in the past and had never troubled the peace. Or *my* peace. My sixth sense told me they were not the ones spying on me.

With another scan, I perused my surroundings. Nothing. Still, I could feel the presence of someone close by.

When I spotted no one, I was about to retreat inside when, as if pulled by a magnet, my gaze landed on the second-story window of the cabin next door. I knew a woman had moved there, but I had yet to meet her.

Fervor spread through me.

My heart rate accelerated.

We fixated our gazes on each other for longer than required. For some reason, I couldn't avert mine. She sported faded pink hair and had the bluest eyes I'd ever seen. Azurite embedded in her porcelain visage. Her lips formed a heart, and her cheeks flushed as I took her in.

I stood there, frozen, oxygen barely making it to my lungs as she stood still, and my gaze roamed over her delicate features.

My throat rippled, and electricity traveled through me as neither of us broke eye contact.

Whoever this woman was, she had a pull on me that I couldn't explain or escape from. My body ignited under the weight of her gaze. I felt like we already knew each other. Yet I was sure if we had ever crossed paths, I would remember. She possessed one of those angelic faces that once you saw them, you could never forget.

A buzz tingled my spine. A sensation I'd never experienced before while facing a woman.

My heart flipped in my chest, and I wondered if it was

a knee-jerk reaction to the lust swirling between us or something else that I had no idea how to define.

My neighbor parted her cherry-pink lips, and the trance we were under dissolved.

A cold wave replaced the warmth that had infiltrated my chest seconds ago.

When she retreated to the side, the towel wrapped around her caught onto something and fell, exposing her bare chest through the glass. To me.

My jaw slackened. I blinked, making sure this wasn't a dream.

A dark-red hue crept up her cheeks, and she met my eyes for half a second before dropping down and hiding from my sight.

Amusement pulled at my lips, and I stifled a laugh.

"Everything all right?" Dahlia asked.

"Yes. Everything is perfectly fine. I think my stay here will be good for me. Yes, I feel it in my bones."

I cocked my head, trying to catch one more glance of the woman, but all I could see was the pink top of her head.

Reality kicked in, and I wondered if she recognized me and her motives for spying on me were less than honorable or if she was embarrassed.

I hoped it was the latter. A diversion appeared to be what I yearned for these days, and I might have found the perfect woman to keep my mind occupied.

Yes, in that instant, I decided this would be my mission. Find out what her deal was.

Because as it turned out I was in Green Mountain for a while, vacationing, away from the limelight, and except for working on my new album and spending time with my family, I had nothing more important to do than to spy on her too.

With determined steps, I followed Dahlia and Jack inside for our cartoon marathon.

———

The three of us sat by the fireplace, and armed with blankets, pillows, and popcorn, we spent the next hour and a half watching Jack's favorite movie, a story about an orphan dinosaur searching for a new family that would take him in as theirs. In a lot of ways, the storyline fit mine. Sure, I wasn't an orphan, not in the theoretical sense at least, but I was on my own, searching for a place where I belonged. I hoped, someday soon, I'd find my place in this world. For now, I was good by myself. Never again would I put my happiness in the hands of someone else. I had learned my lesson the hard way. As my therapist explained, my living-in-hell years should be classified under life experience. A bump in my journey, not my destination.

Earlier, when I woke up and realized Dahlia and Jack had gone for a walk, I missed the cacophony of having them around. The house sounded too quiet without their chatter between these walls.

When she stayed over, Dahlia often went down the road to call her husband. My cabin had poor cell reception, and by the gate, we always got a better signal. Nick and Dahlia lived a few miles from here, in a farmhouse they bought and renovated after Nick moved to Green Mountain and they got together.

The idea Jack and Dahlia would soon go back home had my heart sinking.

Thanks to their contagious happiness, my family's presence healed every piece of my broken heart. When they were around, everything seemed better in my life. Lighter. Brighter. My anxiety levels dropped, my priorities changed, and all the complicated stuff vanished. Even my smile returned.

Since Dahlia met Nick, they hadn't needed me as much as they used to. The four of us formed this unconventional family. It wasn't always easy, but we made it work. And so far, we were happy.

As Jack settled in my arms under the blanket, a hollow sensation lodged in my chest when my eyes landed on his mama. My thoughts drifted to the baby on the way. Dahlia smiled at me, and it quieted the doubts swirling in my head. Then my mind drifted to the new neighbor I couldn't wait to catch sight of again.

———

After his nap, Jack ran toward me. I picked him up and pulled him close to my chest, the beat of our hearts merging together. Jack had grown so much since the last time I saw him. With his dark hair, square jaw, and melted-steel irises, he was the spitting image of me at his age. Talented, he fed his creativity through music the same way I'd always done. However, the kid also had wit, a focused intelligence I envied, just like my brother Jeff.

His presence brought back all the mixed feelings I'd experienced years ago. The tightness in my chest and throat increased, and I pushed away the memories trying to make a return. No need to dig out the past. It wouldn't do us any good. A few years back, Jeff, Dahlia, and I had messed up. We all did. For a while, it divided us. Pulled us apart. Nowadays, that mistake—with a capital M—had turned out to be a blessing in disguise. If we had a do-over, I wasn't sure any of us would change how it unfolded because if we did, life wouldn't be the same. Still, all the unanswered questions haunted my nights sometimes. One day, I'd be brave enough to deal with the lingering mystery once and for all. Yeah, one day. Not today, though.

At the thought, my airways constricted, making my breaths shallow and difficult.

Calm down, Carter.

Tugging at the flimsy threads of my self-control, I kept my discomfort under wraps and faked a smile, searching for an out. A diversion from my troubling thoughts.

"Hey bud, I have an idea. You know the song we've been working on over video chat? Let's record it," I suggested. Jack's tiny fingers squeezed mine in delight, the slight gesture lighting my heart up like a Christmas tree. Moments like this one kept me going; they kept me alive. Thanks to them, I breathed easier.

Together, we made our way to the home studio, a room I had gotten built by some of the best professionals in the industry. With perfect soundproofing, it had two sections. The first one consisted of a navy-blue couch, two upholstered, matching tan chairs, a small end table, and a console, opening to the recording studio through a glass wall. The smaller room contained two stools and a microphone and a designated area for a drum kit and a keyboard. The walls were pale and the ceiling dark, the hardwood floor the same shade as the rest of the house.

"Ready?" I asked him as we positioned ourselves on the stools, holding our instruments, after I turned the console on.

Jack bobbed his head fast, his smile unfaltering. "Yes. Let's do this."

Chapter 5

April

"You flashed your tits to some stranger?" Saunders laughed so much it turned into a train of hiccups. "April, you'll never cease to impress me. I'm so incredibly proud of you, girl."

"Stop making fun of me. It was humiliating enough. He was with his wife and child. Can you imagine this? I hope to never come face to face with him again, or I'll die of shame." My cheeks flushed, burning at the thought of meeting my neighbor up close.

"Is he hot? Please tell me he's a fit bloke. I have nothing against nerdy men or average-looking guys, but for your sake, I hope he's smokin' hot."

Sometimes I forgot Saunders came from the UK and moved to the States to attend college. Then she reminded me with her choice of words.

"You don't understand. Hot is too weak an adjective to describe him. I swear I could've gotten pregnant just from looking at him. He eye-fucked me while my breasts hung there, in all their gloriousness. Seriously, this guy is the most handsome male specimen I've ever seen. Pure spank bank material, I'm telling you. He's what fantasies are made of." I fanned myself with my hand as I recalled his gaze on me, heat stirring low in my belly.

"Now I wish I'd come with you to the cabin. Girl, you need to meet him again. It's an order. Take pictures this time. I want to see if your hormones are messing with your head or if he's that good-looking. Besides, it wouldn't hurt to build yourself a glorious male portfolio. Something to indulge in when you feel lonely at night."

"You're impossible." I sighed at the recollection of the man who saw me topless. "He's *that* hot. I'm telling you, Saund, I didn't dream it. You have to see one of these special creatures to believe in them. I thought they only existed in movies. Put him on a motorcycle or in a cowboy hat, and someone will have to sweep my jaw from the floor. Tall. Dark. All testosterone-y. So damn sexy." I gulped the rest of my wine, clenching my thighs together. "Why are the handsome ones always taken?"

"C'mon, because they're hot. Even if they're psycho crazy, women love them because they're a better accessory than any purse or pair of posh shoes."

"In addition to the hotness factor, he's a family man. No woman can resist a man like that. I'll dream about him for the next month, I'm telling you." For a second, I got lost in a daydream. "I bet there was a set of killer abs underneath his shirt. He's the whole package deal. With one glance, he woke up my hibernating hormones. Now I'm all tingly. And giddy. Oh God." Laughter left my mouth. "Damn, I'm objectifying my sexy neighbor. We shouldn't talk about him this way—"

"Don't shut me out, girl. It's good for you to open up. I

think you're ready to get back out there. Don't forget to send me a visual. Some pick-me-up fantasy for the dark days. My vibrator and I could really use it the nights Reed pisses me off. By the way, we're not objectifying him. We're only assessing his exceptional features." My friend burst into a fit of giggles, and I joined in, both of us sounding like schoolgirls obsessing over their first crush.

"What about Reed? I know you two were having a fuck marathon the other night when I called you on my way here."

"He wants me to move in with him." Saunders let out a long huff.

"What's wrong? You love him, right?"

"I do. His house is nice and closer to your place, which is a plus."

"Then what is it?"

"The idea of having one penis for the rest of my life scares the shit out of me."

"Reed isn't asking you to marry him, at least not yet, only to move in with him. Believe me, if he's the one, you won't even care he's the last penis you ride."

"You're probably right. I told him I'd think about it." She drummed her fingernails on something, probably her desk. "Anyway, I gotta go. I have a meeting in five. A new client looking for an Amazonian retreat. Keep me posted about your hot next-door neighbor ."

I shook my head in disbelief, unable to stop smiling.

We promised to call each other the next day before hanging up.

Hours later, and with endless energy to burn, I ran to my bedroom and got dressed. "I need some fresh air," I told Bernice when we crossed paths on the staircase. Saunders told me a fence surrounded the lot, and there was no risk of facing a bear if I wandered around.

Dressed in a sleeveless peacock-blue puffer vest over a golden turtleneck sweater and black leggings, I slid my feet into my favorite sheepskin boots.

Once outside, I welcomed the crisp January air into my lungs.

The late afternoon sun's rays cast a glow around me.

My feet orgasmed at the sound of fallen leaves and pine needles crunching under my steps.

I never got to enjoy the full extent of all four seasons in Georgia. This, right here, felt amazing.

Oak and pine trees surrounded the property. The cold breeze wavered their tops and sent a tingle to my cheeks. Whoever said the mountain air was addictive didn't lie.

I rubbed my palms against my leggings, warming them up to avoid the slight tremors before I settled to take a panoramic shot with my phone.

Moving slowly slowly in a full sweep, I captured the beauty surrounding me, the view—mountain peaks covered in snow in the distance—taking my breath away.

"Hey. What do you think you're doing?"

A powerful masculine voice startled me from my left. I turned my head and came face to face with Handsome. Damn it. Up close, wearing a pair of washed-out jeans and a tan corduroy jacket over a plaid shirt, he looked even more gorgeous. In a devastating way. My shaky heart free-fell to my knotted stomach, and my breaths quickened.

My nostrils wriggled at the faint scent of pine, cedar-wood, and soap wafting from him. My neighbor even smelled delicious.

I swallowed hard and found my voice. "Are you talking to me?" With a cocked brow, I pointed at my chest with a thumb.

This man meant business, with no trace of friendliness on his face. Attractive and symmetric. Full lips. Straight nose. Melted-steel irises that could swallow me whole. He frowned, the worry lines deepening the storm in his eyes. "Yeah, I'm talking to you. There's no one else around. Were you taking a picture of me?"

His clipped tone aggravated me. I folded my arms over my chest. "Excuse me?"

"You heard me. Now answer the question. Were you— yes or no—snapping a picture of me with your phone? That's a simple question. You should be able to give me a straight answer."

"I should've figured you'd be a prick. You can't look this good and not be a dickhead."

He squinted before his eyes flared and threw daggers at me. "Why can't you just answer the damn question?"

"Wow, that's an enormous ego you have, mister. No wonder you need a house this big to contain it all."

"You still haven't answered the question."

Why wouldn't he let it go?

The wrinkles around his eyes deepened.

"Why would I want a picture of you?"

"Do you always answer a question with a question?" He huffed his aggravation.

I shrugged. "Are you always this nice to people you meet for the first time?"

My neighbor balled his hands at his sides.

Yeah, I noticed.

"We met earlier. Don't you remember?" His full lips tilted at the corner.

I couldn't believe he went there. I prayed my cheeks wouldn't flush under his scrutinizing gaze. "Nah. You must be mistaking me for someone else. I would remember meeting you if I already had. It's not every day I get the chance to run into a jerk in the woods."

His focus descended to my chest

"By the way, my eyes are up here."

"You think you're a smart ass, don't you?"

I pinched my lips together. This was the most fun I'd had in a long time. "Maybe." I offered him my cheekiest smile.

"Stop wasting my time. Did you or didn't you take my picture?" His words now spewed venom.

I sighed. This man had no right to talk to me like that. "I'm glad we've decided you're an ass. It'll be easier not to talk to you ever again."

Handsome's eyes bulged out, and he gave his forehead a scratch with the side of his thumb. "I'll ask you one last time. Did you or didn't you take a picture of me?"

"No. I didn't. Happy now? I took a panoramic picture of this beautiful view." I motioned my hand all around me. "Being handsome doesn't give you the right to be an insensitive jerk and talk to me like I'm worth less than you."

Did I just call him handsome? *Abort, abort. April, retreat. Don't show him any weakness.* I tipped my chin up, turned on my heel, and didn't spare my hot neighbor another glance.

"You think I'm handsome?" Gone was his annoyance. Amusement now filled his tone.

I stormed away from him. Every word he spoke infuriated me, and I wasn't about to indulge him or inflate his ego any further.

"Just so you know, I'm not an insensitive jerk." The irritation in his voice had dropped a notch.

I glanced at him over my shoulder while I swaggered further away. "You've done nothing to prove otherwise. Sorry, but I'll file you under the asshole category. That's where you belong with your over-dimensioned ego and wrongly aimed anger."

"You have categories for men?" Genuine surprise lit up

his gorgeous face. His stare drew me in. He smirked, never breaking eye contact.

My knees buckled under the intensity of his gaze.

"Why not? I think you deserve—" *Bam.* I bumped headfirst into a large, obviously misplaced, oak tree as I turned my head around. I shut my eyes for a second, trying to regain my balance and shake off the dizziness that made my legs feel weak.

"Are you all right, miss?" a small voice asked me in a strong Southern accent.

Blood rushed into my ears and I looked down, blinking. Handsome Neighbor's son was tugging at my sweater sleeve, worry filling his eyes. Where had he come from?

"Yeah, I-I'm good…huh…I think. I hope I gave this tree a big pounding headache. It shouldn't stand in my way." I winked at him, and he giggled.

Handsome Neighbor hurried to join us. "Are you sure you're okay? You seem a little pale. Do you want to sit down for a minute?" He had switched to a softer tone while addressing me this time.

I saw concern swimming in his gray eyes, the shade reminding me of agitated ocean water minutes before a storm. When I stared into them, I drifted away, lost in their depths. Why did everything about my neighbor have to be so damn hot and enticing?

I wobbled on my legs, and he caught me before I humiliated myself further, his strong arms holding me upright. Heat developed where his palms rested on my waist, a sensation foreign to me. Not sure how to interpret it, I pushed away from him and adjusted my sweater, avoiding his eyes. "Huh, I'll be all right. And…and I should go. Sorry for the a-hole comment." I rubbed my forehead with a hand, trying to dissipate the soreness thumping in my skull.

I sidestepped, and dizziness made my head spin. Handsome Neighbor clutched my elbow from behind, and I leaned into him for a quick second. The same warmth I felt seconds ago returned. His touch erased all traces of the uneasiness we shared. Something passed between us, fiery and potent, that sent a discharge through me, but I chose to ignore it.

His hand lingered on the small of my back, and I breathed him in. His smell was addictive—and manly. A part of me wished I could bury myself in his chest and stay there, just to feel his arms wrapped around me once more and the security they provided.

"Miss, why is your hair pink?" the little voice next to me asked, clueless to my inner thoughts. "Is it real? Because my friend Beatrix wants pink hair too. She thinks that it will make her a fairy. If you have pink hair, it means you're a fairy. Beatrix was right. Fairies exist. This is *soooo* cool."

Aware of his eyes on me, I ignored HN's amused gaze. In my head, I renamed him HN. A simpler and shorter version of Handsome Neighbor. Or Hot Neighbor. Or Highly (Annoying) Neighbor. Yeah, HN fit him fine.

I squatted a little to level my eyes with the boy who still watched me with interest and awe, ignoring the throbbing in my head. "What's your name?"

"Jack," he quipped, a genuine smile stretching his lips. He held out his tiny hand, and I shook it, his striking resemblance to HN impossible to ignore.

"I'll tell you a secret, Jack. Beatrix is right to believe in fairies. Life is full of magic. Most people choose to ignore it, but if you look close enough, you'll see magic everywhere. My hair turns pink whenever I focus on everything amazing in my life. It makes my days much more exciting. When my hair is blonde, I feel like a grown-up, and my life isn't as much fun. If you believe in magic, it will find you."

His eyes sparkled, and HN mouthed a silent *Thank you* in my direction.

Without another word, HN reached for the boy's hand. My ovaries did a happy dance. "Come on, buddy, I'm sure dinner is ready by now."

"Bye," the boy said with a wave. "Beatrix will not believe me when I tell her I met a real fairy."

I waved back, and as they walked away, I stood there, watching father and son waltz to their cabin, hand in hand, confused and amazed, all at the same time.

At least, from what I saw, HN seemed like a hands-on dad. I had yet to meet the wife. I winced at the thought. She had to be an angel to deal with his huge ego and attitude problem.

I shot Saunders a few quick texts, hoping the reception was better out here.

ME

Met HN face to face.

HN = Hot Neighbor

Wet my panties. Much better than from afar.

Kind of a jerk, though.

Met his son. Sweetest boy ever. Has a thing for pink hair.

Won't be able to send you a visual, though. He got angry when he thought I snapped a picture of him.

Long story. He's not friendly. Just mouth-watering hot.

Come visit if you wanna see for yourself.

I roamed around with the phone in my hand above my head until the chimes announced the messages had gone through.

As I walked back to my cabin, I wondered what my neighbor's panic was all about. With one last glance over my shoulder, I tried to catch a glimpse of him.

In vain.

Once inside, with my back pressed against the closed door, I cupped my heart. I wasn't allowed to fantasize about him. This was wrong. So very wrong.

And yet, even his broodiness ignited my hormones.

Saunders was right. It was about time I got back on the dating scene because having filthy thoughts about my married neighbor was so not the way to go.

The next day, I was sipping tea on the back deck, wrapped in a fluffy blanket, my feet propped on the small wooden table by the jacuzzi when I heard voices next door. I couldn't make out what they were saying, but I swore there was another man in the driveway. Curious about the commotion, I stretched my neck to see what was going on. And who knew, maybe HN had an equally attractive single brother, and fantasizing about him wouldn't be a sin. I slapped myself mentally. Since when did I become a nosy neighbor? Could I blame being isolated here as the cause? Deep down, I knew what the source of my nosiness was. Since the first time I caught sight of him, HN had been on my mind all the time. *He's married, for God's sake.* How many times would I have to repeat that before my mind got the memo? What was worse than dreaming about him was that I didn't even like the guy. I found him attractive, yes. And he ignited something deep inside me, yes again. But then I recalled his erroneous accusations and *assholeness,* and it killed the fantasy.

My neighbor and the stranger hugged and laughed at

something. His wife joined them, but instead of cuddling with him, she went to the other man and kissed him.

Wait...what did I just witness? Three of them? I blinked, not sure what was going on. Were my neighbors... in some kind of polyamorous relationship? Even though I begged myself to mind my own business, I couldn't look elsewhere, waiting to see how the scene would unfold.

Was that why I was asked to sign a non-disclosure agreement before I came here? Because the sexual activities of my neighbors were controversial?

Many questions swirled in my head as I watched their interaction.

The two men exchanged a few words, but I was too far away to hear anything they said. And I wasn't good at reading lips.

Jack disappeared into the idling car, then the wife dropped a kiss on HN's cheek before following the other man to the vehicle.

Straight back and chin high, my neighbor stood there as they trailed away, not moving. What did I just witness? Polygamy wasn't allowed in the United States.

This whole situation was becoming all the more interesting.

My nose tickled, and before I could hold it in, I sneezed.

No, no, no. I shut my eyelids, wishing I wasn't about to get caught spying.

Was my life so not entertaining these days that now I had to live vicariously through other people's?

When HN's eyes snapped in my direction, I retreated inside, hiding behind the curtains in the living room.

He cocked his head toward me like he knew I'd be standing there, and I begged the ground to open up and swallow me whole when our eyes met.

Chapter 6
Carter

Three days into my stay in Green Mountain, Nick picked up Dahlia and Jack. I offered to drive them home, but he was already on his way. "Hey, Carter," he said, giving me a side hug when we met him outside. "You don't look so bad."

I scrunched up my nose. "Well, it's a"—I held in the curse about to leave my mouth—"nightmare I'm trying to navigate out of. I still can't believe I put up with her for two years." I shook my head and shoved my hands into my pockets. My pulse raced just at the thought of the Evil Queen.

"Don't be too hard on yourself. This stuff can happen to the best of us. Listen, if you need someone other than Dah to talk to, I'm here. Whenever. Call me."

"Thanks, man. Shit, I forgot. Congrats on the baby."

A smile lit up Nick's face. One radiating with pride. He had a gleam in his eyes. The last time I saw something similar was on his wedding day. Their baby would be beautiful. I had no doubts. Nick reached the six-foot mark and had tanned skin and broad shoulders from years of working as a carpenter. He had a chin dimple, which I knew Dahlia found cute as hell, and golden-brown eyes. I could already imagine a toddler with his blond hair and Dahlia's green eyes running around.

"Thanks. We're thrilled."

Dahlia inched closer and wound her arms around her husband's midsection. He kissed her, and when they looked at each other, something passed between them.

Love.

My heart sank in my chest. I wanted that. Someone to share my life with. Hopefully, one day, I'd find it. Or it would find me.

To avoid staring at them, I lifted Jack in my arms and nuzzled his neck. "I'll see you soon, buddy. I love you." I kissed his cheek, and he tightened his grip around me.

"I *looooove* you too."

I lowered him to his feet, and he hurried toward the car.

"See you, Carter." Nick clapped my shoulder before following Jack and helping him into his car seat.

"Call me anytime," Dahlia said. Rising on her tiptoes, she dropped a kiss on my cheek and squeezed my arm before following in her man's footsteps.

A sound from next door caught my attention. When I turned, I spotted my nosy neighbor standing on her back deck. Without acknowledging me, she disappeared inside. Was she spying on me?

"Bye." Jack's small voice pulled me out of my thoughts. I spun in his direction and waved back when I noticed his tiny hand through the open window.

In the driveway, standing next to my SUV, I watched

them retreating, holding my breath, a piece of me leaving with them.

Even after the taillights disappeared, I stood there, my hands stuffed in my pockets, a million thoughts circling through my mind. From the corner of my eye, I caught a glimpse of my neighbor through her living room window. Her hair was tied in some sort of a half-do on the top of her head. She averted her eyes and scurried away, leaving me to my own devices.

The next morning, I woke up early, oversleeping not an option with the never-ending night I had. The entire time, my brain raced with *what-ifs*. After breakfast, I locked myself in my music studio, only to emerge thirty minutes later, my brain a blank slate. Restlessness had invaded me after my family left yesterday. I missed them. And I missed the noise. The one preventing my mind from going haywire.

To keep myself busy, I cooked, ran fifteen miles on the small country roads, took a nap, lifted weights.

Nothing distracted me long enough.

Hours ticked by.

The sun disappeared beyond the tree line.

Slouched on the couch in the media room, I ate leftovers for dinner while watching a hockey game, the TV on mute, and dumb scrolling on my phone. What a waste of time. When I stretched my legs, the clicker fell on the floor and changed the channel by accident. It stopped on a late-night gossip show. I leaned forward to grab the remote but stopped halfway when my face filled the screen. Minus the beard and the untrimmed, disheveled hair. *Goddammit.* With the clicker now in hand, I unmuted the TV. Savannah Prince's diabolical eyes stared back at me. I swallowed the pool of acid filling my mouth.

"There are rumors that longtime lovers, Savannah

Prince and Carter Hills, have broken up for good. Everyone thought there'd be wedding bells in the next year. Insiders believed Carter Hills proposed during the holidays. A source reported an unexpected pregnancy. Miss Prince, who said in a statement she's still in love with Carter Hills and that he broke her heart, has resumed her activities in Hollywood, while Mr. Hills is nowhere to be found. Another source told us the country music star dumped the actress for a famous model. Sadly, it seems like sex rehab might not have worked for Mr. Hills. We'll keep you updated. In other entertainment news, Pierce Callaway…"

I hit the remote and turned the TV off.

Fucking fame.

I loved the music, hated the spotlight.

Lies, lies, and more lies. Wedding. A baby. Mistresses. A model. Sex rehab. Nothing they reported other than the breakup being final was even close to the truth.

When had my personal life become more important than my musical talent? I loathed scandals. I should've thought about that before linking my name to Savannah Fucking Prince.

By tomorrow, our faces would be plastered on the front pages of every trash magazine around the world. I threw the clicker across the couch.

Breathe in. Breathe out.

Those tabloids spread lies, the same way Savannah Prince spread her thighs to get what she wanted, and people bought that shit without second-guessing anything.

When I dumped her ass, I knew she'd paint me as the bad guy despite all the watertight precautions. Although, with Dahlia and Jack around for a few days, I kinda forgot about all of the shit show.

My eyes shifted to the cabin next door, and I wondered

what my neighbor was up to. For reasons I refused to analyze, she kept me on edge. Yep, if I was being honest with myself, this blunt piece of a woman with pink hair intrigued me. There was something about her that appealed to me. It wasn't just the vibrant blue of her eyes that captured my attention and jumbled my heart, her angelic face, or her pink hair. No, it was something more. Her energy. That one time in the woods, we pushed each other's buttons, and it left me with a hard-on. I could've found a smarter way to engage with her than to pick a fight. Juvenile, right? But it worked. I got her attention. Under all the fieriness that infuriated me like nothing else ever did before, she fascinated the hell out of me. She held her head high and didn't refrain from arguing with me. I enjoyed that she was her own person and had enough confidence in herself not to shy away from her opinions. Self-confidence was sexy on a woman. Most women crossing my path tried to seduce me, to take advantage of me. Pixie didn't. She couldn't care less about my name or what I did for a living.

When I caught her after she bumped her head and her knees buckled, I could swear our bodies reacted to each other. A surge of heat had traveled through me, and for an instant, I had found it disorienting because I had no clue where it came from and why it would arise with my neighbor in my arms.

When she confided in Jack about fairies, the sparks dancing in her eyes, the way she spoke to him like his questions mattered, it unleashed emotions inside me. This woman wasn't just fun to banter with, she cared. That made a big difference in the grand scheme of things. I was more used to people demanding than people caring, and the latter weighed more in the balance of my heart.

Fairy hadn't taken my picture that day. I was well

aware. For a short instant, I just enjoyed riling her up and having her attention on me. Now that Jack was gone, I couldn't use him as an excuse to meet her anymore. I'd need to resort to new tactics.

I switched positions on the couch, praying I'd see some movements next door so that I could go for a walk and pretend to bump into her. Even though I refused to acknowledge it, I wanted to test a theory. See if the pull I felt for her the two times we faced each other was a product of my imagination or something tangible.

And also, there was a story here. One I couldn't wait to uncover. The reason she had rented a cabin on a mountaintop by herself for a month. Was she running away from something like I was—an ex-boyfriend, a divorce, or her life—or did she need some time off far from the rest of the world? A breather in the hustle and bustle of her everyday life?

If she was hiding, it raised a bunch of new questions in my mind. From what? From who? Did someone hurt or fail her? Did she leave someone or something behind?

When the agency informed me about the last-minute change of tenant a few days ago, I thought this April Simmons would be much older. Never had I anticipated my neighbor would be an attractive woman about my age. I hadn't planned for this, but now that she was here, I was curious. Most people renting my cabins were either older folks or businessmen, not attractive single women under thirties.

Right now, my life was a clusterfuck, and focusing on something, or rather someone else, would be a more than welcome distraction. The moment I caught sight of her bare tits through her bedroom window, I knew she'd be trouble. And yet, considering my rap sheet, it seemed that lately I was seduced by it.

As if someone had heard my prayers, I spotted my neighbor through the living room window. She was struggling to carry a pile of wood to her cabin and looked like she'd crumple under its weight. I rushed out of the media room and crossed the house. In the entryway, I slid my arms into my lined-denim jacket and exited into the night. Humming a song, I ambled her way, my hands stuffed in my pockets, projecting as much nonchalance as I could muster.

"Hey, Neighbor. What a great night, huh? Need a hand?"

If only looks could kill. "Hmm, no. I'm fine." Feisty and proud. I liked that. A lot.

I circled her until we faced each other. "Come on, let me help you." I leaned forward and grabbed the firewood from her arms, which were shaking from the effort. Our fingers brushed, and a zing worked through me, strong enough that it took me by surprise, and I almost dropped the logs in my grip.

Arms crossed and chin lifted, she held her ground with unwavering confidence. "I was fine, just so you know."

I pinched my lips together to avoid smiling and pushed her a little more. "Keep telling yourself that. Someday you might believe it. Don't overestimate yourself. You're drenched from your exertion."

She snorted.

"Thank you would have sufficed. It was my pleasure to come to your rescue. Good neighborhood manners and all that."

"My rescue? I can see your ego is still a problem. Don't hide your superiority complex under the pretense you're here to help me. I won't fall for your schemes. Sorry. Better try something else if you wanna impress me. Because, so far, your attempts are pretty lame. And those big guns of yours aren't cutting it."

My eyebrows shot up. "Lame? I'm the one helping you out, and you decide it makes me lame? What kind of jackasses do you hang out with? Please enlighten me."

"You know exactly what you did. Don't play innocent. I'm not some damsel in distress." She tipped her chin up, looking defiant. But she couldn't trick me. This woman couldn't hurt a fly. Even when she spewed insults at me.

"Okay, now you've got me confused. Don't mock me with your words. I've met angry women before. Take a number."

A shadow crossed her gaze, so fast I wondered if I dreamed it.

"Anyway, being thankful isn't a weakness. It's just basic civility. You should try it sometimes, I'm sure you'd like it." I smirked. Because I knew it would rile her up even more.

Her eyes rounded for a fraction of a second before she regained her composure—and her angry frown. My words had rattled her. She pointed an accusing finger at me.

"Are you, out of all people, trying to teach me to be civilized? Funny how some people are clueless about what's right in front of their eyes." She eyed me with disdain. "Since the moment we met, you've been insufferable. Nothing but obnoxious. And you think I'm the one with the attitude problem. Enlightening."

My head fell back, and a loud laugh escaped my lips. It released the pressure building up inside me.

She blinked, looking confused. "Why are you laughing? I just told you how I feel about you, and you think it's funny? Something is definitely wrong with you."

"You're cute when you're angry. I didn't know fairies had it in them to be hostile. I'm impressed. You're not as innocent as you look."

"Innocent? You have no idea who I am and what I'm made of." A loud growl left her mouth, and I was pretty sure smoke came out of her nostrils.

"Calm down, dragon, it was a compliment," I teased, trying to ease the tension between us. "Am I not allowed to say nice things to you? Is this some rule I'm not aware of, or are you allergic to niceties?"

Her brows furrowed. Okay, my attempt at being nice had failed.

Without thinking, I inched closer to her and touched her elbow with my free hand, trying to show her I wasn't the bad guy she portrayed me to be.

Our gazes locked. The deep pool of her eyes swallowed me in. Her lips parted, but no sound came out. I noticed the pulse point in her throat pounding, and I wondered if she felt the pull as much as I did. Her tongue swept over her lips, and I followed the movement, unable to look away.

She tipped her face up, and for a quick instant, I wondered how it would feel to kiss her. It was stupid. We didn't know each other, and I'd been burned in the past. I was in no hurry to play with fire again. And yet, every bit of me was attracted to this woman. As if a force greater than us was pushing us together. I couldn't explain it, and it scared the shit out of me. But still, I was too weak to walk away.

A cocktail of emotions filled her baby blues, and as if injected by a truth serum, I babbled like an idiot. "You're beautiful. And I-I'm...sorry." I closed my eyes and reopened them, chastising myself for my bluntness. I cleared my throat and tried a new approach. "I think we should start over." Releasing her, I extended my arm. "Hi, my name is—"

My neighbor's eyes widened, and she snorted before I

could finish my sentence. "Sorry? You are sorry?" The short-lived truce between us vanished as an expression of incredulity entered her eyes. And just like that, the spell we had both fallen under shattered. She jumped back, putting distance between us.

I scratched the side of my head. "That's all you heard from what I just said?"

She raised a hand between us. "Stop. Don't try to seduce me. It's too late for you to kiss my ass and pretend you're this white knight in shining armor. You've ruined our neighborly relationship. Don't come knocking if you're out of sugar. I won't have any left for you."

Wow. She had really decided I deserved no second chance. Did I imagine the last minute we shared? I flashed her my best smirk, wrapping my hurt under a layer of humor. "I love it when you're being sweet. Keep going, Bubble Gum. If you're ever out of sugar, I'll keep a cup just for you."

"Argghhhh… I'm not sweet, and I'm no candy. That little thing you're doing, it's not working."

"What little thing? I complimented you, again, and you acted out, again."

"Flirting. And faking being nice. I'm not interested in anything you gotta offer. Here, you can go now."

"Tell me, do you hate men in general or just me?" I asked, now curious.

"I don't… I don't hate men." She dropped her shoulders, looking vulnerable for half a second. "I don't like people in general—not just men—who think they're better than others. I never asked for your help, and yet, you believed I wasn't able to deal with a pile of wood on my own. Assumptions. Those make me upset."

"Glad to know it's a *me* problem, then. Want me to give

these logs back to you if it helps preserve your ego? Maybe if I do, we can start over."

"You're so infuriating, you know that? Why would you give them back to me? It makes no sense because you didn't want me to carry them in the first place. Whatever. Go play your mind games elsewhere. I prefer quiet to the sound of your voice. And my cat's company to your face."

"Ouch. You're wounding me."

She averted her eyes. "I didn't mean… It's not… Your face is kinda nice to look at." As if she'd heard her own words, she slapped a hand over her mouth, and her cheeks turned an adorable shade of pink.

"Glad to know my face makes up for my full-of-assumption character. Too bad each time we meet, you read me wrong."

"So far, all you've done is prove to me you are, in fact, an ass. Stop pretending otherwise, and maybe there's hope left for you." A tiny curl of her lips made me believe she wasn't that indifferent to our banter after all. Or I hoped that was what it meant.

"Are you succumbing to my charm?" I asked, unable not to engage with her once again.

"Oh gosh. You're the worst. I said your face was nice, not that you were charming. Big difference."

"But the other day you said I was handsome too. Did you forget about saying that after you bumped your head?"

"It just means I need to stop saying what's on my mind out loud." After a moment, she shook her head, her aggravation back and straining her features. "Just drop the wood on the porch."

With a look her way, I noticed how my neighbor's hands were now balled into fists. I bowed my head and nodded.

Okay, this was not going as I expected. I thought our

banter the other day was hot. And I believed she felt the connection too. Had I been wrong all along?

Sure, our first encounter had been surprising, to say the least, but I hadn't dreamed of the electricity I experienced when our skin connected minutes ago and the way we eye-fucked each other right before I had the audacity to say I was sorry.

A big part of me enjoyed her fieriness and the fact she wasn't making it easy on me to gain her trust. It was a nice change. Too often, in my life, people gave in easily when they realized who I was. I loved how my neighbor wasn't impressed with me by any means. It was oddly refreshing.

With my back to her, I sensed her eyes drilling holes through my clothes. The heat of her gaze sent shivers down my spine—the good kind—and my dick jerked up in my pants. *Easy, boy.*

With her in such proximity, something in my chest snapped. A restraint? A chain? I ignored what it was, but I knew my heart had changed its tune. My body tensed for a quick second before it adjusted to the new rhythm. I watched my neighbor over my shoulder. With her arms folded over her chest, she stepped back, forcing me out of her personal space. I grinned. She frowned. This woman was a ball of attitude. In many ways, she reminded me of June. Except, I wasn't attracted to my personal assistant.

I placed the wood in a neat pile on the porch and turned around, not knowing how to navigate the hate slash attraction vibe simmering between us.

I stuffed my hands in my pockets, not sure what to do with them.

"So." I pointed with a thumb behind me. "You're all set. Want me to bring more in case you go through those by the morning."

Without saying a word, she shook her head.

Her throat worked, and it captured my gaze before I brought my eyes back to her face.

The ire I'd seen on her features since I came over faded away.

Like a magnet pulling me in, I inched closer to her, hoping for one of her feisty comebacks. She turned her head to the side and breathed out, her eyes locked on mine. Baby-blue laser beams. I shivered under their intensity.

"Well…I should go now," I said.

Her attention moved back and forth between my eyes and my mouth.

Before I had time to analyze the meaning, the wind picked up and sent the stray strands of her hair flying.

My mind didn't catch up with my action when I padded forward and brushed the tendrils back. My fingertips skimmed the side of her face as I did, and electric bolts traveled throughout my body. Pixie's scent, a mix of lavender perfume and lemon shampoo, swirled around us and filled my nostrils. She watched me, remaining mute while we faced each other.

As if I'd been tased, I jerked my arm back and let it hang at my side. "I'll return to my place. I know you need no help, so I won't offer anymore." What was I saying? It made no sense. I sounded ridiculous. I should shut up now.

"I'm all good on my own." Her tone was definitive and left no place for argument.

"O-kay."

With her arms still wrapped around her body, she walked me down the steps of the front porch, avoiding my eyes. The tight-lipped smile that grazed her lips displayed the lingering specks of her annoyance toward me. My chest puffed out in response.

"Thank you for this," she whispered, the words

tumbling out her mouth like they were scorching her tongue.

My eyebrows bunched together in a silent question.

"For your…huh…unsolicited help."

A grin formed on my face. "You're welcome." I shook my head and waltzed back home. Feeling her eyes still on me, I looked over my shoulder, only to catch sight of her, in full spy mode, peeking in my direction from behind the curtains of her living room now that she had retreated inside. Again.

Okay, this had to be one of the most awkward, yet confusing encounters of my life.

"Guess I'm not the only one who's curious now," I said to myself. She could pretend as much as she wanted, but I'd spotted my neighbor spying on me more than once. She said things, but her actions spoke louder. Perhaps I intrigued her as much as she intrigued me.

From her expressions to her actions, I was certain the lust I felt wasn't just one-sided.

Every time we butted heads, my attraction toward her increased.

I doubted this woman could hold a grudge. From what I'd seen, she lacked a sense of wickedness. Her act didn't fool me, though. Her fake fury only made her more adorable. More alluring. More interesting. It tripled her sexiness. Everything about her captivated me, and I prayed she would crack at some point and reveal her true self. And let me in. For a reason hard to explain, everything about her mesmerized me. From her brightly colored hair to her sass. She held her own, not having a care in the world who I might be. That impressed me, and even at just twenty-six years old, I was hard to impress. Unbeknownst to her, cracking my neighbor's armor had become my newfound mission.

Chapter 7

April

I woke up and lay in bed for a little while, feeling fresh and well-rested, which hadn't happened in a long time. Bernice padded on the mattress, and getting closer, butted my chin, ready to be fed. "Can you just oversleep for once, sweet girl?"

She let out a loud meow as I patted her furry head. She had no intention of going back to sleep. Traitor.

"Okay, fine. Give me a minute." I stretched my arms above my head, my body swallowed by the fluffy bedding. My smile faltered as I swung my legs over the edge of the bed, disappointed to leave the comfort and warmth of my cozy nest.

While brushing my teeth in the bathroom and glancing through the window, I looked over at my neighbor's cabin. I rolled my eyes, thinking about how we bantered every time we met. Three days ago, he took it upon himself to help me carry wood to keep my fireplace running, and that was kinda nice of him. Until I realized his intentions weren't noble and he opened his stupid—but kissable—mouth. Nobody in their right state of mind could stay indifferent to his full lips. No matter what, HN infuriated me like no one else. Both times we met in person, he pushed my buttons as if he knew exactly what would make me tick. I hated the idea he possessed that piece of information about me. Since that night, I'd been asking myself the same question. Did we really share a moment, or did I dream the entire interaction? The latter made more sense since we had proven so far that we couldn't stand each other. The most infuriating part was that he left afterward as if nothing happened. *Ass.* Still, I had no idea what his deal was. Since they left the other day, I hadn't seen the woman or the child around, which intrigued me more than it should, feeding the mystery surrounding him.

Slipping into an oversized knitted sweater, I was fixing my hair when movements outside caught my eye. Talking on the phone while pacing the driveway, HN appeared like he was about to blow a gasket. Taut features, ramrod straight back, tensed shoulders, his entire being screamed infuriation. Still, my skin tingled as I drank him in. Even angry, he projected confidence. And appealed to the woman in me.

I promised myself I would stop spying on him, but for a reason I couldn't explain, I stayed in the same spot, unable to avert my eyes. HN dropped his head and shook it, then ran a palm over his face, looking dejected. His entire demeanor changed, and he appeared younger. Less cocky. In that instant, I wished I could go to him and give him a hug because it seemed like he needed a friend.

Soon enough, his head jerked back as if he'd been

stung by a bee, and his mask of displeasure returned, erasing the vulnerability that had flashed across his face seconds ago.

He kicked the tires of his SUV multiple times, fisting his hair with one hand, his aggravation on full display. Whoever was on the phone with him was at the receiving end of his wrath. Anger darkened all his features, and I felt even more attracted to him. He was this mysterious, hot-as-hell male and the first one in the last couple of years to get my hormones into overdrive.

HN paced across the pavement, his fury unmistakable, even from a distance.

Without thinking any further, I rushed downstairs, filled Bernice's bowl with kibbles—because by now, her meowing had turned into uninterrupted background noise —and went outside, aiming for my car.

Looking for the novel I remembered leaving there the night I arrived, I rummaged through the console between the front seats. When did I become so lame? Was I really snooping on my neighbor again? I wanted to slap myself. The guy wasn't available, but I yearned to find out why he got so angry when he thought I was snapping his picture the other day. Or why he couldn't seem to stay away three nights ago when he carried my firewood or brushed my hair back. Without trying to eavesdrop on what he was saying, I still heard fragments of his conversations.

He flexed his jaw. His eyes had become a sea of gray lava. He changed direction mid-stride, all his movements jerky and stiff. His magnetism pulled my gaze in.

"…she won't get away with it that easily…"

"…no, I won't do it. Forget it…"

"…and you think I'm not aware this is manip-ulation…"

"…no fucking way. That's not up for discussion…"

"…Never mind. I'm over this craziness. For good…"

I held my breath, trying to make myself as invisible as possible, not wanting my neighbor to think I was listening to his phone call, even though I was kind of doing that. *A little.* I winced. *Not really. Totally.*

He hung up, shook his head, and took two deep breaths, erasing all traces of anger from his model-like face. His eyes dropped to the screen of his phone, and he laughed at something he saw. Or read.

My hope deflated inside me. HN didn't need me as a friend or anything else.

Entertaining thoughts about hugging a perfect stranger, because he looked conflicted, wasn't smart either. It had to stop. No more eavesdropping or trying to catch sight of the man next door.

There. I had a new resolution.

Before he could acknowledge my presence and realize I was a desperate cause, I rushed back inside, holding up a tire pressure gauge instead of the book in my hand. *Real smooth, April.* I dropped my head, twisted my mouth, and creased my eyebrows, feeling so dumb. Why was I acting like a child? I ignored the reason why my neighbor's mood mattered to me. Not wanting to give my erratic behavior too much thought, I made tea, and with my laptop perched on my knees, I settled into the hanging chair, intending to write and forget all about the sexy slash obnoxious, probably married, man next door. After what I witnessed the other day, I now had some doubts about his marital status, which didn't concern me, no matter how tempting snooping around sounded.

"Get a grip," I said aloud. Bernice, who was stretched on her side in front of the window, soaking up the warm rays of the sun, purred. "I'm glad you agree, girl."

Focused on my work, the hours slipped by without me realizing. I emerged from my writing bubble at dinnertime. I patted myself on the back mentally when I realized that in my trancelike state, I had written over thirty pages. I stood to fix myself a snack, and sitting at the dining table, I reread everything. I fought the urge to cry my relief and fist-bumped my cat when I grasped how good this first draft was.

Have I been cured of my writer's block once and for all?

I flopped back into my chair and sighed, a grin pasted on my face. I emailed the pages to my agent and decided to treat myself tonight. I deserved a little fun. I cooked chicken fajitas and opened a bottle of wine. Then I snapped a photo of me with my wineglass in hand and sent it to my best friend.

ME

Getting my groove back (I hope). Cheers

It took almost a minute for the message to go through. The internet connection here was all or nothing. Then, when I didn't expect it, I received a text from Saunders.

SAUNDERS

You rock. Glad the mountain air is helping.
Love you xx

After dinner, still feeling festive, I aimed for the jacuzzi on the back deck. The darkness and absolute silence surrounding me made this night perfect. A bit cold, but nothing the heated water of the hot tub wouldn't fix.

With the bottle of white wine resting on the little wooden table and my glass in hand, I sank my white-string-bikini-clad self in the bubbling water.

A whimper escaped my mouth when my cold skin met

the hot water. All my muscles relaxed, and I slipped in deeper.

Mellow country music played on my phone, and I sipped on my wine, gazing at the open sky. I'd never seen so many stars in my entire life. The night swallowed me, and I became one with the starry display. Nothing else around me existed, except me atop a mountain in the middle of nowhere.

I thanked Saunders in my head.

She couldn't have come up with a better spot for a month-long writing retreat slash vacation.

My thoughts wandered from my new book that finally got me excited to my best friend afraid to take the next step with her longtime boyfriend, then to the little boy next door who asked me about fairies, and finally, to Travis, who, I imagined, was staring down at me from a shiny star above.

Raising my glass, I cheered at the sky. "I hope you're happy and safe over there. I miss you."

A star twinkled, and I imagined it was his way of telling me not to worry about him. Travis loved stars. "We're just dust particles, part of a bigger plan. Life doesn't end with death," he'd once said. I loved believing he was right. More than ever, I loved the idea that he lived somewhere out there, watching over me. It somehow lessened the void left inside me that his departure had caused.

A shooting star, bright and glittery, crossed the sky.

Closing my eyes, I made a wish that everything would fall into place in my life.

I had many things to hope for, and they all fit under this big umbrella wish.

Completing my book.

Finding my true purpose in life.

Getting out of my comfort zone.

Falling in love again. True, head-over-heels, *I am yours, you are mine* kind of love.

Health, adventure, fun, friendship, and family.

My ultimate goals.

I'd work hard until I had checked them all.

I yawned. The late hour combined with the hot water had melted away the remnants of my energy reserve.

Craving my bed, I staggered out of the hot tub. My feet slipped on the cold deck, and I held myself steady, thanks to the small table.

The high temperature of the water had magnified the effect of the alcohol in my blood. I was tipsier than I thought I'd be. Off-balance, it took all my might to put the lid back on the jacuzzi. Soon enough, the warmth from the water dissipated. Looking around, the realization hit me. I'd forgotten a towel. *Great.* The winter night was freezing my bones under my soaked skin.

In four strides, I reached the door. Whatever I did—push, pull, turn—it didn't budge. My frozen fingers fought with the doorknob. In vain. *Did I lock myself out?* Bernice appeared on the other side, stretching her body against the glass. "Bernice, let me in. Please. I'm freezing." She purred and sauntered away. "Come on, girl, help me here." My chest deflated.

My fingers shook, turning into popsicles. With my phone in hand, I staggered down the deck and circled the cabin to unlock the front door. Dying from frostbite would be a lame way to go.

The crunchy leaves littering the ground felt like thorns under my bare feet.

As it did on my first night here, the indicator light on the super-sophisticated electronic latch refused to turn green. I placed my hands under my armpits, longing for some warmth. Shaking from head to toe, I tried to focus on my task and the fireplace awaiting me inside. With trembling fingers, I rebooted my phone and tried positioning the device a dozen different ways over the latch. Nothing.

Panic swirled through me. The cold air I breathed hurt on its way in, and I couldn't stop the tremors shaking my limbs.

As I stood there, half-naked, wet, and freezing cold in the night, with no idea how to improve my fate, I felt minuscule. Thanks to the frigid air, even my thoughts were sluggish now. When I blinked, my eyelashes weighed heavy. With a numb hand, I pushed my damp hair away from my face. Icicles had formed at the tips of my locks. My feet burned from the contact with the frosty wooden porch.

What should I do? I had nowhere to go, no one to call to help me out. Even if I wanted to, I wasn't sure I'd be able to dial my phone, my fingers unresponsive.

Out of options, I staggered to HN's cabin.

Misty clouds exited my mouth with each breath I blew out.

Uncontrollable shivers ran through me.

Each step was a struggle.

My teeth chattered, the sound reminding me of Morse code telegraph machines used in old movies.

My skin was turning blue from the biting cold.

My lungs idled.

I tried to wiggle my toes, but they felt like concrete. Stiff and leaden.

Perhaps I should go back into the hot tub. My energy levels were empty. Even if I wanted to, I couldn't get there. Anyway, it wouldn't help anything but my shivering.

A translucent version of Travis appeared in front of me. He nodded his head. Like he was delivering a message from wherever he was. That I could do this. And survive. And fight.

With one last strained effort and a leap of faith, I lifted my balled fist to knock on the door. Frozen, I'd lost all my strength. The muffled sound of my fist on the wood panel disappeared under my jagged breath.

Hugging myself to stop the shivers, I dropped my forehead on the doorbell button.

Now HN or his family would hear me. *Please, please, rescue me.* My eyelids grew heavier, and I resisted the urge to curl up into a ball on the porch.

Did HN have a spare key to my place? Would he help me out with the stupid lock once my body temperature reached a decent-enough degree?

The door opened. I almost fainted. Black spots danced before my eyes. My vision blurred.

A wall of muscles greeted me. It towered above me by almost a foot.

HN's eyes flared when he noticed me. A worried expression colored his face. "What the fuck. Have you lost your mind?"

I shook my head. "Stupid lock—" I mumbled the words as loud as I could muster.

My neighbor pulled me into his arms, and his heat spread through me. He kicked the door shut and walked me to the living room, positioning me in front of the fireplace. In seconds, I had two blankets wrapped around me. When he sat on the floor behind me, he pulled me into his lap, his whole masculine and intoxicating body circling mine.

Exhaustion spread through me, and I fought to keep my eyes open.

April, you're safe now. My thoughts were still languishing.

In an attempt to send hot blood to my extremities, I wiggled my fingers and toes. I could barely feel my body.

Survive. That was the only word popping up in my head on a loop.

My neighbor fastened his arms around me. *I'm safe.*

The more I warmed up, the more tired I felt.

My blood burned like lava in my veins as it flowed through me.

I buried my face in HN's chest, and the sound of his strong and steady heartbeat rocked me to sleep.

Chapter 8

Carter

I sat in the middle of the living room with my neighbor nestled in my arms, the heat emanating from the fireplace radiating over us. Listening to the steady sound of her breathing, the night replayed in my head. How did I end up here?

Before Fairy barged into my house—and my arms—minutes ago, I had spent the evening locked in my home studio, strumming my guitar. The peace music brought me, which had been missing in the last year, had finally found me. For once, I succeeded at shutting out all the noises in my life. The pollution that grabbed hold of my mind way too often these days. Surrounded by soundproof walls, it took me a minute to register the faint sound of the door-bell. Since I was alone in here, I didn't bother closing the door after me when I settled in. I did a double-check when I fished my phone out of my back pocket. *Ten seventeen.*

Except for Dahlia, nobody ever visited me this late. Anyway, they had to go through the gate first, which clearly didn't happen just now because only Dahlia, the rental company, and my handyman had the code. The people renting my cabins used an electronic key fob to come and go, and any visitor had to be announced a day in advance to go through the background check. I hadn't received any such notice. Whoever stood on my front porch had no reason to be here and hadn't been invited.

I rubbed my eyes with the heels of my hands. With long strides, I padded through the house, my hands clenched into fists, ready to punch the fucker standing on the other side of the door. I prayed gossip hunters hadn't climbed over the fence to find me. Ready to give shit to whoever stood on my front porch, I stopped myself when my hand clamped around the doorknob. *Don't get into trouble, Carter. It's not worth it.* I swallowed my anger and looked through the peephole. My eyes widened at the sight of my neighbor wearing nothing but a white string bikini, soaked, her hair frosted, and her lips blue.

Seriously? How could she forget to put on winter clothes?

"What the fuck. Have you lost your mind?" I screeched, opening the door, ready to send her back where she came from. I sighed. I didn't feel like dealing with her right now. She'd just interrupted my creative process. I narrowed my eyes and steeled my back, hoping she'd get the message loud and clear.

Her eyes flared, and her lips quivered. No words came out. Her eyes pleaded with me to let her in.

Her teeth chattered, and she shook her head. "Stupid lock—"

All the color drained from her face, and she faltered.

My blind impulse took over, and I wrapped my arms

around her. Her small body sank into mine, and the smell of chlorine and lavender filled my nose. The wetness of her frigid body made it through my own clothes.

I held on to her, trying to stop her from shivering.

Without even thinking, I wrapped her in blankets and curled my body around hers, hoping my body temperature would be enough to spread warmth through her so she wouldn't get hypothermia.

Except for Dahlia the other night, I hadn't held a woman in my arms in months.

I had a few rules in my life, but the ones I had, I never backed down from.

Stay healthy. Whatever it meant.

Be there for Dahlia and Jack. No matter what.

And lately, I added, stay the fuck away from Savannah Prince. Or any woman gunning for me.

As much as my neighbor intrigued me and I liked getting a rise out of her, I knew I should keep her at a distance. After the mess I'd just gotten out of, even though I was still set on finding love one day, I wasn't ready for another relationship. Much less with a woman who was just passing through my life. And certainly not one who had all my instincts kick in every time I was in her vicinity.

Fairy, with her pale-pink hair framing her face, big eyes, and luscious mouth, had shattered my walls with one look. When she flashed her tits at me in her bedroom, I believed she might have been after my fame.

After the way she bantered with me in the woods, challenging me, I concluded she was clueless about my identity.

Our argument over firewood the other night confirmed my beliefs.

My face was plastered all over the Internet, magazines, and TV. My neighbor either lived under a rock, or she hadn't been paying attention to the world around her.

Either way, I enjoyed being a regular Joe around her. Her spirit and the memory of the way she confided in Jack played with my heartstrings.

Tendrils of her hair tickled my nose.

Buried in my chest, her body grew heavier and her breathing, steadier.

Did she fall asleep in my arms? *Who does that?* I blinked. How could she trust me? We didn't even know each other. And so far, she had proven not to be my biggest fan.

I twisted to look at her face. Yup, she was out of it.

I hesitated to wake her up. Maybe the warmth after freezing so much had messed with her body thermostat or something and she needed to sleep it off to reset it? Or regain her strength?

I was no doctor or hypothermia expert, but I decided letting her sleep could do no harm. I tightened my arms around her, shifting her so that her side pressed against my chest, and I could watch her face for any sign of discomfort.

Entangled together, we sat there for a long time. I was in no hurry to move, in case it woke her up, because I was enjoying this moment of peace between us. Even though I doubted she would remember it once the morning came.

My heart frisked in my chest with Pixie in my arms. Like she belonged there. Like a long-lost puzzle piece, now recovered.

I brushed the crown of her head with my lips as I debated my options. What should I do?

Not ready to wake her up, but needing reassurance her body had thawed enough, I slid my hand under the blankets until my fingers grazed the softness of her creamy skin. A shiver ran through me, and my dick swelled in my pants. I shut my eyes and inhaled. *One, two, three, four.* I exhaled.

Why was my body so reactive to her all the time?

My hand found the curve of her waist and lingered there for a moment. The contact of our flesh toyed with all my willpower. With a tight grip around her body, I let my frozen neighbor sleep in my arms for the next hour, captivated by the sound of her breathing.

I tucked the wild strands away from her angelic face with my fingertips, unveiling her delicate features. Plump lips, button nose, soft-angled dark-blonde brows—probably her natural hair color—thick eyelashes.

Out cold, she looked serene and didn't budge when I tried to wake her up. With a gentle movement, I lowered my hand down to her throat. Her pulse beat at a regular pace. Our heartbeats synched, and a deep sigh escaped my lips.

I should send her back to her place. Or ask for explanations.

Instead, I tightened my grip around her, refusing to let go of her.

I tried to convince myself that keeping her here was a bad idea. I didn't need the complication the morning would bring, and still, my gut won the tug-of-war against my reason.

Ready to go to bed and clueless about the right course of action, I shifted to my feet, and with my neighbor still asleep in my arms—the woman was a lightweight—I climbed the stairs to my bedroom. I laid her on my king-size mattress, wanting to look after her in case she struggled in the middle of the night. One by one, I examined her every finger and toe. None of them was still cold or blueish. The only thing I knew about hypothermia was that it affected the extremities first. My current assessment confirmed she should be okay.

Relieved, I tucked the blankets around the woman in

my bed, undressed to my boxer briefs, and slid under the sheets on the opposite side. No woman had ever slept in this bed with me, but somehow, the idea of her sleeping here didn't freak me out like it should have. Lying on my side, I propped myself up on my elbow, the heat of my body rising and making my breathing harsh, at a loss, unsure how to act. Should I pull my neighbor in my arms or were the blankets enough to keep her warm? A part of me, the one that made no sense, itched to hold on to her like my life depended on it. To be her knight in shining armor as she once accused me of. The other half knew it was a bad idea.

Unable to make up my mind, I scanned the room, but soon my eyes returned to her silhouette. My neighbor stirred in her sleep, and I waited, all my senses on high alert. Her eyelids fluttered, and she stretched her body, but never woke up. I let go of the breath I was holding and relaxed. Extending my arm, I turned off the bedside lamp and fell onto my back, still wondering how I ended up sharing my bed with a stranger.

I grimaced, ran my hands over my face, and finally gave up the idea of pulling her to me. Flipping over to my other side, after making sure she was still out of it, I closed my eyes and chased sleep.

———

The next morning, I woke up with my neighbor's body entangled in mine. Tendrils of her pink hair spread on my skin. Her soft breasts, under her white bikini top, pressed against the side of my torso. With my eyes closed, I breathed her in.

Fuck. How did this happen?

My thoughts froze in my head at the idea I would have to explain our predicament to her as soon as she woke up.

I held my breath and wiggled to get out of bed, but Pixie's arms tightened around my midriff, and she moaned. *Kill. Me. Now.* Her breaths tickled my skin. I exhaled through clenched teeth, enjoying the feeling, but fearing her reaction. If it turned out to be anything like our previous interactions, no doubt it'd be explosive.

Why did I strip down to my boxer briefs last night? I should've slept in pajama pants with a T-shirt on. Or on the couch.

My neighbor's eyelids fluttered open, and her baby-blue doe eyes locked on mine. I offered her a tight-lipped smile and a small shrug. Like a sixteen-year-old caught staring at a girl he had a massive crush on.

Half-awake, she let out a loud shriek, and cold sweat pearled on my nape.

Stay calm. Explain everything. You cared for her. She can't get mad at you. You did nothing wrong.

"What did you do to me?" she asked point-blank, propping herself up.

I hopped to my feet, anger building up inside me.

What happened to keeping my calm? Breathe in, Carter.

"Relax, Pixie." I held my stance, unyielding. "Why would you assume I did anything to you? I saved your ass last night. You came to me, remember? I watched over you the entire night to make sure you wouldn't lose your fingers or toes after your spectacular hypothermia scare, which you still need to explain to me."

A dark blush colored her cheeks when her gaze scanned my body. I rubbed my jaw with my hand before pulling a pair of gray sweatpants on. No doubt my neighbor had a full-frontal view of the outline of my morning wood, my boxer briefs doing nothing to hide my erection.

She surveyed the bedroom, looking anywhere but at me. Until a deep frown creased her forehead and her cheeks turned a shade darker when she realized she was only wearing that ridiculous tiny bikini. Guess we made a great pair. In one swift movement, she pulled a blanket and fastened it around her half-naked self.

With bed hair and a sleepy face, she looked younger in the morning light.

"Why am I in your bed, hooked onto you?" The muscle in her jaw flexed, and she folded her arms over her chest, mirroring my stance, her eyes flashing with challenge, her face set in stone—a look she had mastered perfectly as if she'd been roughened up by life before and had to learn to stand up for herself.

My breath sounded like a whistle when it caught in my lungs. "Christ, did you hit your head last night? Would you have preferred I let you sleep on the couch in a house you might not even remember coming to? Maybe I should've let your toes and fingers fall off—"

Pixie's gaze dropped to her hands. My eyes flared when, one by one, she counted her digits. And then her toes from where her feet peeked out from under the blanket. I bit my lips to avoid laughing. After a deep sigh, she brought her attention back to me.

"Listen, I'm sorry for snapping at you. I don't know you. I don't even know your name, and I woke up in your arms, in your bed. Put yourself in my shoes for a minute. That's awkward." She tucked her hair behind her ear, and her features softened, chasing her troubled expression away.

I resumed my normal breathing. Desperate to cover up, I snagged a dark hooded flannel shirt from my closet and buttoned the front. "I'm just the guy next door. I'll fetch you something to wear and help you get back inside your cabin."

On the second floor, I rummaged through Dahlia's stuff and came up with a cream sweater and a pair of gray yoga pants, before rushing back upstairs.

"Is your wife going to be okay with my sleeping in your bed and wearing her clothes?"

A laugh, loud and harsh, escaped my mouth. "Wife?"

"You know, the person you share your life with, the mother of your child, the pretty redhead I saw you with."

"Did you spy on me, sweetheart?"

"Don't ever call me *Sweetheart*." Her eyes threw bullets at me, and I lifted my hands in surrender before me.

"What's up your britches, lady?" I asked.

Her eyes rounded. "Who says that?"

"You're unbelievable. Let me say it again. Don't get your panties in a twist, lady. There. Better?"

"Don't patronize me."

"Geez, relax already. It's not even nine o'clock yet."

Her tone hardened. "Where's your wife? Or maybe she's your mistress and the boy, your love child? You guys look like you have one of those open relationships. Not that I'm judging. I'm only stating the facts."

Fury boiled in my veins. Whoever Dahlia and Jack were to me didn't concern her. I tugged at the roots of my hair and paced the room to calm the fuck down before I blew a fuse. I had endured another woman talking shit about my family for two years. I wasn't about to let anyone else express their nasty opinion about them. Much less a woman I'd just met.

"Stop talking. You have no right to say anything bad about my family. They're all I have. I don't need to explain them to you. Don't disrespect them ever again." The words bruised my tongue on their way out. "Did I make myself clear?" I dragged my hands down my face, unable to settle the wrath bubbling inside me.

My neighbor neared me and placed a hand over my forearm. The tension building in my shoulders evaporated under her touch. "I…I'm sorry. I didn't mean to upset you. They're obviously important to you. By the way, your son is adorable. He has your eyes."

Her words pierced my heart like swords, making me bleed inside. How could she have read the situation and concluded they were mine? *My* wife. *My* son. *My* eyes. She couldn't know what kept me up at night sometimes. All those secrets hovering over me I had yet to address. A surge of unwelcome heat rooted in my stomach, and I placed my hand over my chest to quiet my throbbing heart.

The woman, standing inches away from me, infuriated me, and I should get her back to her place and keep my distance from her for the rest of her stay. We were done playing games. She wasn't worth the trouble.

Every time she opened her mouth, it stirred up all the things I worked hard to keep settled inside me.

Fifteen minutes later, armed with her cell phone, I fumbled with the digital lock on her front door. When it refused to unlock, a few curses left my mouth before I could reel them in. "This thing is useless."

Now dressed in Dahlia's clothes, Fairy stood beside me, arms crossed over her chest, lips pinched together, a frown creasing her forehead. I wondered whether her annoyed demeanor was her usual stance or if it was reserved just for me. "I told you it's not working. I'm not tech-savvy, but I can tell when something is broken." She lifted her chin, her defiant expression unwavering as we locked eyes.

"Yeah. No kidding." I returned to the latch and grumbled as I fought the urge to tell her to shut up. She could keep her sassy attitude and her *I told you so* to herself right now.

After a few attempts, the stubborn lock gave up the fight, and the light flashed green. I blinked. *Finally.* I studied it for a minute, as if the reason it'd been difficult would appear by magic. *I should get it looked at.* I made a mental note to reach out to my handyman later.

"Don't worry. I'll get someone to fix it. I know a guy… Hopefully, today." I couldn't risk a repeat of last night. Fuck that. Without asking, I entered the cabin and pounded across the first floor toward the rear door. It was locked from the inside. Fairy didn't lie to me last night. I silenced a sigh of relief. She'd genuinely locked herself out of her cabin. "I'll ask my guy to change the back door deadbolt. Just in case," I informed her when I returned to the living room.

The cabin smelled like her. Lavender. Soft music played on a wireless speaker on the kitchen counter. A sweater and two pairs of socks lay forgotten on the couch, while five empty mugs cluttered the coffee table. Without being a slob, my neighbor had made the cabin hers. It pleased me that she felt at home here, probably more than it should. Instead, I should call her on that. Surveying her mess once more, I decided it was better and safer to think of her as untidy. Yeah, untidiness grated on my nerves, just like her. Couldn't a grown-up woman pick up after herself? If I noticed all the things that annoyed me, I wouldn't be tempted to get to know her better. It sounded logical. At least in my mind.

When I turned around, I took in the sight of my neighbor bent over a few feet away, stacking wood in the fireplace. My gaze lingered on her backside before I caught myself and stepped closer. "Let me help you with that."

She turned around as if she'd been burned and crossed

her arms over her chest. Again. That had to be her signature move. Guess I wasn't special after all. "Who do you think you are?"

I blinked twice, her cockiness making her irresistible. "The guy helping you out. Now move, I'll start the fire."

"I thought we already concluded I *don't* need your help."

"So how do you explain last night? You knocking on my door and needing my warmth? Me saving you? What would you have done If I hadn't been home?"

She growled.

"Yeah. You would have been screwed. I fucking saved your life, Fairy. Kill that pride of yours and admit it."

She shot to her feet, planting her heels with the kind of defiance that needed no words. "Ohmygod, are you one of those sexist males who think women are idiots and that we require you, Neanderthal specimens, to save the day? Please, tell me you're not that dumb."

"What? I never said that."

She murdered me with her blue laser beams and harrumphed. "You implied that since you're a *man*, you're better at dealing with the fire than *I* am. And the last time I checked, I'm a woman. Which means you think men are superior."

"Are you high? I only offered because I was being a nice neighbor and was happy to help you out. Jesus, woman, sheathe your claws. It's too early for your little tantrums." There, I said my piece.

Red clung to her cheeks. "For your information, I'm a very capable woman, *HN*, and I can start a fire by myself. We're not in the fifties anymore, in case you didn't get the memo. And by the way, last night was a one-time thing. I didn't plan on having to warm up at your place. Don't get used to my asking anything from you."

"Go on, play your own hero. Why would it be so bad if you needed someone else's help for a change? I understand you have one of those egos, but don't you think you're overreacting?"

"Easy for you to say. You don't know me. Stop judging."

"I'm not. I'm trying to understand." I angled my body to face her and crossed my arms over my chest, mirroring her stance. Why was everything with this woman a confrontation? Couldn't she let go for once, or did she have to always have the last word? Lifting one eyebrow, I asked, "HN? What does that even mean?"

"Whatever." She stamped her foot like she was defending something. "It's none of your business."

"I wanna know. Spill it."

"I won't. See yourself out." She pointed in the direction of the front door with her chin.

I huffed. This woman enraged me to no extent. "Tell me, and I'm out of here."

"No way. I'm not telling you." *Really mature.*

With a step forward, I shrunk the gap between us. "You know you're infuriating, aren't you?"

"Not my problem, *HN*. You're the one acting like an ass."

"No, you're the one implying I am." I paused for a second before using her own words against her when I added, "You think I'm handsome, that I have a nice face to look at, and that I'm an ass. You think you've got me all figured out, huh?" I let the words sink in. "You're wrong. I'm not an ass."

The woman clenched her teeth, fury radiating from every pore of her petite frame. "Then stop acting like one, *HN*."

"I swear I am not."

A grunt slipped from her sassy lips, the words garbled. "What?"

"You're also a jerk, you are obnoxious, and you think too much of yourself."

"Do I?" The air between us frizzled.

With a pout, she nodded, conviction never leaving her face.

"You were quick to run to me last night, though. I bet you didn't think I was an ass when you jumped into my arms, did you?"

Those blue laser beams closed in on my face, and an audible groan escaped her mouth.

The sound reverberated deep inside me. "So, now you're speechless. After insulting me, of all things."

"Don't take my silence for weakness. I'm just not sure if you're worth my anger…and my words. Still debating here." She tapped the side of her head with a finger. "One moment, you're nice and the next, you're a prick. Decide. Here and now. Which one are you?"

I tipped one eyebrow, giving her my most charming, panties-melting smirk—the one I knew women couldn't resist. "Why can't I be both?"

The woman facing me clenched her hands and groaned once more. "Ohmygod, you're impossible. Why can't you act like a grown-up and stop messing with me? And you just said you weren't an ass. Wow, impressive," she shouted before turning on her feet, about to stomp away.

Not ready to end our banter, I added, "Yeah, leave. You're the one acting like a petulant child."

She halted, and from where I stood, I noticed how her fingernails dug into her palms.

She sighed. "I'm not a child. I'm just trying to be the better woman here and walking away." When she spun around to face me, her eyes glistened. Not with tears, but with something much more intense.

"Okay. Prove it. Only a child would bolt in the middle of a conversation."

Her nostrils flared. Her eyes got so big I thought she'd popped an eyeball. "This is no conversation. It's just that your thinking you're smarter than me." She relaxed her hands. "Anyway, I've got nothing to prove to you. I'm not the one playing stupid games."

"You sure about that?" I asked, eyeing her. "There's no shame in admitting defeat or asking a man for help. Isn't that what you did last night? God, I thought you were a wise woman."

She brought her fists to her hips. "Ugh. And I thought you said I'd figured you all wrong." She cocked a brow, and I sucked in a long breath, trying to cool down, every inch of my body sizzling under the intensity of her gaze. We were now facing each other, both panting, neither of us bold enough to break the silence.

My gaze traveled from Pixie's blue eyes to her pink mouth and lingered on her breasts, focused on the movement of her chest with each intake of air. My entire body stiffened. Yeah, every part of it. I felt lightheaded. Was oxygen even reaching my brain anymore? Everything about this girl sent my body into a blazing mess. I wanted to hold all her attention and have my name lingering on her lips. She tsk-tsked, and I brought my attention back to her face.

Her cheeks had turned a dark shade of red.

Cast under her spell, my eyes locked on hers.

Holding her stance, unflinching, she blinked but never looked away.

A fat minute passed.

Her gaze turned to heat—scorching heat. Hot enough

to melt all my defenses, and any retort hanging on the tip of my tongue.

Her breathing accelerated.

She parted her lips, and her tongue grazed the rim of her mouth.

The fury that had colored her face until now faded.

Her eyes roamed over my features, gave me a slow once-over, then locked back on mine.

Particles of electricity swirled around us. Time stopped as we faced each other without another word.

I was transfixed, nailed to the floor. Air barely reached my lungs. Even swallowing turned out to be a challenge. My mouth was dry. My wild heartbeat was all I could hear.

Frustration and lust mixed together.

"I can't stand you," I said, my voice lacking conviction.

"You are the most infuriating human being I've ever met." Her pupils dilated, and for once, her words didn't sound like an insult.

My throat worked, and her stare dropped there.

From where I stood, I noticed the pulse point in her neck quickening.

Neither of us motioned to leave.

Fairy's eyes darkened until they were almost midnight blue. If I were scared easily, I'd run for my life, her hold on me growing by the second.

Awareness bloomed on my skin, and I shivered under the weight of her dedicated attention.

Without another word, I stepped forward and erased the distance between us. Pixie gasped when my hands connected with her hips, and I lifted her up in my arms. Her legs wrapped around my waist holding me against her at the same time I crashed my mouth on hers.

I devoured her lips like I depended on them to stay alive. I took a handful of her firm ass cheeks as she moaned against my mouth. She played with the hair at the back of my head, and a croaky groan passed my lips.

Unapologetic, I cupped one of her breasts over her sweater, and she melted under my touch, her body fusing with mine. The image of her bare chest the other day flashed through my mind. Her tits felt fuller in my hands than how they'd appeared from a distance. I'd been obsessed with feeling them from the moment I got a peek of them almost a week ago.

She nipped my bottom lip and my earlobe. I curled my hand around the back of her neck, angled her head, and ate her mouth like it could satisfy my hunger. The tips of her fingers dug into the skin of my shoulders.

In one swift movement, she peeled the sweater off. I caught it and tossed it on the floor. I tugged at the loose string of her bikini top with my teeth and untied it, leaving a trail of kisses on her chlorine-scented flesh. The tiny piece of fabric joined the sweater at my feet.

I tightened my hands around her waist, and I feared it'd leave bruises on her pale skin.

I flicked my tongue over her hard nipples, one at a time, and feasted on them, tasting, licking, and biting her flesh. Pixie arched her back, begging for more.

"Fine, you're not a child," I whispered, breathless.

She moaned in response, shattering every restraint I had left.

My dick pulsated in my pants. A surge of warmth coursed through me.

The image of her body clenching around my shaft increased my arousal. My mouth watered at the thought of her sweetness lingering on my lips while I ate her up.

Our tongues entangled together, and Fairy sucked on mine. For a half second, I watched her. Her eyes rolled back in her head before they captured mine. Enough to confirm she needed this as much as I did. I plunged my hand into her bikini bottom and swept my fingers over her wet center, so ready for me. I slipped one digit inside her tight channel, her flesh feeling like velvet around mine, and her inner walls tightened. I licked the corner of her lips, swallowing all her whimpers. I spread her wetness over her folds, and rubbed her clit with my thumb as I entered a second finger inside her, gliding them in and out, helping her ride the orgasm building deep in her core.

Pixie's body clenched over my digits as I bit on her lower lip, her lids fluttering close. Her ecstasy coated my fingers. Not wanting to jizz in my pants, I focused on my breathing. *God, it's been too long.*

The woman dissolved in my arms, and I drew her into me as pleasure rippled through her in soft waves.

Her big blue eyes, with flecks of green, drew me in when they opened, taking me hostage. I panted, at a loss for words, admiring all her beauty. Plump lips. Flushed cheeks. Swollen breasts.

Smart. Sexy. Sassy.

My neighbor checked every box on my *Ideal Woman* list.

For a minute, nothing else existed but us.

All the tension in her body faded, and she turned into a puddle in my embrace.

She blinked when she came back to her senses, and it broke the daze we had fallen into.

She pushed my shoulders with both hands. "Put me down."

I complied.

She stepped back.

"What the fuck, Fairy?" I asked, my cock throbbing inside my pants, my control hanging by a thread, in desperate need of a release. "We're just starting." My eyes zoomed in on her reddened lips, and I wondered how they'd feel wrapped around my dick, licking and sucking me until I saw stars.

She raised her hands in the air, annoyed, ready to murder my aroused self. "Don't touch me. You might have a wife and a kid. I won't be the girl you cheat with. No way. You may be hot, but you're not worth it."

Yeah, I thought the same thing about you ten minutes ago.

I would've thought the mention of Dahlia and Jack would get my dick to surrender. But no. The storm in my neighbor only made it harder.

She pulled at my sanity every time she opened her damn mouth, but it made me crave her even more. Damn, she looked fucking adorable when pissed at me.

"I thought we'd already ruled this out. Listen to me. I don't have a wife. And I don't have a kid."

"You're impossible. God, you're such an ass. I hate liars."

I stepped forward. Pixie stepped backward. Two could do this dance. I had all day—and nowhere else to be— except buried balls-deep inside her.

"I'm not lying." And now I had to justify myself.

"Huh, I saw you with them. You know, while you ogled me. You're a pig, HN. I can't believe I allowed you to touch me. Must be the aftermath of my hypothermia. My brain hasn't thawed yet."

I neared her, invading her personal space, forcing my eyes to stay on hers, while they kept wanting to drift to her full lips and naked chest. "I want to fuck your dirty mouth right now and fill it so tight you won't be able to say another word. I want to be deep inside you until you forget your own name and only remember mine."

Her eyes widened, and for a second, I thought she'd slap me.

"I made you come. You make me come. It seems like a fair deal, don't you think?" I raised my brows at her.

I extended a hand in her direction, my palm upward, a gesture meant to settle the peace between us. Now a cock-block, my neighbor balled her tiny hands on her hips, a superior air etched on her flawless face.

At six feet five inches, I was at least a foot taller than this woman.

"Come on, Pixie, don't be a prude. You know you want me as much as I want you. My dick here is tired of waiting for you to give up your protest."

She gasped before flipping me the middle finger and spinning around on her heels.

"Tell your dick it won't happen. Not in this lifetime. You're such an ass," she growled, and I rolled my lips over my teeth to avoid smiling.

Hiding her bare tits with the sweater she picked up from the floor, she left me in the middle of the living room, speechless and with my lower self hard and pulsing, and darted away.

Angry Woman, that's what she should be called right now, slammed a door behind her.

"You keep saying that. Believe whatever you want."

No reply.

"I'm not done with you, woman," I said mostly to myself. "No. I am not."

I stood in the middle of the room, hoping she'd come back. In vain. A yellow cat neared me and arched its back. I squatted to pat its head. "Hey you. What are you doing here?" The feline purred in response and butted my leg, pushing me. "Okay, fine, I'll go."

The cat and I ended up in a staring duel. After a minute, it turned its back on me and followed the direction to where my upset neighbor had disappeared. I clenched my teeth and pounded through the cabin, my cock still hoping she would change her mind and give it a chance to prove itself.

What's wrong with these people?

Wait, did I just consider a cat a person? Fuck. I was more screwed than I thought. With fury boiling in my veins, I let myself out and slammed the door behind me, ready to take my dick out of his misery myself. *Yeah, right now, I considered it a person too.*

Chapter 9
April

"Who does he think he is? He toyed with me, then thought I'd suck his dick like a perfect housewife? He might be married, though the jury is still up on this one. Ugh, he's such an ass. I was right. I don't care how hot he is. He keeps arguing he's not a jerk, but he's never proved me wrong."

Saunders snickered. "I can't believe you let your hunk of a neighbor finger you. Girl, you should've told me all you needed was a change of air. It's about time you come out of your shell. I'm so proud of you, Bubble Head. My girl has finally graduated from Slutty School. You're getting your groove back."

Wrath sliced my words. "After everything I told you, that's all you have to say, that you're proud I almost let a complete stranger, one who drives me nuts, by the way, fuck me." I huffed a loud sigh. "Did you forget he could be married?"

"Gosh, he told you he wasn't. So, I don't see a problem."

"Listen to you. You're ridiculous. HN acted like a prick. He thinks he can do whatever he wants." I paused, my body so tense it could rip at the seams. "Not with me. He'll never get his dick in my precious mouth. Fuck him."

My friend giggled, and my anger left me. I slouched my shoulders forward and buried my face in my hand.

"Does he kiss like a god?"

"Better. I've never been kissed like that in my entire life. It was animalistic. He possessed me with every flick of his tongue. I swear I could've come only from his lips on mine. And from what I felt, he's huge down there."

Saunders whimpered. "Oh yes, that's exactly what you need. A big dick to get back in the game. I think your HN is the perfect specimen to help you reach that goal. You've been alone for far too long. A real man's touch will do you good. You need some human connection. Some flesh on flesh. If he fucks like he fingers, you're in excellent hands, girl. Hang up. Put on something sexy and a thick coat of red lipstick. Go ring his doorbell. And suck his dick. He's worth it. You'll thank me tomorrow."

"He's *maybe* married, for God's sake. He looked cozy with that woman. And stop saying I'll thank you for everything good happening in my life, Saund."

"You should. Your publishing contract, the cabin, your hot neighbor. When was I ever wrong? I'm your voice of reason. Your guardian angel. You need me to push you to do things you're too afraid to do on your own."

"Okay, fine. Send yourself flowers. Put the same effort you put in my love life into your own relationship. Stop screwing around with your man. If you love him, move in with him, and stop avoiding any kind of commitment. You're better than this. Take the next step."

"I know Reed is perfect for me."

I grinned, glad the focus had shifted away from me. "He is. And he loves you. Always has."

Saunders and Reed met the same night I went on a horrible blind date two years ago. They actually met because of my disastrous date. Their love story made this night one to remember.

———

"Saunders, I don't do blind dates. And I'm not looking for a boyfriend."

"Bubble Head, go on this one date. Do it for me. Just put yourself out there for once. I know you're not ready to date, but meeting new people won't kill you. And who knows? Maybe you'll get a new friendship out of this. You've been pretty lonely since Travis. If you promise to give this guy a chance, I promise to save you if he's an arsehole. Deal?"

I forced a breath out through gritted teeth. "Okay. Fine. I can't believe I'm doing it. This is crazy. I'm so not ready."

"I know, but you need a first time. The next will be easier."

I closed my eyes and mouthed to myself, Sorry, Travis. You know Saunders, she won't give up. I love you. *I kissed my fingers and directed them toward the ceiling. Then I brought my attention back to my best friend. "Let me get the details, and I'll let you know. Not sure I still love you, though."*

"I know. Trust me. You need this." We hung up, and I threw a pillow across my bedroom.

Why did I agree to have dinner with——? Wait, what's his name again? Oh yes, Paul. The first time I texted him, tears streamed down my face. Somehow, I felt like I was betraying Travis.

I sat across from Paul in the restaurant, a glass of Chardonnay in hand. Everything about this night felt forced. Even my smile. Paul wore a light-blue sweater and beige pleated pants. He parted his light brown hair to the side. Why did Mrs. Mayers, the old lady living down the street, match me with her nephew? We had nothing in common. He sat there with a stick in his ass and a cocksure grin. The pants alone should've been a hint to run away.

Before I even finished my appetizer, I texted my girlfriend.

ME

9-1-1. It's HORRIBLE. Please, please, please get me out of this.

SAUNDERS

Coming. Hold on. You got yourself a blighter?

ME

YES. Hurry. Dying here.

My best friend entered the restaurant less than five minutes later and strode into the upper-end Italian bistro, ready to create a diversion.

How? Had she been waiting in her car all this time?

In perfect Saunders fashion, she caused a scene to remember. Our gazes met for half a second, the fire already burning in her hazel eyes. The one telling me my date was in big trouble. My best friend put her best game face on, grabbed a glass of red wine from an adjacent table, walked toward us, and started yelling at my date.

"Paul, are you kidding me right now?" My date's eyes widened, and his forehead wrinkled. "You're cheating on me with this"—Saunders turned her head toward me—"this skank. I hate you." In one epic motion, burned into my memory forever, my best friend hurled the drink in the guy's face.

"Miss, I think you've got me mistaken for someone else," Paul protested, wiping the dripping red liquid from his chin with a cloth napkin.

"No. You're a bugger. A cheater. A womanizer. Get out of here." My friend took a step back and pointed at the entrance. My date wasn't brave enough to argue with a crazy-acting Saunders. He lacked

not only balls but decency too. He tossed his napkin on the table, and without even excusing himself, he pussyfooted away with his head hanging low, under the stares of the entire restaurant.

I felt bad for the guy, but not really.

Paul kept disparaging women like we were still living in the nineteenth century. "Women shouldn't work." "Women shouldn't vote." "Women are only good for raising children."

I tried to express my point of view, but he cut me off every time with a flick of his wrist, his opinions ingrained in his fundamental values. Jerk. I could've picked up my purse and left, but I preferred to let my best friend give this guy a run for his money. He deserved a lesson in humility.

Saunders dropped into the seat facing mine and smirked my way. "So, what are we having for dinner, girl?"

I pursed my lips to avoid chuckling.

Soon after, things took an unexpected turn.

The man Saunders stole the wineglass from neared our table, sat next to my friend, and offered her a fresh glass of wine. He had light-brown, almost gold, hair, and bright blue-green eyes. He must have been a little over six feet and was lean, his shoulders not wider than his hips. He looked handsome in his black slacks and silver-gray button-up shirt, rolled to his elbows, with the top three buttons undone. A silver watch with a thick black leather bracelet adorned his left wrist. The guy had a smart, successful, no-nonsense look in his eyes.

"Here. You deserve this. I think I'm in love. Do you believe in love at first sight?" He cocked an eyebrow at Saunders. "You were amazing. A superhero, sexy and badass, coming to your friend's rescue. That guy was a dickhead. No offense. He deserved each drop of the wine—my wine—you threw at him. I forgive you."

They clinked their glasses and forgot all about me. The guy held out his hand. "I'm Reed, by the way."

"Saunders," my friend said with an enormous grin, almost Joker big.

"Wow, you can throw your wine at me any day if you let me take *you out on a proper date. I promise your friend will never have to barge in and save you."*

The rest was history.

———

When I hung up the phone, my head and heart had reached a new level of insecurity. Saunders was wrong. I wouldn't make a move on HN.

For the rest of the day, I immersed myself in my writing, and in just a few hours, I'd written four more chapters. Being angry and sexually frustrated helped my focus, and it made creativity bubble up inside my head. Who would have thought? My fingers typed on their own, and I got lost in the words popping up on my laptop screen. No time to reread anything, too busy trying not to miss a scene, an expression, or a line of dialogue.

After dinner, afraid to lock myself out again—the locksmith guy HN called hadn't come yet—I ended up in the giant, freestanding bathtub instead of the hot tub.

Small candles flickered around the room, plunging the bathroom into semi-darkness. The moon, half-full, shone through the window. The trees danced under the winter breeze.

I added some bubble bath and two drops of blood orange essential oil to the hot water and soaked my body.

With all my attention centered on my breathing and my eyes closed, I tried to put my mind to rest.

My lips mouthed the lyrics of the song playing on my phone.

My mind swam between Saunders back home and HN next door. I wondered what his deal was. The other day, he barked at me in the woods because of a stupid picture, then helped me out when I struggled to stack the firewood, and last night, he cared for me like I belonged to him. This morning, he did everything to push my buttons, then he ate me up as if he'd die without a taste of me.

Like I was the oxygen he needed to breathe. Even his broodiness when he argued with me or was riled up played with my hormones. Was I that sex deprived? *Maybe. Yeah, no doubt I was.*

I contoured the rim of my mouth with the tip of my index finger, reminding myself how HN's touch felt on my flesh. How intoxicating his kisses were. I parted my lips and licked my finger, my tongue circling the tip slowly, making me ache in all the right places. I sucked on my digit while my other hand traveled down my body. Stopping at my breasts, I rubbed a stiff nipple between my fingers, fancying his hands playing with my skin. My hand lowered further down, and I spread my thighs to make room for it.

The climax built inside me, ripping at my core as I dipped one finger into my moist center, smearing my wetness all over my aching self. My sensitive bundle of nerves throbbed under my soft touch.

I dived a second finger inside me and thrust them in and out at a slow dizzying pace—the same way HN did earlier—the heel of my palm grazing my clit with each movement.

I hiked one leg over the edge of the bathtub, giving me more space to pleasure myself.

My spine arched, shivers tracing each vertebra, electrifying my every cell, rivers of ecstasy furrowing inside me.

My swollen clit vibrated, and a jolt of pleasure, raw and powerful, tore through me.

I removed the finger from my mouth and brought my hand to my swollen breasts instead, kneading and pinching, seeking a second release.

My hips moved in sync with my fingers as they hit the sweet spot inside me, over and over, consuming me.

As a loud moan escaped my lips, I threw my head back, and the orgasm shook my entire body. It took me a few minutes to regain complete consciousness.

The whole time, I pictured Hot Neighbor in my head.

Damn it, how could I be so screwed up?

———

The next morning, HN still haunted my thoughts. I'd been flipping over the entire night in my bed, unable not to think of him. I cursed at myself. When I accepted the offer to come to Green Mountain, it was to clear my head. To get my creativity into high gear and pen the first draft of my new novel. Not fantasize about some unavailable man living next door.

I grimaced because I was really doing good…great even…

Until him.

Now I feared my creative mind had left me once again.

Only HN occupied the corners of my brain. And my dreams.

My hormones took over. The bathroom mirror, when I showered earlier, reflected the image of a sex-deprived horny teenager back at me.

Dilated pupils.

Rosy cheeks.

Plump lips.

Swollen breasts.

And it didn't even take into account my state of arousal and my need to rub myself with anything at any time. When did I get so horny?

Last night's pleasure session in the bathtub didn't cut it.

I needed a penis. Flesh. The real thing. Stamina. Warmth. Thickness. Arms around me. Fingers tangled in my hair. Lips to kiss. Eyes to drown myself in.

The guys renting the cabin facing mine were all business-type people over fifty. They wouldn't do it. I double-checked them, just to be sure. No, none of them would cure me of my constant state of arousal.

Pacing the living room, restless and unable to stay still for a full minute, I slipped my feet into my sheepskin boots, wrapped a blanket around my shoulders, and stood on the front porch, relishing the mix of cold winter air and hot sun's rays caressing my skin. With my eyes closed, I took a full breath in. Exhaled. And started over again. There. I could feel the peace and quiet spreading through me and erasing the throb that was wreaking havoc on my body. Another inhale and I blew out the remaining of my angst.

I enjoyed the sunshine on my face a bit longer before opening my lids.

All my zenitude dissipated when I locked eyes with my broody neighbor standing a few yards away from me, his hands shoved in the pockets of his denim jacket. The deep frown wrinkling his forehead made him look lethal. But the intensity in his gaze could set the house on fire. The mix of the two sides of him played with my hormonal state and sent packing my newfound calmness.

Leaning my head backward, I shut my eyes and prayed my mind had conjured him and he wasn't really there, watching me. I craved space away from him—for my sanity—and every cell in me he troubled with his presence. In vain. When I brought my gaze forward again, he hadn't moved.

I sighed and fastened the blanket around me. "Why are you here?" Could he sense the disdain in my voice? "I was having a great day. Why did you have to spoil it? I'm not in the mood to engage in a battle of wills with you. Scram. Go back to whatever it is you do, and let me be. Not interested in taking part in your childish games today."

"Oh, you're sassy even at an early hour. Shame on me. After the rant yesterday morning, I should've guessed. My bad."

I killed him with my eyes. "Are you done? I have a big day in front of me, and you are disturbing my energy… and my peace. Again, leave me alone. Want me to spell it out for you? Go bother someone else." I flicked my wrist toward his cabin. "Go. Now."

He stayed put, not moving a limb.

I growled my dissatisfaction. "Ohmygod, you're so annoying. What do you want from me?"

He shrugged. "I was coming back from running errands and saw you there. I thought you had locked yourself out once again."

"Oh." I relaxed a bit. "I..huh…I have not. I just needed some fresh air. You know, I-I was suffocating inside."

"Ok, then. Thanks for letting me know. Being friendly and welcoming in the morning isn't a skill you have mastered very well. I'll be aware from now on."

He turned to leave, and somehow, for reasons I failed to understand myself, it upset me.

"That's it? You came over here to check on me. Instead, you spied on my little calm-myself-down routine, then you throw an insult my way, and you leave? Don't you have anything better to do with your time? Where's the fight in you?"

He halted and spun around so fast I was startled, then padded in my direction. He climbed the two stairs leading to the front porch and stopped, bringing his eyes level with mine. A smirk curled the side of his lips, a contrast to the menacing image he projected otherwise. "Tell me, Fairy, you want us to fight?"

His proximity sent a wave of neediness through me. Why couldn't I stay indifferent to this man? I squirmed at his closeness and tried to hide it under a shiver. Being that close to him did nothing to quell the arousal that had been plaguing me since our kiss.

He gave me a slow once-over, as if he was aware of the effect he had on me. His smirk widened, and I screamed inside. I refused to let him see through me.

"You didn't answer the question. It's really something you should work on because you're failing at the basics of a conversation."

Anger radiated through my being. "You're condescending. Take a good look in the mirror before accusing me of lacking communication skills."

His deep baritone laugh worked through me.

"What's so funny?"

He shook his head. "You. You let yourself believe you're all rough and tough when you're fairy tall. It's cute. Really."

I stepped forward, eating every inch of distance between our bodies. "Don't talk about me like you know me. You have no idea what I can and cannot do."

HN's face neared mine, and I held my breath. "I love it when you get angry. It's kinda hot." Before I could add anything, he leaned forward and spoke into my ear. "Bet you touched yourself replaying our encounters, right? Tell me I'm wrong." He angled his head, watching me, waiting for me to say something.

Instead, I stayed mute. What else could my neighbor read on my face? Was I so predictable even a stranger could perceive my inner thoughts?

"See? You can't deny it." His mouth returned to my ear. "I'll see you later then." Before he stepped back, his nose traced the side of my face, leaving goose bumps behind.

Tremors invaded me. I closed my eyes, trying my best to maintain my composure. Biting my lower lip to stifle a moan, I said nothing, unable to form coherent thoughts. Until his small action registered and I pushed away from him, my eyes fully open now. "Did you just sniff me? What kind of a sick psycho are you?"

HN climbed down a step, a red hue coloring his cheeks. "Stop mixing your fantasies with reality, Pixie."

I growled under my breath. "Stop pretending you know better." Without another word, I twirled around and returned to the safety of my cabin, deciding to put him in my rearview mirror once and for all.

———

Curled in the hammock chair, a cup of hot chocolate in my hand, and Bernice dozing in my lap, I prayed this would heal me from my horniness.

"Hot chocolate is supposed to heal everything," I said out loud, mostly because I needed to believe it. Badly.

My mind wandered, needing a distraction. Unable to sit still, I got up and went for a walk. I trapped my cat in the first-floor bedroom and jammed the back door with a rock, to prevent it from shutting completely. The fresh air stung my cheeks, and the tip of my nose tingled under the crisp breeze.

Bathing in the cold late January sunshine, I did a few yoga poses. Warrior one, warrior two, triangle pose. I welcomed the flow of energy coursing through me.

Energized, I jumped, stretched my legs, raised my arms

over my head—my fingertips tickling the clouds—bent over, rotated my hips.

Warmer and calmer, I roamed down the path leading to the gate, the fallen leaves and pine needles crunching under the soles of my boots, twirling on myself with open arms, letting the mountain air flush all my fears, uncertainties, and dirty thoughts away.

Upright, standing a dozen feet away from the cliff, I closed my eyes and let the sounds of nature rock me to peace.

When I came back, the front door of the cabin was wide open. What the—I'd locked it when I left.

Panic knotted my stomach.

I skulked toward the door, my hands clenched in fists, ready to defend my five-foot-three self against an intruder. Or a bear. Could a bear break in? *No, silly.* In elementary school, Nana used to tell me I should project assurance even if I lacked self-confidence when I doubted myself . "Fake it until you make it," she used to say. Now I'd be strong and fearless. I put my Mighty April suit on and padded toward my cabin.

My hand relaxed, and I blew out a sigh of relief when I noticed HN, kneeling, stacking wood in the fireplace. My eyes took in his firm ass through his low-cut jeans, the ridges of his back muscles underneath the light fabric of his long-sleeved black cotton shirt, his muscular hand holding the poker. He looked younger with his dark hair untamed and messy, like he'd run his fingers through it multiple times. His focus stayed on the burning wood, and I studied his square jaw, still cloaked in the same dark stubble from yesterday. It seemed he hadn't shaved in quite a few days.

My hormones kicked in, and I felt like eating him for lunch.

HN whirled around, and I snapped out of my daze.

Our eyes met, and I swallowed hard, at a loss for words, my mouth hanging open.

His stare burned holes in me, and I steadied myself against the wall. His Adam's apple bobbed, and I blinked, wanting to avert my gaze. Impossible. My lips pursed, but nothing came out. Handsome Neighbor stepped forward, and I sucked in a ragged breath.

His own breathing quickened. His pupils dilated, and for a second, I thought he'd make me come just by the way he eye-fucked me.

With his single gaze in my direction, I soaked my panties. It should be illegal to be that hot. That male. That enticing. *Take me. Play with me. Fuck me.* I blinked my dirty mind to silence.

His stormy-gray irises, now a shade darker, liquified me. I became a puddle at his feet, burning for him to touch me, to fuse my skin with his, to eat me alive.

I blinked again.

Smitten, with his glazed eyes full of need, I took a step in his direction. I lost all control over my body. Like a magnet, HN's was my lodestone, the one with whom I'd readily clash. The sexual tension between us had grown tenfold since yesterday. The air around us was electrified. We risked catching fire with every breath.

He prowled forward, eating up the space between us.

He grazed his bottom lip with his tongue.

My eyes flared.

We got lost in our own world.

He was about to swallow me whole, and I had no intention to put a stop to it.

On their own, my feet carried me forward, but I halted when someone cleared their throat behind me.

"Hey, how is it going? It's been a long time." A small,

chubby man stomped in our direction, his face flushed and a wolfish grin playing on his lips. "Sorry to interrupt. The door was open, and since you said I could come by anytime this morning, I didn't ring the bell. I hope it's all right."

HN approached him, and they exchanged a handshake. My neighbor found his composure in a heartbeat, like we weren't about to rip each other's clothes off ten seconds ago.

"Your timing is perfect, Desmond." HN coughed. "The wireless lock is giving the lady here some trouble, and the knob on the back door needs to be checked. The other night she got locked out of the cabin in the cold."

"How are things back home?" Desmond asked, opening a red toolbox.

HN shrugged and stuffed his hands into his pockets, raising a wall around him, clearly not in the mood to discuss his personal life with the man.

Desmond bent down and peered at the back door lock. "Let's not take any chances and just change the deadbolt. I might even have a spare one in my truck. Can you check for it? Back shelf. Third row on the left."

HN disappeared outside, and I forced a smile at the man eyeing me a bit too closely. I hugged myself and offered him my best fake smile.

Soon enough, HN came back empty-handed. "Desmond, you're out of luck, man. No spare lock in your truck."

"I'll come back another day to fix it then. Let me just look at the front door first. These high-tech latches are fickle sometimes."

"You don't mind if I stay here while Desmond does his thing?" HN asked me in a low voice, his warm breath tickling the shell of my ear.

I shook my head. No way would I stay in here alone with this Desmond guy. I hated when some men stared at women for no apparent reason. It made me feel self-conscious. So, not a fan of people staring at me. Neither did I enjoy engaging with unknown people or starting a conversation with them. Except for my neighbor. I couldn't seem to resist bantering with him. He, too, seemed to have no problem breaching the walls I'd erected around myself. In all honesty, if the attraction wasn't mutual and parts of him didn't appeal to the woman in me, I wouldn't let him get close to me either. For some reason, though, I enjoyed his attention and our face-offs, so I let it slide.

But the handyman wouldn't get a free pass. Glints shone in his eyes when his gaze collided with mine, but I wasn't interested in him. Nope, there was no lost lust there.

Keeping a neutral expression, I spun around and aimed for the kitchen. Nothing like putting as much distance as possible between two people and not carrying on small talk to show your nonexistent interest.

With my back to the guys, I busied myself making tea. HN joined me, and his hands brushed my hips from behind for a nanosecond. The simple touch made my heart bounce in my chest and ignited my skin. I sucked in a shaky breath and swallowed a gasp, keeping my gaze down, not wanting my neighbor to witness the effect his closeness had on me.

Chapter 10
Carter

Desmond stared at my sexy neighbor like he craved a piece of her. I noticed. Fuck him. Not under my watch. She was destined to be mine. Our mutual attraction had reached new heights, and suppressing the sexual tension between us now seemed impossible. Every fiber of my being crackled around her. Not touching her became less bearable each time we were near each other.

Now that I knew how she tasted and felt, I was hooked. I needed more. A lot more. Her scent was my drug, her lips my kryptonite.

If I didn't stake a claim, Desmond would try to get into her pants. That I knew. I was a man too, and I'd known Desmond for years. The guy was a player.

He'd been my on-call handyman since the day I bought my first cabin in the area. With the small resort I'd created here, I needed someone I could trust to do all the small work and make sure everything stayed in order.

Desmond proved himself to be that guy.

The man didn't care about my celebrity status or the money in my bank account. For all the work he did around here, he charged me next to nothing. Each year, I thanked him with an expensive bottle of scotch on Christmas Day.

His wife died a couple of years back, and I'd seen him in action multiple times, trying to charm the ladies down at the dive bar on the outskirts of town where I hung out from time to time.

My sassy neighbor had everything he had a boner for.

Petite and delicate, with curves to fill a man's hands.

Enough edge to banter with me endlessly and indisputable sex appeal to bring any man down to his knees.

Big, bright blue eyes and a gorgeous smile that could melt Antarctica.

Pixie was dynamite in our little town.

Dangerous and mesmerizing.

Even Jack fell under her charm the other day. And he was five, for God's sake.

Fairy busied herself in the kitchen, and my hands met with her hips before I could think about what I was doing. A sense of calm washed over me like a wave on the shore. It felt like the natural thing to do, as if we'd rehearsed this dance before.

My hands brushed her hip bones, and I wasn't even sure she noticed. I pulled myself together before she could say anything. She avoided my eyes, keeping herself busy, but I caught the faint blush coloring her cheeks.

I had this urge to be close to her but feared scaring her away, not in the mood for another one of her angry ramblings.

Go slow, Carter. Baby steps.

My lips itched to kiss hers. There was no way she would agree if I simply asked. I'd learn my lesson. It was better to let our sizzling attraction do the work for me. That, she seemed to have no problem resisting.

"Okay, here's the thing," Desmond explained, disrupting my daydream. "I'll be able to fix the back door, but there's something wrong with the front electronic latch. Unfortunately, I don't keep any in stock. I can order a replacement, but it'll take a few days. Those things are tricky."

"Can we still use the front door in the meantime?" Did I say *we*? Fuck. I slapped myself mentally.

Baby steps, Carter. Focus.

"Sure, but I can't guarantee it won't act out again."

Pixie stood beside me, her arms folded. "I'll stay in. I have nowhere else to go anyway." She shrugged. "I'll jam the back door with a rock just in case if I go outside." She swiveled on the balls of her feet and walked back into the kitchen. My eyes widened in awe. Nothing ever seemed to bother her. Except for my attitude.

I bet something, or someone, had hardened her up. Made her tough. I saw it in her eyes. A few times already. A dark shadow. Sadness. Or fear. And resolve. I couldn't decide.

"Okay, I'll come back in a day or two. Will call you beforehand." Desmond let himself out after waving at me over his shoulder.

An idea flashed through my mind.

A perfect way to break the extra layer of ice that had settled between Fairy and me after we made out yesterday.

Getting her doors fixed would probably earn me some brownie points—important, sure—but I needed something more immediate for now.

I excused myself and went back to my place to get everything ready.

———

Later, I rang her doorbell, my hands full. A lopsided smirk stretched my lips. My neighbor greeted me wearing skinny jeans so tight it looked like someone painted them on her, making her curves even more delicious than I remembered, along with a black metallic top. Her feet were bare, her toenails painted in a golden hue.

My jaw popped open at the sight, and I asked, spellbound, "Are you going somewhere?"

A hint of a smile bent her lips as she twirled a strand of pink hair around her forefinger. I grinned. Like a fool.

"No. Remember, I'm stuck here. I felt like dressing nice for a change, that's all. I've been wearing my share of sweats and leggings since I arrived in Green Mountain."

"You look beautiful."

With her chin, she pointed at my overflowing arms, choosing to ignore the compliment. "What's all that?"

"Huh, I forgot. How do you feel about the real estate market?"

"Wait. What?" Her brows knitted together, confusion spreading over her face. Her blue eyes glistened, the sparks emphasized, thanks to the shimmery gray eyeshadow and her thick, mascara-coated lashes.

"Since you're stuck here, I thought keeping you company tonight was the least I could do. I brought dinner and Monopoly. Hence the real estate market interest." I quirked one brow, waiting for her to invite me in.

Her soft laughter rippled through me. "I'm here every night, HN. Being stuck at home doesn't faze me." She crossed her arms over her chest, tipping her hip forward, unimpressed. Her eyes remained on me, giving me a slow once-over, a tiny smile curving her lips.

Okay, she liked what she saw. I could work with that.

She searched my gaze when she asked, "Unless it's you who can't fathom the idea of spending a night on your own?"

I loved the challenge in her defiant tone. Fucking turn-on. I repositioned my stance to ease the tension in my groin.

"Yeah. You caught me. I need a five-foot-tall, pink-haired woman to look out for me in case a broad-shouldered, three-headed, six-eyed alien lands here tonight. Or a grizzly bear."

Fairy chuckled, and I joined in.

"I'm here. Ready to defend you with my five-foot-*three* height, by the way, against hardcore criminals who may want to attack your weak ass." She straightened her back. "I'll let you in on one condition."

"Name it," I agreed, ready to dye my hair blue and howl at the moon if she asked me to.

Her shoulders tensed, and she narrowed her eyes. "And this is the moment you tell me the truth. No bullshit."

I nodded, a million thoughts running through my head, splinters of ice lining my spine. Did she know about me? Was she about to expose my lie by omission and confront me about not being honest about my identity? Adrenaline shot through my system, and my blood pressure soared. I rolled my shoulders back and held my breath, ready for her to deliver the punch.

"Is the redhead your wife?"

What? I stumbled back a step. The tension in my back vanished. *That* was her question? Okay…I was safe.

"Why does it matter? You're interested?"

"Answer the question. I won't have dinner with some-one's husband."

"I'm not married. Never have been. She's my family, but I won't explain her to you. Not yet at least." My grip tightened around the pot in my hands. Telling her about Dahlia would put my anonymity in jeopardy, and I wasn't ready to throw myself under the bus just yet.

"And this is the truth, the whole truth, you swear?"

"I promise you she's not my wife or my girlfriend."

She studied me for a minute, her lips pinched in a thin line, her jaw set, and her brows wrinkled, looking like one of those tiny Angry Birds. With a sigh, she moved to the side and opened her arms to invite me in. "Then come on in, big guy, make yourself at home. I'm starving, and you mentioned you brought dinner."

In my head, I high-fived myself as I kicked the door shut.

One point for me.

I breathed easier, and my body warmed up at the thought.

"Wine?" my neighbor asked as I dropped everything on the kitchen counter once she lifted the board game out of my arms.

A wireless speaker set beside a small essential oil diffuser played soft music, giving the space a cozy, homey vibe. The fresh scent of lavender filled my nose, and I relished the atmosphere the setup created.

"No, thanks." I shimmied out of my jacket and adjusted my navy-blue plaid shirt I'd rolled at the elbows. "I'll stick to water." A song of mine, "Forever," started playing, and she hummed the first notes. My body tensed, and my back stiffened. "Country music fan?" I asked, doing my best to busy myself in the kitchen and avoid staring at her.

"I love just about any music. But country soothes me. There's something about it." She shrugged. "I must sound silly." She swayed her hips. "I love this song."

A tight feeling gripped my chest, and I forced out a breath.

"Why don't you relax while I set the table? Everything should be ready in ten minutes."

She neared me. "Oh, this smells good. And it looks divine. Gnocchi?"

"Yeah. With tomato pesto. Here," I said, bringing a piece to her mouth with a fork. "Taste it."

She pursed her lips, blew on it, and took a bite.

Fucking hot. Not the food. This woman was a vision.

Fairy licked her lips but forgot a little drop at the corner. With a sharp intake, I wiped the smear of red sauce with the pad of my thumb and brought it to my mouth. She bit her bottom lip, and I thought I'd die of a heart attack. Lust clung to us, making us its prisoners. Before I did something my whole body was burning to do, I stepped back. The knuckle of my thumb found my forehead. My pulse quickened.

I was dying to finish what we started earlier, but I refused to make a move and spoil the evening.

My neighbor lowered her gaze. "Thanks. This is delicious. I'll set the table while you finish up here." She poured herself a glass of Chardonnay and chugged half of it in one mouthful. Soon color crept up her cheeks.

Why did I think coming here tonight was a good idea?

I plated our food and added fresh herbs from the container set on the windowsill to give it a chef's treatment. With a step back, I admired my work and smiled. Yeah, that looked good.

When Jeff turned eighteen—I was fifteen—Mom gave us cooking lessons for months. She feared he would only eat takeout in college. She told us people ate with their eyes, so my brother and I learned how to present our food in a tasty way. Now I'd mastered the skill. It was useful when I wanted to impress a girl. Yep, it worked every time. It didn't hurt that I liked to cook either.

I placed both plates on the wooden table, along with the bottle of wine, where Pixie had already set two glasses of water. She lit up a white candle centerpiece while whistling a song I didn't recognize.

"What are you singing?" I asked as we sat on either side of the table, the candle projecting shadows on the wall behind us.

"Oh, that? An old jingle from a cereal ad I watched too many times when I was a kid. Every now and then, it pops up into my mind, and I can't get rid of it for days."

She grinned. I grinned back. Tonight, it looked like someone had tattooed a permanent smile on her face. All the restraints I saw every other time we crossed paths had melted away. I loved every second of it.

I lifted my glass. "To our first dinner."

Fairy clinked her glass with mine. "And to greater—"

"Company?" I asked, hoping she would agree.

"That's what I was about to say."

"Oh, I can read your mind." I took a sip of iced water.

With her elbows propped up on the table, she studied my expression. "Let's see if you're a mind-reader." She drummed her fingers on the wooden surface. "My favorite color."

I snorted. "Pink. Duh."

She cast a glance up. "Duh. Really? What are you? Ten?"

I laughed along with her. "Sometimes I wish."

"Let's try again. I have a tricky one."

"Bring it on." I clasped my hands together.

"What's my favorite perfume?"

My lips stretched into an easy grin. "Come on, you can do better than that. Lavender."

Fairy watched me with a surprised expression. "Why? How? You noticed?"

I shrugged. "Did you forget you slept in my arms for hours the other night?"

She hid her face in her palms.

I extended an arm and pushed her hands away. "Don't."

"It's embarrassing." She shivered at the reminder. "Gosh, I was so cold. I thought my toes would fall off."

I took a gulp of water and leaned back in my seat. "Well, it could have been worse. I'm glad you're okay."

We exchanged timid, tight-lipped smiles.

"And you got mad when you thought I sniffed you earlier? Don't forget that." I winked, and she shook her head, laughing. The sound clear and contagious. "I guess I'm forgiven?"

"So, you are admitting you took a whiff of me this morning."

I lifted both hands between us. "I'll never admit nor deny it."

"And yet, here I was thinking you were a reformed ass."

"Stop trying to pretend I'm not charming."

She flushed.

"I think it's a good thing you love pink so much."

"Why?"

"Because. It looks good on you."

Her lips separated, but no sound came out.

I extended my arm to rest my hand on her forearm. "Let's eat."

Fairy spread her napkin over her lap. We studied each

other for a beat, exchanging smiles and something more potent I couldn't define. Whatever lies she tried to feed herself, our relationship wasn't neighbor-like anymore. Had it ever been? If the charged air surrounding us was any indication, we'd burst into flames by the end of the night.

As the first bite crossed her lips, a sound that I could only define as a deep-throat cry of pleasure left her mouth. It sent a signal right to my groin. I coughed, trying to keep my composure. "Having an orgasm?" I covered the lust I could barely contain with a tease.

"*Mouthgasm*," Pixie replied with a huge smile. "It's creamy and tasty, what's not to like, right?" She dipped a fingertip into the sauce and brought it to her mouth before sucking her digit clean. Another whimper filled the silence.

I blinked multiple times, still unsure if I heard her right. When I parted my lips to speak, she winked. She fucking winked as if it was all a game to her. Right then, I almost shot my load in my pants. Was this woman for real? I hadn't had sex in a very long time, and her dirty little games were screwing with my sanity.

"Keep doing what you're doing. Don't stop on my account." I brought a forkful to my mouth, trying to busy myself—and my mind—to avoid thinking about other creamy and tasty things I could provide her with.

The sound of my neighbor's voice brought me out of my filthy fantasy. "Tell me the truth. Are you a chef? Because you cock like one."

She pinched her lips together, and her eyes grew big. Mine did too. Did I hear her right, or was my mind so screwed I was imagining words she didn't speak out loud?

She sipped her wine, avoiding my gaze for a second, then corrected herself. "No, what I meant was *cook*. C-O-O-K. You *cook* like a chef. Gosh. Sorry for the slip-up."

"Don't be," I mumbled.

"What?" She dropped her fork, staring at me.

"Nothing. I'm happy you like it and enjoy the creamy texture."

She blushed darker, and her hotness multiplied. Did she look this irresistible on purpose?

I smirked, then lifted my water to my lips. "No, I'm not a chef. Maybe I should rethink my career choice."

Fairy regained her composure. "Please. If you do, let me invest in your business."

A loud laugh escaped my lips. "You can't stand me, but you wanna invest in my business?"

"I'm not kidding. This tastes amazing," she said, pointing to her food. "And I have to admit, you're not always being an ass."

A broad smile lit up her face, and my knees weakened under the table. "If only I'd known the way to a compliment was through your stomach, I would've cooked for you days ago."

She scrunched up her nose, and I freed the laughter bubbling inside me.

The rest of the dinner went down smoothly. I was in no rush for it to end, and by the look of it, Pixie mirrored my thoughts. The entire time, I fell under her charm a little more. I pushed back my chair and started clearing the table. When she motioned to follow, I stopped her with a raised hand. "Let me. What about some Monopoly now and some dessert later?" I quirked a brow.

"You brought dessert?"

"Sure did. I told you, I'm not just a handsome ass. I can also be a gentleman." I watched her from the kitchen. "Unless you want me to feed you a treat right now?"

She coughed her wine but regained her composure quickly, the tilt of her lips matching mine. "All good. I'm full. And we, women, prefer when the pleasure lasts. Sure, a quick fix is satisfying…on occasion. But enjoying what's good for a little longer is usually worth the wait." As if she just didn't fuck with my mind—and my throbbing dick—she moved to her feet and offered me a blinding smile.

What did happen here? Was I dreaming the entire night?

How could all the words she spoke sound so dirty to me?

We set up the game on the coffee table in the living room and sat on pillows. My neighbor placed the half-drunk bottle of wine beside her on the floor after refilling her glass.

Her eyes sparkled in the dim light. Keeping my hands —and my mouth—to myself was sweet torture. How could the connection between us be so effortless? Like we'd known each other inside out. Like we'd been friends for years.

"Okay, HN. I hope you're not a sore loser because I thrive at Monopoly. And I'm heartless."

"I'd expect nothing less from you. But never underestimate me. I was a real estate shark in another life."

I winked.

She gasped.

I threw the dice.

Pixie switched the playlist for a jazzy one. Everything about her oozed sex. She was so easy to get addicted to. Her laughter rippled through me, and her scent left me dizzy. A mixture of lavender, fruity shampoo, and happiness. Something exclusively hers.

From the fleeting glances she cast my way to the shimmer in her eyes, I noticed everything about her. The woman loved the game. She was fierce and unapologetic.

"Eight hundred dollars, HN. You'll see, I'll wreck you." She held out her hand.

"Please do," I whispered under my breath. "I'll give you everything."

She ignored my innuendo, but her face flushed, proof she'd caught every word that left my mouth.

Her features told me everything I needed to know. A twitch of her eyebrows meant she was about to pay me a large sum of money. The gleam in her eyes appeared each time she had the upper hand. Her lips curved whenever she cashed in on her properties. We weren't playing Monopoly anymore. We were playing self-restraint—at least I was.

I bet she knew the effect she had on me, even without catching sight of my erection under the coffee table. A fever stirred beneath my skin, and every inch of me felt it. In my mind, I pictured myself laying her on the kitchen table and cherishing every inch of her flesh with my tongue. She would ride me to oblivion, and I'd pound into her with purpose, shattering both our worlds. Or maybe she'd wrap her lips around my shaft, and I'd forget everything, my only goal to coat the back of her throat with my cream. Fuck. I swallowed, hopped to my feet, and made it to the kitchen. I refilled my glass of water, taking care to keep my back to the woman who was killing me softly.

"Dessert?" I asked once I regained some of my weak self-control.

I brought the plate of fresh fruit dipped in dark chocolate that I'd prepared earlier to the living room. Sitting back beside her on the floor, I fed her a strawberry. All my blood rushed to my groin. I was playing with fire but didn't care if I got burned doing so. Pixie closed her mouth over the juicy fruit and moaned, and for a second, I imagined it was my cock she was feeding on. My throat worked as I tried to put to sleep the storm raging inside me. I inhaled through my mouth. Once. Twice. Three times. I was hard as a flagpole.

As if she sensed my growing uneasiness, she rose to her feet and lit a few candles all around the room. She beamed in the flickering light. How could she waltz through the sexual tension like it meant nothing? She bent over to pick up the matchbox she'd dropped on the floor, giving me a front seat view of her perfect heart-shaped bottom. Was she tempting me on purpose? Testing my self-control? She put the matchbox back on the fireplace mantle and sat down on the opposite side of the coffee table.

"Get ready, HN. I'm going to end you."

Yeah, I know you will.

Chapter 11
April

Ohmyfuckinggod. We were playing Monopoly, and it felt as if I was being fucked senseless. My body vibrated the entire time. Could someone die from horniness? At that moment, I wondered. For real. When I opened the door and saw HN, all man and gorgeous on the doorstep, I feared my jaw would hit the floor. For a second, I was tempted to pinch myself to see if I was dreaming. No. I wasn't. I was wide awake. His navy-blue plaid shirt looked good on him. It fit snug to his chest in all the right places. I stuffed my hands in my pockets, resisting the impulse to touch him.

Okay, I had to be honest. HN was not only good for the eyes, but he was also an impressive cook.

All night, his presence ignited every one of my senses. Like fireworks on a summer night.

We were halfway through our game of Monopoly

when he got personal. "Tell me why you're here, in Green Mountain."

I hesitated a moment before answering. "I needed a place to unwind. To get a fresh start." Why did being honest feel like laying my inner secrets on the table? "What about you? You're here for pleasure or work?"

"You want the truth?"

"Always."

A dark shadow passed over his smoky irises. "I needed an escape. A moment to stop and breathe. To reassess my life."

His throat rippled, and I feared our night would turn sour, so I changed the subject. "Okay. Let's raise the stakes here."

His full lips curled upward. "What do you propose?"

I tapped my chin with a finger as I thought about what we could do. "The winner will cook breakfast tomorrow morning. People always assume the losers must pay some price, so why don't we change things up? Make it more interesting."

HN leaned forward and held out his hand. "Fine with me. You'll be lucky to taste my vegan sausage if I win."

His words sucked all the air from my lungs. I shifted in my seat, my body an aching mess. When I regained some sort of self-control, we shook on it. He winked, and if I weren't sitting on the floor, I would've fallen off my chair. HN exuded confidence and sex appeal like they were tailor-made for him. My body was hot and bothered, and I wondered when someone had cranked up the thermostat in here.

A ball of lust settled down my throat. I coughed and found my voice. Two could play this little game. "Well, I'm not sure I'll let you enjoy my buns, but how do pancakes sound?"

For the first time tonight, I noticed a slight pink flush rising up his face under his dark stubble. My eyes lingered on his throat, where I witnessed his pulse spiking. I clenched my thighs when our gazes met. HN swallowed hard, and the movement sent jitters between my thighs and down to my toes. My skin burned, and my heart quivered. Ohmygod, his grin could, without exaggerating, liquify me on this floor.

"Show me what you've got."

All my inhibitions died right there. His eyes ate me up like I was some sort of candy melting on his tongue. He grazed the side of my face with his knuckles, and I shivered. With a glint in his eye, he leaned back and settled onto his side of the coffee table.

His intoxicating presence sucked every molecule of the air from the room, leaving me breathless, and all my senses heightened.

His genuine laughter and soft chuckles made me dizzy. With desire. And need.

When I won the game after he went bankrupt, HN cupped his heart. "You own me, Fairy." The way he'd faked I bruised his strong male ego made me shiver. I tried to ignore the game we were playing, but I couldn't stop. Every time I bent over, pushed my boobs up whenever I folded my arms over my chest, or wet my lips with my tongue, he missed nothing. And the more his eyes darkened, the more my inner thighs pulsed. Monopoly was just an excuse to test each other's restraints. No matter what, I wouldn't give in to temptation. HN would crack first.

———

The next morning, after just mere hours of sleep, I woke up with a purpose. Since I won last night's game, according to our terms, I was on breakfast duty. Armed with freshly mixed pancake batter and chocolate-dipped fruit leftovers, I paced the kitchen for long minutes before mustering the courage to go next door. On my way over there, my heartbeat was louder and more out of tune than a little kid's orchestra. I slid my hands into my sweater sleeves and stretched my neck muscles in all directions, trying to calm the flock of birds taking flight in my chest.

Last night had been amazing, but what if, in the morning light, things felt awkward between us? My neighbor had occupied too many of my thoughts since he had walked away the night before.

Whenever we were together, the world around us stopped existing. Nothing could happen between us, and yet, I kept going back to him as if I had become a glutton for punishment.

No matter how many times I told myself I should stay away since I woke up, my feet couldn't care less and brought me next door of their own volition. Now that even my legs were on his team, my body had been forever categorized as a traitor.

Standing on the front porch, I tried to collect myself and act cool, but inside, I was all but calm.

When I heard HN's hurried footsteps on the other side of the door, I held my breath, not sure I was ready to see him again, fearing the emotions it would stir in me.

Nothing had prepared me for the sight of my just-woken-up neighbor, standing bare-chested mere inches in front of me, with unruly bed hair, an unconcealed erection, and an adorable sleepy smirk grazing his lips. His abs. Gosh. They looked as if they had been sculpted on him. They had haunted my dreams since the morning I woke up in his bed, entangled in his warm, toned body, after my hypothermia scare. My mouth watered as I stood there like an idiot, picturing him wearing only boxer briefs in my head, his tanned, rock-hard chest on full display.

No amount of blinking could coax my voice back to life.

Travis was handsome, but my neighbor was out of this world. Had I become so rusty with men that just being this close to one was enough to send my hormones into a frenzy? Last night, in a moment of weakness, drunk on more than the wine in my glass, I had feared my ovaries would take over and beg him to ram into me, on repeat, till next year. Because I missed sex. And until I moved to Green Mountain and met him, I had forgotten just how much.

All evening, I caught him checking out my butt—more than once. And each time he got busted, he didn't shy away or offer any excuses. Instead, he offered me a shrug and a smirk that sent surges of heat through my being. Loving the effect I had on him, I took pleasure in swaying my hips a little more whenever I got the chance.

From the doorway, HN studied me without a word, his head tilted to one side. For an instant, I feared he had forgotten I was coming over and felt my blood rising in my cheeks. I was ready to bolt and lock myself in my cabin when he snapped out of it and ushered me inside, killing some of my will to flee. His warmth bled through me as I passed him in the entryway, and right there, I knew I was completely in over my head with my neighbor.

Chapter 12

Carter

Ding. Dong.

I woke up to the sound of the doorbell.

I pried my eyes open and rubbed them with my fists, my eyelids still half-closed from sleep. Squinting, I unplugged my phone from the charger on the nightstand. *Eight o'clock.* I exhaled in one big huff knowing I hadn't slept more than a few hours.

Ding. Dong.

I blinked. "Go away," I whisper-yelled. Who could it be? No one had announced themselves from the gate.

I slipped my naked self into a pair of dark-blue cotton pants and tucked my morning wood in, to prevent flashing a tent at whoever stood on my front porch.

My hand raked through my hair, trying to comb the tousled dark strands I knew were pointing in all directions.

Two at a time, I ran down the stairs, not bothering to put on a shirt. I stretched and scrunched up my facial muscles to remove all traces of sleep and unlocked the door.

Fairy.

She stood there, a soft smile drawn on her lips, dressed in a sleeveless puffer vest over a black sweater, silver leggings, and sheepskin boots, looking freaking gorgeous.

Her night had been as short as mine—four hours at most—but unlike me, she was every shade of radiant.

Holding a plate wrapped in aluminum foil in her hands, she singsonged, "Morning, HN."

I cleared my throat, my larynx clamped from sleep. "Morning to you."

Was her presence here a dream? I shook my head as my mind drifted to last night.

Dinner. Monopoly. The best night of my life in a fucking long time.

Around three a.m., she had ended me for real. I had no money left and went bankrupt.

I had even raised my hands in surrender. She owned me. Yep. I was ruined in all the ways that counted. Her incredible smile told me she knew it.

Later, we had both yawned, then stood to put the board game back into the box.

Even now, I remembered my attention zeroing in on her lips. All night, I'd resisted kissing every smile, every pout, every word that fell from them. *You just landed in the friend zone, Carter.* We'd reached a truce, and I wasn't about to screw up everything. Not yet at least.

Desperate not to let her know how affected I was last night, I'd shoved my hands into my pockets. Rocking on my heels, I'd hesitated for a moment before bidding my farewell.

She had nodded and walked me to the door. Then she

did something that stunned me. Without a word, she wrapped her arms around me and gave me a hug. One that lasted longer than required. It was awkward and magnificent at the same time. I felt tipsy as I breathed her in. My heart had leapt to my throat the entire walk home, and my mind kept asking the same question throughout the night.

What the fuck just happened?

Facing me in the morning light, my neighbor cleared her throat. The memories of the previous night faded away, and my attention returned to her.

She flashed me a ten-thousand-dollar grin. "Made pancakes. Hope you're hungry." She handed me the plate. "Wait? Did I wake you up?"

I grabbed the dish she offered me and nodded with a lopsided smile.

"I'm sorry. It's a beautiful day, though, and I intend to make the most of it. Time to get moving, neighbor."

I turned my head to the side, my eyes fixed on her. "Are you for real?"

She raised her gaze to meet mine, and a slight flush tinted her cheeks. Her lips parted, but she stayed silent, her blue irises swallowing me in. "You forgot?" A frown marred her forehead.

"No, I didn't…huh…yeah…well, I kind of did," I said, rubbing the back of my neck.

She pivoted on her heels. "It's okay. I can go."

My heart thundered in my chest, and I held out a hand to grab her elbow. Tingles tickled the pads of my fingers. She turned her head toward me, her molten irises burning with lust. Did she feel it too? My throat tightened, and I cleared it before speaking again.

"Don't go. You're already here. Come on in." She followed me to the kitchen where I set up plates and silverware on the island, before offering her a stool and taking the one next to hers.

Just like the night before, the conversation flowed naturally between us. None of the silences were uncomfortable.

My neighbor's blinding smile reached her eyes and her face became a ray of light in my darkness.

Before we knew it, it was past noon.

"I need to go. I have work to do," she said.

"Sure. I'll hit the gym." I needed to release the exponential tension growing in me with every passing minute in her company.

As soon as she left, that was what I did.

I sweated on the treadmill until my clothes were drenched. I lifted weights until my muscles trembled. And then I locked myself in my music studio, doing what I did best in life.

Write music.

Chapter 13

April

Hours later, as I sat in front of my laptop, the memory of all the moments HN and I shared since last night still got me all tingly and giddy. The stolen glances. Long stares. Barely-concealed lust.

When I left his cabin around noon, I believed I'd get some writing done. Who was I kidding? I shifted in my seat. Fidgeted with my digits. Chewed on my purple pen. Not even the fantastic hammock chair with the perfect view of the mountains was appealing enough today. Like a caged lioness, I roamed around the cabin, not knowing what to do with myself. My fingers itched to do something but refused to comply on the keyboard. I fanned myself with a hand, a wave of fire rippling through me. I rolled a bottle of cold water down my nape, between my breasts, over my forehead. Carved into my nose, HN's manly cedarwood and pine scent was all I could smell.

The sound of my own fingertips tapping on the pad of

my laptop drove me nuts, and I aborted the idea of writing for now. Instead, I layered a soft blanket over my lined jacket. Slouched in an Adirondack chair on the back deck with a fantasy novel in hand, I welcomed the winter sun above, hoping it would clear my mind and make me forget about HN's hotness.

The story, dark and exciting, kept me on the edge of my seat for hours as I immersed myself in the pages. My heart did a little dance. Mission accomplished.

I fixed myself a quick dinner, sprawled on the couch, and dozed off. Bernice curled up beside me, her furry body resting against my belly, my dreams spiced up with everything I wished my hot neighbor would do to me.

Some time later, a loud thud woke me up. I flinched and leaped to my feet, wondering whether it was part of a dream or not. My heart scrambled in its cage and felt heavier in my chest. The sun had settled down hours ago. I scuffed to the far corner of the living room and flicked on the light. The room swam in a warm, golden glow.

Another loud bang thundered outside, startling me. I held my breath, all my senses waking up.

Was it a raccoon going through the trash can? A skunk? Or a bear?

No. The fence. Saunders told me it prevented bears from getting too close to the property.

While my heart tumbled down to my stomach, I padded across the room and grabbed the TV remote on my way to the front door, ready to hit anyone standing in the dark.

I caught a glimpse of myself in the reflection of a window. Armed with only a remote, I wouldn't even scare a baby. I sighed.

For a second, the idea of calling my hunk of a neighbor to my rescue flashed through my mind, but I shook my head and pushed the thought to the back of my mind.

We never exchanged numbers, or even names. Our nickname game sounded silly and juvenile right now.

Anyway, I could take care of myself on my own. *You can do this, April. Be fearless.*

I didn't need some tall, handsome, obviously fit guy with corded back muscles and a six-pack to save me from whatever wandered around my cabin. Nah…I was fine on my own. Another thud. I jumped three feet up. Seriously?

On my tiptoes, to avoid making noise, I flung the front door wide and growled, the guttural sound piercing the now quiet night, ready to chase the intruder away, a death grip on the TV remote in my hand. My options to protect myself were limited, and I couldn't think clearly, my brain still foggy from my nap.

A loud chuckle resonated in the dark.

A familiar figure appeared under the porch light, flashing an amused, wary eye. "Who do you think you're scaring away?" my neighbor asked, his arms overflowing with a pile of wood. "Wait, is that a TV clicker in your hand?" HN shook his head, and his smile reached his eyes.

I stuck my tongue out, annoyed at the way he teased my attempt at self-defense. I loved his smile, though. It lit up his features even more than usual, giving him a boyish look. A grown-up boy with stubble. "What are you doing here? It's late."

"It's cold outside, and the weather forecast said it'd snow tonight or tomorrow morning. I'm making sure you've got enough wood to keep the fireplace running." He shrugged like it wasn't a big deal.

I blinked.

It'd been a long time since a man cared enough about me and my well-being to make sure I had everything I might need at hand. I relished the idea. A bit too much. Flutters danced in my stomach. The small gesture meant a lot to me.

"Wow, that's nice of you. Really."

HN flashed a small smile my way and dropped the wood under the covered porch where we stood.

Another loud thud echoed in the night.

I'd barely ever seen any snow in my life. The thought of being stuck in a snowstorm or buried under truckloads of white frozen flurries got me on edge. In my head, snow was a threat. Yeah, I was that girl.

My gaze traveled to the pile of wood my hot neighbor already brought over.

I'd be fine. This time my own lips stretched into a grin. "Thanks."

"Glad I could help." He stuffed his hands in his pockets and ambled away.

My eyes stayed fixed on his firm ass as he disappeared into the night.

"Good night, neighbor," HN yelled over his shoulder, waving at me.

Uneasiness sprawled inside me as I watched his back as he retreated. I had no clue what the right thing to do was. Should I have invited him in?

For a fat minute, my feet remained glued to the wooden porch as I stood there, swept by the chilly breeze, wondering what to make of him. I glanced at his cabin, where he had already vanished, unable to make up my mind about his confusing personality.

My attention zoomed in on the pile of logs by the door. Peace settled over me.

He cared.

Electric happiness prickled along my skin at the thought he really did.

The next morning, a thin blanket of snow covered the ground and the treetops. Not feet high like I feared, but about an inch. Breathtaking. With a mug of hot tea in my hand, I watched, from the hammock chair in the living room, the perfectly defined snowflakes falling. With the sun already shining, I knew this white wonder wouldn't last long. Still, the snow filled me with a rush of giddy energy.

I changed into warmer clothes, put on my jacket and a black beanie and my sheepskin boots, and ventured outside. With my arms stretched wide on either side, I spun around, my eyes fixed on the sky, a giant smile splitting my face in two. Unable to resist, I hummed a Christmas song. A fervor radiated through my body, pooling in my heart.

"The kid in you happy this morning, Fairy Girl?"

I was so mesmerized by the winter display that I hadn't seen my neighbor standing nearby. My chest flipped when I noticed his smirk as he caught me spinning around. Flutters, akin to butterfly wings, invaded my stomach.

I halted and, without thinking, hugged the man standing beside me, wrapped up in my own little world. Nothing could temper this moment.

His scent made my head spin as I buried my face in his chest.

HN stiffened under my touch, and I stepped back. "Sorry. Huh…got a bit swept away by all this beauty."

He tucked a loose strand of my hair behind my ear, and shivers raced inside me.

I sucked in a breath and met his eyes for a nanosecond before averting my gaze. I hoped he couldn't hear the hammering of my heart from where he stood. His attention stayed locked on my face, shifting between my eyes and my mouth. Just to tempt him and see what he would do, I bit my bottom lip in a way I knew was both sensual and sexy. His Adam's apple bobbed. This game of seduction we were both fully engaged in was getting more fun each day. I'd never indulged in foreplay like this before—not one to attract much attention from guys in general—but I was sure I could master the art perfectly by the end of my stay. As long as all we did was flirt with each other, there was no harm done, right?

After a moment, HN broke the silence that had settled between us. "Desmond will be here after lunch to change the back door lock. I'll come over to deal with him."

I nodded, staring at his mouth. "Great," I mumbled with a shuddering breath.

He kept talking, but I didn't process anything he spoke.

"Hey, did you hear a word I said?"

My eyes landed on his. I pursed my lips, having no clue what HN just told me. "Mm-hmm. Sure."

He touched my forearm, and I snapped out of my daze. I shook my head, blinking, rebooting my confused brain.

"Hello?" he asked again.

"Sorry. Got lost for a moment. What did you say?" I straightened my back, projecting fake confidence.

"I said I'm going into town this afternoon. You need something? Groceries? A pair of boots? Anything?"

He fixed me with a heavy stare, waiting for me to say something.

Instead, my organs failed, and my breath caught in my lungs. I opened my mouth to speak, but no sound passed my lips, so I closed it a second later.

"Did you hear me? Pixie?"

Liquid lust stirred low in my belly at the sound of my neighbor's deep, husky voice. With a step forward, he closed the distance between us, his body now grazing mine.

When he spoke close to my ear, I stopped breathing for a beat. "So, do you need anything?"

"I-I'll go later…by myself," I stuttered, my voice shaky and low.

"No offense, but the roads are icy, and your car will never make it up here on the way back. We'll take my truck."

The spell I was under broke. "Excuse me, are you making fun of Miss Dolly?"

"Miss who—? Oh crap, did you give your car a name?" He raked his fingers through his already tousled hair sprinkled with snowflakes.

"Don't look so surprised. Lots of people do." I gave a single nod, hoping it would lend weight to my argument. "Anyway, I bet your dick has a name too. Not judging." Why was I fixated on his penis? Damn it. *Keep your thoughts to yourself, April.*

"I…never mind," he said before his eyes drifted down my body. His voice lowered, and when our gazes collided, I found myself under a familiar trance. "What if my dick has a name? You—"

I swept my tongue over my lips, breath catching in my throat. I had no oxygen left in my brain to argue. His palm brushed my shoulder, and I closed my eyes, inhaling his masculine scent, the addictive mix of pine and cedarwood. Everything inside me screamed to kiss him again. His warmth reached my core. I leaned into his touch, butting his palm the same way Bernice always did when I petted her.

"I… What?"

HN's sudden intake of breath sent shivers down my body. His focus descended to my mouth before climbing back up to my eyes.

I squeezed my thighs together, my already flimsy composure slipping away.

My neighbor, without a doubt, the most handsome male specimen I'd ever laid eyes on—according to my sex-crazed hormones—seized my forearms with both hands and flashed me a grin. My chest rose and fell in quick succession. I was panting like I'd just run a marathon, even though my feet were glued to the snowy ground. I stepped forward, the gap between us shrinking. My breasts swelled. My lips tingled. And my lungs idled.

Without saying anything, he released his grip on me, pivoted on his heels, and walked away.

Frozen in place, I stood there, thoughts tangled and the snow forgotten. What had just happened?

"See you later, Pixie." His voice pulled me out of my stunned daze. With long strides, he reached his cabin in no time, leaving me speechless and spellbound, aching and needy before I could even form a reply.

The heat radiating from me could melt the freshly fallen snow blanketing the entire town. I had to regain some control around my neighbor before this thing between us ignited and consumed us both.

Chapter 14

Did only my presence steal away my neighbor's ability to speak? I closed the door behind me, shrugging off the snowflakes clinging to my hair. Even in the comfort of my house, I could still feel the heat of Pixie's big doe eyes as they licked me up from head to toe, only to linger over my mouth for a beat longer.

Earlier, when I had noticed her from my kitchen window, twirling around in the snow, I found her so irresistible that I had to come up with an excuse to go to her under any pretense.

Desmond had called me at the same time, giving me the perfect reason to talk to her. She never saw me coming, and the surprise on her face when I appeared before her doubled her adorableness.

I could tell she'd barely ever encountered snow before. Her astounded eyes had given her away. Anyone accustomed to winter's sparkling dust wouldn't be this smitten by a few snowflakes. But Fairy totally was. She looked like a little kid enjoying the tiny crystals falling from the sky as if they were the most precious and rare diamonds she'd ever seen.

Then her gaze had landed on me, capturing me and making my body acutely aware of her proximity. The more she stared at me, the deeper and darker her vibrant blue eyes had become.

My lungs constricted, and my mouth went dry at the memory. The entire time I had stared at her, my heart had hammered against my ribs. Even now, I could still feel the lingering echoes of the last few minutes.

For some reason, I always felt like a stupid, starstruck teenager around her. Never before had a woman had this much effect on me. This was all new to me and a bit confusing to navigate.

When she had wrapped her arms around me, I had stood frozen, torn between hugging her back and stepping away. My dick, already semi-hard, had enjoyed the contact. All the air had left my lungs when she had leaned back, and I had to take a few deep breaths to calm the zing coursing through me.

Until she admitted she had fucking named her car *Miss Dolly.* I shouldn't be surprised. But somehow, I was. She always found new ways to astound me. But out of nowhere, she'd started talking about my dick, and the attraction brewing between us had returned. The sucker loved hearing its name. Its throbbing against the zipper of my denims had been a telltale sign. And now, in the privacy of my own home, it was still standing tall, ready for some playtime of its own.

Was Fairy aware of her dirty mouth, or was she innocent enough that she didn't think before uttering those words?

In the heat of the moment, I had been tempted to kiss her. To shut her up once and for all, instead of engaging in one of our face-offs.

The words had frozen on the tip of my tongue, and instead of revealing the dirty thoughts swimming in my head, I had walked away while I still had some self-control left.

My neighbor had woken up something in me that I thought had died a long time ago. Feelings. Addictiveness. The need to connect. I had no idea how to resist her charm anymore. The worst was that she had no clue how sexy she was or how enticing I found her. Entering my kitchen, I readjusted the crotch of my pants and sighed. The last thing I needed was to be pussy-whipped by another woman who'd walk away from my life in just a few weeks after destroying me.

Easier said than done.

No matter how many times I tried to erase the image of Pixie from my head, it stayed front and center in my mind.

A scary-large grin appeared on my face as my thoughts swam back to last night when she had tried to scare me away with a growl and a TV clicker. The picture had stayed with me for hours afterward. That was funny as hell. And stupid. But damn hot. My body temperature had shot up at the sight of her. My neighbor was fascinating. A breath of freshness in my life. A vision to lose myself in. All I could think about was her lips on mine, her tight and curvy body clenching around my fingers as she orgasmed in my arms. The memory filled all my thoughts, all my dreams.

I raked my hands through my hair, a tightness squeezing my insides. She was just passing through my life. I shouldn't get attached or become bewildered by her.

Maybe fucking her for real just once would erase the tension between us and free me from my blue-balls syndrome. That was it. A case of unrequited lust. Nothing more. She was the only woman in my life right now. She wasn't special. I had an itch to scratch, and Pixie was here. I'd fill two needs with one deed if only I could get into her pants. Damn. New goal. Yeah, I needed to set goals.

First one. Fuck my neighbor until I got her out of my system.

Second one. Keep her at a distance afterward. For my own good.

I squeezed in an hour of training before lunch, yearning to expend all my excess energy, bury my unsatisfied needs, and clear my head. After a much-needed jerk-off session in my shower with images of the woman with cotton-candy hair dancing in my mind, which left me raw and sore, I toweled down and got dressed into a pair of denims and a beige hoodie to meet the girl haunting me at her place to wait for the handyman to show up.

"The back door is all fixed," Desmond said matter-of-factly, fifteen minutes later.

"Great. Thanks, man. We can still use the front door, right?"

"Yeah. But you won't be able to lock it, though. I dismantled the whole thing. I thought I might be able to fix it until I get the new one. I watched a tutorial last night and believed I'd give it a try. Now it's not working at all. It got stuck, and when I pried it apart, it broke. I'm sorry. I'm not a tech-savvy guy, and I don't know how to put the remaining pieces back together the right way." He gave me an embarrassed smile and lowered his voice. "With your status, I wouldn't risk leaving this woman here alone without a fully working lock on the door."

I blinked. My neighbor had no idea who I was, and I

intended to keep it that way. She frowned as her eyes traveled between me and the handyman. Not wanting him to spoil my anonymity or say something he shouldn't, I urged him outside, my hand between his shoulder blades, blocking Fairy from eavesdropping on our conversation.

"Don't say a word around her. Please."

Desmond clapped my shoulder. "You're a lucky man, Carter. She seems like a keeper." He winked and stored his toolbox in the back of his van. *If only.* With one hand in the pocket of my denims, I waved at him before his truck pulled away.

Back inside, I accepted the cup of tea my neighbor offered me, hoping she wouldn't get mad as a new idea formed in my head.

———

"Move your piece of garbage, asshole," I said, my anger directed at the car blocking the narrow mountain road. It'd been obstructing the only way down for the last five minutes. Outside, most traces of the morning snow were gone, leaving us with a brownish-gray scenery.

"You sure know how to keep your calm around the ladies," my neighbor teased, a glint in her eye.

I chuckled. "Yeah, well…sorry?" It sounded more like a question. "I'd like to be able to go to town and come back before next year."

A ghost of a smile appeared on her pink-painted lips. Pixie had put on a little makeup after Desmond left. Combined with her loose turtleneck cream sweater, black faux-leather leggings, and pink hair, she made winter look sexy.

The bald man wearing a plaid flannel jacket, who blocked the road, got out of his car and rummaged through his trunk. His eyes lit up when he found a pack of cookies. *Really?* A car honked behind us, and more cars lined up on the opposite side of the road.

Fairy rolled down her window and propped her head out. "Hey you, dear gentleman. Yes, you who's stalling everyone. Do you need help?"

The man swiveled to look at her.

Before he could say anything, a man in his late forties, with a salt and pepper goatee, wearing a brown trucker hat and corduroy jacket, jumped out of his old pickup truck and swaggered, spitting anger toward Cookie-Eater. "You better move your car, bald man, or I'll move it myself."

Cookie-Eater turned his head to face him but said nothing, his chubby cheeks now a dark shade of red.

Without a warning, Fairy climbed out of my truck and bounced in Cookie-Eater's direction. I rolled down my window, a mix of surprise and wariness simmering inside me, ready to intervene if I needed to. Adrenaline coursed through my bloodstream, all my senses on high alert. I hated the idea of her inserting herself in an about-to-explode face-off. However, I also knew my neighbor could take care of herself. Words were her weapon of choice. I held my breath, not wanting to miss anything they said.

Trucker-Hat continued, ire coloring his words. "I know you're hungry and can't wait to fill this belly of yours with empty calories, refined sugar treats that look oh so yummy, but I'm sure you can manage to shut your stomach for a mile or two and do all of us a favor. Stop being a jerk and move your *not of this decade* piece of junk out of the way."

My hot as fuck and fearless neighbor neared the older man and placed her hand over his shoulder in a protective gesture. Round at the waist and short on legs, Cookie-Eater was only an inch—or two—taller than her. "Sir, do you need help?" she repeated in the sweetest possible voice, concern clear in her tone.

"That's it, sweetheart, ask him to move his woody wagon off the middle of the road," Trucker-Hat said.

I gulped down a breath. Poor guy. He had no idea what he just did. Fairy's little hands clenched at her sides, and a blood-red flush crept along her neck and cheeks. She pivoted on her heels to face the cocky bastard who'd just called her *Sweetheart*. I cringed, my eyes glued to the scene unfolding before me. My stomach filled with a handful of pebbles. Would they merge into a big giant rock, or would they turn into proud fireworks?

"Don't ever call me *Sweetheart*, you jerk. You better shut your dirty mouth, or my boyfriend over there will shut it for you. If you want a lady's help to control your temper, all you need to do is ask. But don't get on my last nerve because I'm in labor right now, and you're about to assist in delivering this nine-pound bundle of joy. I'm sure you'd like to be on the receiving end of my placenta. Hope you played football in college. Could end up being useful. By the look of it, you probably won't be a big help. Unless you have something smart to say to this man, I suggest you go back to your dump and mind your own business." She rested her fists on her hips and glared at Trucker-Hat.

"Don't be a smart-ass, lady. You can't be pregnant. You're like child-size. What are you, twelve?" Underneath her loose sweater, Fairy could be hiding a pregnant belly, and nobody would know.

"Are you willing to bet on it?" Fury crossed her usually peaceful face.

Trucker-Hat eyed her for a moment. Part-spooked and part-confused, he rubbed his bearded jaw before climbing back behind his wheel, giving my neighbor a long stare.

Fireworks. Yeah, the whole show.

Once Trucker-Hat was out of the way, she turned her attention back to Cookie-Eater and whispered something that made him smile. They exchanged a few words, and she hugged him before he hauled himself back into his car and resumed his drive.

Pixie flashed me a proud smile as she opened the door. "That's how it's done, HN. You're welcome."

I clamped my mouth shut, my eyes wide and unblinking.

Who was this girl, and where did she come from?

When I finally found my words again, I side-eyed her. "Impressive. But not very ladylike. You called Trucker-Hat a jerk." I winked as my passenger punched my upper arm and stuck her tongue out at me with a wrinkled nose. The air thickened in the car. "Boyfriend, huh? Something I should be aware of?"

"Don't flatter yourself. Would you have preferred husband?" She cocked an eyebrow, challenge dancing in her blue eyes—bluer with the mascara coating her long lashes. Yeah, I noticed.

I shrugged, trying to look unaffected. "Maybe."

The girl snorted, and we stayed silent for the rest of the drive while she fidgeted with the ring on her right hand, looking through the window, her face unreadable as I parked on Main Street.

"Is the baby mine?" I asked.

"Why? Do you want it to be yours?" She studied me with her ocean-deep gaze, and after a minute, I shrugged.

I swallowed, my throat working a double shift, all my hair standing on end at the way her stare burned a tunnel straight into my soul.

Parked in the lot next to the grocery store, I turned the upper half of my body and stretched my arm to grab a cap from the back seat. I placed it on my head, and without removing my shades, I made my way inside the building.

"Wait for me." Pixie jumped out of the truck, and in small strides, she followed me. "Stop acting like you're being chased by paparazzi, HN. Oh, dear God, you look ridiculous with your sunglasses indoors."

If only she knew.

June had texted me this morning that she'd received over fifty phone calls, offering her a lot of money if she revealed where I was hiding. She'd never betray me. At least, that I knew for sure.

"The fluorescent lights. My eyes are sensitive." Lame. I'd lied better in the past.

"Do you want me to unfold the red carpet for you? Perhaps you'll feel more in your element."

I poked her arm, and her giggle went straight to my dick.

"Hollywood is this way." She pointed toward the front of the store with her thumb and grabbed a bottle of barbecue sauce from a shelf on her right. "I can even present you with an Oscar if you like and give an emotional feel-good speech, complimenting you on your tear-jerking performance."

I bit the inside of my cheek, refraining from unmasking my identity by revealing I'd much prefer a country music award.

"Come on, woman, let's do this." My fingers knitted with hers, and I led her toward the back of the supermarket, not wanting to draw anyone's attention to us. Locals knew I owned a house around here. They rarely cared. However, tourists were unpredictable for the most part. I couldn't risk their recognizing me.

A little girl, with white-blonde hair and big, doll-like honey-brown eyes, stopped us in our tracks. "Hi, my name is Alicia. Can I take a picture with you?" My heart jackhammered in my chest. The air froze in my lungs. *Fuck.* Here I was, fearing tourists, when I should have been wary around kids. Were they the new weapon used by paparazzi to get closer to their victims? I swallowed the rock in my throat. *Relax, man. It's just a kid.*

"With me?" I faked being surprised. Perhaps this girl would think she'd mistaken me for someone else. A little prayer never hurt anyone.

"No, silly. Her," she said, pointing her finger in my neighbor's direction. "I love your hair."

Fairy placed a hand over her heart. Her priceless reaction got me tongue-tied. "Awww. You're so cute. Sure. I've never done this before."

The child walked over and handed me a phone—probably her mom's—using a bossy tone to address me. "Here, mister. Take the shot but not before I tell you to."

Enjoying the dynamic a little too much of not being the one chased around, I snapped half a dozen pictures when the kid ordered me to.

My neighbor was flustered. Beautiful, shy, and radiant all at once. "This is weird. It has never happened before. Next thing I know, I'll be signing autographs."

I bit my lips to avoid laughing. Pixie made it almost impossible not to want to kiss her. Her eyes glistened with happiness. I wondered how her pink lips would feel around my shaft. *Stop.* Feeling involved in the conversation, my dick swelled in my pants, and I forced my mind to wander elsewhere. The old lady on our left. Desmond. Savannah. I swallowed and filled my lungs with much-needed air. That did the trick. Kinda. A little. And I huffed in relief.

"Believe me, you're a natural. You should wear your shades inside too."

She poked her tongue out at me once more, and I

resisted the urge to kiss the life out of her, right here in the middle of the deli section.

My fingers itched to brush the soft flesh hidden under her sweater and to get her hands all over me. I wanted to taste every inch of her skin. To finish what we'd started the other day. I had no idea for how long I'd be able to resist her. My body shook with all the dirty thoughts that crossed my mind. I was *so* doomed.

Together, we sauntered down the aisles, and Pixie added chicken breasts to our buggy when we reached the meat section. I turned around and put them back on the shelf.

"Hey. Give it back."

"No meat for me, Fairy. You should try it."

She laughed, and I cracked a grin.

"It doesn't matter. We're not sharing a fridge, Big Guy."

"Big Guy, huh? I think I prefer HN. Whatever it means. Sorry to tell you, but you're not going back to your cabin. Starting tonight, you're staying with me."

With a scowl, she planted her hands on her hips and stopped, daring me despite her petite frame. The sparks in her eyes faded. "Excuse me, who are you to decide where I should live? I'm a grown woman, and I'm not gonna do whatever you say because you feel entitled. Don't assume I'm some weak girl who believes you're the one who'll save the day. When we get back, I'm going to *my own* cabin. Thank you for the offer, but I'll pass."

"Don't be difficult. Geez. I'm helping you right now. There's no way you're sleeping in your cabin if you can't lock the front door properly. The latch is broken."

"Don't be a chicken, Hotshot. No pun intended. There's a gate. Nothing can happen to me. I'm a big girl. I can take care of myself. Thank you for your concern, but no thanks."

"Yeah, right. You're fully capable of defending yourself, I forgot. Armed with a TV clicker? Yep, you're invincible."

She threw daggers at me with her eyes, but it rather felt as if she were throwing kittens my way. She stayed silent, her arms folded and her stance rigid. She studied me, as if trying to read something in my offer I hadn't spoken out loud.

"Why do you even care? I'm not a child, and I'm not your responsibility."

"You'd be surprised the freaks you can come face-to-face with when you're least expecting it."

"Okay. First, there's a gate around the lot. So, your 'freaks' argument isn't good enough. And second, I love my cabin. I don't want to move. Considering we both know you can be an ass, I prefer avoiding being around you for too long. I wouldn't want to risk your cynicism rubbing off on me."

"I'm not cynical. And I already proved to you I am not an ass. You don't have any logical reason to refuse. You're not my responsibility, but gate or not, your safety matters to me."

She eyed me. How long would she fight me over this?

"Where will I sleep? No way are we sharing a bed…or a room. The last time we did, it didn't end well."

"Yeah, my dick still remembers."

Pixie nudged my arm. "You know what I mean. Don't be an ass."

Amusement bubbled inside me, and I bit my inner cheek, silencing the wheezy snicker threatening to escape my mouth. "You'll never let it go, will you? Anyway, I bet I can find a guest room for you to sleep in. We won't even be on the same floor. I'll be a happy camper, I promise. And a very discreet roommate."

"No funny business?"

I raised my hands in surrender. "Not unless you want it too." I winked.

Her face turned crimson.

"Okay, fine, no funny business." *We'll see about that.*

Since my stubborn neighbor ogled me every chance she got—yeah, I had noticed—this roommate situation should be fun.

My full attention returned to her when she harrumphed. "I have conditions."

"Yeah, I assumed nothing less from you. We'll discuss them in the car. Now let's decide on something for dinner."

We roamed through the aisles.

"Cheese?" she asked

"Nope."

"Cream?"

"No."

Pixie gave me a puzzled look and sighed. "You're impossible."

"No. It's called being healthy."

"Whatever, take the lead, I wanna see what you get."

Just like that, we bought groceries together, and it felt like the most natural thing in the world. Again.

When we neared the cashier's, I stopped in my tracks. My own face looked back at me. Multiple times. On the covers of four different magazines. Each in dozens of copies. My airways tightened, and my legs weighed a ton.

"Where's Carter Hills?" one title said. *Fuck.*

"Carter Hills dumped Savannah Prince for one of his mistresses," said another.

The muscle in my jaw ticked, and I clenched my teeth.

Seconds later, my legs regained their function, and I

slid my body between the buggy and the magazine stand to block my neighbor's view. I crossed my fingers, hoping she had no interest in flicking through gossip rags while waiting in line at the grocery store.

Probably not.

If she did, she'd know who I was. I had appeared on so many front pages in the last two years that I lost count. Not giving her time to think about anything else, I kept the conversation going.

"Should I be worried about that cat of yours moving in? It doesn't seem to like me very much."

She chuckled, the sound fucking delicious. "C'mon, HN. Bernice is harmless. She won't attack you in your sleep. Ohmygod, are you scared of a fifteen-pound feline?"

"Don't be ridiculous. Just trying to get to know my new roommate, that's all. I'm sure we'll be best friends in no time." I smirked. "What's not to like? I'm irresistible."

She snorted. "Yeah, well, we'll see about that."

A mass lodged in my throat. I hated lying to her. I should come clean before she learned about me from another source, but a big part of me liked our relationship as it was. Telling her the truth might destroy what we were building. I clenched and unclenched my fists at my sides again and again, battling with my conscience. I faked a smile when my future roommate said something I didn't quite catch. *Relax, Carter. Breathe in. Breathe out.*

When we reached my truck, a guy pointed his phone at us. With my hand on the small of Fairy's back, I rushed her into the passenger seat, after dropping the grocery bags on the backseat, and closed the door after her. I cursed under my breath as I rounded the vehicle to slide behind the wheel, my insides sizzling with anger. I ignored the guy on the opposite sidewalk, keeping my head down.

Shit.

I prayed in silence he hadn't gotten any significant pictures of us. Fucking fame.

My neighbor didn't need to have her face plastered on the covers of tabloids all around the world because she bought groceries with me this one time.

I had no idea how to explain my celebrity status to her. She seemed so clueless about me and my life, and I'd love to keep it that way as long as possible. Maybe I was being egoistical about it, but I'd been burned in the past, and the last thing I wanted was a repeat of the tragedy my life had been.

One day, I'd tell her. Not today, though. Today, I'd keep my anonymity.

I peeled the cap off my head and ran my fingers through my hair before pulling it back down. All my insides were knotted together. The selfish part of me wasn't ready to let the woman occupying the passenger seat walk away from my life. I wanted to keep her all to myself for as long as I could. From experience, I knew that the truth—and who I was—would mess everything up. Why couldn't it be simple for once?

Not willing to let the press drag my clueless neighbor into the dirt, I sent June a quick text message while waiting at a red light, keeping my best poker face on. I prayed Fairy couldn't read me. She didn't know me well enough, and all my friends agreed my poker face was shit. They always made fun of me for not being able to hide my emotions. Just this once, I hoped I could pull it off.

"Are you okay?" she asked, her fingers grazing the skin of my forearm.

"Yep. All good." I tried to inject cheerfulness into my words, but it fell flat. Inside, I was coiled tight and ready to burst.

"Tell it to that frown of yours," she teased.

"It's nothing. Just something I have to deal with. Don't worry."

"If you say so." A tiny smile formed on her lips, and the sight of it chased my grumpiness away.

"I do."

"Then let's get rolling because I'm starving. Never keep a pregnant woman waiting when it comes to food."

Peals of laughter left my mouth. I couldn't resist her humor. "Fine. I hope this imaginary baby loves my cooking too."

"He sure will." She winked, and I shook my head.

My attempt to stop smiling failed. "By the way, I can catch a football. In case it ends up being useful," I said, using her earlier words about delivering that fake baby.

We exchanged a grin and this time, she was the one who burst into laughter. God, I freaking loved making her laugh.

How could Fairy's bubbly personality always have a way of adding colors to my toneless existence? Even though I couldn't explain it, it grew on me. And I relished every second.

———

While Fairy went next door to pack some of her stuff, I attacked dinner. Tingles of excitement swirled in the depths of me and lifted up my mood. No woman, except for Dahlia, had ever stayed over with me before. Not even Savannah. I thought the idea of having someone else living with me would freak me out. Truth was, I loved the thought of sharing my personal space with the woman living next door.

Fairy kept a low profile as she settled in, not asking for a house tour or to repaint the bedroom walls. I appreciated her even more for this because the last time I let a woman in, she made everything about her and turned my life upside down in the worst possible way. Even though I wanted my neighbor to feel at home, I wasn't ready to let her all in. My defense mechanisms wouldn't let me lower my walls. Not all of them, anyway.

After freeing Bernice from her carrier, she disappeared upstairs to unpack her suitcase in the guest room. I showered real fast and dressed in a pair of dark sweatpants and a white T-shirt. When my guest returned to the kitchen, now wearing a pair of pearl-gray lounge pants and a black fleece, looking at home in my space, I offered her a glass of white wine from the bottle I uncorked for the risotto.

"You want me to pour you a glass?" she asked.

"No, I'll pass."

Keeping my back to her, I added another cup of vegetable broth to the rice simmering on the stove. This way she couldn't read my expression. Or distract me. My new roommate seemed to have a special key to my soul when her eyes locked on mine.

Tilting my head, I watched her over my shoulder as she chopped mushrooms and shallots on a cutting board, her hips swaying to the rhythm of the music playing low in the background. Some country ballad she said she adored. For an instant, I imagined her moving her hips and humming the melody of one of my songs, like she did the night I invited myself over to her place and we played the hottest game of Monopoly known to humankind. My lips curled up at the memory. A *but* lingered, though. Would she even be here with me if she knew the truth?

Glass shards crept along my spine, and not being ready to assess the *what-ifs*, I pushed the thought away.

I returned my focus to the dish simmering in front of me, knowing I would have a hard time resisting this woman if I looked at her, and let the sweet aroma of dinner envelop my senses instead.

Every time we faced each other, her baby-blue eyes acted like magnets to my steel-gray irises. They called to something inside me, and I felt naked as she assessed me. This was something I never experienced in my life before. A connection I lacked words to describe.

"No alcohol, no meat, no dairy? Something else I should know? Are you a sugar freak too?"

Not looking away from the pot on the stove, I chewed on my lips and rubbed the back of my neck. "Well, I started eating clean six years ago. My brother…he was in the army…huh…died of sudden cardiac arrest. He had completed a tour overseas a couple of months earlier. You would've thought that would've killed him. Nope. He died on his way back home from the gym one night. I-I used to love my Tennessee Whiskey, but after his death, I promised to take care of his wife and unborn child. Somehow, I always believed if I took extra good care of my health, I wouldn't abandon them too. After my brother passed away, I hired a fitness coach, and he changed my entire philosophy about food and health. I cut off all animal products from my diet, and it impacted more than just my overall health. It increased my energy levels, my stamina, my creativity. I'd never go back."

I had never confided in anyone about my family like this. About Jeff's passing.

The air thickened in the room, but then something in me shifted. A weight I'd been carrying around for years lifted from my shoulders. My back straightened. I inhaled, and some of the knots in my stomach slackened. The lump in my throat melted, and I breathed easier. My fists unwound.

Why did I feel safe telling a woman I barely knew the

story of my life? Why did I feel like my heart could beat again when she was around? That her presence only could heal the scars of my heart?

Her soft voice brought me back to reality. "Are they the ones who stayed with you the other week?"

I blew out a long breath. Legitimate question. Jitters tickled my stomach.

She's not snooping. She's genuinely interested. She's just making conversation.

Relax, Carter. Breathe in. Breathe out.

I pushed strands of my hair away from my forehead with the back of my hand. I was in dire need of a haircut.

"Yeah. Dahlia and Jack. Their names." A small smile lit up my face at their mention. "Dahlia and I, we kinda grew up together. She was my first love. When I mustered the courage to tell her I loved her, at fifteen, it was too late because she had fallen for my brother…Jeff. His name was Jeff. He…he died when she was four months pregnant. They'd just gotten married." My throat bobbed. I closed my eyes and inhaled through my mouth to keep my emotions at bay. "After his death, I took over. They're family. They are my entire world."

Back when Dahlia and I were members of Carter Hills Band, we made the covers of magazines countless times. People's interest in us escalated once they found out about the pregnancy. Every time we ventured outside of Nashville, fame-sucker enthusiasts tried to snap pictures of us. We had to lie low to escape the hell our lives had become.

One day, Dahlia cracked, packed her stuff, and kissed me goodbye. She moved here and never looked back.

Three years ago, she opened a bridal shop on Main Street. She had this new life and was happy. That was what I'd always wished for her. For the last six years, I'd been devoting all my free time to Jack and her. Nobody else in this world meant as much to me as they did. Whatever I did in my career, wherever I was in the world, they remained my top priority.

Fairy brought the mushrooms and shallots over. Our hands brushed. I sucked in a breath. Her other hand lingered between my shoulder blades. Through her touch, she healed a broken part of my heart. A tiny piece that went missing years ago. I took a deep breath to stop the tears threatening to fill my eyes. When was the last time I felt alive? And hopeful? Emotions blocked my airways. I forced my shoulders to relax and cleared my throat, chasing the surge of emotions inside me.

Change the subject. Quick.

"You play any instrument? Musical instrument, I mean."

"Nah. I tried piano when I was like ten, but I had no talent. I sang a duet in the garage band of this guy I had a crush on in high school, once or twice to impress him. Didn't work. I had no singing talent either. Anyway, I'm pretty much a music-playing virgin."

I whirled around and brushed her shoulders, the need to touch her so strong, my heart throbbed in my chest. "Wait here. We'll change that."

"Now?" Panic filled her blue irises.

I snickered and hurried to my studio to pick up my Taylor, one of my acoustic guitars. I put the risotto on the back burner and led her to a chair. She wasn't just my neighbor anymore. She was becoming so much more. I ignored what exactly that was, but I was thankful we had crossed paths. That life placed her on my journey.

Inhaling a cleansing breath, I forced myself to let go of the tension straining my body and prayed the music would ease the tightness spreading through me. It always soothed my nerves. My roommate stared at me, her eyes wide and filled with questions. The heaviness of our earlier conversation had spread goose bumps all over my skin. Time to lighten the atmosphere and present her with a happier side of me. Her tongue darted out, wetting her lower lip, as she watched the guitar in my hands, a deep frown etched across her forehead.

Oh, did I make her nervous?

A smile broke free on my lips.

Fairy scrunched up her nose. "Don't get your hopes up, HN."

I gripped her hand in mine, and the pounding of my heart decreased at the touch of her skin. The now familiar sensation of her palm in mine. The softness of her fingers. "Don't be too harsh on yourself. Everyone must start somewhere."

She hissed a low laugh, and it quieted my mind.

I forgot all about the world outside my cabin.

Her eyes rounded and darted between the guitar and me, and I battled with myself not to drop a kiss on her forehead. To pull her to my chest and promise everything would be all right. All colors drained from her face, and she appeared scared as if I had told her we were going bungee jumping over a river filled with crocodiles.

"You'll be fine. I swear." Oxygen came in and out of my lungs easier around her, the sensation of my chest being crushed under piles of rocks dissipating. "Come on. Let me give you your first lesson."

Chapter 15
April

As I sat on the kitchen chair, I sucked in a breath and dug up some courage from deep inside me. Maybe I could do this. How hard could it be, right? HN squatted in front of me and placed the guitar in my hands. A drift of his scent washed through me, and for a fleeting instant, I wondered if he tasted as good as he smelled. The temptation to find out grew stronger every time we were together. *Shut down your crazy, needy hormones, girl.* I closed my eyes and evened out my breathing. There. Better.

"Place your fingers right here." I did as he instructed. "No, this one needs to be higher. Yes. Perfect."

Our eyes met, and all the air in my lungs left me. I could do this. All I needed was to focus. HN's fingers brushed mine, and I combusted from my core to my skin.

"Ready for your first chord? I'll show you an Em." He positioned my digits. "Try this."

I glided my thumb against the strings.

"Not bad," he said, grinning. He looked so handsome when he let go of whatever walls he kept high around him. Carefree. And happy. "See? I knew you were better than what you credited yourself for."

Pride shot through my bloodstream.

"Now let's try a C." Once again, he repositioned my fingers, and I strummed the guitar chords the same way he showed me.

In the next fifteen minutes, he taught me three more chords before we started from the beginning as I tried to remember all five of them. I wasn't the most promising student, but he didn't seem fazed by my lack of musical talent. My fingers tingled each time he moved them, and on a few occasions, I faked not remembering a chord so he'd touch my hands again. My eyes traveled all too often to his lips. I wanted to feel them on mine once more. To savor their addictive fullness. The only time we kissed, I was so hungry for him that I didn't take the time to brand the feel of it into my memory.

When I stopped obsessing over his mouth, I listened to him—for real this time—and enjoyed his teaching. The best part? HN's smile lighting up his face throughout the hour-long private guitar lesson. At some point, he placed himself behind me and leaned forward, pressing his chest to my back. My breaths caught in my lungs, and my entire body pulsed in his presence. I coughed and shifted in my seat. His steady fingers blanketed mine, and his soft breath fanned over my nape, catapulting my heartbeat into a wild, new tempo.

During dinner, the tension between us faded a little.

"Are you living here full-time?" I asked.

"No. Sometimes I think I should move here for good, though."

"You own the cabin?"

HN nodded. "And yours. I own a few more in town. My dad always told me real estate was a good investment, so—" He shrugged and took a sip of his sparkling water.

"Now I get why you acted like you owned the place every time you came over. It makes more sense. It wasn't an act."

My neighbor smirked at me from behind his glass.

Later, I went to bed with a fluttering heart and a grin that lingered well into the night.

When we prepped dinner and he opened up about his brother's story earlier, with each word he spoke, his pain tore at my heart. It rang too close to home and sent sharp, painful chills up and down my spine. I didn't open up about Travis. I couldn't. Sorrow and pain swam in HN's stormy irises, and I fought the urge to hug him and tell him everything would be fine. He was still struggling with his grief, and I could relate to it in ways he'd never know. Not trusting myself to resist the urge to kiss him to soothe his pain, I kept a safe distance between us, only allowing myself to press my palm to his back to let him know I was there.

Dahlia and Jack were his brother's family—not his. I had misread the entire situation from the start. A sigh of relief escaped me even though I already knew the red-haired woman wasn't his wife. It shouldn't matter to me who they were, but in a lot of ways, it did.

His caring for them was such a selfless and loving act. New sensations ran through me. Tonight, every time he said their names, his eyes glowed, and a smile tugged at the corner of his lips, making him look way younger, giving me an insight into the boy he must have been years ago. No wonder I thought the redhead was his wife that day through my bedroom window. They had this strong bond that couldn't be faked. It showed even from a distance. He admitted she was his first love. But after everything they'd been through, was he still in love with her? After all this time? What was their relationship like nowadays? Plenty of questions swam in my head for which I had not enough answers. The only thing I knew for sure was that Jack was his mini lookalike. A tight knot formed in my stomach. So much mystery surrounded my neighbor, and for some reason, it made me feel queasy. It didn't make sense, yet somehow, it did. I felt like a complete nutcase.

Under the covers, in a bedroom I didn't recognize— hardwood floor, white walls, steel-blue accents—I closed my eyes, images of him filling the darkness.

Our night and the closeness we shared replayed in my head. Tonight, HN's confessions, the vulnerability in his eyes and in his words made him even more attractive than usual. Like he had stripped a part of himself bare before me, and now I had no idea what to do with it. One thing was certain. I needed to move back to my cabin. For my mental health. And my sanity. This roommate thing would be too hard on me. I could sense the chaos coming our way. My neighbor was trouble, and I should stay away.

The next morning, I woke up and stretched before grabbing my phone to look at the clock. *Eight fifty-eight.* Another night of uninterrupted sleep. I wished I could have high-fived myself. My eyes adjusted to the morning light peeking through the curtains, and I swallowed hard as I scrolled through my notifications and saw that i had two missed calls and four text messages from Saunders. I frowned. What did she get herself into this time?

SAUNDERS

OMG April, WTF?

Call me. NOW.

Blimey! Call me already, girl.

CALL. ME. BACK. ASAP *9-1-1*

Saunders and I only ever used the 9-1-1 code in case of extreme emergencies. Breakups, Travis's death, walk of shame, broken condoms, or dates gone wrong. Those types of situations.

I dressed in a pair of leggings and a fluffy sweater and hurried downstairs. HN had left a note on the kitchen counter next to a cup of tea. I lifted it and realized it was still warm.

Good morning, Bubble Gum.

I laughed at the term of endearment.

Went to town for a meeting.
I'll be back for dinner.
HN – Heavenly Nice? Hot and Natty? Or Handsome and Neat? Pick one.

I cupped my mouth and snickered. *Hot and Natty.* I loved it.

So far, living with him hadn't been that bad. Anyway, he left me no choice. He'd moved furniture around yesterday to create a writing nook in the den for me and filled the kitchen with the widest range of tea I'd ever seen because I mentioned I was a fan. He even let Bernice venture all around his place. *Sweet.* It was just one of his many layers. Spending my day alone in his place made me a bit uncomfortable. In all honesty, the grandeur of the place intimidated me a little. It wasn't decorated like a mansion—nothing too grandiose or overly expensive—but still, I was used to much smaller spaces. Here, the windows were so large, I felt like I was living outside while still being inside. At least he trusted me to be on my own, and the realization sent a flutter to my chest. In the den, I sipped the mug of tea he had left behind, basking in the sun's warm rays streaming through the floor-to-ceiling windows.

This room had stolen my heart the first time I'd stepped in. Not that I'd seen every room, but there was a warmth between these walls that made me feel at home.

The cell phone reception wasn't any better here than at my cabin, so after walking around with my phone held above my head for a few minutes without getting a good-enough signal, I shrugged it off, put on my puffer jacket, and strolled toward the gate with a pep in my step. I hummed a song, trying to guess why Saunders would use the 9-1-1 emergency code. Was she freaking out about moving in with Reed? The Saunders life crisis. Typical. I grinned, putting my best friend suit on.

I neared the gate and dialed my friend, who answered on the first ring.

"What took you so long? Why are there pictures of you and Carter Hills all over the web?"

My eyes widened at her inquisitiveness.

"Hello to you too. Sorry, who?"

"Carter Hills. The country music legend. The sexiest singer on the planet. Also known as the fit bloke who makes an entire stadium wet their panties when he plays his guitar and sings love songs."

"Carter Hills?"

"Yes, Bubble Head. C-A-R-T-E-R-H-I-L-L-S. The one and only."

"It must be a mistake. I've never even met him. Are you sure it's me in the pictures?"

"Sexy, pink-haired girl with sparkling blue eyes. Who else could it be?"

I sighed loudly, grinding my teeth. "I don't know. Maybe we were at the same place at the same time once, and I ended up in the pictures somehow. Who cares, right? Anyway, what's the emergency?"

"Okay, you know I love you, but get real here. April, your Handsome Neighbor *is* Carter Hills." Saunders paused to let the words sink in.

I laughed so hard I thought I'd choke. My eyes watered, and a fit of hiccups exited my mouth.

My friend sighed. I imagined her rolling her eyes. "April. Stop."

Why couldn't she let it go?

"This isn't a joke. The pictures were taken in Green Mountain. Yesterday."

I sucked in some air. Carter Hills? *No.*

HN looked nothing like the country singer. Did he? *Okay, maybe a little.*

Although, it couldn't be him. If so, he would've told me. *Wouldn't he?*

My neighbor, a big country music star? No way. This made no sense. Wait... Unless he shaved off the stubble on his jaw and cut his hair shorter. *Fuck. No, no, no.*

Was it really him? Had he been playing me all along?

The air sliced through me, making me dizzy.

My hand shot to my chest, pressing against my pounding heart as it skipped a beat.

Anger surged through my veins.

Did HN lie to me? *No. Not really.* Unless a lie by omission still counted as a lie. *Did it?*

This was a nightmare. He was the first man I'd trusted in years, the first one I'd let get too close, and it turned out he was a liar. Gosh, my asshole radar was spot on at first...

Except he wasn't an asshole. Not really. My liar radar, though? Defective, kaput, broken. How did I not see it sooner? How much more of an idiot could I have been?

How much fun did he have messing around with my ignorance?

But, on the other hand, we never even exchanged names... Did that count as a lie? It had to, right? Or was it fair game, and I shouldn't hold it against him?

My thoughts spun in dizzying circles, racing through my mind.

Ohmygod, how could I have been so blind? The guitar lesson, the shades he kept on at the grocery store, the note I found on my countertop the day I got here. *Your host, C.H.* A tightness spread deep in my stomach, like a knot that wouldn't untangle. I'd been living with Carter Hills. *The* Carter Hills. And he kissed me. We laughed together. We bantered. Oh God, he put his hand in my panties, his fingers inside... Dry heaves rattled my body.

I scratched at my throat, my airways tightening as a cold feeling crept up my spine.

Saunders spoke, but my brain locked her out. I dropped my phone on the ground and placed my hands over my ears, silencing the buzzing sound reverberating in my head. A chime caught my attention, and I lowered my arms. I picked up my device, brushing off the dead pine needles from the case as I skimmed over the screen with shaky fingers. I held my breath and opened the message Saunders just sent me. A picture. No. Not a picture. Pictures. Like lots of them.

The first one showed me and HN, or should I say Carter Hills, buying groceries together yesterday.

The second one was a shot of us in his truck the same day, exchanging smiles.

A third one captured his hand on the small of my back, talking close to my ear.

I felt as if someone had violated my privacy. This was worse than a nightmare. It was a goddamn clusterfuck of epic proportions that I'd gotten entangled in without even knowing it. I bent at the knees, gut-punched, desperate for air.

The fourth picture, a cover of *Star News Magazine*, displayed a close-up shot of Carter Hills—yes, that was definitely him—and a photo montage of us together with the title *Carter Hills has moved on. Who's the new girl?*

Another cover claimed he left Savannah Prince for one of his many mistresses. A.k.a. me.

My knees buckled, and I almost collapsed on the ground.

I kept scrolling. More pictures. More shots of us looking awfully close, sharing smiles and touching.

More gossip magazine covers.

More exposure.

More invasion of my privacy.

More lies for everyone to see.

"April, are you still there?" Saunders asked, worry lacing her voice.

"Y-yeah." I stuttered the word, my eyes clouded with unshed tears. My chest hurt. I placed my hand back over my aching heart. My lungs seized. I coughed, trying to ease the discomfort creeping inside me. More dry heaves.

My world crumbled beneath my feet. I was the butt of the joke. I thought HN and I were friends and that he trusted me… After all, he told me about Dahlia…and his brother. I thought we shared something real. How naïve.

Fuck.

"I gotta go, Saund."

"No, April. Don't hang up on me. You're not in a great state of mind right now. You need your best friend."

I snorted. Tears pricked the back of my eyes.

"Let me in, girl. I'm worried about you."

A sarcastic laugh left my mouth.

"April, I'm coming to you. I'll spend a few days in Green Mountain and help cheer you up."

"Don't. I'll be fine."

"No games. I know what the word *fine* means, pal. I'm a girl. Give me a day or two to sort out my schedule, and I'll ring your doorbell." My friend paused for a few beats. "Did you really have no idea who he was?"

I shook my head, feeling so dumb. "No… Yes… He's not the same guy you see on TV, in magazines, or all over the internet. Around me, he's relaxed. His scruff's longer, his hair too, and his smile is genuine. And he looks much younger." My entire body shook, the truth slicing my heart open. HN was Carter Hills. *HN was Carter Hills.* "It's like all his guards are down and he's himself. He doesn't have a mask on. HN looks nothing like Carter Hills." Tears streamed down my face, and I let them flow.

"April, you're falling for him." She said it in the sweetest possible way, trying to protect my heart and my feelings.

"No, I'm not. I just thought we were friends. Friends don't lie to each other." Anger replaced my sadness. I wiped my soaked cheeks with the sleeve of my sweater. "You don't have to come here. I'm a grown woman, and I'll deal with this on my own."

"Whatever. I'm still coming. It might be my only chance to meet him. Call me a groupie, but you know how I've always thought he's one of the finest male specimens on the planet."

A high-pitched laugh came out. "You're being ridiculous, Saund, but that's why I love you. He's human. No need to start fangirling over him."

"I love you too. Talk to him. Listen to what he has to say before running away. I know you. You guys are really friends now?"

I shrugged. "Yeah. Or I thought so." I withheld the fun fact that we were now sharing a house together.

"In that case, let him explain. He may surprise you."

"No promises. If I go to jail after killing him, will you bail me out?"

"Always. And April, I don't want you to end up with another broken heart. Be careful."

After we hung up, more tears streaked down my face, a storm of mixed emotions raging inside me.

With a constricting throat and a hitching breath, I dragged my feet back toward Carter's cabin. *HN is Carter Hills.* How many times should I say it to start believing it?

The tears I couldn't stop blurred my vision.

In that instant, I hated myself. How could I have been so clueless?

Once inside, I climbed the stairs to the guest room, where Bernice lay on my bed, stretching. I collapsed on the mattress, face first, and she inched closer, purring into my ear. She'd witnessed my crying so many times over the years this new surge of sadness wouldn't surprise her. She slid her head under my chin, her way of comforting me, and I patted her soft fur.

"I hadn't seen this one coming. I…I feel cheated." My voice cracked on the last word. "I'm such a fool. Never trust people, Bern. They all…they all leave at some point. Now I'll be the one leaving first. Remind me to never get attached to anyone else, okay? Not that I'm attached to him…it's just…I-I could feel some sparks between us. They mean nothing, though… How could they? We're from two different universes. He's a freaking rock star. And I'm…I'm just plain me. A regular girl. Not that it's bad. It's just… I'm just not cut out for a guy like Carter Hills. God, I still can't believe this is his house and I'm living here *with* him. That he touched… Damn, I've been so stupid."

I snuggled up against my cat, holding on to her like a lifeline, and closed my eyes. Using my sleeve, I wiped away more tears from my cheeks.

For the next hour, I dozed on and off. When sleep evaded me, a new resolve steeled my back and firmed my shoulders. Moving to my feet, I emptied the closet and the dresser, dropping all my belongings on the bed, and started packing.

Amidst everything, I had forgotten why I agreed to move in with HN. Oh, yes, the lock. Now I understood his panic when he thought I snapped a picture of him in the woods and why he refused to let me sleep in a cabin with a broken latch, even though we were surrounded by a fence. Carter Hills probably had tons of crazy fans out there. The mere thought of them gave me the creeps.

I dried a new batch of tears with my fingertips. My vision clouded once more, and I dropped to the floor, my head between my folded knees. *Don't cry over a liar. Someone who played you. He's not worth it.*

A woman's voice drifted up from downstairs—clear and soft. "Cart, are you here? Your door is unlocked. That's very unlike you."

I closed the bedroom door, deciding hiding was my best option. No more humiliation for the day. *But what if the woman calls the cops or thinks I'm a crazy stalker?* I should show my face…just in case.

From the bedroom, I called out, "Carter's not here. He's gone into town"—my voice sounded croaky, and I coughed to clear my throat—"and should be back in a few hours."

Unsteady on my feet, I stepped down the stairs.

"And who are you?" the voice asked.

"A…a friend. The neighbor. I-I'm not sure anymore. Anyway, I'm supposed to stay here until my cabin gets fixed." In my rambling, I came face-to-face with Dahlia. I stopped in my tracks. Up close, she appeared even more beautiful than I remembered. She was this gorgeous redhead with pale freckles sprinkled over her straight nose and high cheeks, wearing minimal makeup. There was an unmistakable calmness about her, and sparks danced in her moss-green eyes.

Dressed in black jeans and a simple gray, off-shoulder knitted sweater, she beamed. Her gaze swept over the length of me. "Oh, it's you." She didn't seem surprised to see me here.

I frowned, unsure about what I should say.

Her smile acted like a soothing blanket.

"You know who I am?" I asked, my eyes widening.

"Carter and I have been friends for many years. We can read each other like an open book. I heard the smile in his voice when I talked to him yesterday. In fact, he called to talk to Jack, my son, but we ended up having a long chat."

"He did? Wait. He…huh…he talked about me?" My eyebrows bunched together as I was having a hard time believing Carter Hills had anything to say about me to his dearest friend.

"You're kidding? He talked about you nonstop. He told me he met this amazing woman. Carter has never said stuff like that about any other woman in the past."

"Oh." *Did he?* Lava pooled in my cheeks.

She stepped forward and held my forearms in a

comforting gesture, like a big sister would do. "I can see what he sees in you. Your heart is pure." *Or that I'm stupid because I had no idea who he was.*

Flustered, I had nothing to add. She dropped her hands and took a step back, probably noticing my uneasiness.

"I'm sorry. I'm really protective of him. Carter is family."

I nodded. My lips parted like a fish, trying to suck in some air. Dahlia said nothing about my glossy, red-rimmed eyes, and I thanked her in my head. Before coming down-stairs, I'd grimaced at my reflection in the bedroom mirror, but had no time to do anything about it.

"Are you leaving?" Her eyes traveled to the suitcase in my hand, a confused expression drawn on her face. I kind of forgot about it.

I cast a glance down and shrugged. "It's, huh, compli-cated. I-I've learned some things today, and I… Let's just say that I can't stay here. Carter… He lied to me." My voice wavered. I hated showing weakness. Taking a deep breath, I shoved my emotions down and squared my shoul-ders. "Anyway, I shouldn't stay here. It's not right." I sighed and placed my piece of luggage on the floor.

Dahlia grabbed my hands in hers. "You're not going anywhere before you and I have a girl talk. You'll tell me what Carter lied about, and we'll go from there. Then if you decide to leave, I'll know I did everything I could to convince you to give him another chance." She snaked her arm through mine and led me to the kitchen.

Was she for real? Why would she want me to give Carter Hills, the country superstar, another chance? My curiosity got the better of me, and I followed her.

"Tea?"

I nodded.

"Carter doesn't drink coffee, so I hope you're not a caffeine junkie because I'm sure we won't find any in here."

"No, I'm more of a tea, hot chocolate type of girl, actually."

"Perfect," she said, clasping her hands in front of her. "You and I will get along just fine."

I watched as she filled the kettle and placed tea bags in two mugs. She was a natural in HN's kitchen. No doubt she came here a lot. I reached for the plate of chocolate chip cookies I baked yesterday and slid it between us.

"Hungry?"

Her eyes rounded. "You baked those?"

I nodded with a tight-lipped smile.

"Sorry, I didn't introduce myself. I'm Dahlia Ellis, Carter's oldest friend." She held out a hand for me to shake.

I slipped my palm into hers. "I'm April. April Simmons. I live in the cabin next door. Or at least, that's where I'm supposed to be staying."

The woman leaned her back against the kitchen counter, bringing the cookie to her mouth. "These are amazing. It's nice to finally meet you, April. Oh, and I love your name by the way. What brings you to Green Mountain?"

"It's a long story. I'm an author, and I was having writer's block. Or rather a creative outage. My friend Saunders, who owns a luxury vacation rental company, had rented the cabin next door for one of her clients, and he had a change of plan at the last minute. She offered it to me, hoping it'd unblock my creative flow." I shrugged. "I guess you could say life brought me here."

"That's amazing. Living here is like an addiction.

When you've breathed the mountain air once, you always need more."

We both exchanged a smile.

"How long have you been here? In Green Mountain, I mean."

"Well, I moved here while pregnant with Jack. You've met him, right?"

"Yes, and he's adorable. He looks a lot like Carter."

"He does." Something dark passed in her eyes. A memory. "Enough talk about me. I want to know why you want to leave and what Carter lied about. Men... They can be idiots sometimes." Dahlia filled our mugs with boiling water and took a seat facing me. "Carter is a complicated man. However, once you get to know him, there's not a more passionate and selfless man in the world." A soft smile spread across her face.

I fidgeted with the handle of the mug, hesitant to confide in her. I knew nothing about this woman, except that Carter had been loving her forever. Dahlia offered me a hearty smile. I tucked strands of my pink hair behind my ear and fished my phone out of my back pocket.

After unlocking it, I slid the device toward her across the counter. On the screen were the pictures Saunders had sent me earlier. Dahlia swiped them, one by one, a deep frown marking her porcelain face.

"I see. And you were clueless about who he was. Am I right?"

I buried my face in my hands. "Yeah. It sounds so stupid, but I really had no idea... I swear. For me, he was just this half-annoying, half-sweet neighbor." I lifted my head to meet her gaze.

Dahlia rested her chin on her open palm, her elbow propped up on the counter.

"April, I'll tell you something. That's what makes you

even more special in his eyes. The truth is that you don't care about who he is outside these walls. You treat him like a man. Not a country star or a celebrity. You see the real Carter Hills, not the image he creates for the media. Only a handful of people have access to this version of him, and you're lucky to be one of them."

"It doesn't change the fact that he lied to me," I said, my heart pounding in my chest.

"Carter loves how normal his life is around you. He should've told you. You're right about that. But he also did it to protect you. April, you don't need this circus in your life, believe me. It's not good for anyone. Not many people are built for this kind of attention. I walked away from the music industry and fame because I refused to let my baby be a part of this." She blew out a long sigh. "Carter must be with June as we speak, trying to find ways to keep you away from the press." She brought her mug to her lips but didn't take a sip.

"June?"

"Juniper. His assistant manager. The media will create any story they see fit if it helps them sell copies and captivate their audience. Carter despises everything about this side of the business. He loves the music. He's the best songwriter I know. I don't say it because we're friends. It's the truth. But he struggles with fame…daily. That's why he comes here every chance he gets. To escape. To ground himself. To clear his mind and just be."

I pondered her words for a moment as we basked in the confidences she just shared.

After I promised her I'd talk to Carter before deciding on anything, Dahlia left. She hugged me on her way out, and I realized I'd just met my first woman crush. Right then, I understood why HN loved her so much.

I was sitting at the kitchen island, writing with Bernice

curled up at my feet, snoozing, when Carter walked in three hours later. With dark circles under his eyes and worry lines etched into his face, he looked ten years older than he did last night.

He erased the distance between us, caged me between his arms, and kissed me on the cheek.

He hadn't shown me any sign of affection since the day we practically devoured each other's faces in my cabin when I first arrived. Yet somehow, my heart fluttered at the simple gesture. It felt like something normal between us… As if he'd done it a hundred times before. Like I belonged here. With him.

I shivered at the thought. A big part of me loved how I felt around him—like everything finally made sense when we were together, and I didn't have to overthink every little thing. Like I could just be myself.

After my talk with Dahlia earlier, my anger toward him had subsided. The voices in my head telling me to run away had quieted.

I loved her honesty, and our girl talk helped me see the situation from another perspective. His.

"How was your day?" I asked, swiveling on my stool and resting my hand gently on his forearm, the cord of his muscles flexing under my touch.

Carter sighed, bent over, and scooped Bernice up, petting her head and nuzzling her fur. "Painful. What about yours?"

"Eventful."

He furrowed his eyebrows.

"Dahlia came by earlier."

His frown deepened. "She did?"

He had no idea? My girl crush intensified. I appreciated her discretion. "Yeah. She's nice. We…huh…we talked. She's really a fan of yours."

"What did you two talk about?"

"You." I averted my gaze, scared he would be mad I talked to his best friend about him behind his back.

"Cool. I hope you said wonderful things." He leaned forward and laid a kiss on my lips, again, as if it were the most natural thing in the world.

My eyes flared, but I said nothing. Butterflies danced in my belly when he pressed his mouth to mine. It awakened all my senses and filled me with renewed energy.

"Glad to be home. I'll change and cook dinner." He turned around to walk away, but I caught his wrist. I felt his pulse, strong and steady, beating under the pads of my fingers.

"No offense, but you look like shit. I can prep dinner."

He grazed my shoulders with his fingers, and his voice softened. "I want to. I insist. Give me ten minutes. I'll be right back." His lips connected to my forehead before he disappeared upstairs.

What the hell's going on?

Carter Hills was acting like we were dating. What did I miss?

Now, I refused to spoil the night by venting my frustration. Deep down, I wasn't even sure I was still angry. Hurt, maybe, but my anger had faded hours ago. I cringed inside. Gosh, I was so screwed.

———

We finished our dinner, and I sat back in my chair, my half-empty wineglass in hand, looking at Carter over the rim. His dark hair was disheveled, the way I liked, and the sleeves of his Henley black shirt were pushed up, revealing his corded forearms and the leather cuff around his left wrist. Even dressed in a casual outfit, he looked handsome.

I should've picked up on the signs about his identity sooner. Now that I knew who he was, I couldn't unsee it. He stabbed the last piece of food on his plate, his face strained and eyes unsettled, something that had been there since the moment he walked in earlier. He didn't look upset, but rather dejected. With a roll of my wrist, I spun the clear liquid around in my glass, thinking about my next course of action. I loathed secrets. Bringing the glass under my nose, I took a whiff of the alcohol, the gears in my head spinning to find the right words as my heartbeat sped up.

You can do this, April. You have to.

My gaze wandered all around me, avoiding my host's, and I cleared my throat. "I know about you." Clear and concise. Straight to the point. I struggled to keep my voice low and even, too many emotions bubbling up inside me.

His eyes locked on mine for a split second, and his lips tightened in thin line.

Something passed between us.

Carter pressed the heels of his hands over his eyes and leaned forward, resting his elbows on his knees. "You do?"

I nodded, keeping my gaze down.

"Fuck, this wasn't supposed to happen. I'm sorry. I never meant for you to learn it this way. How did you—?" His voice cracked, and it drowned his last few words.

The same way I did with Dahlia today, I pushed my phone across the table, a picture of us visible on the screen. "My friend Saunders sent me those. Thought I knew about you and kept it a secret."

Carter raised his head, grabbed my phone, and swiped through the pictures with devoted focus.

His Adam's apple bobbed with an audible swallow, and he breathed out. "Listen, I-I'm sorry. I messed up. Shit. I'll understand if you want nothing to do with me anymore."

I extended my hand to grab his, but he leaned back

and punched the table. "Stupid press." He stood up and dragged a hand over his face, smoothing the worry lines, and started pacing across the kitchen.

I watched him for a minute, his expression morphing from anger to a painful one. For the longest time, I stayed silent, not sure what to say.

"I fucking despise this side of my life. I hate that you found out like this. It's not fair to you. I should've...I should've thought it through."

Curiosity won the battle inside me, and I finally asked the question I'd been holding onto all evening. "Wh-why didn't you tell me?"

Carter stopped pacing and faced me. "I love how I'm just HN around you. You expect nothing from Carter Hills. You're yourself, standing your ground, not afraid to call me out on my bullshit. People always treat me differently when they know who I am."

I failed to hold in the smile stretching my lips. Rising to my feet, I joined him in the kitchen. He slid an arm around my shoulders, and when he pulled me close, I buried my face in his chest.

"I was mad earlier. Super mad. Extra mad. You lied to me, and I wanted to leave before you came back home. But then Dahlia stopped by, and she explained stuff to me. About fame and how you hate it. She told me you left this morning to take care of that," I said, pointing to my phone on the table with a grimace.

"Yeah, I did. Wait. You wanted to leave? Without saying goodbye?"

He was so much taller than me that I had to crank my neck back to meet his eyes. Carter did a poor job of hiding the hurt shadowing his face.

I nodded and swallowed through the shards lining my throat.

"That's why your suitcase was in the foyer, isn't it?"

I bowed my head, and he grabbed my hands in his muscular ones.

"Honestly, I didn't know what to think of all this, and I still don't. I felt betrayed because I thought you and I were friends. You…you hurt me."

He brushed his thumb across my cheek. "I took your luggage back to your room earlier. That's where it belongs."

"Thanks," I said, avoiding his heavy gaze, my head still hanging low.

He extended his hand to shake mine, and I blinked before lifting my gaze to meet his. "April Simmons, I'm Carter Hills. Nice to finally introduce myself."

I gasped. "You knew my name all along?"

He lowered his eyes, a pink flush coloring his cheeks, and winced. "I know the names of all my guests. Wasn't fair to call you by yours while withholding mine. Sorry about that."

I blinked again. "If it means anything," I said, "I loved the nickname game we were playing. I enjoy a bit of mystery now and then. It keeps things interesting."

His intense stare liquified me. I kept my eyes locked on his. Heat flooded my cheeks, and a flurry of emotions swirled in my chest.

Carter pulled me back to him, and I breathed him in. A shiver traversed my body, and he wound his arms around me, bringing me much-needed warmth and shelter. The emotions of the day seeped through me, and my eyes burned as I fought back tears. The reality of my neighbor's identity still sounded unbelievable to me. Right now, I, April Simmons, was nestled in *the* Carter Hills's embrace, and it didn't even feel weird.

Not knowing what to do with my hands, I fisted his

shirt, not ready for him to release me. His lips rested at the crown of my head, and after a beat, he planted a soft, lingering kiss. I swore I saw stars.

Carter Hills and HN were the same person. I felt silly for never catching onto the truth. Somehow, a part of me was relieved I hadn't, because I couldn't help but wonder how different our relationship—or whatever it was—would have been if I had known.

"I flashed you. That first day...I...huh...flashed you. Oh, this is mortifying. You must have thought I was some sort of crazy groupie chasing after you."

He snickered, his chin resting on top of my head. "It wasn't even the first thought that popped into my head. I wondered if we had ever met before... I got entranced by the blue of your eyes. Even from a distance, they fascinated me and took me hostage. Sure, I appreciated the view, but your eyes were to blame for my growing interest in you."

Our laughter died down, and we remained silent for a long while, both of us unable to break apart.

"I'm glad you didn't run away earlier." Carter's deep voice vibrated through me.

"Well, for what it's worth, I'm glad I stayed."

One arm released me, and seconds later, low music played on his phone. "April, dance with me."

I leaned back and lost myself in the gray of his irises. My own personal storm. The one that could be the death of me if I wasn't careful.

I bobbed my head, and Carter repositioned his arms around me. With my eyes closed, I followed his movements, losing myself in the slow melody and the sensation of his body pressed against mine. In his masculine scent. In the safety his arms provided.

Our feet fell in time, and our hearts followed. Soon, our breaths matched in perfect rhythm.

Time stopped.

The man holding me right now wasn't a famous country music star. He was the one who cared for me. The one who kissed me earlier when he arrived like we were a couple. He was the one who enraged me but also fascinated me. Who rearranged his furniture around to create a writing space for me when I moved in and taught me how to play the guitar.

He was just that. A man. No matter what I tried to let myself believe at first, he was an incredible one.

And I was a woman who was trying to keep her heart under lock and key to make sure that man wouldn't shatter it to pieces.

When did we become more…so much more?

The song ended, but Carter didn't release me.

The first notes of a song about love and forever started, the heartfelt lyrics enveloping us.

"This is yours, right? The song? Isn't it?" I asked, my voice barely above a whisper.

"Yep." He grazed the length of my back with his fingertips, eliciting shivers in their wake.

We slow danced in silence, melting into each other, for a full minute.

"Thanks for dancing to my words with me, April."

"Anytime." I pressed my cheek against his beating heart, loving how both our bodies fit against each other. How his enveloped mine and I felt safe in his embrace. "Your songs are inspiring. Filled with love and so many emotions, I feel them all. It's a rare gift you possess."

After the third song, I risked a gaze up. Carter's eyes captured mine. I swallowed, not prepared for the heat I saw on his face. Every particle aimed at me.

"I trust you." I felt the need to reiterate the fact in case there were still doubts lingering between us.

"Thanks." He nodded, never breaking eye contact.

At the same time I moved to my tiptoes, he leaned in. Our lips brushed together as if it was the first time. A zing tingled the tip of my spine. The tentative kiss evolved into a languorous one, and my entire being got electrified when our mouths danced together like a perfectly rehearsed choreography.

Carter's hold on me tightened.

Swaying to the music, we kissed some more.

It was nothing like our first kiss. We were in no rush this time. No desperation. It wasn't about sating a thirst, but more like a promise. Filled with trust, respect, and something I couldn't quite name.

We were equal.

No celebrity status or exes stood between us.

We were Carter and April, two people who had no idea how to navigate the connection they shared and the reality they both stepped in when they met.

Our lips moved together, and soon we were devouring each other's mouths without restraint, the heat enveloping us palpable. We were both starving, kissing as if the world would end any second.

Carter's palms moved up and down my back, and I twisted his shirt in my fist, craving a physical connection other than him to keep me grounded in the moment.

Heat shot through me, ribbons of lust coiling around me and making me their prisoner.

Light-headed, I wasn't sure how I ended up here but wished to be nowhere else.

The proof of his desire pressed against my lower belly, and I rubbed myself against him, searching for some much-needed friction that would tame the flames licking my skin and turning my insides into molten lava.

One large hand cupped my cheek, angling my face so

Carter could deepen the kiss. The one that had my toes curling.

I lost contact with everything around me.

I looped my arms around his neck and pulled him down, relishing how his teeth toyed with my lower lip. Moans I couldn't keep inside for another second escaped, burying the sound of our combined frantic breaths.

Carter lowered his hands to my ass, grabbing a handful before lifting me onto the kitchen counter, leveling our faces. Even through layers of clothes, his touch felt like a burning caress. My legs wrapped around his, keeping him close to me, trying to erase any space left between us.

With his lips, he cherished the corners of my mouth, traced my jawline, and kissed the column of my throat. He sucked on my pulse point before licking his way down to my collarbone and returning to my lips.

My head swam in a blissful haze of pleasure, and I couldn't tell who broke the kiss first. With our faces about three inches apart, we stared at the other, breathless, neither of us saying anything.

Carter's chest rose and fell in quick succession. A glint shone in his eyes, and his lips curled into a lazy smile.

I grinned, never letting go of him, feeling vulnerable when he watched me like I mattered to him and I belonged in his arms.

A new song began playing, and until that moment, I had forgotten all about the music. The only sound I could hear was the drumming of my own heart.

Carter lowered me to my feet, and his arms pulled me back to his chest. Tangled together, we danced some more. Each time our gazes fixated on each other, there was a sense of peace settling between us that wasn't there before. Some sort of silent agreement.

Whatever happened, Carter had my back. And I had his.

"Listen, I'm giving a show next Saturday in Nashville. June, my assistant manager, convinced me it'd calm the storm surrounding us. Some sort of gift to my fans. I'd like for you to come along, but it's up to you. If you refuse, I'll understand."

Carter Hills said *us*. I wanted to fan myself but refrained. After a rock and roll morning, my day had taken a wild, unexpected turn. "I'm not sure I'm cut out for all this attention."

He shook his head. "It won't be like this. I promise. You'll stay with June the entire time. She's part of my team. I trust her. You'll be backstage. It's gonna be an acoustic show, not a big concert. Me and my guitar. Nothing too glamorous. You know, a few hundred fans, maybe even less. My team is setting it up as we speak. I don't have all the details yet."

Since when did HN ramble around me? He slouched, releasing a heavy breath through his nose.

After a beat, he gently tipped my chin up with a curled finger, and we gazed into each other's eyes. I saw the plea in his melted-steel irises.

"I'll think about it."

He curved a hand around the back of my head, pulling me closer, and pressed a kiss to my forehead. "Thanks."

My frantic heart rate dropped a notch.

And time stopped.

Chapter 16
Carter

"Okay, there are quite a few things I enjoy. Let's see. What I like the most about Green Mountain are the feet orgasms I get while walking on crunchy leaves covering the ground and the sunsets."

Feet orgasms? I mirrored April's grin. Even her words sounded like poetry.

"I also shed tears every time I see old people kissing. The ocean breeze gives me goose bumps, and fireflies on summer days entice me."

"Anything else?"

"I adore candy apples because they remind me of my childhood, and I believe wishing upon a star makes dreams come true." She took a sip from her mug.

I leaned in to wipe the hot chocolate off the corner of her lips with my thumb. Our gazes locked, and for a minute, I forgot how my lungs worked.

Fairy averted her eyes. "Where was I? Oh yes. Hot

chocolate heals everything…"—her voice dropped to a lower and huskier tone—"or it should."

My entire body pulsed with need. Sitting on the couch, next to the chair I was in, with her legs tucked under her, she tightened the white fluffy blanket around her shoulders. After we slow danced and kissed earlier, keeping a safe distance between us seemed imperative. Until we figured out the specifics of our blossoming relationship—and what it all meant. The fire crackling in the fireplace and the cat's slow, steady snoring were the only sounds in the house.

"What about you? What do you like, Carter?" April's words had turned into a guttural whisper…or was that just my imagination?

My heart shuddered each time my name—my real name—fell from her lips. *You*, I wanted to scream. I swallowed hard, doing my best not rip her clothes off and ravage her with my mouth like I did mere hours ago. "I love music. It's an addiction, a drug. Without it, I'm lost. It keeps me sane. Don't tell anybody, but I also enjoy watching rom-coms." I scratched my jaw. "I already told you about Jack and Dahlia, so… Oh, and I like sledding. It's something I do with Jack. A tradition. We should do it together. You and me."

"Huh, you're sure it's a good idea? I'm not even sure I like winter yet."

"How about we go tomorrow? Everything about flying down a snowy slope feels like magic." I didn't exaggerate. "For a minute, you're back to being a kid again. You don't have to like winter to enjoy this."

"Okay, you make it sound fun. I can do this."

"Now that you know all about me, tell me why you're staying in Green Mountain for a month by yourself. And what are you writing all the time on your laptop? You spend hours a day glued to that screen."

She sighed and rolled her jaw back and forth. Did she not trust me? I didn't have too much time to ponder this possibility when she started talking. "I'm writing a book. A novel. I'm an author…huh…for now."

My eyes widened. "Nice. You said, *for now*? Why?"

She shrugged. "I don't know. It just kind of happened, but this wasn't a dream of mine. I love it, believe me. I'm good at it when I put my mind to it, but I'm not sure it's what I'm supposed to do. Sometimes I feel like I'm missing something. My true purpose. I haven't figured out what it is, though."

"You published anything yet?"

Fairy nodded. "Two books. And they're doing quite well."

"Anything I might have read?"

Her laugh rang out, sending a zing through my entire being. "No. Unless you're into magic and fantasy worlds kind of literature."

I shook my head. "Nah. I don't think so. Perhaps I should try it. Do you think it would suit me?"

Her sweet laughter doubled in intensity. "Please don't. I refuse to picture you as my typical reader."

I puckered my face and pretended to stab my chest. "Ouch, that hurts. Anyway, I think it's great. Might explain why we're so good at bantering. I found my word-lover soul mate." I winked, and April shook her head, her smile not faltering.

"Well. Anyway, even if you tried searching for me online, you wouldn't find a thing. I'm using a pen name, and my picture isn't out there. I relish my privacy too much."

My interest grew even more. "What is it? Your pen name, I mean."

"If I tell you, I'll have to kill you afterward because

only a few people know. Not sure it's worth the risk. I'll keep it a secret, so your life is safe."

She winked, and I almost melted in my seat when I realized she wouldn't tell me, for real. Should I be impressed or run for my life? April Simmons was dangerous around me. She was both a drug and a mystery, all wrapped up in one bubbly and sexy woman. I fixed her with a stare, speechless—and spellbound. Had I finally met my match?

The crackling of the fire filled the silence, and both our gazes drifted toward the burning logs. The rich smell of the brownies April had baked after dinner clung to every particle of air around us.

Here and now, I felt content. And relaxed. It'd been an eternity since I last felt fully at ease around anyone who hadn't been part of my entourage for what felt like forever.

After a long moment, she fought a yawn. "Well, I'm going to bed. I have no idea what time it is, but I'm exhausted. Today was an emotional ride."

"About that, I'm…I'm sorry. I never meant for you to find out this way. I was afraid you'd run away if you knew who I was. In the past, I've been… Let's just say I've been burned and learned my lesson, and now I'm more careful."

"Don't sweat it. It's fine. Maybe if I had known early on, it would have freaked me out. You're kind of a big deal out there. Some part of me relishes the fact we got to know each other beforehand. Still, gimme some time to get used to it, though."

We eyed each other for a few beats. April hugged herself with her arms, and I cleared my throat. "Okay. I can do that. Thanks for giving me another chance to make things right. I'll let you go to bed now. Good night, Fairy." There was so much more I wanted to tell her, but I couldn't find the words. "I'll see you in the morning."

"Yeah. Night, HN." She waved at me and walked away, leaving me all alone with my thoughts. And a massive hard-on.

I raked my fingers through my hair, leaned back, and breathed out, the pressure of the day melting away.

Once I was sure April wouldn't come back downstairs, I turned off all the lights and made my way to my bedroom. I undressed, and butt-naked, I collapsed, face first, on the mattress and fell asleep in no time. Images of my roommate filled every one of my dreams.

———

The next day, April and I spent the morning working. She was writing in the den while I was locked in my music studio, sitting on the couch, trying to come up with a melody for a song I wrote. After lunch, we drove to Dahlia's.

"*Carrrter*," Jack shouted, running into my arms as we climbed out of my SUV. He lowered his voice. "Is the fairy your friend?" A loud chuckle left me as he looked at me with wide eyes.

"Yes, she is." I extended my arm to grab April's hand in mine and pulled her forward. "April, you remember Jack?"

Letting go of my hand, she dropped to her knees, bringing herself to his eye level. "Hey, Jack. It's nice to see you again. How is your friend Beatrix doing?"

The boy's eyes flared. "You remember her name?"

"Yes. How could I forget the name of the biggest fairies fan?"

"You want to meet her?" His voice was full of hope. And excitement.

April grinned. "Sure. I'd love to."

Jack lifted a finger to stop her from moving or talking. "Okay. Wait here. I'll be right back." He hurried inside, leaving us in the driveway.

"Guess we should go inside," I said, pushing her forward after I helped her up. Some sort of electricity passed between us from where my hand rested on her lower back., and my heart jolted. I swallowed hard and kept walking.

Dahlia appeared in the doorway before I had time to knock. "Hey guys." She rose on her tiptoes to kiss my cheek and greeted April with a genuine smile and a hug. "Nice to see you again, April. Glad you two made up."

April offered her a small, lopsided smile. "Nice to see you too."

"Carter told me you need winter clothes. I'm taller than you, but we're about the same size. Follow me. We'll find you something." Dahlia grabbed April's hand and led her away. "Give us a few minutes, Cart."

"Where's Nick?"

"Working," my friend said from a distance. "Some emergency."

In the kitchen, I was pouring myself a glass of water when Jack came running. "Is April still here?" he asked, breathless.

"Yes, why?"

He bent forward to catch his breath. "Bea will be here in five minutes. Her mama is dropping her off for the afternoon. We're having a playdate."

"Does your mama know?"

He bobbed his head quickly. "Yes. She told me I could invite her over."

When the doorbell rang, I greeted Mrs. Foster and Beatrix, just as April and Dahlia came back, my roommate dressed in navy-blue snow pants and a bright pink jacket.

My lips curled at the sight. "For someone who's not a winter fan, you pull those off pretty well," I teased, throwing in a wink.

A rosy hue spread across her cheeks.

Jack disrupted the moment when he tugged at her sleeve. "This is my best friend, Bea. Bea, this is April, Carter's fairy friend I told you about."

Just like she did earlier, April squatted and held out her hand to shake Beatrix's little one.

The girl's hazel eyes grew big as she offered April her best smile.

"Hi, Bea. I'm happy to meet you. Jack told me all about you."

The questions spilled from Beatrix's mouth in rapid-fire succession. She barely had time to catch her breath before launching into another one. Beatrix didn't even notice her mom slipping away, her face lit up with a giant grin as she watched her daughter in full awe mode.

I snickered behind my hand, watching the two five-year-olds embroiled in a serious debate about hair color.

"Well, if you wanna go, I guess I need to break this party up," Dahlia whispered in my ear. "Either that or April will faint from heat stroke underneath all these clothes." Her hand found mine, and she gave it a strong squeeze. No words were needed.

"You've made quite an impression," I told April as we climbed back into the truck a few minutes later. "You're lucky those kids let you go."

She laughed—a clear and happy sound that went straight to my heart. For a long time, I had to deal with Savannah Prince's pretenses, and right now, it felt good to witness a woman being herself fully, not playing a role or wearing a mask.

"I'm not joking. Ever heard of being abducted by kids

so they could experiment with strands of your hair and steal your magic? It's some serious shit. Being a fairy, you should know all about it. For your safety."

She laughed some more, and I joined in.

Ten minutes later, we arrived at my special spot, the one I'd been bringing Jack to since he was old enough to stand on his feet by himself. My heart beat a little faster, knowing I brought someone else here. April was the first woman I allowed around him without a second thought. For a reason I ignored, it felt right. A rock grew in my stomach. Her time in Green Mountain had an expiration date, and I needed to remember that. My heart had been broken too many times already, and I wasn't interested in putting it through the wringer again.

"I'm surprised there's snow here." Her eyes traveled all around us. "Everywhere else, it has melted."

I snapped out of my daze and cleared my throat. "The valley is always feet deep covered in snow. This and the ski resort. Everywhere else in town, it comes and goes. Ready?"

She followed me close, glee radiating from her. We'd parked at the top of the hill, and the view from there was breathtaking. Snowy mountaintops. Valleys. A glimpse of Main Street below. The slope was a fraction of a mile long and not too steep.

"It's peaceful here. I understand why it's your special spot." Fairy's eyes were wide as she took in her surroundings, and a piece of my heart expanded.

We settled ourselves on the sled, way too small for two grown-ups. With my height, it was a bit of a challenge to fit both of us on the wooden sleigh, but April was so small that we made it work. She positioned herself in front of me, and I wrapped my legs around her.

"Zip up. You don't want to turn into a snowman."

"All done," she said, excitement clear in her voice. "I can't believe we're doing this."

"Hold on tight," I warned her as we launched ourselves down the snowy hill. With a push of my hands, I propelled us down the slope before wrapping my arms around her waist. It satisfied some of my urges to touch her. Whenever April was nearby, my hands itched to brush her skin.

The sled hopped. She yelped. My heart swelled in my rib cage.

This girl lit up like a Christmas tree for things most people would consider boring. Snowflakes. The crisp crunch of fallen leaves beneath her feet. Hot chocolate. Her cat snoring. Sunsets. Winning a game of Monopoly. Buying groceries.

The sled tipped over at the bottom of the slope, enveloping us in white flurries. April's contagious laughter resonated around us in the valley. We were in our own world when we tumbled in the snow together. The kid in me was having a blast.

"Oh. My. God. That was insane. I can't believe I've never done this before."

We were both lying on our backs on the ground. I turned to my side, removed one of my gloves, and using my fingertips, dusted off snowflakes from April's nose and cheeks. The air in my lungs turned to ice. Her bottom lip shuddered when the pad of my thumb smoothed the contours of it. She closed her eyes. This was it. The moment when I abandoned all my restraints. Our lips were a hair's breadth apart, breath mingling, hearts racing, the world narrowing to just the space between us.

April cocked her head and sneezed, breaking the moment. "Sorry," she said as she sneezed again and sat upright. I rose to my feet, grabbed her hand to pull her up, put my glove back on, and dusted off the snow covering her hat and coat.

"Can we go again?" She looked at me with her best puppy dog eyes.

"Come on." I turned around, adjusted the erection in my pants, and squatted low. "Hop on." She locked her thighs around my waist and her arms around my neck, and I carried her on my back the entire way up. Even from under all our winter clothes, her heartbeat, strong and fast, thudded against my back and vibrated through me.

At the top of the hill, April fixed her hat, her smile never faltering. "Thank you, Carter. I'm glad you insisted I wear proper winter clothes. This is so much fun."

Yeah. One hypothermia scare was more than enough.

———

"Today, I'm giving you a snowboarding lesson. I bet you've never tried it before."

April shook her head. "Isn't it dangerous? Can we break our backs or something?"

I dropped a kiss on her wrinkled forehead. Pixie was clueless about everything related to winter. "You're cute. I'll never let anything bad happen to you. I promise. You're safe with me."

"Okay, then. Let's gear up."

I burst out laughing. "It's a bit more complicated than that. We gotta rent you a board and boots first. Get changed, and meet me in the truck. I'll gather my gear."

The lesson lasted half a day, and the entire time, every cell in my body ached to touch her. I locked my hands around her waist, helping her with her balance too many times to keep count. It wasn't much, but it fulfilled some of my touch-April needs. With a reluctant smile and a high dose of trust in me, she held on to me with a death grip. We exchanged heated stares, and I forced myself to think about olives, a fruit I hated, and gooey snails, a mollusk that grossed me out. Focused, she worried her bottom lip between her teeth, and it almost pushed me over the edge. *Relax, Carter.* My roommate had a way of enchanting every parcel of me. I jumped up and down, faking I was cold and trying to shake off the tightness in my pants, the fabric suddenly feeling a little too snug.

"I did it. Carter, I did it." April carved a few turns without falling and jumped into my arms when I finally came to a stop next to her, ecstatic, her feet still strapped to the board.

My level of pride skyrocketed to outer space.

We hugged for a bit too long, unable to break apart.

I breathed her in. Lavender. And mint lip gloss.

Another wall around my heart crumbled, leaving it exposed.

"I'm fucking proud of you, Fairy." I held on to her before lowering her back down. My thumb brushed her lips when I cupped her cheek and she shivered under my feather-soft touch. With a step back, I released her and broke the spell. "Let's go again."

———

"Tomorrow, we're leaving for Nashville, but what about ice skating this afternoon? You can get some writing done before we go. Anyway, I have a song to finish. Work in the morning, fun later. How does it sound?" I asked April as we finished breakfast, sitting side by side at the kitchen island, both in sweats and bare feet. Half of her hair was tied in some sort of knot on the top of her head, and with flushed cheeks and her lids still heavy from sleep, she looked adorable.

"I'm not a very athletic person, HN. Don't be too optimistic here. Also, all my muscles are still aching from snowboarding and sledding."

"You'll be fine. I'll be right beside you the entire time, holding your hand."

Ice skating was another one of April's first times. From now on, I wanted them all—all her first times.

And her lasts.

During the entire ride to the ice rink, she kept her hand firmly lodged in mine.

Once we arrived, we sat on a bench and removed our boots. I put my skates on in less than a minute and kneeled in front of April once she slid her feet into the pair we rented for her, eyeing them as if she had no idea where to start.

I curled my fingers around her shin and positioned her foot between my knees to keep it in place.

"What are you doing?" she asked, watching me with a curious gaze.

"Tying these. Let me know if it's too tight."

"Oh. You don't have to do this. I-I probably can do it myself."

"Let me do it. If they're too loose, your ankle will roll. They gotta be tight, but just enough. You'll understand what I mean." I laced the first skate, enjoying being able to do this for her.

April snickered, studying each of my movements. "But you're kneeling in front of me."

I winked. She blushed.

On unsteady feet, April glided forward, her hand never leaving mine. We took a few tentative steps on the ice, so she could get the hang of balancing on blades. With a soft pull, I guided her closer to me, turning my back to the other skaters so we were facing each other.

"See? One foot, then the other. You can do this."

With panic flashing in her eyes, she tightened her grip on my hand, draining it of blood, but she did as I said.

She looked out of her element on the ice at first, but after half an hour, she found her footing. I missed her touch the moment she let go of me. April glided on the surface on her own, feet apart from me, sparks of pride shining in her eyes. I got drunk on her laughter and light-headed on her lavender perfume.

"Hot chocolate?" She jumped to her feet, her rental skates removed and hanging from her fingers.

"Sure, I'll—"

"You stay here, and get those off your feet," she said, pointing to my still-laced skates. "I'll be right back. My treat." She waltzed away, and my eyes stayed glued to her retreating figure. Was that drool that pooled on the ground? My drool? I pinched my lips together, gave my head a small shake, and finally freed my feet from the skates.

Later, we sat on a wooden bench, watching a teen hockey game on the second rink, a big icy rectangle. A light breeze swept across our faces. I pushed strands of April's hair behind her ear and smoothed her beanie into place over her head. Families surrounded us. The ice rinks were in the middle of River Park, the largest park here in Green Mountain. Behind us, two little boys ran around, chasing each other. A husky puppy neared us, and April gaped at his sight. Both of us leaned forward to pet its head before its owner pulled on the leash. My eyes traveled back to the two boys, now laughing their hearts out, sitting on the ground.

"My dad played hockey all his life and would've made

it to the pros if he hadn't messed up his knee in college. He taught Jeff and me how to skate when we were still in diapers. We spent most of our Sunday mornings on the ice growing up. Neither Jeff nor I shared a passion for hockey like our dad did, though. We loved the game, but I've always preferred music and words, while Jeff enjoyed building stuff. He'd never really been into sports either." A low laugh escaped my mouth.

"Did your dad encourage you to follow your dreams, or was he the kind of dad who only wanted you guys to follow his own?"

A small smile tugged at the corner of my lips. "One winter day, when I was maybe seven or eight, our dad woke Jeff and me up early to go to the rink first thing in the morning. Both of us begged our mom to let us go to the winter fair instead. There was a band playing and some sort of *build a mailbox for Santa* workshop for kids. You should have seen my dad's face. He tried everything to discourage us. In vain. We ended up spending the day at the fair." Nearly twenty years later, that day remained vivid in my memory. "He let us follow our own path. I think the idea we'd never play hockey was a gut punch at first." I shrugged. I hadn't thought about my parents in quite some time. "What about your parents? Did they encourage you to follow your dreams?"

April's smile faded. She rolled her shoulders back and inhaled. "I don't know my parents. Never met them."

I angled my body to face her, keeping my face neutral. "You were in foster care?" Not that it mattered.

"No. My mom's aunt raised me. It forced me to grow up faster than any kid should. My mother got pregnant at sixteen. After she gave birth, she panicked and left me on Nana's doorstep one morning and disappeared. Nana was already over fifty-five when my mom left me. If it hadn't been for her, I would've ended up in the system. Nana lost touch with her after I turned six. The last letter she sent to my mother bounced back. Over the years, I never tried to reach out to find her. I have nothing to say to her. And my sperm donor? Nobody even knew who he was. I've forgiven my mother a long time ago and always refused to live with the ghosts of my past. In my head, and in my heart, Nana is forever going to be my mom. Biological or not, she'd been my only parent growing up.

"Saunders, my best friend, the one who sent me here, is my only family now. We met in college, and it was love at first sight. We shared a dorm room freshman year and haven't been apart since. After Nana passed away, Saunders became the only person I could count on." April gazed at me, a tinge of pink coloring her cheeks. "We had little money growing up. Over the years, I've been knocked down more times than I can count. I learned to be independent and resourceful early in life. And resilient."

I draped my arm around her shoulders and cradled her close. "I'm sorry. I didn't know."

"It's okay. I struggled for a long time, scared to let people in. Nana died during my freshman year of college. At eighteen, I was all alone in this world. Saunders and Travis, my college boyfriend, showed me I mattered to some people and that I wasn't as lonely as I thought. It took me a while to accept their unconditional love—" She averted her gaze and toyed with the lid of her hot chocolate to-go cup. "I'm a better person because of them. They showed me every day I was worthy of love."

I kissed her temple, and April relaxed in my embrace. We exchanged a ghost of a smile and watched the rest of the game in silence, her head resting against my shoulder the entire time. Something shifted inside me, and an urge to protect her, no matter what, grew inside me. Unlike the last time when I dated the Evil Queen, this time there were no voices in my head pleading with me to run for my life.

————

How come the trip from Green Mountain to Nashville seemed shorter this time? As if more than a hundred miles had vanished. April had this way of making even the most boring things in life colorful. Forget Nashville, we should've aimed for a thousand-mile road trip instead. Vanish into the sunset. Fuck under a palm tree. Never come back.

We grabbed green tea to go and settled in my SUV, playing each other's music playlists on our phones.

"Okay, I have to tell you something. It might hurt your feelings, and I'm sorry about that." I sucked in a breath and put my best poker face on. "This song sucks. Big time. I can't understand why sane people would listen to this. There's nothing good about it. Sure, the chorus is catchy, but other than that, it's punishment to endure the"—I looked at the in-dash entertainment slash navigation screen—"entire three minutes fifty-seven seconds of it. There's no vocal technique and too much Auto-Tune, it's distracting. Nails on a chalkboard would sound less painful."

"Shut up, HN. What do you know about pop music?" April cocked a brow, and I burst out laughing like a kid, choking on a sip of scorching hot tea.

"Did you forget I'm the professional here, Pixie?"

She made a funny pout. The kind I'd die to kiss. Ignoring the rise in my body temperature and my permanent hard-on, I nudged her arm. April played another song on her playlist.

"Whoa, that is even worse. Where's your taste in music, woman? My ears are bleeding right now. I thought I could trust you as the honorary DJ on the road. Kill me already. I was wrong. You're fired."

Her laughter—a sound I had come to associate with her—was clear and genuine, and I couldn't help but laugh along with her.

"Please stop this massacre you call music. New rule. My truck, my music."

Her eyes glistened every time I teased her, and I suffered from not kissing her a little more each time. She wiped off the tears welling up in the corners of her eyes with her fingertips before regaining her composure, a long-lasting grin imprinted on her pink lips.

Eyes shut, she sighed, her palms touching as if in prayer. "Okay," she said once her fit of laughter had subsided. "I'm really disappointed in your lack of open-mindedness about other music genres. You get one free pass. Let's settle on classic rock and country. Truce?"

"Yeah, better. There's this guy, Carter Hills...huh...I think. Don't know if you've ever heard of him. He has had a few hits. You should give his music a try. I heard it's amazing. Just sayin'." I shrugged, and April kept her face emotionless.

"I've heard about this guy. Such an ass. I hope his music is better than his attitude."

We drove a few miles, the silence comfortable between us.

"This pen name of yours, are you going to tell me what it is?"

She tapped her chest with her open palm. "You sure you want to risk your life for this?" She arched a brow, challenging me with her gaze.

I dropped my shoulders, trying my best puppy-dog eyes, hoping she'd crack. I was certain I could master it too if I gave it a try.

"You're not fooling me, Big Guy. Nice try."

We arrived in Music City mid-morning, and after a quick late breakfast, I walked April to her suite. My team had booked each of us a suite at City Garden, Nashville's finest hotel. There would be a small after-show party in mine later. I had hesitated between staying at my penthouse overlooking the city skyline or the hotel. Somehow, I feared inviting April to stay with me at my place would scare her away, which sounded ridiculous. After all, we'd already been living together for almost a week now. Had we stayed in town for more than a night, I might have offered her the choice. Not this time, though. I preferred to play it safe.

Deep down, a selfish part of me hoped she'd stick around long enough for us to come back here. Together.

I had no idea why I kept referring to an *us* when I thought about her, but somehow, I couldn't help it.

To avoid any weirdness between us but also not wanting her to feel all alone, here I was, staying at City Garden too for the night.

Since it was April's first time in Nashville and her first time in this world of mine, I wanted her night to be ultra special. I loved this city so much that I couldn't wait to give her a taste of it.

The fun part, at least.

Never in my life had I invited a woman to join me backstage at one of my concerts. Savannah didn't care about my music, and except for movie premieres or galas, she barely ever left LA, her only interest being my fame—and my money.

This, having April here with me, was a huge deal for me, and I intended on making every second of our time in Nashville count.

Chapter 17

Carter walked me to my suite right before leaving for sound check and whatever else he had to do hours before a gig.

I gasped when I entered the room. The entryway with its white walls and eight-foot-tall paintings framed in gold reminded me of a museum.

Down three steps, it opened to a living room area worthy of a multi-million dollar house. High ceiling, panoramic windows, thick dark velvet curtains, a matching set of couches, and a plush carpet. This was the fanciest hotel room I'd ever stayed in.

A long dining table big enough to seat ten people separated the living room section from the state-of-the-art kitchen. On my left, a hallway led to what I assumed was the bathroom and bedroom.

"This is our suite?" I asked, still surveying the space, slack-jawed.

"No. This is *your* suite, Fairy. I'm staying down the hall."

"I-I… This is all for me?"

He shrugged like it was no big deal. "Yes. All yours."

"O…huh…okay. Wow. I'm—"

He swiveled to face me and grabbed my upper arms. "You okay?"

"Yes. It's a bit much. Didn't they have like regular-size rooms with a queen bed and a balcony?"

Carter tossed his head back and laughed before planting a kiss on my forehead. "No idea. I told you I would make it up to you. Enjoy." He checked the time on his phone. "June will be here in one hour to take you shopping."

"Shopping?"

"For a dress. For tonight. Let me spoil you. Just this time."

I froze there, mute.

"Anyway, before she gets here, you can either go to the spa on the second floor or take a nap or plunge into a bubble bath. Anything that helps you relax." His hands moved to my shoulders, and he massaged the tension away. "Are you gonna be okay on your own?"

I found my voice. "You're kidding, right? I'm still not sure I'm not dreaming."

He lowered his lips to mine, grazing them in a soft, fleeting kiss. "Enjoy, okay? I'll see you later."

I bobbed my head. "Yeah. Sure. Don't worry about me."

He turned to leave but stopped midway. His eyes captured mine over his shoulder. "And June barks but doesn't bite. Unless she has to. Don't let her scare you, okay? She's very protective of me."

"Huh… What do you mean?"

"Stand your ground. You two will get along just fine, I swear." His lips curled up, and he shook his head as if thinking about something funny. "Yep. You two will hit it off."

As if Carter had predicted our first encounter, June wasn't exactly thrilled at the idea of me attending his concert tonight. This became clear when she came to pick me up to go shopping. She didn't offer to take me as an act of grace but only to assess me and my intentions toward him. She didn't trust me. It was written all over her face, from her tightly pinched lips to her defiant glare. She acted all friendly and shit at first, but once we sat side-by-side in the backseat of the SUV, she went straight for the jugular without flinching, her mama tiger suit on.

June studied me with a frown, her arms crossed over her chest. "What do you want from Carter?" The words sliced the already thick air in the car as one of the security guys drove us around. "And don't fuck with me. I won't let another crazy bitch profit from him. Not happening again. Not under my watch." Disdain had dripped from her words. She never broke eye contact. Though she was shorter than me, I didn't doubt she'd kick my ass if she ever had to.

Carter had warned me she was protective of him, but I didn't think I gave her any ammunition to doubt my character. I wouldn't let her intimidate me. If he thought June and I would hit it off, I trusted him enough to believe it was true. Even though, at first, I couldn't see it happening in the near future.

"Okay, I think you sized me up wrong. I'm no crazy bitch." I raised my hands between us. "I'm here because he invited me. Nothing more, nothing less." My cheeks flared in anger.

"I'm sure you're after something he has. They all are."

I harrumphed, balling my hands under my thighs. "I really do not care about anything else but him. None of this matters," I explained, motioning one hand around us. "Carter and I are friends, and none of it is your business. Maybe I should go back to the hotel since you clearly don't want me around. I didn't even want to come, but he insisted. It was *his* idea. But now that I'm here, you gotta deal with it." I folded my arms over my chest, mimicking her pose.

June opened her mouth, but nothing came out. She clamped it back shut, her gaze never leaving mine. "I think you and I will become friends. Welcome to Nashville, April."

And just like that, we reached a truce, and her guard-dog attitude vanished. The wrinkles around her mouth softened. "Let's find something incredible for you to wear tonight." She snaked her arm through mine like we'd been best friends for years, and I blew out a cleansing breath, shifting in my seat, the weight on my shoulders fifty pounds lighter.

My skin itched at the idea of spending Carter's money, but when I turned down the sixth dress after a quick glance at the price tag, June took matters into her own hands. She grasped my upper arms and forced me to look at her. "April, pick anything you like. It's Carter's treat. Ignore the price tag. Just this once, okay?"

I nodded, my head hanging low.

"I stopped arguing with most of his orders long ago. Don't worry. I have your back. Also, he gave me specific instructions, so you don't really have a choice." June shrugged, no doubt used to this.

Once she drove me back to the hotel one hour later, I locked myself in my suite and lay down on the expensive couch, thinking about how my life had changed since moving to Green Mountain. I could hardly believe I had been that lonely woman unable to put the pieces of her life back together for so long. This new life was temporary, but it had given me a taste of what I could accomplish, what I could aim to be. My stay in Green Mountain had transformed me, and the month wasn't even over yet. I was happy again. Smiling didn't feel like an effort anymore. And my insomnia was a thing of the past. Even Bernice appeared happier since we arrived.

For an instant, I wondered if it was the result of the mountains or the man who played a huge part in getting my groove back and stealing bits of my heart with every smile.

My phone chimed with an incoming text notification from Carter, and I held my breath as I unlocked my device. I hadn't been in Nashville one day, and already I had been swept off my feet multiple times, living the princess dream. The suite, the dress, the concert tonight. It all felt surreal.

I read his words, and despite myself, my heart banged in my chest.

Carter Hills was messaging me.

My lips tipped into an oversized grin.

The guy had a way of making me feel weak in the knees without even trying.

I controlled the tremors in my fingers as I texted him back, trying to act like I was not freaking out about this entire weekend, when in reality, I was nothing close to chill inside.

Unable to erase my grin, I wrote a simple reply, pressed *send*, and exhaled.

I downed a bottle of water to ease my nerves, waiting for him to text back.

After I left the hotel, I used my free time to check on the venue and decide on the playlist for tonight.

Acoustic shows with only a small crowd had always been my favorite. Sure, the rush I got from playing sold-out stadiums compared to nothing else, but I always preferred the intimacy of small venues.

At that moment, I wondered why I hadn't thought to focus my energy on smaller gigs before, since they brought me more joy and serenity. The idea of scheduling a string of unplugged concerts instead of a worldwide tour next year began to grow on me.

Me. My guitar. My music. My rules.

Riley, my long-term manager, greeted me. He'd organized this last-minute show using all his contacts after our emergency meeting days ago.

Alone in a room with my phone on speaker set on the

table in front of me, I got connected to my favorite radio station. The one we teamed up with to announce my show.

"Carter Hills will do a surprise performance tonight, folks. We'll draw tickets throughout the day. We'll reveal the location at the last minute. Stay tuned for more details."

Then the host, Mark, a decent guy I went to high school with, took my call. I wouldn't have done an interview with anyone else. I thought it'd be nice to chat with him on-air since we hadn't seen each other in person in quite some time.

"Hey, Carter. Thanks for talking to us today. How are you doing?"

"Good, Mark. Excited about tonight. Thanks for having me."

"I and everyone else in Nashville are glad you're doing okay, Carter. With all the fake news out there about you, you had us worried for a moment."

I laughed and shook my head, even though nobody could see me. "You're a smart guy, Mark. Don't believe everything you hear or see. In all honesty, I'm better than I've been in a long time. It's good to be back, even if it's just for a night."

"Do you have any scoop about tonight's show? It's the talk of the town right now."

"All I can say is that it's going to be unplugged, and I may have a surprise up my sleeve. I guess we'll see how it goes."

"That sounds amazing. I'll let you get ready for tonight then. Always a pleasure to talk to you, Carter. Have a great show."

"Thanks, Mark. Have a good one."

"That was Carter Hills, folks. All y'all, ready for tickets? I—"

I tuned out and hung up. I sighed, a small smile grazing my lips.

My entire team believed getting back on a stage with a pop-up concert would help deflect the attention my love life had gained lately, and that fans would love the intimate setting.

I trusted my team. And my gut.

Apart from the Savannah Prince fiasco and some stupid suggestions from Carla, my ex-PR person who had since been fired, I never had any major reason to battle with my management team or my label in the past. Sure, we'd had our share of disagreements over the years, but nothing of importance. The biggest mistake of my life had been the clusterfuck I had brought upon myself by dating Hollywood's Evil Queen. Probably the lowest point of my existence.

Tightness lodged in my chest every time the memories resurfaced. I could write a book about all the craziness our relationship brought into my life. I was sure it'd be a bestseller. People would definitely wonder if I made it all up. Yeah, it was that much nonsense.

For the longest time, my personal life had lacked direction. While my career had its ups and downs over the years, it remained the one constant—the one thing I could always count on when everything else seemed to burn to ashes. For years, I felt stuck, unable to commit to anything worthwhile outside of my music. But after everything I went through, I could see the clouds parting. Perhaps I would finally get the new beginning I'd been craving for so long.

Lately, things had turned around, and in a short span of time, the positives had begun to outweigh the negatives. As this sank in, my thoughts wandered far from here.

Dahlia and Jack. Who were happy and living fulfilled lives.

The future. Which appeared much more encouraging than I would have thought a few months ago.

Fame. Which had its perks, but oh so many downsides. I was still debating sometimes if it was all worth it.

April. How, with her pink hair and quick wit, she had brought a wave of fresh air into my life in the short time we'd known each other.

How she infuriated me but also mesmerized me.

Her freedom. Her sass. Her magnetism. Her childlike ways of being amazed by small everyday things.

At the mere thought of her, my body relaxed. My thoughts got sorted out. Never before had I expected another person to have this much effect on me one day.

And truth be told, I needed her energy in my life.

She possessed some special powers strong enough to soothe all my inner demons. My doubts. My insecurities.

Amid everything I put her through, photos leaked to the press, becoming fodder for the gossip mags, she deserved to have some fun tonight.

And I planned on making her night one to remember.

———

I high-fived my musicians and turned toward my manager. "Did I lose my magic touch?" I asked in a teasing tone.

Riley neared me and pulled me into a one-arm hug. "You? Losing your magic touch? Nah, never. I'm glad you're getting back out there. It was about time you walked on a stage." He let go of me and stepped back, grinning.

"Well, I missed it. A whole lot. We should talk about booking a few shows in the next few months. I have new stuff I wanna try, and at this rhythm, I may have enough material for a new album soon."

"That's what I'm talking about. The Carter Hills standing in front of me is the star I recognize. Green Mountain is good for you, man. Your smile is back. And you seem happier. Dahlia always says the mountain air is addictive. I guess it's time I believe her."

I scratched my neck, glancing down as I debated my next words. "The mountain air is great, Ry. Fantastic even. I love it. But…huh, there's also that girl."

"I thought you said she was just a neighbor living in one of your cabins?" He quirked a knowing eyebrow, taking a sip from the to-go cup in his hand.

"Yeah… well, about that… We kinda live together now?"

He choked on his coffee, studying me for what felt like an eternity. "Is that a question?"

"Huh, no."

"You said, *We kinda live together now?* As if you were asking me."

"The electronic lock at her place broke. I didn't like the idea of her living on her own in the cabin until it got fixed, so I moved her into mine."

My manager stared at me, his lips forming a line, and his eyes assessing my level of stupidity—or that was what it looked like.

"You moved a woman you barely know in with you. Okay… And when we met to talk about this gig after pictures of you two leaked, you didn't think to share this piece of information because?"

"It is new. I didn't know how long she would stay. It's… huh…complicated." He parted his lips, but I kept going to avoid him bursting my bubble. "She's here. In Nashville. With me. June took her shopping." He raised a hand to shush me, but I kept talking. "You'll meet her later. Don't make up your mind before you do., okay? Please. Do it for me. You gotta trust me on this. You said I look happy. Well, April is the reason."

Riley slapped my shoulder. "I won't. Not my style, man. All I want is for you to be thriving, you know that. I'm just careful this time around. We've all been burned by your previous relationship, and I don't want a do-over."

"I'm not in the same state of mind that I was in the last time. And did you once tell me during the length of my relationship with you-know-who that I looked happy?"

He shook his head. "Nah. You looked every shade of miserable." He paused, and we exited the venue after he gave all of us instructions for tonight. "Tell me more about April then. I wanna know why she's so special."

For the next ten minutes, we talked about the woman I couldn't get enough of.

"I can't wait to meet her." He turned to haul himself into his car when he halted and turned around. "And for what it's worth, I trust you, Carter. I've always done so, even though, sometimes, you let your emotions run the game and get the better of you. You always find your way back when the clouds part. Remember, I'll always have your back. See you later."

I nodded. His words pleased me, a lot.

Riley was like my true north in the chaotic whirlwind of my professional and personal life. He helped me stay on track, even when I derailed or whenever we didn't see eye to eye on something about my career. I respected him enough, both as a human being and as a manager, to never go behind his back. In the end, we always found common ground that worked for both of us. Over all these years, he knew me so well yet never tried to impose his vision on me. Riley respected me too—as a man and also as an artist.

When I messed up, he always offered me a hand to help me get back on my feet. I understood his reservations about April, but deep down, I knew he would change his mind once he met her. This woman left no one indifferent. Me included.

On the drive back to the hotel, I called June. "Hey, how is it going with April?"

"Drove her to the hotel half an hour ago. We had a great time. My bitch radar didn't detect anything suspicious. Still, be careful. You don't need a repeat of Savannah Prince's story."

"I'm not asking your permission." I clenched and unclenched my fists. I knew June meant well. As did Riley. "All I'm asking is for you to treat her with respect."

"Will do, Carter. No worries. We hit it off."

Stopped at a red light, I texted April next.

ME

> Late lunch in my suite? I'm on my way to the hotel.

I would've made a reservation at one of my favorite restaurants in town—the barbecue shack on Broadway or the southern bistro in East Nashville—but people were looking for me, so I preferred lying low.

For her sake.

And my own sanity.

APRIL

> Sure. Text me when you want me to come over.

In Nashville, most people let us *celebrities*—God, I hated this word—be. They didn't care to share their everyday life with famous athletes, Hollywood stars, or country singers. It didn't impress them. It was just the way things were. A far cry from Hollywood. Things would be different now that the press was hunting for juicy pictures of me and "my new lady." Anyone with a cell phone became a threat. A hunter ready to make a few bucks selling pictures of me as I bought toilet paper or drove around town with a woman.

I cringed at the idea they'd sell shots of April without her knowledge or consent.

Over the years, I'd grown a thick skin to protect myself from these vultures. She hadn't. She had no idea how careless these fame-seekers could be or the extent they'd go to get a great shot of my taking the garbage out or eating a burger. Fury boiled in my veins as it did every time those thoughts consumed me. Desperate to keep my calm, I forced myself to relax my white-knuckled grip around the steering wheel. I pictured April's smile in my head, and a wave of calm washed over me, leaving me with a stupid grin tattooed on my face instead.

———

I walked April back to her suite so she could get some rest before tonight's show. Sitting on the couch with my guitar, I played for a little while before giving Riley a call because I had made some last-minute changes to my set that I wanted to go through with him. Once we both agreed, I dialed June. She met me, holding her tablet in one hand and her phone in the other, ready for whatever I asked of her.

"Hey," I said when she crossed the threshold of my room. "It won't take long."

She brushed past me and took a seat by the kitchen counter. "I ordered tea. It should get here soon. I also sent bubbled water, an assortment of juice and chocolate, and a basket of fruits to April's room. I thought she might need a snack before the show." She scrolled through her notes. "The hotel will see to it. Food will be delivered to your suite around eleven tonight. I asked for the usual. They'll set it in here, on this counter, so when we have that little gathering later, we won't have to go out to eat or order in."

I stood in front of her, my palms pressed on the counter, waiting for her to finish her spiel.

"Anything else I missed?" She was almost out of breath.

I flashed her a smile. "Nope. All fine." I peered down at her, before asking the question burning the tip of my tongue. "You and April, you're good?"

A wrinkle etched across her forehead. "Yeah. I told you earlier. Why? Did she tell you she hated me when you two had lunch together?"

I stepped back and hooked my thumbs into my pockets. "She only had wonderful things to say about you. I wanted to thank you. For having her back and giving her a chance."

"Cart—"

"I'm not gonna go all sentimental on you, June. I just appreciated it. That's all."

"Carter, I'm just doing my job." She shrugged as if it was no big deal.

"We both know you do much more than what's on your job description. You're not just my assistant or Ry's assistant, you're my friend. And I wanted to thank you, for always having my back but also doing the right thing. I know I've pushed you away in the last two years, and I wasn't very open-minded when you tried to tell me I was making huge mistakes, but I never stopped looking up to you. Sometimes, I need to fuck it all up to understand the lesson. I'm just happy you never held it against me." I paused, looking down for a second before bringing my attention back to her. "I talked to Ry earlier. I'm doing better, and I'm feeling better. I'm not sure I'm ready to headline a world tour just yet, but I do want to get back out there. A few shows. Test some new material. Write new music. Record an album."

By the door, we hugged for a minute.

"Carter, I've missed you. I'm relieved the real you didn't get buried under all that shit. Take as long as you need to unwind and get back on your feet. And don't worry about April. I'll take care of her."

"Thanks." It was about time I made amends with the people who had stood by my side when the storm rocked the boat. In the grand scheme of things, the people who stayed in your corner when your life fell apart were the only ones who ever really mattered…the true friends you'd fight for anytime, without hesitation.

Jack called the moment my assistant walked out. That kid had a sick sense of timing.

We had this tradition going where we'd call each other before all my concerts. Jack would tell me about his day, and hearing his voice always helped with my mindset and defused the before-show jitters bomb inside me.

We talked for a little, but then I could sense his restlessness on the other end of the line. "What is it, buddy? Something you wanna talk about?"

"Can Bea and I come over soon?" he finally asked in one breath. "We want to spend a day with April."

"Let me check with her, but I'm sure it can be arranged. My fairy hunch tells me she'd like to see you both again."

"Cool. Thanks, *Carrrter*. Bye."

"We'll talk later, buddy."

"Wait. Mama wants to talk to you. She keeps asking me to give her the phone when we're done." He lowered his voice. "She has this weird look on her face. You know. *The* look." He snickered. "Good luck with that."

A soft chuckle bubbled out. I knew the look. Dahlia's *I mean business* frown.

"Thanks, buddy. I'll take all the luck I can get. Be nice to your mama."

"Hey, Carter," Dahlia said in greeting.

"Dah, everything all right?"

"Yeah. What's going on?"

I dragged my hands over my face. "Not much other than trying to get the press off my back, I reckon. I'm doing a pop-up show tonight. Something to ease every-body and make everyone forget about Fairy."

"Fairy? You mean April?"

I closed my eyes and nodded, even though Dahlia couldn't see me through the phone. "Yes…huh…April."

"She's one of the good ones. I can tell."

My thumb found my forehead and grazed it. "I know." I stayed silent. In my head, I counted to three.

Dahlia finally spoke up like I knew she would. "It's none of my business, but you're family, Carter, and I love you too much not to say anything. You're falling for her… more than you realize yourself. And I can tell she's falling for you too. Call it feminine intuition or whatever you want. I saw the glint in her eye when you two came over. And when you lied to her, she was devastated. This whole fame thing you've got going on is scary. I've been there…" She paused. "What I'm trying to say is, if you like her as much as I think you do, don't rush things with her. If what you two could have is worth it, give her some time to ease into the idea this is your life. If you move too fast, she'll run away. She…she almost did once. It's intimidating to date someone in the limelight, Carter. Think about it. You know I love you."

I closed my eyes, taking deep breaths in to ease the knots strangling my heart. Love. Falling. The idea sent waves of dread through me. I'd been to war, and I still bore the scars. Over the years, my relationship rap sheet had been less than glorious. While my best friend spoke to me, one thing became perfectly clear: like clouds parting after a storm to let the sun shine, I deserved love—and everything it entailed. Her words didn't rattle my soul but filled me with courage instead, and something resembling determination. It took me a long time to understand Dahlia and I were better as friends, but right now I was quietly grateful our relationship had never become something more—because when I thought of April, she was the one woman who could slip under my skin and stir something deep in me. The one I couldn't get out of my mind. No one else.

"I don't want you to end up with another broken heart. That's all," she added. "Last time, it really took a toll on you."

Riley, June, Dahlia. They all worried about me, and it broke my heart knowing I was the reason. Like I had already done with my manager and his assistant, I tried to reassure my best friend.

"You're right, Dah. I love you too. You and Jack will always be my family. And I'll be careful with April… There's something there. I can't quite name it, but it's powerful. Exciting and frightening all at once. I need to explore what it means and see where it can go."

"You're allowed to thrive, Carter. You're allowed to find happiness. To love and to be loved. For what it's worth, I'm glad you're putting yourself out there again. I can tell April is the one who's putting that smile back on your face, and it pleases me a lot."

After she sent me positive vibes for tonight's show, we hung up.

At six, I knocked on April's door, rocking on my heels. I breathed in and rubbed my hands over my denims. A sense of peace filled me.

My heart rate slowed to a steady rhythm as I waited for her to open the door to her suite.

When she did, my jaw hit the floor, and my breath stuck in my lungs. A tidal wave of heat rippled through me, and no words came out. I stood there like an idiot, unable to avert my eyes, tongue-tied.

Hot as fuck in her short ombre sequin dress, I stared at her without blinking. A wide smile brightened her face as she twirled around. My dick throbbed when I noticed the low-cut back, the V of the dress ending just above the swell of her ass. April had curled her jaw-length pink hair in soft waves and wore cowboy boots on her feet instead of heels. I closed my eyes and evened my breathing. My tongue darted across my lips. She did this thing where she swayed her hips, which drove me crazy.

She had to be aware of how the simple movement sent my body into overdrive and my libido skyrocketing.

I rubbed the heels of my hands over my eyes, desperate to calm the desire awakening in me. I tried to push away all the dirty thoughts racing through my mind. *Olives, gooey snails, Riley, Savannah Prince.*

My sight clouded, and my heart soared into my throat.

Air whistled through my lungs.

The vision of April in her dress—too short for anyone's eyes but mine—jolted my heart back to life. It resuscitated my dormant state, shattered my walls, and the last threads of self-control left in me. Her legs appeared longer, her skin creamier, her hips fuller.

"Fuck." The low curse passed my lips, and I scratched

my jaw, my gaze laser-focused on the sequin number she was wearing, unable to look away.

"Something wrong?" Her grin vanished. "Oh, you don't like it? I should've picked out the black halter dress. I knew this one was too short. I can go and change." She mumbled, doubt flickering across her face, cheeks flushed, her features strained.

I harrumphed and adjusted the crotch of my pants. They had tightened so much that I feared my dick would die of asphyxiation. April's eyes widened and followed my hand. "Babe, I love it so much that all I want to do is watch you all night and forgo the show." My voice cracked. "We should go. Now. I cannot come inside your suite, or neither of us will ever get out." My sinful mind was in high gear. I clenched my teeth, fearing all the dirty thoughts would spill out of my mouth without permission.

She flashed me a shy smile, and I turned around to lock away what was left of my willpower.

My wild heart banged inside its cage. I pressed one hand over my chest. *Is this what a heart attack feels like?* I paced the hallways, trying to will the blood that had pooled in my groin back up to my brain. How could I ever focus on my set tonight, knowing she'd be watching me from the wings, looking so sinful?

Drawing a shaky breath, I slid my thumbs into the belt loops of my dark denims and exhaled. *There. Better.*

After a few deep breaths and some quiet self-talk, I pivoted and held out my hand for her. Shivers raced up my arms where our skin touched. It was as addictive and thrilling as it was disconcerting.

"Fairy, you look amazing. I wouldn't want anybody else by my side tonight."

A genuine grin spread across her face, and all traces of

hesitation vanished. To ease any lingering doubt, I leaned forward and pressed my lips to her forehead.

Dahlia's words replayed in my head.

If what you two could have is worth it, give her some time to ease into the idea this is your life. If you move too fast, she'll run away. She…she almost did once. It's intimidating to date someone in the limelight, Carter.

Out of the corner of my eye, I glanced down at my date, hoping she'd give me a chance to show her how good we could be together. That we could make this thing between us work. *Small steps, Carter. Be yourself. That's all April will ever need.*

The venue looked amazing. About two hundred fans screamed my name when I walked onstage of the old barn turned into an auditorium. I'd missed this. The energy from a crowd. The feeling I was where I belonged. I'd never performed here before. On the outskirts of town, it gave this private, exclusive concert a more intimate and meaningful atmosphere. The owner of the barn had kept the original wooden plank floor and walls and beamed ceilings but had added acoustic panels and other decorative elements to achieve the best possible sound and eliminate any reverberation. I wasn't convinced it would work at first, but he proved me wrong. I loved everything about this place. The cachet. The history. The ambiance. But tonight, I couldn't seem to enjoy any of it. For the entire set, my eyes kept drifting to my girl offstage, in that sexy dress. *My girl.* It made no sense to think of her as mine, and yet, it made perfect sense.

Without even trying, she occupied each corner of my mind. All the time.

Every song I sang, I sang for her.

After finishing the last one, "Someday You'll Fly," one of my greatest hits, I bent down from my stool to take a sip from the water bottle at my feet, my thoughts spinning faster than ever. With newfound confidence, I gave in to my inner will.

"Hey guys, thanks for coming tonight. It means the world to me." I loved small, intimate concerts because they gave me time to talk to the crowd and soak in their energy. "I have a special gift for you. Please don't tell anybody; they'll be jealous." Laughter rippled through the audience. "I have this new song I've been working on, and I want to share it with you tonight."

The small venue buzzed with cheers. People whistles and howls.

My pulse spiked, and I breathed in and out at a steady pace, trying to ease the bundle of nerves knotting my stomach.

My eyes drifted to April, a goddess in her sequin dress.

My fingers strummed the first chords of "Pink and Country."

> **I couldn't see the light**
> **I thought I had it all**
> **figured out**
> **But I didn't, I had no clue**
> **And then you came my way**
> **You disrupted everything I've**
> **always known...**

I kept my eyes closed, letting my voice and my guitar do the talking.

> **... Girl, I just want you to know**
> **I want my life to be pink like**
> **yours**
> **Babe, I'll never let you go**

You're my absolute favorite color.

On the last words, I blew out a nervous breath. My voice and fingers, steady and self-assured, were a far cry from the way I felt inside. My stomach was a puddle of jelly, and my heart a mushy ball.

The applause from the crowd filled the space, and it tugged at my heartstrings. I cocked my head, and April captured all my attention. She wiped the tears rolling down her cheeks with the tips of her fingers and shot me the most dazzling smile.

There was no going back now. I had laid my heart on the line.

The only way I knew how.

Chapter 19
April

Carter sang the last verse of *my* song. *My* song. Carter Hills, the one and only, wrote me a song. My heels were glued to the floor, my fingers laced, palms pressed together in prayer, resting under my chin. I stood tall, my body rock-solid, a stark contrast to the jittery chaos roiling inside me. A flow of tears streamed down my face, and my heart danced around in my chest. A tingling sensation traveled throughout my body, leaving a trail of goose bumps behind, like raindrops on cobble-stones. Carter couldn't feel this way about me. We barely knew each other. However, the idea that I inspired him to write a song made me all kinds of emotional.

I, April Simmons, the girl who always ended up alone, had inspired the lyrics of a song written by a famous country music star. Speechless, I pinched myself—three times, just in case. The pain didn't wash the dream away. Euphoria took roots inside me, and all my thoughts dissolved, my eyes and ears consuming the emotionally charged, *it won't happen twice*, best four minutes of my life.

Carter wrapped up his show, and I heard the applause and cheers, but my feet refused to move. People talked to me—June, Riley, and a bunch of other people—but I didn't register anything they said. The idea Carter Hills saw me, really saw me, shattered a boulder the size of Australia that had been buried deep inside me for as long as I could remember.

The one I pushed aside years ago after I met Saunders and Travis. The one that made me believe, for a long time, I wasn't worthy of anybody's time and affection, thanks to my biological parents. Now it was gone, for good. From offstage, I let my eyes linger on Carter.

With purpose in his stride, he waltzed toward me backstage. My body shut down. I couldn't breathe, my heart frozen, and my limbs numb. When his hands circled my waist, I snapped out of my daze. I cupped his cheeks, my eyes wet with a mix of confusion and amazement. I brushed my thumbs over his short stubble and crashed my lips against his, forgetting about June beside me and ignoring everyone else around us.

Excitement tickled my spine.

My emotions trapped the words, so instead of speaking, I allowed my lips to express the vortex of feelings trampling my heart, leaving it raw and unguarded. Our mouths feasted on each other. My knees buckled, and I tightened my grip around his neck. *Carter Hills wrote me a song.* His mouth tasted like mint and sweat, a deadly combination wreaking havoc on my hormones. With a swirl of his tongue around mine, he ignited me and turned me to ashes in his arms. Our friendship—I cringed, lacking a better word to describe what we were—made no sense, yet our lips fusing together felt as natural as breathing. He leaned back, one large hand cradling my nape, the other hooked on my hip, keeping me upright. The raw desire in his eyes scorched me, and the smug grin on his face glistened, giving him a devilish edge.

Hours later, in his suite, sitting amongst some of his closest friends, his musicians, and his managing team, I still couldn't believe this night wasn't a dream. A fantasy world. A parallel universe.

Carter introduced me to the people he cared about as if I'd always been part of his life. As if I belonged there, with him.

I took a sip of my champagne, the aftermath of the concert sinking in.

In the folder of *Crazy things that had happened in my life*, tonight stole the top spot, by far.

A foreign thrill blistered inside me, and I rubbed my throat to ease the air coming in and out of my lungs. I closed my eyes and inhaled through my mouth, hoping to erase the crippling sensation knotting my stomach. My memory would fade over time, and I wished I had the first time Carter Hills played my song captured on video. One I could replay over and over every time I had a bad day or the urge to listen to it, the exact way he sang it tonight, not the one he'd record or the tenth time he'd sing it, but *this* one time. The very first time. I wanted to bathe in his words and drown in his melody.

All my senses heightened as I listened to his friends tell stories about the good old days, as they called them. When the world wasn't ruled by social media and cell phones were a shit substitute for cameras. His pine and cedarwood scent, now that he'd showered and changed into a clean pair of jeans and a plaid shirt, filled my nostrils and made me lightheaded. His calloused fingers, roughened due to years of playing the guitar, sent tingles straight to my core as they skimmed my skin, making me wish we were alone. The essence of him lingered on my tongue, hours after we kissed, and I wished it'd never fade away.

Carter Hills possessed me in a way I never thought possible. Tonight, he rocked my world with a song and a kiss. A pretty memorable kiss, though. The reminder of it made my toes curl, and a twitch rumbled deep inside me. *Ohmygod.*

My heart cartwheeled in my chest every time my brain wandered back to the song. *My* song. He sang for me and made me his with only his words. I pressed my thighs together, heat pooling low in my pelvis.

Saunders. I needed to reach out to her and tell her about my night. And the song. Mostly the song. She'd go batshit crazy over this.

As if she'd read my mind, my phone vibrated inside my little golden clutch, and my best friend's face lit up the screen.

SAUNDERS

> Bloody girl, are you kidding me right now?
> Tell me I dreamt the whole thing. I'm arse
> over tit over this.

With my lips pinched together to avoid smiling too big, I typed a reply.

ME

> Have no idea what you're talking about.

SAUNDERS

> Stop playing dumb. He wrote YOU a
> freaking song. It's all over the web.

ME

> Kidding, right?

> Shit. You're not. How would you know?

SAUNDERS

Girl, get real, Carter Hills professed his
feelings for you, and now the entire world
can see it. Or hear it, I guess.

ME

STOP.

It's nothing like that.

SAUNDERS

You're living under a rock. Or in a cave. Not
in the mountains. There's a mix-up. You're
lacking oxygen in your brain. Altitude can
do that to you.

ME

We're friends. Who care about each other.
That's all.

SAUNDERS

April, your song is Carter Hills's new hit. It
has over six million views already.

I reread the last message a dozen times. Still, it didn't register.

ME

Can't be. Are you sure?

So, a video existed somewhere of my song being sung for the first time. My body temperature flared. I wanted to fan myself with my hand. To jump to my feet. To scream. To laugh. Just the thought people could watch Carter perform it sent shivers through me. Why did I want to keep it under wraps? Somehow, I felt possessive of my song, and I wished it was only meant for me. I sucked in a breath. I was being silly. I swallowed, hard. The entire night was a whirlwind I wasn't prepared for. I liked it as much as I feared it. The vibration of my phone stopped my racing mind and my galloping heart from bouncing out of my chest.

SAUNDERS

> If you two wanted to hide your little country fling, you failed. BIG TIME.

ME

> No relationship here, Saund. Don't get ahead of yourself. Carter and I are friends.

SAUNDERS

> [Link to video]

> Check it for yourself.

My fingers itched to click the link. Right now. I closed my eyes and exhaled. This could wait. It had to. I was surrounded by people, and now wasn't the time.

SAUNDERS

> Believe what you want. Reed's jaw is still somewhere on the floor. He watched the video ten times already. Your man got himself a new fan. April, you're in denial.

> Reed wants me to tell you you're getting banged tonight if you haven't already figured it out or haven't already been fucked many times *winking emoji* And also to get stocked on condoms 'cause you'll need a whole king-size box.

I placed my hand over my mouth to silence the chuckle threatening to escape.

ME

> No comment.

SAUNDERS

Enjoy your night with your there's-no-
romance-between-us hot piece of country
ass. We'll talk later. I need to glue Reed's
jaw back to his face. I'm happy for you.
Love you x

A little smile tugged at my lips, and my heartbeat quickened. The charged air in the room soared and suffocated me. I fidgeted with the gold band around my right ring finger. Was I blind or stupid or were my friends right about Carter's feelings?

Carter arched a brow and stretched his arm, his hand finding the small of my back. "Everything okay?"

I nodded. My pulse skyrocketed at the sound of his hoarse, low voice.

"Everything's perfect." I mirrored his grin, zooming in on his lips for a fraction of a second.

Saunders's words replayed in my head. *If you two wanted to hide your little country fling, you failed.* Carter and I were just friends, right? My head said yes, but my heart vetoed it since there was a big flashing, warning neon sign stating we were so much more.

Maybe I was really fucked after all.

With an appreciative smile aimed at me, June refilled my champagne glass for the fourth time. The bubbly alcohol helped dissipate part of my discomfort, and I felt more at ease amongst Carter's entourage.

I forced an upward curl back to my lips as my heart continued to thunder inside my rib cage.

As more alcohol was consumed and the hours ticked by, the chatter in the suite grew louder—and so did my heartbeat.

Carter placed his hand on my thigh, and I gasped, sucking in a breath. Dizziness blurred my senses, and flutters danced in my belly. I squeezed my legs together, trying to ease the ache building up inside me.

Deep in conversation with Tim, his tour manager, about a show scheduled in Berlin next summer, Carter looked handsome with his closely shaven jaw—leaving only stubble—shorter hair, a relaxed stance, a look I'd only seen on him for the first time this afternoon. He turned and flashed me a grin. A panty-melting grin. One no girl in her right mind could ever resist. His eyes burned holes into my skin, and his fingers dug deeper into my flesh.

I grinned back, and some of the tension in my back left me.

He traced lazy circles on my bare flesh with his thumb, just above my knee, and I scooted closer, his touch intoxicating.

My insides melted. I drew in a deep breath, stifling the soft moan rising in my throat.

The pulse in his neck throbbed. Carter tried to act nonchalant, but his body's responses gave him away. His palm, the one still attached to my thigh, got clammy. He scraped the other through his hair every few minutes, and a tightness appeared around his eyes. The air in the room heated another few degrees. I wasn't sure how to act with all these people around. His hand moved higher. I chewed on my lower lip to distract myself from writhing under his hold. Whatever game he was playing, he made me feel like the ultimate goal, the endgame, the coveted prize. I struggled to stay put, wanting more. More of this…more of him.

June sat beside me, and I welcomed the distraction. We chatted about her last trip to Europe and exchanged numbers. Around midnight, she rose to her feet and picked up her things. "I need to go, y'all. My munchkin, tomorrow morning, won't care if her mama got less than five hours of sleep." She hugged everyone in the room. When she reached Carter, she whispered something to him that brought an upward curve to his lips. I stood as she inched closer and hugged me. "April, I hope to see more of you soon. I don't know what you've done to this grumpy fellow," she pointed her thumb at Carter, "but I haven't seen him smile like this in a very long time. Whatever your secret power is, please don't stop. He's usually much more withdrawn after a show. I'm glad we're good." She winked, and her words touched my heart.

First Dahlia. Now her.

Truth be told, I had no clue what they both meant. Carter and I weren't even dating. For all I knew, I left him with a serious case of blue balls after our make-out session that morning in my cabin when I locked myself out after the hot tub incident.

We were friends with *no* benefits. Two people enjoying each other's company without the complications of sex or a relationship.

Around one-thirty in the morning, everybody left the suite, and Carter and I ended up alone in the dimly lit room.

His face turned serious after his last guests walked out. The lightness in his features faded, and his lips pressed into a thin line.

Did I piss him off somehow? Was I clingy or awkward tonight? No. I got along with everyone, and he seemed to like having me around. Chasing away the crippling thought, I waited for him to say something. A second later, his melted-steel irises darkened, and his heated gaze took me hostage. A chill ran through me under the intensity of his stare.

I held my breath. The air between us crackled with sexual tension.

A few feet separated us, yet I stood frozen, fingers twisted together, unsure what to do

In four strides, Carter closed the distance between us and crashed his mouth on mine, his lips soft and demanding. Startled, I almost lost my balance. His strong arms wound around me, holding me against his firm chest. No matter how much I wanted to resist him, I failed. Instead, I indulged in his kiss, parting my lips to welcome him, forgetting everything. Where I stood. What day it was. What decade we lived in. I combusted inside out, dissolving under his touch. He cupped a breast over my dress with his hand, and I almost lost it. My nipples hardened into stiff peaks, begging to be taken care of. His tongue tangoed with mine, stealing my breath away. My entire body tingled. With a hand around his nape, I pulled him to me, wishing no more space existed between us.

Could I catch fire from just a kiss?

The moans that left my mouth sounded foreign. This time I didn't silence them.

A force stronger than me had taken over my whole being. At this moment, he could consume me, and I wouldn't put up a fight.

I yelped when he grabbed my ass cheeks and lifted me until my legs could circle his waist. My dress bunched up around my hips, and Carter ground against me, leaving me panting and aching, needy and lusty. The outline of his manhood sent thunderbolts throughout me. I raked his muscular back over his shirt with my fingernails, and shivers woke up in their wake.

He ran his tongue along my collarbone and bit the skin of my neck softly.

Whimpers passed my lips, and I arched my back, about to ignite from too much sensory overload.

I rubbed myself against him, needing friction to tame the fire burning inside me.

My panties, already soaked, stuck to my flesh. I shivered under the pads of Carter's fingers, arching my back to allow him more space to devour my skin.

Desire throbbed deep in my core, and a throaty moan escaped my mouth. My dress slid down my arms and exposed my bare chest. It had a low-cut back, and wearing a bra hadn't been an option. His primal growl pulsed through me and confirmed I had made the right choice when I chose this outfit earlier. Scorching heat emanated from the man facing me. He licked one of my hardened nipples, rolling and sucking the dark-pink tip with tenderness and hunger. He assaulted the second nipple with his mouth, giving it the same delicate yet greedy attention.

Breathless and never letting go of me, Carter stepped further into the room until he landed on the loveseat by the window with my legs still wound around him. Our mouths reconnected, our tongues restless and our lips starving.

His short stubble rubbed against the sensitive flesh of my cheeks, no doubt marking me.

He drew a line with his finger over the crotch of my black lace panties, tracing the seam between my thighs. "God, you're so wet."

I swallowed hard, torn between crying from pleasure and turning into a puddle in his hands. I let my head fall back, drawing his attention to my neck once again.

With his other hand, he cradled my face, fingers tracing my jaw, his kisses a mix of intensity and tenderness. He took his time to cherish my mouth with his, tasting every corner. My toes curled, and my body hummed under the devoted attention.

"All night, the sight of you in this dress was fucking torture. I can't wait to taste all of you, Fairy." He pushed my drenched panties to the side and grazed my clit with his thumb. I quivered, using his shoulders to ground me.

"Please…I—" I couldn't even form a coherent sentence anymore. "Don't stop."

My hips rolled in sync with his hand, desperate for his fingers to dive inside me and put out the fire burning me alive.

"Fuck, you're gorgeous." He tugged at my lower lip with his teeth, then licked the sting with his tongue.

I purred, unable to contain the sounds spilling from my lips as sensations swirled inside me.

Yearning to feel him too, I shifted one hand downward and rubbed him over the fabric of his pants. His hard-on throbbed under my touch, begging to be freed. I accelerated the up-and-down motion, relishing each jolt of his thick erection against my palm.

His breathing caught, and the playfulness vanished from his face. He increased the pace of his fingers, rubbing my clit in delicious circles.

Desperate to feel his skin on mine and unable to wait any longer, I peeled his shirt off over his head, not bothering with the buttons. I traced the ripped muscles of his chest and abs with my hands. I didn't have enough fingers to explore each inch of his tanned skin the way I wanted to.

In one swift movement, Carter lifted me from him and laid me on my back. I gasped before framing his face with my hands and pulling him down on me. Our tongues battled for the upper hand. He positioned himself on top of me, supporting his weight with his stretched arms.

We were both panting, breathing hard, and hungry for each other.

Carter lowered himself, his hard chest pressing against my soft breasts.

Every cell in me shuddered with an ache only he could quench.

He entangled one of his hands in my hair, and I tilted my head up when he sucked on the flesh of my neck.

Lifting myself up on my elbows, I pushed him back just enough to be able to unbuckle his belt. We both couldn't take our eyes off my fingers as the strap glided through the loops when I tugged on the other end.

Carter kneaded one naked breast, his mouth returning to mine.

I licked the length of his jaw, nipping his earlobe and reaching for the button of his dark jeans.

A low, guttural growl rumbled in his throat, drowning out the sound of our harsh breathing.

I pushed a hand inside his boxer briefs, the warmth of his length seeping into my palm.

Before I could stroke him the way I had been dreaming of, he leaned back and stopped me with a hand. His thickness quivered under my fingers.

"April. Stop." He sounded breathless. "I-I don't want us to rush this. Whatever this…us…is, I don't want to ruin it."

Wait. What? I released him and blinked, unsure if I heard him right. Was he pushing me away? My cheeks burned, and my breath hitched.

The expression on his face, something that said *I can't believe I'm doing this, but I have to*, told me this was indeed not a joke.

I had no idea how to react. Part of me wanted to laugh, thinking he was messing with me, while another part wanted to cry, feeling humiliation creeping in.

I couldn't tell whether I should be pissed or proud that Carter was acting like a decent guy. Right now, I didn't want a decent guy, though—I wanted a man. Hard and powerful. Passionate and insatiable. Wild and unstoppable. And I wanted the sex. Dirty and animalistic with a side of tenderness.

"Ruin it?" Trying to catch my breath, I could barely utter the words. Carter's index finger traveled the length of my lips, and I sucked on the tip, my vision already blurry from the building desire. "Tell me you're kidding," I said through the whimper I couldn't keep inside. Gosh, I wanted him to take me in every possible way, right now, until I was completely satiated.

In the last few hours, my desire for him had reached new heights. That was saying a lot, considering I'd been yearning for him since the first time our eyes met. Each day, my need for him grew stronger. Every time our skin touched, my longing became harder to conceal. Inside, I was a ticking time bomb.

Right now, it was a miracle I still had any restraint left after ceding control to the rock star who had been moments away from ravaging me.

My pulse throbbed between my legs, the ache refusing to be put out.

Every inch of me trembled at the thought that I might not come undone tonight. I was wound so tightly that I could detonate at any second.

Every bit of me craved Carter's intimate touch—his caresses, his love—but the resolve I could read on his face acted like a cold shower.

He isn't kidding when he said we should stop. This wasn't a joke.

With a strong grip around my body, he lifted me to straddle him once more, the feel of his big, calloused hands on my soft skin almost enough to bring me over the edge. His hooded eyes sucked me in.

I wanted to beg him to keep going, to continue what we were doing, but I knew it would be futile.

He released me and raked his fingers through his disheveled hair.

Still aroused, I blew out a shuddering breath at the sexiness of his gesture.

"Don't be upset. Fuck, I can't believe I'm doing this. I…I must be crazy. No one has ever affected me the way you do, April. I can't…I can't just fuck you and forget all about it. Please. End me already." He closed his eyes again and breathed through his mouth as if his body and mind were at odds with each other.

He dragged a hand over his face and with a shake of his head, opened his eyes. We stared at each other for a moment.

"April, this…you…me…us… You must be certain this is what you want. Because once you're in, we won't be able to hide forever, and you must agree to all that it means to be with me. I know it's unfair to both of us, but it's my reality. If we do this, it won't be a one-time thing because I'll never be able to stop. I'm fucking sorry. I want you so bad right now…all of you. Everything you're willing to give me. You could never be just a fuck. Not to me. This would be wrong, and I would never go through with it if that was what you wanted." He dropped his head in the crook of my neck. "Not sure my dick will ever forgive me for this. I hope your pussy will."

When his attention returned to my face, his lips quivered, and he claimed my mouth. In slow motion, he curled his hands around my nape, and he kissed me as if it could somehow soothe him, but also his fears and his doubts.

I rested my forehead against his, panting.

"Pixie, I want to bury my face between your thighs so

bad. The taste of you is all I'll ever need to stay alive. I'm starving."

How could his words hit me right where they felt good? Where I longed for him?

"Don't shut me out." I nipped his lower lip. "We both need this. Let's be bad tonight. We'll talk tomorrow. We don't have to decide everything right now."

Carter leaned further back, putting more distance between us, stealing the heat that had been swirling between us, and shook his head. "Can't. It's all or nothing."

A lump dissolved down my throat. "You serious?"

He nodded and offered me a tiny shrug. "I'm not playing the field. Not interested."

"Wow. And some people think you're a womanizer who only cares about getting laid, whatever be the consequences."

A soft grin grazed his lips, and he moved closer, winding his arms around me. With the gentleness I had come to associate with him, he peppered kisses on my eyelids, his lips warm and soft.

When we stared at each other, he combed my hair back with his fingers, the small gesture sending a flock of butterflies to my stomach. With his free hand, he adjusted the crotch of his jeans, a painful glaze shining in his eyes, his erection straining at the seams.

I sighed. *What a waste.* With a tentative gesture forward, I caressed the bare skin of his torso, the need to touch him still running high inside me, and met his eyes. "Thank you…for tonight. And for the song. *My* song. I still can't believe it."

"April, you inspire me in so many ways. If only you knew…"

We sat there for a moment, breathing each other in,

my head pressing against his bare chest, his hands playing with the waves of my hair.

After a while, I inhaled some courage. "I should go."

He nodded, and we both moved to our feet, fixing our clothes. After putting his shirt back on and tucking his erection back into his pants, Carter escorted me to my suite. An air of sweet torture settled over us. I ached to slide my palm into his, yet I had no idea how to navigate this new status of our relationship—or lack thereof.

I unlocked the door to my suite, but before I could hide inside my room and freak out with no witnesses around, his mouth found mine, and his teeth toyed with my bottom lip for a second, making me tingly and horny for him all over again. I pushed him back with both hands. "Go. Now." My tone betrayed the smile in my voice.

Carter walked backward, a huge grin plastered on his face, his eyes capturing mine, refusing to let me go. I cupped my chest with both hands, calming the pounding of my overexcited heart.

Once in my suite, I pressed my back against the door and let go of the air I'd been holding in my lungs for far too long.

I smiled at the realization.

Tonight, Carter Hills had rocked my world…several times. My night had been nothing like I imagined it would be. Exceptional in so many ways, I didn't have enough words to describe it

With resolve in my steps, I walked to the bedroom, needing a release more than ever. Where was my vibrator when I needed it? Without a care in the world about how late it was, I filled the giant bathtub, too big for just one person, and sank my pulsing body into the warm water. I itched to invite Carter over, but he made it clear. This wouldn't happen tonight. Once again, I was condemned to pleasuring myself without any outside help. I closed my eyes, and the images of his lips on mine took over. I felt his hands on my breasts and sucked in a breath. A tidal wave of pleasure rocked my body. The temperature of the water rose. My fingers found my tight channel and slid in and out of me with ease. My skin vibrated with need. Damp heat filled my lower belly. I out soft, breathy cries, unable to keep all my arousal locked inside.

Less than a minute later, I was panting, recovering from the climax that had reduced my body to jelly. This—bringing myself to orgasm—wasn't enough anymore. I craved the real thing. The flesh. The shivers. The kisses. The man. "Carter Hills, put me out of my misery already," I whispered, my pulse deafening me as a new wave of desire crashed over me.

———

I woke up with an untamable grin on my face. Whatever I did, shower, make tea, or meditate, that grin refused to wash away.

My song.

From the moment I pried my eyes open, I tried to sing it from memory, but I failed. I could only hum the melody. Sort of.

With one goal in mind, to listen to it again, I clicked the link my best friend had sent me last night, surprised at myself for having resisted watching it for so long.

Goose bumps blossomed all over my skin when the first words left Carter's mouth. This time, I listened to each verse. Butterflies took off in my stomach. Nobody had ever done something as huge as writing a song for me before. A song about *me*. The chorus started, and it took all my inner strength not to cry right there.

Girl, I just want you to know
There's no one else like you
You are the sunshine in my
    storms
You color my night sky
You are the star I wish upon
    every night
You hold my heart, I'll never
    let you go
Babe, I'm blind without you.

Flashes of last night surged through my mind.

How devilishly delicious HN looked on that stage with his guitar.

How his voice soothed every fiber of me, down to the dark corner of my soul.

How every chord he played made my heart vibrate.

How his lips tasted.

The sequin dress, folded on a chair, reminded me the night hadn't been a dream after all. I held both hands to my heart, still overwhelmed with emotions.

A soft knock on my door disturbed my daydream.

I pressed pause on my phone and tripped over my feet, trying to get to the door. Frozen for a second, I broke out into a loud laugh when my eyes locked on Carter standing in the hallway. The sight of him rendered me speechless.

He stood there with two disposable teacups in his hands, wearing baggy cargo pants in a questionable shade of beige, a puffer lime-green jacket, a mustard-yellow beanie, and some oversized shades. My eyes overflowed with tears, and I patted the moisture under my eyes with my fingertips. "Ohmygod, HN, Halloween was months ago. What is this?"

His gaze licked me from head to toe, lingering on my

breasts, showcased in my tight white shirt. My laughter died in my throat. Did I forget to put on a bra? I cupped my chest, just to make sure. No. I didn't. No clothing mishap. Carter swallowed before meeting my eyes again. I clamped my legs shut and exhaled. His heady gaze ignited flames that ran the length of my spine.

I blinked, tongue-tied.

I stopped fondling myself, dropped my hands, and took a calming breath.

"Good morning to you too, Fairy. Today, I'm giving you a tour of my city. I don't want us to be chased down, so I decided we'd get creative and dress up for the occasion." Carter walked in with resolute steps and handed me a bag full of equally mismatched clothes.

"You can keep your jeans and shoes on, but you must hide your pink hair. I'm sorry. I love it. Very much. But if we don't want to be recognized, we must play the part. Today we'll be tourists. It's a shame to hide this shirt, though. Perhaps we should stay in."

His gaze lowered to my breasts again, and I snapped my fingers. "Eyes up here, Country Boy."

He shrugged, and his lips curved into an irresistible boyish grin as he raised his eyes.

"Not a chance. I've been dying to discover the city. Stop ogling me."

Carter pushed his bottom lip out, pouting, but it didn't last. "Go get ready. I'll wait in the living room." He closed the door after him with a kick. His security details, two men I saw for the first time yesterday, stayed behind in the hallway, dressed in street clothes.

Astonished and unable to utter any coherent words, I disappeared down the hallway into the bathroom.

"Usually, we don't have to hide in Nashville. People let us be. But after last night's show, my team thinks I made the matter worse instead of helping it." Carter was talking about my song, his voice echoing through the hotel suite. He continued, his tone changing to a more serious one. "I'm sorry you were brought into this. Again. I never meant for you to be drawn into this mess. The song meant a lot to me, and I thought you'd like it too. It was an *in the heat of the moment* thing, and I didn't think it through."

I came out of the bathroom, dressed in my new clothes, only to be met with the sad expression on his face when I stepped into the living room. His hands were stuffed in his jacket pockets—a gesture he did when he was either uncomfortable or trying to act detached—and his head hung low. My pulse rattled at this sight. I treaded through the room and placed a hand on his forearm.

"I know you didn't mean to. It's okay. We'll deal with it. I'm sure some young actress will forget to put panties on or a wannabe rock star will trash a hotel room or burn down a house. Soon enough, we'll be old news." I offered him a reassuring smile. "And the song means everything to me. Never apologize for it, okay? This is the best gift I've ever received." I rose on my tiptoes and dropped a kiss on his cheek.

The worry lines around his eyes smoothed. "Are you sure? People will make up all kinds of stories about us... About you..."

"How bad can it be?"

His face darkened, and he opened his mouth to say something, but I silenced him with a finger pressed against his lips. "We'll deal with it later. Now tell me who picked up these horrible outfits."

Genuine amusement lit up his face, replacing the somber expression. "June. She said she had a blast selecting each piece for us. She knew your size and let her imagination run wild. I bet her daughter is to blame. That kid has the weirdest taste. She's heartless, I'm telling you. She has something against me and made it personal." He flashed his pearly whites. "Anyway, June said she got inspired."

His manager or personal assistant, or whatever she was, chose a large purple knitted sweater for me, white aviator shades, a matching purple beanie to hide my pink strands, a long mustard-yellow scarf, the same shade as Carter's hat, and a sleeveless royal-blue puffer vest.

Carter gave me a slow once-over, and holding the lapel of my vest, he smirked—a giant, wild smirk. "Even when it looks like you got dressed in the dark, you still look beautiful, Fairy."

I curtsied, and admiring ourselves in the full-length mirror, we chuckled together. Each expression of joy I drew from him felt like a small victory.

Still giggling and looking ridiculous, I followed HN to the elevator. Feeling brave, I inhaled and slid my hand into his. He intertwined our fingers and looked at me. No, looked into me. In that small gesture, he said much more than his words ever could. My heart doubled in size, and prickles woke up inside me. I stopped breathing as the elevator doors closed, and my pulse spiked with a mix of anticipation and excitement.

Chapter 20
Carter

April and I played tourists for the rest of the day. We ate sweet potato pancakes at this little place mostly visited by locals, far from the tourist hot spots, where I knew we wouldn't be disturbed, and strolled through Centennial Park.

After lunch, we sauntered across Music Row. "I recorded my very first album here," I said, pointing to a little craftsman powder-blue house with white columns.

"With your band?"

"Yeah, before we all went our separate ways." I stifled a laugh as memories flooded my mind. "God, we were just kids… It seems like a lifetime ago."

Later, we hopped into one of those golf carts that transport tourists all over the city.

"Broadway and Fifth, please," I asked the elderly man who took it upon himself to give us a tour. April listened to everything he said, asking questions. The next thing I knew, they were talking about the man's grandchildren, and he was showing her pictures on his phone. April gave him her full attention, and I watched the exchange in silence, a wide smile stretching my lips.

"So, where are y'all from?" he asked.

"Georgia," April answered without missing a beat. "We're in town for the weekend. Huge fans of country music here." She elbowed me in the ribs.

"Sure," I said, scratching the side of my head. "The biggest fans."

She smirked and brought her attention back to our tour guide, squeezing my arm with her small hand.

The man dropped us in front of the Ryman Auditorium. "Y'all enjoy your trip."

"Frank, tell Rosa to try frankincense essential oil for her arthritis. It should help. She can contact me if she has questions. You have my contact info in your phone."

Who was Rosa? His wife? If so, when did April have the time to learn about our tour guide's spouse and her health? Lost in my daydream, I hadn't paid attention to much they said.

"Will do." Frank turned around to face me. "Take good care of your wife, sir, she's a keeper." He winked, and I stopped in my tracks. *Wife?* How much did I miss?

At lunchtime, we grabbed vegan tacos from a food truck on Second and traipsed down Broadway. The entire time, April's face sparkled.

"All the bars are already open." This was more an affirmation than a question. Even at this time of the day, bands were playing live music. "Did you ever play here?" she asked me, pivoting on her heels until we faced each other. I nodded. April watched me, and I had a hard time reading her eyes through those shades.

My mouth went dry as echoes of the past consumed me.

"I wish I'd heard you play back then." She rose on her tiptoes and brushed her lips over mine, not quite kissing me. We breathed the same air, and I got dizzy.

I locked my arms around her waist, and I drew her toward me. "Let's hang out here for a while."

She turned and pressed her back to my front. I gripped her waist, and she swayed her hips to an old Garth Brooks hit as we listened to the cover band through a large, garage-door–style window from the sidewalk. Pixie couldn't miss how much I loved having her in my arms. My appreciation pressed firmly against her lower back.

I'd spent years shielding my heart, keeping it unreachable. Why was it so different with her? Why did I feel like opening up to her, spilling all my secrets, including the one that had been eating me alive for a long time?

"Riley and my friend Tucker own this place." I pointed to the bar across the street. "It's the hottest spot in town. And Jeff used to work there." I motioned to the establishment right next to it.

"I thought he was in the army."

"Yeah. But he moved here after high school. He dropped out of college after a few months and started working there instead. He's the reason we got signed at eighteen to a big label. He made some contacts, and one day, Riley came to see us play. The rest is history."

"Wow. Were you guys close? I've always wondered what it'd be like to have siblings."

Growing up, my brother and I got ourselves into impossible situations more times than I could recount. Up until his death, Dahlia and he were my two best friends.

"There was this time. When I was about nine years old...I think. We built a soapbox out of the junk we found in our neighbor's backyard. We used the little money we had, the money we earned mostly from doing chores, to buy paint because we wanted our cart to look fierce. For two months, we hid our secret project under a tarp in the back of the garage. Our parents were clueless about it…or rather, we thought they were. Anyway, we worked on it for weeks. It helped that Jeff was good with tools. Proud, we took our soapbox out for a road test, wearing helmets and elbow pads. To this day, I'm still grateful we did.

"I remember that day perfectly. The sun was shining high and glowing in the blue sky. Jeff sat in the front, both hands on the old, rusty trash can lid serving as a steering wheel. He told me to hold on tight as I sat behind him, my little arms wrapped around his waist. *Don't be nervous, Carter,* he said, trying to reassure me in his big brother way. We wheeled down the hill at high speed. I remember how I felt. Free. Invincible. Excited. I remember the breeze on my skin and messing up my hair. We laughed the whole time. Until we realized, too late, we forgot to install some sort of brake on our little cart. One wheel broke, and the soapbox tipped over, ejecting us. Jeff ended up with a broken arm, and I broke two ribs and chafed the skin of my back on the pavement." I smiled. "That minute of freedom was worth every broken bone and every burn."

April's grip tightened on my forearm. "Ohmygod. Did you get grounded? What happened afterward?"

"Wait, that's the best part. Once we both fully recovered from our injuries, our dad surprised us with an improved version of our soapbox. He'd fixed it and added two sets of brakes, just in case. Jeff and I entered the town's annual derby competition at the end of the summer, and we finished in second place."

"That's amazing. I would've loved to witness the troublesome Hills brothers at that age. I missed the action growing up. Nana wasn't much of an adrenaline junkie or a prankster."

"Ask Dahlia. I'm surprised our parents didn't die from children-induced stress."

"Carter, I'm sorry Jeff is gone."

I inhaled a shaky breath. "Me too."

She pivoted and planted a kiss on my lips, so soft it freed me from years of pain. The twinkle in her eyes glued back together more pieces of my heart that'd been hanging around in my chest for years. Pieces I thought were lost forever. April had this way of making everything in my life better. Even my sorrows.

In Centennial Park earlier, I'd kissed her under a tree. I couldn't resist. She made all these cute sounds whenever I showed her something new, and it turned me on. Big time. When her eyes flared, I knew she saw something exciting. When she scrunched up her nose, something was bothering her. A lopsided smile meant she wasn't sure. Without a word, I could read her like an open book. I'd pushed her against the trunk of a willow tree, caging her with my arms, and the hunter side of me had taken control, craving to claim her as mine. Our mouths fused. Hungry. Yearning. Desperate. She whispered my name, and my chest cavity expanded to make room for my swollen heart. Her lips on mine deprived my brain of oxygen. Every lap of her tongue against mine reminded me how stupid I had been last night to push her away instead of holding on to her like I should have. Time stopped. April liquified in my arms, and I never wanted to let her go.

We continued our stroll down Broadway, heading toward the Cumberland River.

"The other day, you said you didn't know if you were supposed to be an author. When you were little, what was your dream job?"

She lifted our joined hands and brushed my knuckles with the pad of her thumb. "It's silly. I always knew I wanted to be a writer. When I was little, I was obsessed with poetry. Not sure I could've made a living out of it, though, so I picked journalism as a major in college. Seemed like a smarter choice at the time." She shrugged.

"Do you want to be a journalist? Right here, right now, tell me the truth."

"Hell, no. I prefer writing fun things. Creating worlds…from scratch."

"Ever wrote song lyrics?"

She stopped in her tracks and stared at me, her lips parted and her eyes big.

"It's a bit like writing poetry. You should give it a try. Just a thought."

She stayed silent as if what I'd asked required some in-depth analysis. As if I'd spoken a different language. Or I'd opened a door she never knew existed before.

"If you're interested, I know a person who does that for a living. He's an ass but a charming one. Think about it." I kissed her still-open mouth and winked.

April didn't say anything. I could probably see the gears working in her head if I looked close enough. Her eyes were focused. Her lips slightly twisted. Her nose wrin-kled. She was processing my words and looked fucking adorable.

Halfway down the pedestrian bridge, Fairy fished her phone out of her purse and stepped on a concrete bench, now standing as tall as me. "Scoot closer, HN, I want a picture. This is one of those days I want to remember forever." She snapped pictures of us, our back to the Cumberland River, her lips on my cheek, her eyes as bright as fireworks on the Fourth of July.

My gaze landed on her face as she scrolled through the

photos she'd just taken. My clothes felt too tight and itchy. I removed my beanie and ran a hand through my hair. *Breathe in. Breathe out.*

April jumped into my arms to kiss me just as we were about to climb into my truck and drive back home. *Home.* Green Mountain. The cabin. Anywhere with her felt like home.

"Thanks for everything, HN. It's like we spent the last two days in a snow globe where everything is magical."

I dipped my head, and our foreheads met. The air us seemed charged with a million tiny sparks. I said nothing, struggling to keep my hands to myself—and other parts of my body too. At the moment, I wished I could bend her over the hood and thrust into her until neither of us could stand upright.

On the ride back, we entwined our fingers, and I traced circles on her palm with my thumb, fully aware of each movement.

"Tell me. Any crazy fan stories?" Her eyes flashed with interest. "Any women who threw their panties at you mid-show?"

I mirrored her grin. "Let's see... Where should I begin...? There was this one guy who bypassed the security, way back when I bought my first house, and ended up naked in my bed. Somehow, he knew when I'd be back from tour and wanted to surprise me."

April's hand flew to her mouth as she tried to suppress a laugh. "Ugh, I would have freaked out."

"It's was pretty memorable. Another time, a guy convinced everyone he was my half-brother and landed a backstage pass, giving him access to places he shouldn't have. He followed me into the green room and threatened me with a blade."

Her eyes nearly popped out of her head. "You're not joking?"

"Nah. I wish. I have funny stories too." I told her all about the girl who got my face tattooed on her chest and the one who wore no panties when she interviewed me on live TV, flashing me her hairy pussy the entire time.

"It's kinda gross. How did you keep a straight face?"

"No idea. I was young, and let's just say it took a long time for my brain to erase the images of that day."

We stopped for gas, and April bought the biggest assortment of snacks I'd ever indulged in. And slushies.

For the next hundred miles, we talked about everything and nothing, our conversation flowing effortlessly. Even the silences felt comfortable. I had no idea what to make of the familiarity settling between us.

Two hours in, she fell asleep, slumped against my side. The corner of my lips lifted as I pressed a gentle kiss to the crown of her head. If only I could drive all night and never have to wake her, knowing we shared this moment of peace together, I'd be a content man. Left alone with nothing but my thoughts and the soft sound of her breathing, my mind wandered into uncharted territories. Places I tended to avoid. Doubts crept in slowly, occupying the corners of my mind where the past still lingered. My throat tightened as memories swept by, and each breath became heavier. Deep inside, fear bubbled, threatening to surface and suffocate me. Reservations about my burgeoning emotions teetered on the edge, threatening to derail the fragile connection simmering between us. Lust. Desire. Trust. Happiness.

I didn't know if I could trust what I was feeling at the moment. Pixie was creating chaos in my life, upsetting the twisted balance I had set for myself a few months ago. Looking at her, I knew she wasn't the typical woman you banged on the side and left behind with the bedsheets still covered in hot sweat. She was a girl you planned a future with. A keeper—like our tour guide had said. A girl you introduced to your parents. The kind of woman you'd see yourself married to. The one you'd never forget or get over when she stepped out of your life.

The one you'd give forever to.

This relationship needed time to blossom and lots of patience. Did I have that in me? Besides, the attraction between us was an inferno, threatening to leave only ashes behind. Such an attraction could be a dangerous game. How hadn't I realized it sooner? I was sinking in too deep, my thoughts consumed by her. After my last experience, how had I removed the icy walls around my heart so easily? Now my organ longed to beat only to her rhythm. Even the idea of not being able to spend days without feeling her skin on mine or getting a whiff of her lavender perfume had become unbearable. She was seizing my control, and I was willing to give up my freedom for her. How did that happen? When did I drop my guard down long enough to let a woman get close to me all over again?

I strangled the steering wheel, my knuckles turning white and my palms clammy. No, I shouldn't bear feelings for the woman sitting next to me. Not only did it not make sense, but it was too much too fast. I had escaped my last relationship not so long ago. Was I ready to dive right back into another one? With no safety net? And with a trusting heart?

Just the thought of everything that could go wrong sent my heart into a chaotic tempo. The cab of my truck grew smaller, stealing all the viable oxygen and suffocating me. I was insane. How could I risk another heartbreak? Didn't I learn my lesson the last time? Didn't I suffer enough already?

A little voice in my head kept telling me to give it a shot. To have faith that this could lead to something amazing.

April stirred in her sleep, forcing my attention back to her. Her relaxed features made her look younger. When we first met, I had noticed the shadow lingering in her eyes. After she told me about her past, her family, I could tell that was what had toughened her up. Right now, the lines around her eyes were invisible, and she looked at peace. If only I could swallow her worries with one kiss. And then fill her with unfaltering happiness with every other one. I'd kiss her every day to make that happen.

I parked my truck in the driveway and turned the engine off but made no move to get out as I watched her sleep a bit longer.

Her eyes fluttered open and landed on me. "Hey," she said.

"Hey."

"How long was I out?"

I shrugged. "An hour maybe."

Her face wrinkled as she studied me. "Are you okay?"

I swallowed my discomfort and nodded. "Yeah. Sure." Before she could gauge the uneasiness troubling me, I leaned over and kissed the back of her hand still connected to mine. "Come on, let's go inside."

The next morning, I woke up early. A train of yawns left my mouth. I grabbed the torn envelope I kept under my pillow. This was my demise. It used to be immaculate and white. Not anymore. It'd followed me all around the globe for years. I traced the faded black ink letters scribbled on the front. *Carter.* Dahlia's handwriting. And the answer to the one secret I'd been holding on to for years. The one neither of us had any certainty about. I turned it around between my fingers, took one last look at the sealed flap, and slid it back where it belonged.

Would I ever be able to open it? I blew out a shuddering breath. Not today. Over the years, I'd asked myself the exact same thing more times than I could remember.

After tossing and turning most of the night, unable to shush the voices in my head or go back to sleep, I got up. As much as I'd miss spending my day with April, I knew a day spent on my own would be a smarter choice. The intensity of my attraction for her had been troubling me all night, and it still did, even hours later. It played with all my insecurities. And scared the hell out of me. Fairy appeared in my life when I least expected it—when I had no plans to let anyone in again, not so soon after the disaster of my last relationship.

The idea she was sleeping a flight of stairs below me topped my anxiety. One side of me wanted her to move back to her place, while the other hoped she'd hang around and become mine. That she'd welcome me into her bed and never let me go. That she could be the long-lost piece of my heart I'd been looking for all my life.

I raked my fingers through my hair, and my pulse spiked dangerously.

Dressed in faded black sweatpants and a brown hoodie, I tiptoed downstairs and grabbed my car keys. With every step toward my truck, I prayed April stayed in bed, not feeling strong enough to face her right now. What would I even say to her? *Leave, but don't go? Stay, but I'm not ready for you? I want you, but I'm too scared?* My insides and my head were a scrambled mess. What I wished for and what I was ready for didn't seem to fit together anymore. Last night, on the drive back from

Nashville, as I watched her sleep, a chain had grown around my heart, squeezing it, each pull and twist more painful than the other. How could I feel something for a woman I had met just a few weeks ago? How had she slipped under my skin and into my heart so easily? The other day, Dahlia said I was falling for her, and at the time, I brushed it off. But what if her words spoke the truth?

April wasn't my ex. The two of them had nothing in common. The time spent together wasn't a game she played. A role she was auditioning for. She didn't make me feel like I owed her something…everything. A meal ticket to a scripted end. We were equals. Friends first.

Still, doubts lingered. Big, fat, persistent ones.

Was I so infatuated with her that I imagined things the way I hoped they'd be? I did that once, and it cost me my soul.

Panic froze my blood. Breathing became harder with each gulp of air.

Outside, the early morning was still bathed in darkness. Riled up, I didn't feel the cold winter breeze across my face.

Breathe in. Breathe out.

I bent in two, trying to quiet the voices in my head. The hand of steel crushing my heart. The rocks sitting on my chest and messing with my breathing.

My own doubts trapped me in. I'd loosened up for a few days, and now my closeness with April was tampering with all the rules I'd set for myself. And the fears of another failed relationship. One that was destined to crash once she went back to her life. And leave me behind.

The aftermath of our weekend in Nashville acted as a cold shower. Where was my self-control when I needed it?

As much as I was attracted to my smart and gorgeous

guest and wanted to see where this thing between us could go, I also feared it would end badly.

Every relationship in my life always does.

The only thing I had, for sure, was my career, even though Savannah tried to wreck it with all her fucking lies. Why did I tell April I wanted us to be serious the other night? Committed to each other? What was wrong with me? Seriously. Was I ready to be consumed by another human being? Again? April's heart was pure. Fame and money meant nothing to her. But would she ever be cut out to be part of a life like mine? Fucking fame. Always in the way.

Last night, on our way back here, she asked me, "Are you sure your people packed my dress? It's the nicest piece of clothing I've ever owned."

"You're attached to a dress?" I raised a brow, not sure I heard her right.

She offered me a timid smile. "Think what you want, Country Boy, but that dress is amazing. I love it."

That girl fell in love with a dress. A *dress*. A fucking piece of fabric with glitter.

My lips curled up at the memory. I'd never met anyone like her before.

How could a grown-up woman be in love with sequins and silk, no matter how amazing and tempting they looked on her?

She even insisted on paying for lunch yesterday. Except for Dahlia and my mother, no woman had ever offered to pay a bill in my company. Nope. Not once. Never happened.

People knew I had more money than I could spend in this lifetime. I never bragged about my wealth, but it was common knowledge. And they always took advantage.

Yesterday, even dressed in her ugly outfit as we played

tourists, I couldn't look away from the woman holding my dreams captive.

I hit the steering wheel with all my strength. *Fuck.*

This wasn't supposed to happen. In the short time we'd known each other, April had taken a front row seat in my life. She'd not only stolen my heart, but also my soul.

The realization hit me hard. My thoughts spiraled in my head. A new surge of panic spread through my being. Oxygen felt scarce when I took a big inhale that didn't fully reach my lungs.

With a hollowed-out chest, I drove to a house on the other side of town that I'd transformed into my escape place three years ago. Nobody knew about my secret hiding spot. Not even Dahlia.

It had an attached garage, making it easy for me to come and go without anyone getting a glimpse of me. The place consisted of a gym, a giant TV hanging on the wall, a small kitchen, an old and ugly, but comfortable, couch, a bathroom tinier than a closet, and a few guitars. No bedroom or fancy things. Basic necessities. A place to unwind. To let go of the things haunting me. It looked more like a teenager's basement than a grown man's hangout spot. Nobody would bother me here.

I parked my truck but didn't get out.

I wrote Desmond a quick text message.

ME

> Hey, it's me. When do you think you'll be able to fix the lock?

But then I stabbed the backspace button many times with my finger. What was I doing?

Did I really want April to go back to her own cabin? No. I wanted her in mine. With me.

Shit. I had no clue what to do. Spots appeared in my

vision. I knew the signs. Seconds later, I was hyperventilating, moving my head back and forth, massaging my temples with my fingertips to calm my overwhelmed mind. A cloud of darkness blanketed me. My blood turned to ice. My body craved to move, but I was frozen. *Breathe in. Breathe out.* My throat tightened. I choked, my eyes filling with tears.

After gathering my thoughts, I stumbled out of the SUV and changed into the workout clothes I kept in the trunk. The back of my eyes blazed with unshed tears as I hit the treadmill. My feet stomped on the running belt with a soft thump. I ran away from my life. And away from my fears. Until all my muscles burned and twitched from exhaustion. My legs weakened by the twelfth mile. My chest heaved. My breathing scorched my lungs. Drained out, I steadied myself against the wall to stretch my calves, quads, and hamstrings. Bent over at the knees, afraid I'd hurl even on an empty stomach, I inhaled slowly. The gears in my head sprinted. What was going on with me? Once the storm in me lessened, I chugged a purple sports drink I fetched from the refrigerator. The drenched fabric of my shirt stuck to my skin, and every inch of my flesh itched. With shaky hands, I peeled it off as if it were on fire.

I was trying hard not to lose it, but the more time passed, the more restless I felt.

My vision blurred.

My stomach grumbled, begging to be fed.

Sports drinks couldn't be considered food.

Desperate to silence my stomach and get over with it, I mixed a protein shake and gulped half in one gulp. I heaved as it went down. I paced the main floor, trying to do those stupid breathing exercises that were supposed to help me calm the fuck down. *Breathe in. Hold. Breathe out.*

Repeat. Doing my best Clayton Kershaw impression, I threw my half-drunk shake into the kitchen sink. The thick, dark-green liquid splattered the backsplash. I shrugged, turned around, and reached the two-car garage. My house-cleaning obsession just went out the window. My episode was worse than I first thought. Darkness thickened around me. It made me a prisoner of my own mind. Of my inner demons. I rubbed my eyes with the heels of my hands. The giant ball of knots filling my stomach made my breaths shorter. This was a fucking nightmare.

"Let go, Carter," I screamed at no one. "You can't embark on another relationship. Anyway, women always fail you." Why would April be different? My therapist would disagree with my assessment. We went over it multiple times in the past. I really believed I was over my mother's abandonment issues, but right now, blaming her was all I could do to soothe the pain surging inside me. After all, she was the first woman I loved unconditionally who'd turned her back on me. She was supposed to be in my corner, to cheer on me, but she quit. The wounds she sliced in my heart ran deeper than anyone could imagine. Myself included.

With a kick, I opened the door leading to the garage. Not risking any injuries, I wrapped my hands and slid them into the worn-out black boxing gloves I kept on a shelf. My muscles were still warm from the running, so without losing a second, I assaulted the heavily taped red punching bag hanging from a beam in the ceiling. I punched the motherfucker like I wanted to end its life. Like it had wronged me.

"Fuck you, Savannah Prince. For trying to ruin me." I punched the bag with a succession of uppercuts. "Take this, Mom. Take this, Dad." I punched harder. "You left me when I needed you the most." I dried off my tears, hot as flames, with my upper arm. "Jeff, take this because you abandoned me too. You were my best friend, and you left me all alone to fend for myself. And Dah. Take this. I loved you, and you always picked other guys over me. I never stood a chance because you never gave me one. All of you, go fuck yourself."

My chest and back dripped sweat. My body trembled from exhaustion.

It wasn't enough. It never was.

It did nothing to keep my mind from wandering back to my roommate. To erase my mixed feelings toward her.

An hour later, on the back deck, I stripped down and welcomed the cold air on my body. The icy breeze tingled my skin. I buried myself, bare-assed, in the hot tub and closed my eyes, stretching my arms on either side.

In the past, I drank my weight in whiskey whenever I needed to evade my mind. Now, except for exercising like a person on the edge of a mental breakdown, I didn't know what else to do.

I pictured April in my head. These days, I always fucking pictured her. Awake. Asleep. Laughing. Smiling. She occupied every free corner of my mind.

All the memories of her resurfaced.

My tongue tasting her flesh.

Her lips locked on mine.

The sultry dress she wore.

Her swaying hips when she listened to music.

Her tits bouncing when she jumped into my arms.

Her ass in those skinny jeans she loved so much.

The memory of her, nestled in my arms that morning in her cabin after we met, her body clenching around my fingers, haunted me even after all this time.

My cock sprang hard, and I pumped it in fast strokes, trying to get rid of the discomfort crippling me.

Yet, jerking off thinking about her was never enough. I tried. Countless times.

My entire body ached whenever I pictured her in my head.

I should've fucked her out of my system in Nashville when she begged me to. Perhaps that would've helped keep her off my mind. To keep me from craving her. April had crept under my skin the day we bantered in the woods and became much more than an itch to scratch.

She had become the center of my world. Fuck. *Fuck, fuck, fuck.*

I had no idea how to do this—how to be with her. That was what had thrown me into this anxiety-driven episode to begin with. I wasn't prone to anxiety when I was younger, but Jeff's death triggered something in me. After he passed away, the attacks began.

April. Why was just the thought of her powerful enough to send me spiraling down?

My head spun. I climbed out of the hot tub, the breeze too cold against my junk, reminding me I was naked. A shiver started in my toes and made its way to the back of my neck. My body shook, and I hurried back inside.

Showered and dressed, I jumped behind the wheel of my SUV and drove without purpose for hours, music blasting through the sound system, deafening my brain, preventing it from going to places I refused to venture.

Why couldn't I have a normal life?

April refused to reveal her identity as an author. If we were to be together, how would she deal with being recognized? Because no matter how hard I tried, people would know we were a couple. How much would she hate me after being exposed by the press vultures? Her face would be on magazine covers, her name whispered on gossip shows. Strangers would criticize her and everything she did, as if it were their birthright—like they were entitled to it because their own lives sucked and they were miserable.

A sour taste filled my mouth.

In a short amount of time, she had become precious to me. A true friend. And a woman I yearned to call my lover. That connection we shared, it couldn't be faked. Like we'd known each other forever, and we were just finally meeting again. Being offered a second chance at love.

My head swirled with unanswered questions.

Could I ever make both sides of my life fit together? The personal and the professional one. I wasn't willing to give up my music, but I wasn't ready to lose April either. Not before we explored what we could be.

My body hurt as if thousands of needles pricked my skin. The fog surrounding me wouldn't disappear. It enfolded me tighter. My lungs were compressed. I fought the urge to get to her. To explain where I stood and pray the celebrity side of my persona wouldn't scare her away. That it wouldn't stand between us once the novelty of a new relationship wore off.

What would happen when her stay in Green Mountain was over? Would she walk away like I never mattered to her and turn out to be a mirage in my life? Or would she be willing to put in the work—and sacrifice her anonymity —so we could be together in the long run?

Would she be a constant in my life or become someone I longed to hold on to, but essentially inaccessible?

Once again, Dahlia's words replayed in my head. *If what you two could have is worth it, give her some time to ease into the idea this is your life. If you move too fast, she'll run away.* My gut told me to move in, to seize my chance. I was tired of listening to everybody else's opinion about my own life. Dahlia. June. Riley. Carla. Savannah. Why couldn't *I* decide once and for all what was good for me? Sure, I had misjudged Savannah's motives, but I was already in a dark place back then—a far cry from the life I was leading these days.

All the scenarios my mind conjured left me dizzy and more confused than ever.

"I'm fucking tired of chasing happiness. Why can't it be simple?" I asked no one but myself.

More crippling thoughts paralyzed my brain.

What if April didn't want me as much as I wanted her? Chills worked through me at the idea.

Abandoned in the cup holder, my phone buzzed with a call. Followed by another one. My focus moved to the road in front of me, and I chose to ignore June's and Riley's attempts to reach out. Anyway, the race in my mind would prevent me from having a normal conversation with anyone.

It had been a long time since I'd had an episode that overwhelmed me so much, and once again, it involved my fear of losing someone I cared about. I itched to call Dr. Diaz, my therapist, but I wasn't in the mood to be asked existential questions I should have answers to but would take me forever to figure out. He would nod, waiting for me to fish out the truth from inside me. Probably something I subconsciously had decided to bury deep down. Then I'd cry, get angry, and cry again. Finally, he would say, "I'm proud of you, Carter. Now how can we fix this?" Yeah, been there, done that. No thanks. Not today.

The chime of an incoming text message grabbed my attention. Just the sight of April's name on my phone screen was enough to twist my troubled heart into another knot. In a swift gesture, I threw my device on the backseat. There, I could breathe easier and swallow the bubbling sobs down my throat. Turning up the volume of the radio,

I sang along to the tune playing until my voice became hoarse.

Around midnight, struggling to keep my eyes open and not ready to face April yet, I drove back to my secret spot and slouched down on the couch. I kicked my shoes off and shifted position, the tightness around my heart not releasing its deadly grip. Panic attacks had been my hell for years. For the longest time, I almost forgot they existed. Until they came back with a vengeance last year.

With shaky fingers, unable to leave her in the dark and not wanting her to worry about me, I shot April a text.

ME

Won't make it home tonight. Have some things to deal with.

Reclining back, I stretched my legs, crossed them at the ankles, and propped my head up on a pillow. With my eyes closed, I did some breathing exercises to silence the voices in my head. The ones that usually helped when nothing else did. My limbs grew heavier. The air in the room trapped me, making it hard to draw a full breath. With a flick of my wrist, I sent my phone sliding across the floor to resist glancing at it all night. A strangled cry of despair lodged in my throat as I fell into an agitated slumber, my body and mind restless.

Vivid dreams and nightmares disturbed my rest.

Chapter 21

April

Carter had disappeared at least twelve hours ago. Nobody had heard from him all day. My gaze drifted outside, the pink and orange stripes of sunset having long faded away.

When I had woken up this morning, I had been optimistic about the day. Even though the moment my lids opened, I made the decision not to push him into something we both might regret. I would draw the line at friendship. Maybe I'd agree to add some groping and kisses to the mix, but that would be it. I wasn't cut out for one-nighters. And sooner or later, it would haunt me if I dropped my guard and gave in to whatever my body vibrated for.

My heart felt lighter.

Yep, limits. They would help our situation stay in the friendship zone. With a new resolve to enjoy my time left here as much as possible, I had extracted myself from the comfort and warmth of my bed, ready to jumpstart my day.

After I had showered and dressed, I added makeup to my eyes and lips, putting a little effort into my appearance, aware HN and I would spend the day together.

Downstairs, there had been no trace of him. Cold had seeped through the cabin's walls, and a shiver ran through me. The fireplace hadn't been lit since we left for Nashville two days ago. Whenever Carter woke up first, he always made sure to start a fire to warm up the place.

When I couldn't find him anywhere, I had concluded that my housemate was still asleep.

Not wanting to wake him up, I had tiptoed around the place. In the kitchen, I had fed Bernice before filling the kettle with water to make some tea.

Once I had lit up a fire, I sat in front of it, hugging myself, until my body reached a comfortable temperature and the chills running through me dissolved.

It was around noon, when I went out for a short walk to clear my head, that I realized Carter's truck wasn't parked in the driveway. The massive black SUV was indeed missing from its usual spot. Carter had left. When? Why? I had no recollection of his telling me about a meeting or some other place he had to be first thing in the morning after we had returned from Nashville last night. Anyway, his whereabouts were none of my business. Carter owed me nothing. Yet, something felt off.

For the rest of the day, I had kept myself busy. The more I had focused on my work, the less Carter had infiltrated my thoughts and the less I had worried about his absence.

Eight-twenty-six.

It'd been a whole day since I heard from him, and here I was now, switching between worrying about him and working on my manuscript, moving chapters around. My mind wasn't into it. I looked at the time on my phone screen again in case I missed his call. In the last hour, I must have done that at least a dozen times.

Unable to focus anymore, I kept myself busy in the kitchen prepping dinner, praying that by the time I was done, he would show up. Wherever he was, I was sure Carter would like a home-cooked meal after his long day. I decided on broccoli and cashew pasta, a vegan recipe I found in one of his cookbooks. I rummaged through the pantry for cashews, but came up short. Maybe if I asked, he would stop by the grocery store on his way back, so I sent him a text.

He never replied.

I ended up making pasta with basil and tomatoes instead. For half an hour, I picked at my food before throwing it away, and I put the plate I fixed for him in the refrigerator and stuck a note on the plastic wrapper.

If you're hungry.
April

Exhausted from the weekend, I sat in the living room in front of the fireplace, with a glass of white wine and a novel. Time ticked, but Carter never made it home.

Around eleven, I climbed the stairs to my room. With one last glance at the driveway through the second-floor window, I concluded he wouldn't be coming home tonight.

After my nightly routine and from the comfort of my bed, I shot him one last message. My heart deflated in my chest when once again, he didn't reply. Whatever happened, I just prayed he was safe and sound. Lying on my back for the longest time, I replayed our weekend in my head, wondering what had changed since we came back. The whole day, no matter what I did, all my thoughts narrowed down to him and our amazing time in Nashville. Gone was the broody man I had met in the woods when I first got here. From what he confided in me, Carter had a complicated life, and he hid behind this angry version of himself when, in reality, there was nothing dark about him. He was not only genuinely nice and caring, but he also possessed a huge heart and could light up an entire town when he smiled. Something I could never get tired of being on the receiving end of.

With a hand, I pressed my chest over my heart, calming its tremors. I was not ready to go back to the real world once this vacation was over.

Even though I enjoyed how Carter made me feel and the undeniable hot and sizzling chemistry we shared, I couldn't envisage a future with him. We were much more alike than I could have ever imagined, but we belonged to two different worlds. He, the famous rock star recognized worldwide. I, the author hiding behind a pen name and refusing to let people in and have access to the real version of me.

The night of his concert, when we kissed, it felt as if the stars were realigning themselves for us. But after much consideration, indulging in the lust simmering between us would have been the wrong move. A bad decision. If we got attached to each other, how would I ever be able to walk away when my time in Green Mountain was up? I knew my heart—and all its weaknesses. Without hesitation, I could already tell Carter Hills was one of them.

When he said if we ever had sex, it wouldn't be a fling, I agreed. What he forgot to mention was what would happen if we ever gave in to the attraction we couldn't deny. I lived in Southern Georgia. He lived in Tennessee.

Our statuses weren't the only thing that would keep us apart. Distance would too.

Bernice came to snuggle in bed with me, her purr lulling me toward sleep. Soon sleep claimed me, and I wished Carter would come back to me in my dreams.

———

I woke up feeling like someone had sat on my chest all night. My shoulders and neck were strained. Wrapped in the white duvet, I stretched my arms and legs. On the nightstand, I grabbed my phone. Carter had sent me a cryptic text message around two in the morning.

CARTER

Won't make it home tonight. Have some things to deal with.

My insides constricted. Something was wrong. Anger surged through me. Was I stupid for being mad at him?

We were nothing more than friends, and I was acting silly. He had engagements and a rock star like him prob-ably had tons of meetings every week. He was a grown-ass man and didn't require my permission to do anything. I knew I shouldn't worry about his whereabouts, but a little voice in my head insisted he wasn't being himself. After breakfast, I went for a walk to clear my head. Last night, for the first time since I came to Green Mountain, I had insomnia. Entangled in my bed sheets from tossing and turning for hours, I often woke with a start, convinced I heard him coming in. How I didn't even notice my phone chime in the middle of the night when he texted me remained a mystery.

Bernice bunted my leg as soon as my feet touched the hardwood floor, begging me for food. "Girl, is that all you ever think about?" I lifted her into my arms, nuzzling her fur.

I was filling her bowl with kibbles when the sudden chime of the doorbell made me jump. Wondering who it could be, I rushed to the front door.

"Hi, April," Dahlia said once I cracked the door open. "Where's Carter?"

"Huh…not sure."

Jack glided through the open door. "Mama, look. Carter has a cat," he said, kicking off his boots.

I turned my head to face the boy and caught his jacket when he threw it off. "Her name is Bernice. I think she'd like to have a friend." The boy flashed me a two-thousand-dollar grin—reminding me of the man I was, despite myself, obsessed with—and ran after Bernice. I brought my attention back to Dahlia. "Sorry, you were saying?"

"Carter's not here. His truck is gone."

I peeked through the doorway to look past her even though, deep down, I knew that once again the black SUV wouldn't be parked in the driveway.

"I haven't seen him since the night we drove back from Nashville two days ago. He's been missing all day yesterday too."

"Did he say anything to you?"

I shook my head. "No. For all I know, it's not like him to leave without a word…or is it?"

Compassion filled her eyes. "It depends. Sometimes, Cart longs for some space from everything and everyone. Usually when he has to think or breathe alone. If I were you, I wouldn't worry. Unless he had stuff to deal with in Nashville. If that's the case, it would make sense he slept there."

"But we just came back from Nashville. Why would he have returned here only to go back?"

"You're right. I'm sure he'll turn up later and explain everything. Guess we'll come back some other time then."

"Can I help you with something?"

She shook her head. "No. Not really. Jack wanted to say hello."

"Huh, I—"

The little boy traipsed in our direction, Bernice in tow. "Look, April. We're best friends."

"I think Bernice loves you very much."

"Jack, we're leaving," Dahlia said. "Carter isn't here. We'll come back another day."

The boy crouched down and patted the cat's head. "Bye, Bernice." Without a warning, he hugged me next. "Thanks, April, for letting me play with your cat." He grinned, and I ruffled his hair.

Dahlia must have seen the puzzled look on my face because she angled her body until our faces met and whispered, "Don't worry, okay? He'll be back."

I nodded, unsure of what to say.

They both waved me goodbye as they drove away.

Standing on the front porch, I watched their taillights until they disappeared, wondering where Carter could have gone. It wasn't his style to leave without a note. Something felt off, now I was certain of it, and yet, I couldn't pinpoint what exactly.

Had I done something to scare him away? Had the whole Nashville thing confused him?

Fear prickled at my spine. The breath I was holding escaped me, and every piece of me prayed he was okay.

Still, I had a hunch something was wrong.

After forcing myself to eat a few bites of oatmeal, my appetite gone with the man I lived with, I got dressed and ventured outside. Close to the gate, I returned Saunders's call.

"Hey, Bubble Head. How is it going with your man?"

I sighed. "He's not my man."

"Did you guys have dirty sex the other night?"

I sighed. Again. "If you mean in Nashville, no, we didn't." I braced myself for the questions that would come.

"Did you panic?"

"Why do you think I'm the one to blame?"

"Well, are you? Tell me the truth." She lowered her voice in the caring tone she often used with me. "It's okay if you're scared. But it's also okay to let go."

"Saund. Stop. Carter was the one who stopped our make-out session. He said he didn't want us to be a fling and walked me back to my room."

"Blimey. You're kidding, right? You snogged, and he turned you away?"

I buried my face in my hand. "It wasn't—"

"He's a wanker. Anyway, I'm coming to Green Mountain on Friday night. I'll assess the situation with my own eyes. Your life is so entertaining."

"You're coming? For real?"

"Yep. Oh, crap. Can we talk later? I have an important call coming in. I'll text you. Bye." My best friend hung up before I could add another word.

I danced in place. Saunders would be here. On Friday. I squealed, unable to contain my joy.

My cabin's lock should be fixed by then, and I'd be out of Carter's way. A girls' weekend was everything I needed.

After lunch, Jill, my agent, called me back, and we went over the first half of my manuscript to discuss my work. Over the years, Jill and I had become friends. We chatted for a bit and brainstormed ideas. Once we hung up, I got back to work and rewrote some pages like we discussed and sent her two more chapters. With a mug of hot chocolate, I settled in the den, my fingers unstoppable on the keyboard. HN's disappearance wouldn't mess with my brain. I wouldn't let him. If he chose to leave, vanish, or ignore me, that was on him. I poured all my restlessness into my work. April Simmons, the author, was in full creative mode. Finally. A wide smile spread across my face. I hadn't felt this hopeful about writing in a long time.

Orange and purplish brush strokes filled the sky as the sun settled down for the night. Done for the day, I found myself alone in this *too big for one human being* cabin, with more knots tying my stomach. I put music on, songs whose lyrics I knew by heart, to keep my mind busy, and cleaned up the place, hoping Carter would come back tonight. Somehow, I missed him and the way he stared at me with interest—and lust. Like he cared. I missed the bantering, the nights by the fireplace sharing pieces of our past, his plant-based cooking, and how he asked my opinion whatever the subject. I even missed his grumbling over my music choices.

My phone chimed on the kitchen counter.

JUNE

April, any news from Carter?

I wrinkled my nose. What should I tell her? The truth sounded better than a blatant lie. I sighed, trying to put to sleep the flock of hyperactive butterflies in my belly.

ME

Not since late last night. Still not home.
Sorry.

She replied almost instantly.

JUNE

Keep me updated. Please.

ME

I will.

You think he's all right?

JUNE

I hope so. Sometimes he disappears for
days. Don't worry, he'll come back. It's his
way to unwind when he's overwhelmed. I'll
text you if I hear from him first.

ME

Okay. I'll keep you updated too.

JUNE

Thanks, April.

Our weekend in Nashville played back in my mind once again. Where did it all go wrong? Even though both Dahlia and June told me not to, Carter's vanishing act worried me. Was he really that overwhelmed? Did it have something to do with me?

The first stars appeared in the inky sky, and I double-checked the doors to make sure they were all locked, knowing how he hated the idea of me being in a cabin by myself with no lock. I wouldn't neglect my security now that I knew why he insisted I move in with him.

Over the weekend, Carter had confided a lot about personal stuff. Why would he open up to me if he wanted nothing to do with me anymore?

What changed between us after we got back to Green Mountain?

No matter how hard I tried to convince myself I wasn't responsible for his disappearing act, my instincts kept insisting I was the cause.

All weekend, Carter acted like my boyfriend. He made me feel special.

A headache took root at the front of my skull. I closed my eyes and massaged my temples.

Bernice purred, and I leaned forward to lift her up. "Hey girl. Ready to go back home?" She arched her back and mewed. "I know it wasn't the plan. But how can I stay here? If Carter doesn't come back, I...I can't stay here by myself. It feels wrong. And if he does come back, things may be awkward between us. Don't be sorry. We had a great time." She stared into my eyes for a long minute. "Don't worry, we'll be fine." I put her back down, and she traipsed toward the music studio. "Yeah, just leave me alone too. Nice job, Bern."

Around midnight, lying in my bed, I felt lonelier than I'd felt in a long time. After Travis's death, I had learned to be on my own. To count only on myself. Since moving in with Carter, I had rediscovered the joy of sharing my time with another human being—with a man. Now I realized how much I'd missed it over the years. I loved the company. Sharing meals and talking about anything and everything. Stealing glances and catching smiles. No more insomnia. No more procrastination.

With Carter, I was back to being alive.

Too bad it was over so soon.

Chapter 22

Carter

I woke up before dawn with a pounding headache. In the mirror, I caught my reflection when I took a leak. Bloodshot eyes with dark shadows underneath, disheveled hair, a few days' long beard. I looked like shit. I rubbed my fists over my eyes and swallowed two painkillers with a tall glass of water. After I forced a protein shake down my throat, and not feeling like spending myself physically for a third day in a row, I opted for the thing I did best in my life. Writing music. The mere thought of it soothed something inside me. I poured all my restless energy into my art, diving into the sound of the guitar.

My whole being ached from what I put myself through over the last two days. Punishing workouts. Hot baths. Falling asleep, exhausted.

Worried my body would give up, I curled up on the couch and napped for an hour. When I woke up, the storm inside me had lessened. I blew out a long breath. By the end of the morning, I had written three new songs, including a guaranteed top charter. Putting my heart on paper eased my mind and shot me with pride.

Even if I tried to deny it, April had inspired most of the lyrics. There was just something about her that roused my creative side and made the melodies flow and the words poured out of me.

As I strummed the last chord of a song I just wrote, my heartbeat slowed, and my mind took a break. I slouched back on the couch, a pillow underneath my head, and exhaled all the lingering anxiety and anger inside me. Music was my drug of choice. No matter what I tried to tell myself, whatever happened in my life, I could never give it up. It answered the question that had been nagging me since yesterday.

I had become a greedy bastard because, this time, I wanted it all. The music, the career, the girl, and I wasn't willing to sacrifice any. I did it once. Never again.

With steady fingers, I turned my phone back on. Notifications of messages and calls I'd missed during the last forty-eight hours popped up on the screen. I winced at the high number.

Dahlia's name flashed on the screen while I scrolled through my messages. For as long as I'd known her, I'd never ignored her calls. But for a second, this time, I debated shutting her out too. She was my best friend but also the first woman who made me believe I wasn't good enough to be loved. Both times we could've been together, she chose the other man. She never chose me. Not once. I rubbed my thumb over the screen of my device, wondering what to do.

What if she needed me to be there for her and I was too busy fucking my entire life up?

What if Jack had had an accident…or…or something was wrong with the baby?

I cursed under my breath. The caring side of me won the battle, and I accepted the call.

"Dear God, Carter. Finally. Where are you?"

I sighed. "Are you and Jack okay?" Nothing else mattered.

"Yes. It's you I'm worried about."

Some tension left my back. They were both fine.

"You're in one of your episodes, aren't you?"

I glanced around, trying to gather my thoughts.

"Carter, talk to me. Where are you? I'll come to meet you." She kept her voice even and low, knowing I needed her calm. She was used to dealing with my racing thoughts and my anxiety attacks.

"I'll be fine, Dah. I'm messed up. It all… Everything was spinning too fast in my mind, and I panicked."

"Hey, it's okay. I'm here. What do you need?"

"Don't hang up. Talk to me. I need to hear your voice. In my head, it's all fucked up. I'm…I'm sore. I'm tired." My voice cracked, and hot tears pooled in my eyes. "I'm so tired, Dah. Like I wanna sleep forever."

She sucked in a low breath. "Don't say that, Carter. You don't want to sleep forever. If you do, I'd haunt you in your grave. You know I would."

I snickered through my tears. Dahlia knew I didn't want to sleep my life off. And she also knew how to lift my spirits.

"What happened? Was it Nashville?"

"Yes. No. I don't know. I'm restless."

She hesitated for a few beats. "It's April, isn't it?"

I stayed silent. How could she always tell what was troubling me?

She sighed and raised her voice a tad. "Carter, is it

about her? Talk to me. Are you afraid to trust someone else with your heart?"

I cleared my throat. "I'm scared….and I-I'm never scared of anything. I'm Carter Hills, for fuck's sake. I'm supposed to be in control all the fucking time. I'm never supposed to mess up because the entire world will judge me afterward. I did something stupid once, and the planet spread nasty rumors about me. In the last two years, my personal life has been reduced to gossip. It's exhausting… I'm exhausted. How can I hide my feelings, my insecurities, and my stupid fears so people won't take advantage of me? I'm supposed to piss gold and shit diamonds." A sarcastic laugh escaped my mouth. "I'm not sure I can even be in a relationship. Last time, it almost killed me. What if once again it becomes a clusterfuck? What if the reality of my life is a turn-off for any sane woman? I can't lose the music again. Where does this leave me?" I fought with my inner demons with all my might. "Tell me how am I supposed to do this? And why would April want to be with someone like me? I'm damaged goods, Dah. Whenever I put my heart on the line, it always gets crushed."

A long silence stretched between us. Neither one of us dared to comment on the confidences I just threw on the table.

"Carter—" Dahlia's voice, familiar and comforting, sounded like music to my ears. "Nothing is damaged about you. Savannah was just a bump in the road. Or what if she was a means to an end? A stepping stone in order for you to follow the right path. Have you ever thought about it this way? Like if you hadn't survived hell, you might have never ended up where you were supposed to be because it wouldn't have given you the opportunity to get stronger and aim for what you really wished all along. All those years you thought you were in love with me…a part of you was…but you were also in love with the image of us you'd created in your mind when we were kids. Together, we wouldn't have been good. We're too emotional around each other. And it took you a long time to arrive at the same conclusion I reached a decade ago. Nothing that happens is in vain, Cart. There's always a reason behind everything… I truly believe that. Sometimes though, it takes longer for the explanation to reveal itself."

We both said nothing for an infinite minute.

"I'll tell you something I never told you before. Because you weren't ready to hear me out. Jeff always envied your talent. He asked me multiple times why he hadn't inherited those music genes too. He never told you because he felt insecure about it. Searching for his place in this world… He found it hard to be in your shadow sometimes." Dahlia's words pierced my heart. I never knew my brother felt this way about me. Most of the time, he was a happy guy, joking around and gripping me into headlocks until we both ended up laughing out loud, whatever bothering us long forgotten. "But one thing was clear. He wanted you to succeed. He would have done about anything to help you get there. No matter what, he always wanted what was best for you… Always. Even when you guys wouldn't talk."

The last memory of us hit me like a freight train. The moment I told my brother I didn't want anything to do with him anymore…or asking him to leave me the fuck alone. A long-buried sob bubbled out. "I did something horrible to him, Dah. If he had known, he would have never forgiven me. Jeff trusted me, and I…and I let him down. And then I shut him out. I. SHUT. HIM. OUT. I'm sure I'm the reason he dropped dead. Me."

"Shhh, Carter. Don't blame yourself. Never. Please,

don't say that. Jeff was aware… He…he knew everything. I told him."

"You did?" I blinked, my jaw hanging open.

"Yeah. I was always honest with him. I'm not certain he knew what hate was anyway. All along, he could tell there was a strong bond that needed to be settled…a story he wasn't part of. I…I dropped the bomb after we returned from Australia, right after he asked me to marry him. I had to tell him the truth. He wasn't happy about it, to say the least. Believe me. He got mad and everything, but he didn't push me away or end our engagement. It took him a while to come to terms with what had happened, but in the end, forgiveness and moving forward were all that truly mattered to him. That's how amazing he was. See? You didn't kill him. None of us could have prevented his heart from stopping when it did. Never blame yourself."

My hands shook. A strange, foreign sensation coursed through me, and I could barely draw a full breath.

Flashbacks that had haunted me for so long, memories I'd carried around for all these years, lifted from my shoulders.

"Don't be hard on April because your mama is gone and your crazy ex-girlfriend hurt you, okay? I met April three times. She really cares about you. Your ex had problems you couldn't fix. And your mother, well, there's nothing you can do about it either. You tried. We all know you tried. She's heartbroken and has no idea how to overcome her grief. Same for your dad. They love you, Cart. They're just failing at dealing with their own broken hearts."

"It doesn't change the fact that they left me, Dah. Even after hours of therapy, when I stop and think about it, it's still a hard pill to swallow. They fucked me good." My throat worked. Could my body shut down from too much pain?

"You're not alone. And you never were. I'm here. We're here. Everyone who loves you. About April… I think you should talk to her. She's a smart girl. You two should figure out what you want…together. Listen to what she has to say. It's not just up to you this time. If you believe she's worth it, don't push her away because you think it's the right thing to do."

A long moment passed before Dahlia spoke again.

"And Carter, no matter what you think, you *are* boyfriend material. You don't give yourself enough credit. All these years, you've only been distracting yourself. Maybe it's time you stop finding excuses, let go of the past, and act like a man. Any woman would be lucky to be loved by you."

Her last words simmered for a moment. "I love you, Dah."

"I love you too, Cart. I always will. Now call back your people because they're worried sick about you. Nobody has heard from you in the past few days. They think you got into an accident or something. About everything else you said, we'll talk about it later. Talk to April. Please. Don't shut her out. She's good for you. I can tell. You need someone like her in your life. Who is grounded and level-headed. Someone who is real and not easily impressed by your career choice. And Carter, remember. It's okay to be scared. Just don't be scared alone."

After promising Dahlia to clean up the mess in my head, I hung up and scrolled through the five text messages April had sent me since I disappeared without a word.

Monday morning:

APRIL

> June called and said you're not answering your phone. I told her you were busy. She said you need to call her back ASAP.

Monday night:

APRIL

> HN, I'm sorry to bother you. I was wondering if you could stop at the grocery store on your way back. Call me if you have a minute.

Monday late at night:

APRIL

> Okay, no news for an entire day. Should I worry? Call me when you get my text. Or text me if you're alive. Kidding. Not kidding.

Yesterday evening:

APRIL

> I'm sorry if I did something to upset you. I should've never tried to have sex with you the other night. It was dumb. I acted like a groupie, which I'm not, I promise. I got carried away in the heat of the moment. Hope we can still be friends.

Earlier today:

APRIL

> Carter, I'm packing my stuff. You don't want to be around me for whatever reason. Your team keeps calling my phone. They're worried. At least let them know you're okay. It's fine if you don't want to see me anymore. Your silence speaks louder than your words. Thanks for last weekend and for the song. I'll cherish it forever. Maybe someday we'll cross paths again. Goodbye, HN. By the way, it might or might not be Hot and Natty... Who knows? The mystery adds a little fun to our short-lived friendship. I wish you the best. You deserve it. You're pretty amazing when you're not being an ass. Never let anyone tell you the opposite. Keep shining xx

By the last one, my heart had plummeted down to my toes. April blamed herself. She was so damn wrong. My only wish was to be around her. Not to push her away.

Last Sunday, on the drive back from Nashville, I had realized being around her was much more effective in calming my mind than any therapy. Her presence alone eased everything inside me. It silenced the nagging voices in my head. That wasn't supposed to happen. Now I was not only mesmerized by the woman, but I needed her too. My throat tightened, and I rubbed my hand over my face. How could I even fathom letting her go? Was I more insane than I thought?

Deep down, I knew I had to be honest with her. About everything. Even the doubts crippling me and my episodes. One day, I would have to tell her about the thoughts keeping me awake some nights and how they affected me. How could I expect a relationship based on communication and honesty if I hid facts from her? And didn't tell her how I felt? Sharing about my inner struggles wasn't something I excelled in, not when it included the fuck-ups of my past, but here I was, alone, exhausted, and miserable without her. I needed her light and optimism in my life, like I needed oxygen to breathe.

If I pulled my head out of my own ass, maybe I could salvage what we had before it was too late. Maybe I could redeem myself…explain stuff. Starting with how my brain worked sometimes or how my fears took full control of my mind and body and asphyxiated me. I could do this. Open up and trust another person with my life and my secrets. I didn't wanna live in uncertainty forever. I owed it to myself to face my worst fears and free myself of the *what-ifs* once and for all. To move forward and not be tied to a past that no longer suited me. To chase my own happiness. And true love. For real this time.

April sent the last message over an hour ago.

If I didn't act—and fast—she'd go back home early to avoid me. *Breathe in. Breathe out.* She would leave. Our cabin. Green Mountain. Me. Forever. I scratched my forehead with the side of my thumb and shot her a text. If I hurried, maybe I could catch her. My heart raced into a frantic rhythm. I had only one thing left to do.

ME

April, don't go. Please. I'm sorry. We need to talk.

I didn't wait for her to reply. Instead, I showered, changed, and drove back home.

When I pulled in, some of the tension in my upper back eased at the sight of her car still parked in the driveway. She hadn't left. She was still here. I pressed my hand against my chest, resuming my breathing. Would she give me a chance to explain? Would she let me in, or had I lost her trust? I swallowed hard. The knots in my stomach multiplied.

Once I regained some composure, I squared my shoulders, straightened my back, and climbed out of my truck.

Pixie and I weren't done yet. I hadn't said my last word.

Chapter 23
April

I blinked a few times and took calming breaths to keep the tears burning the back of my eyes at bay. Carter didn't come home last night. Again. No message this time. He'd chosen to end our story—or whatever we had—on his own terms. Fine. Screw him. I wouldn't define myself through a man.

As soon as I was out of bed, I sent a message to my best friend back home.

ME

> Don't bother driving up here. I'm leaving early to come back home.

SAUNDERS

> Is everything okay?

ME

> Yes. No. Not discussing it.

SAUNDERS

You're sure you're not running away in
typical April Simmons fashion?

ME

Maybe. Not sure. It's complicated. I'll talk to
you later.

SAUNDERS

Everything fine between you and (OMG!!!!!)
Carter Hills?

ME

I'll call you once on the road.

I wasn't in the mood to explain to her that if I stayed here, as soon as Carter came back, my stupid heart would break, and it'd hurt too much to be around him, knowing I had scared him away.

SAUNDERS

April, do I need to worry?

ME

Please don't. I'll explain everything. Later.

I would. Once I'd put enough distance between me and this place and when the memories of the precious stolen moments we shared didn't feel like a stabbing pain anymore.

SAUNDERS

Reed wants me to tell you to be careful.
The roads are icy.

I really wanted to visit you.

ME

I know. Raincheck, okay?

SAUNDERS

Call me when you can. Be careful xx

Then, after some hesitation—and four drafts later—I sent Carter a text message to inform him I was leaving. For the second time in a week, I packed my stuff. My heart quivered, and my eyes overflowed with tears. Not rushing it, I filled my suitcase, hoping Carter would show up in the meantime. But he didn't. *Get real, April. Stop wishing for a happy ending.*

With all my feelings in the pit of my stomach, I zipped up my suitcase and placed it in one corner of the bedroom. Squatting, I lifted Bernice from the bed and cuddled her against my chest. She purred in the crook of my neck, and I felt better. Sort of.

My phone went off, and thinking it was Saunders, I looked at the message. My heart skipped a beat when his name and the picture we took on that bridge in Nashville filled the screen.

CARTER

April, don't go. Please. I'm sorry. We need to talk.

I should've left at that moment, but my curiosity got the better of me. And maybe I wanted to see him one last time. For closure. Yeah, closure was necessary. To move on.

I reread the message for the third time. What did Carter want to talk about? His actions were clear enough. No need to hear him say he regretted befriending me or that kissing me was a mistake. Or that I was just a fling, after all, and what we shared meant nothing. Or that my actions, when we almost had sex, were inappropriate or whatever. My ego didn't need to be kicked to the curb face-to-face. Not by the first man I let in after Travis. Not the first time I dared to be vulnerable with someone other than my best friend.

Carter disappeared three days ago after we spent an amazing weekend together. After we spent a day flirting and kissing as we strolled around his city, as he called it. Was our time together all a joke to him? Did he play me for his own sake? Slouching forward, I buried my face in the bent of my elbow, my arms resting on my pillow, and let out a shaky breath.

How did I end up in this mess? Why did HN have to be so sexy and such an amazing person? And why were my hormones so horny?

I couldn't leave without hearing what he had to say. Even if the truth scared me, it was better than coming up with scenarios in my head for the foreseeable future about why even our friendship didn't work out. I needed closure, otherwise I'd be miserable.

Like the masochist I'd become lately, I sat on my bed and played "Pink and Country" on a loop. By now, I knew all the words. Each time I pressed play, my heart did somersaults, and tears welled up in my eyes. Listening to Carter's raw masculine voice, his heartfelt words, and his rich and bittersweet melody made me feel closer to him. Like he was talking to me. As if our souls were connected in the most primitive way, bare and uncensored.

Last night, Saunders sent me a link to an interview Savannah Prince had given over the weekend.

With a warning.

SAUNDERS

This bitch is crazy. Don't listen past forty-eight seconds. It's best if you hear it from me instead of some low-key gossiper.

Saunders was right. I preferred it when my best friend was the one delivering the news. However awful it was. Until now, I'd done my best to avoid watching the interview. Without overthinking everything, I clicked the link, and the actress appeared on the screen. Flawless makeup, dressed to impress, and shiny hair that appeared silky even through a screen.

"How are you feeling about Carter moving on so quickly after your very public breakup?" the interviewer, a tall brunette with injected lips and perfectly shaped eyebrows, asked.

"Carter is a hard man to tame. Women are his ultimate weaknesses. I'll never stop loving him. I hope he remembers how good we are together and stops fighting what we have. I'll stay by his side to help him overcome his challenges. We'll figure it out together as a couple." Savannah flashed a pearly-white smile to the camera.

"So, you've seen Carter lately? We're all wondering where he's been. Can you tell us more?" the interviewer continued with a cheesy smile and wide eyes, fangirling over the movie star.

"All I can say is that you'll see more of us together soon."

"And what about the song he wrote for the mystery woman he's currently seeing?"

The actress rolled her eyes at the camera. "Come on, Cindy, you can't be serious. Carter wrote that song a long time ago. It has nothing to do with this—" I held my breath and closed the browser tab, ending the video. Enough. *Forty-nine seconds.* My stomach churned, and I inhaled deeply to calm the emotions storming inside me. Savannah Prince had nailed the act of the manipulative bitch to perfection. For a second, she even almost got me convinced Carter was the bad guy. That was why I never watched entertainment news or read gossip magazines. People vomited words to sound interesting and sympathetic when, in fact, they had nothing meaningful to say. How could Carter ever fall for her and then be interested in someone like me? His ex-girlfriend oozed confidence and sexuality—the exact opposite of me. I sighed, feeling completely out of my league.

The day I found out who he was, Carter had straightened out some facts about their relationship before I heard things and panicked. Everything he'd said that night kept running through my mind, and I couldn't seem to stop thinking about it.

"We're both to blame for this mess," he had told me. "I agreed to this relationship when everything in me screamed I shouldn't. I didn't get out when I should've. At first, we seemed like a good fit. It changed once we moved in together. She became some sort of evil, and I stayed because I wanted to make it work. To prove to myself I could be in a long-lasting relationship. And do things differently, I guess. I was lost."

"Did you love her?" I had to ask, but regretted it the moment his eyes had met mine—wide and startled, as if I'd said something terrible. I had lowered my head, feeling like I was intruding on his personal life. "Sorry...it's none of my business."

"It's okay. No, I didn't love her. I wanted to, but I couldn't. Maybe that's why I endured this nightmare longer than I should have. Because I wished, one day, I'd feel something. Anything. In the end, I learned facts I'd been blind to. Lots of them. A part of me still thinks it's surreal. But then I remember I lived through this and it's nothing but the truth. Everything about that woman is fake. Her laughter. Her orgasms. Not just her tits or her lips. She told every one I was a sex addict to portray me like a cheater. I wasn't sick. I was sexually frustrated, and she had been the one playing me… Let's just say she reached new lows to secure a role. Not long after I moved to Los Angeles to be with her, I began a dry-spell diet. She always had a far-fetched reason to keep me at a distance. Too tired or too stressed. Too everything. Her nails got done, or she refused to mess up her styled hair. One time, she even told me she'd cleaned her aura and that close contact with me would misalign her chakras or some shit. And then she became someone else entirely. No kidding. I was literally living in hell. She thought she was being sexy when the truth is that she was scary as fuck. At some point, I was afraid for my sanity."

"You're joking, right?"

"I wish. The day I left, I wanted to rip my eyeballs out. Still, months later, she's telling the media we'll get back together. Our relationship was one big clusterfuck. A gigantic mistake. She hated me. So go figure." He had then risen to his feet and disappeared into his music studio while I had attacked the dishes, fiddling with the dishcloth in my hands, wondering why I had opened that can of worms.

Carter had joined me in front of the fireplace an hour later, his smile back, our conversation about his ex-girl-friend forgotten.

The Carter Hills I'd gotten to know had nothing in common with the one the actress described in interviews.

Now, with my eyes closed, his song did all the talking, and I wondered how long it'd take for him to come back home. When did I start considering Green Mountain and Carter's cabin as *home*? Not ready for an internal freakout, I pushed the thought away. None of this mattered anymore since I was leaving today. Ginger Creek was my home.

Green Mountain was more like a fairy tale. No matter how exciting they seemed in books or on TV, fairy tales didn't exist in real life. As long as I remembered that piece of information, I would be all right. Adjusting my position on the bed, I relaxed my shoulders, my brain half-awake, and got lost in Carter's voice. To hell with what his ex-girlfriend had said. This song was mine.

Every word he sang. Every single note of it.

Lost in my head—and my song—I didn't hear him coming in. He pulled the earbuds from my ears, and I jumped. My eyes sprang open, and my breathing hitched. It took a second for my brain to reboot.

Carter's eyes locked on mine. Dark and penetrating. Lustful. With him so close, I struggled to remember why I had been mad at him in the first place, or why I had wanted to flee his house just hours ago. He looked tired and stressed, yet still handsome, with his unshaven jaw and untamed hair. The time we spent apart didn't mean anything anymore. His metal irises swallowed me whole, and I lost myself in them, swimming in their depths.

And right now, I had a hard time remembering why fairy tales didn't exist in real life.

———

Continue the story in **Forevermore**
emmanuellesnow.com/products/forever-more

Thank you for reading the first part of Carter and April's beautiful and emotional story.

———

Did you miss Carter's prequel story?

ACKNOWLEDGMENTS

When my editor offered to revisit this story (which was my debut novel), I jumped on the occasion. I remembered how in awe I was of Carter's and April's characters when they first appeared on the pages and how hard I fell in love with them both.

After everything they had overcome in their lives, they needed to find each other and embrace the happiness they both deserved. They were made for one another…not just on paper. *Blindsided* is book one in the *Heart Song* duet, and my new re-edited version of their love story.

Back when I wrote this book a few years ago, I knew it couldn't end there. It just didn't feel right. Carter and April and their friends and family had so much more to experience. Along the way, my country music standalone novel became a series that I'm so proud of. Fast forward a few years later and you can now see plenty of Carter and April in other books of the Carter Hills Band universe because they are the heart and soul of this world.

I want to thank my husband, without whom I wouldn't have started to write my first novel yet. You've always believed in me even back when we were young and clueless, and you've stuck by my side, no matter what. I love you. I'm lucky I found my soul mate early in life.

I also want to thank my kids. All four of them. You guys have been patient and selfless through this whole project and the many that came afterward, giving me the space I needed when my fingers itched to write one more page or one more chapter. The love and pride you show me every day are priceless. Thanks, guys, for being my biggest fans.

I also want to thank those people who helped me through this adventurous journey as an author.

Shalini. Thanks for sticking by my side and helping me write the best version of Carter and April's story and revisiting it when the timing was right. You're the best!

To my readers, none of this would be possible without you. Thanks for giving me the chance to do the thing I love the most—writing love stories.

Ashley, Miriam, and Sara, thank you for your help and unconditional support.

And to the Bookstagramers, influencers, Booktokers, Booktubers, who helped me share this book with the rest of the world, I can't tell all y'all enough how grateful I am.

Hope you enjoy reading this book as much as I did writing it.

Cheers
Emmanuelle

WANT MORE EMOTIONAL LOVE STORIES?

WHICH COUPLE WILL YOU PICK NEXT?

False Promises

★★★★★ "The angst, the utter heartbreak, and protectiveness I felt for Carter during this book is unreal!"

★★★★★ "Emmanuelle Snow really knows how to tug at all of your emotions and does such a great job of bringing her characters to life!"

A gripping story of sizzling passion, lust, and the price of fame.
Start Carter Hills's story now

———

Sweet Agony

★★★★★ "If I could give more than 5 stars, I would."

★★★★★ "This is not a romance, it is a story about first love, first heartbreak and growing up."

A compelling tale of love, friendship, and self-discovery that will tug at your heartstrings.

Start Dahlia's story now

———

Cruel Destiny

★★★★★ "Wow. Just wow. If that could be my review, that is all I would write."

★★★★★ "Emmanuelle has done it yet again. She found a way to slip into my mind and heart with her words and the creation of characters you can't help but fall in love with."

★★★★★ "This book broke my heart in the first twenty five percent and sewed it back together."

A story of healing, second chances, and the risks of opening your heart to someone new. Can they trust each other with their hearts, or will their pasts keep them apart?

Read Nick and Dahlia's love story now

———

Wild Encounter

★★★★★ "This is by far one of the most well-written book I've read this month. It is dynamic, intriguing, interesting, unafraid to go there and most of all touching."

★★★★★ "I personally wouldn't call this book JUST a romance novel because it's so much more. I 100% recommend it no doubt in mind."

A tale of passion and perseverance that will leave your heart racing and your spirit soaring.

Read Tucker and Addison's love story now

————

Last Hope

★★★★★ "This book was not only about the darkness but it was about pure love, hope, spice, family, and friendships on point with just the right amount without overpowering the storyline at all."

★★★★★ "Devon and Riley's story is a beautiful one with a lot of emotions. The subject matter is intense but it is handled very gently."

A tale of resilience and second chances in a world where love and danger intertwine.

Read Riley and Devon's love story now

————

Midnight Sparks

★★★★★ "The characters, the love, the humor, the steaminess, the emotions… it's everything I hoped and more."

★★★★★ "I think that is one Emmanuelle Snow's sexiest novels yet."

Welcome to the island where Holiday magic meets unexpected romance and a chance at a fresh start.

Read Gavin and Aisha's love story now

———

Fallen Legend

★★★★★ ""The love that grows, not only through tough angst but through unconditional moments had my heart. This is a spicy and riveting book"

★★★★★ "Emmanuelle Snow doesn't just tell a story, she creates an entire world."

A poignant and uplifting journey of hope, love, and the power of second chances.

Read Sam and Madison's love story now

———

Snowbound

★★★★★ "5 big stars from me for this amazing story. Absolutely loved it!"

★★★★★ "Emmanuelle Snow's stories are always full of angst, and Snowbound is no exception."

The intertwined lives of two strangers bound by fate in the midst of a snowstorm.

Read Anderson and Abigail's love story now

———

All available at emmanuellesnow.com

ABOUT THE AUTHOR

Soulfully Beautiful Love Stories

USA Today Bestselling Author Emmanuelle Snow is an author of contemporary YA and women's fiction love stories, who gives life to strong characters who'll fight with all they have to reach their life goals and find their own happiness. She loves her characters to be relatable and realistic.

Emmanuelle is in love with love. Especially complicated, deep, and passionate feelings that make a relationship extraordinary and complex all at the same time.

In her spare time, when she's not writing or reading, she likes to go on road trips—with her four kids and her own soulmate—watch movies, paint, or do some DIY, always with a cup of green tea in her hand and listening to country music.

She splits her time between beautiful Canada and the small US towns she adores.

Find all of Emmanuelle's books here:
emmanuellesnow.com

———

ALSO BY THE AUTHOR

CARTER HILLS BAND UNIVERSE

(suggested reading order)

Carter Hills Band series

False Promises

HEART SONG DUET

Blindsided

Forevermore

Whiskey Melody series

Sweet Agony

SECOND TEAR DUET

Cruel Destiny

Beautiful Salvation

BREATHLESS DUET

Wild Encounter

Brittle Scars

Upon A Star Series

Last Hope

Midnight Sparks

Love Song For Two Series

Read them all

emmanuellesnow.com

All available on author's bookshop

EMMANUELLE
USA TODAY BESTSELLING AUTHOR
SNOW
WILD ENCOUNTER
a love story
Whiskey Melody series - book four
SAVE THE DATE
LOVE
HOCKEY

WILD ENCOUNTER

ADDISON

I slumped down on the couch of the posh hotel we were staying at all weekend and huffed, a wine bottle hanging from my fingers by its neck. Glasses were overrated, anyway. "That's it. I'm over men. I'm done." My childhood best friend snickered. "I'm serious, Dah. This time I mean it. You know I do."

I scanned the space around me. Large windows with a direct view of Nashville's busy streets below, high wooden beam ceilings, dark flooring, and handcrafted wood furniture. Chic and tasteful, with an unmistakable country vibe.

"Yeah, right. I'm sure you won't last a week. Two at the most," Dahlia teased.

My friend, and the bride-to-be, inched closer, and I zipped her up. Her cut-out mermaid gown was a gray-lavender hue and looked both sexy and demure, showing just enough skin without being indecent. Perfectly Dahlia Ellis.

Before I could sink back into my lazy position on the couch, she beckoned me with a finger to follow her. Sitting on the edge of the bathtub, I glugged the wine straight from the bottle and watched her apply mascara.

"Addi, there are good men out there who would appreciate your light. Don't punish all of them because you dated a few who were total dickheads." She grinned at her reflection, but it was meant for me. And it warmed my heart as she continued, "I'm confident you won't last in your quest to ignore them all when they turn on the charm."

"Laugh all you want, girlfriend. You'll see. Be prepared to be shocked. This time, I'm not backing down. Anyway, remember Felicia from college? She messaged me last week. It's destiny."

"The one you 'experimented' with?" my friend asked, curving her fingers into elaborate air quotes, her gaze fixed on her eyelashes in the mirror, not sparing me a look.

Another sip. "The same. We could have been in love and lived happily ever after. The timing was just not right back then."

"Huh, you said the same thing about Carter once. Besides, I thought women weren't your thing," Dahlia added with a quirked brow.

"It's not the same. And perhaps I changed my mind. Who knows? I might be into women more than men after all. Think about it, we should have been a couple, you and I. Everything would have been much simpler."

"You think?"

I shrugged. "We get along fine. And we're friends, so our relationship would have had a solid foundation. Look at you and Nick. Friends, then lovers. I believe that's the secret to long-lasting love. Back to business..." I sighed. "Felicia and I experienced some pretty memorable moments together. It's just Shawn happened to cross my path, and I couldn't resist him. Stupid me. Stupid men. I'm telling you their species is old news. You're lucky you found two awesome ones in your lifetime. What are the odds? God knows I've tried. I usually don't back down easily, but hey, maybe it's time I try something else. That I understand once and for all what life has been trying to tell me all these years…"

Dahlia shook her head, focusing her attention on me for the first time since I started the conversation about my disastrous love life. "Addi, you know how much I love it when you're not being overdramatic, right?"

I poked my tongue out, and we both burst out laughing. Peace washed over me. Dahlia Ellis had that effect on me. Her presence was always enough to ease all my doubts and bring a curve to my lips even when I didn't feel like expressing joy. "That's why you love me. I'm entertaining…despite myself. Anyway, where are the bridal shower festivities taking place? I can't wait to party the entire weekend. The distraction will do me good."

My best friend reached over and landed a kiss on my cheek, her eyes searching mine. Worry shimmered in them. "You okay?"

I nodded.

"You'd tell me if it wasn't the case, right?" I sensed the apprehension in her question.

"Always. You're the only one I willingly confide in."

With a warm smile that promised everything would turn out just fine, she went back to applying her makeup. "All over town. Tonight, we're having dinner with only the people closest to us. And tomorrow, a get-together with some of my good friends and the guys on a yacht before splitting up and maybe meeting them again later."

"Rewind for a sec. We're having your bridal shower with your future husband and his friends?"

"Yep. His best friend. Guys from work. That's the idea."

"Yeah, I should've been the one organizing the whole thing." Dahlia raised a hand, ready to argue, but I kept going. "For what it's worth, I'm sorry I let you down. I was really looking forward to throwing you the bachelorette party of the century."

A new weight grew heavy on my shoulders. In the fog of my latest relationship blowing up, I had lost focus on what really mattered. This time, my tears had knocked me out more than ever. But I was back now, and no way was I failing the girl I considered a sister again.

Dahlia pulled me into a hug. "It's okay. Don't chastise yourself. It'll still be fun. And you did plan most of the wedding already. You deserve a night off…to enjoy yourself… You, me, booze, music. And the man I love and his friends."

I leaned back, studying her for a moment. Dahlia had no ounce of evilness in her. She really meant everything she'd just said.

"What is it?" she asked, a frown marring her forehead.

"Real sweet, Dah. After I told you I was done with men, you're going to make me spend hours with a bunch of Nick's buddies. And alcohol. If I didn't know your heart, I'd think this was a test. To check my newfound determination." One more sip of wine. *Be strong, Addi,* I repeated in my head. I flicked my hand and pasted a smile on my lips. "Know what? It doesn't matter. I won't back down. I'm done with men, and I'll prove it to you. Tonight. I won't flirt, and I won't kiss. Nope. Nada. D.O.N.E. Just watch and learn, girlfriend."

I held out my hand, and we shook on it.

———

Read Tucker and Addison's story,
Wild Encounter, now

emmanuellesnow.com/products/wild-encounter

"Tucker freaking Philips!!! Wow! Emmanuelle Snow has written another beautiful, rollercoaster, sneakily emotional romance."
(Goodreads)

"This is without a doubt Emmanuelle's best work yet!" (Goodreads)
Wild Encounter is book one in the ***Breathless*** duet.
Read the first part now

Wild Encounter

https://emmanuellesnow.com/products/wild-encounter

Author's bookstore at emmanuellesnow.com